A TOURIST
IN THE YUCATÁN

A NOVEL BY
JAMES MCNAY BRUMFIELD

TRES PICOS PRESS
CALIFORNIA

Published by
Tres Picos Press
116 Martinelli Street, Suite #1
Watsonville, CA 95076
www.trespicospress.com

Originally published by Hollis Books 2000
Second edition 2004, published by Tres Picos Press

First printing May 2004
Second printing September 2004
Third printing July 2006

Library of Congress Catalog Number: 2003098933

ISBN-13: 978-0-9745309-0-1
ISBN-10: 0-9745309-0-5

Also by James McNay Brumfield
Across the High Lonesome

For Mom and Dad,

Thank you for everything.

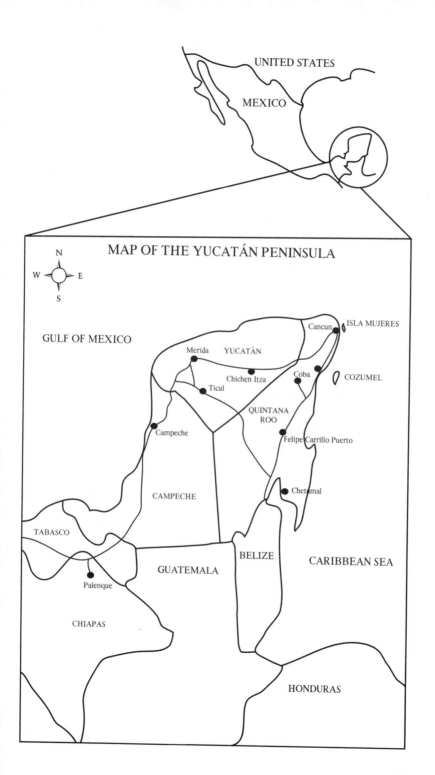

MAP OF THE YUCATÁN PENINSULA

N
W E
S

UNITED STATES

MEXICO

GULF OF MEXICO

YUCATÁN

Cancun
ISLA MUJERES

Merida

Chichen Itza

Coba

COZUMEL

Ticul

QUINTANA
ROO

Campeche

Felipe Carrillo Puerto

CAMPECHE

Chetumal

TABASCO

BELIZE

CARIBBEAN SEA

GUATEMALA

Palenque

CHIAPAS

HONDURAS

"Que bonito es el Mundo;
lastima es que yo me Muera."

"How beautiful is the world;
it is a pity I must die."

A song sung by the girls of the
village of Nohcacab during the fiesta
of Santo Cristo del Amor, as recorded in
"Incidents of Travel in Yucatán,"
by John L. Stephens, 1843.

CHAPTER 1

Sam Peters paid four pesos for the ferry ride to Isla Mujeres. It was double the fare, but he did not feel like hassling the swollen-eyed ticket man for gouging him; after all, it was less than one dollar American. The Mexican smiled as he took the money, revealing a set of stained and crooked teeth and the smell of last night's tequila heavy on his breath.

Ticket in hand, Peters started down the gangway to the Punta Sam car ferry. An iguana scrambled out from under the walkway onto the hot, white sand. Once at a safe distance, the lizard froze and stared at Peters with a suspicious reptilian eye. This was not Mexico's most picturesque coastline. The rocky beach was littered with debris, flotsam from off the Caribbean: an old rubber flip-flop, discarded plastic motor oil containers, chunks of a Styrofoam buoy, and the stripped and rusted hulk of a beached fishing trawler. The Cancún Tourist Bureau was not going to put this stretch of sand on a poster.

The gangway rocked with each step as Peters walked out over the water. His nostrils filled with the pungent smell of the tropics, while the morning sunlight felt pleasant upon his skin. It was a sparkling day, but it might be short-lived. The early morning breeze was gaining momentum, and a wall of dark clouds brooded on the horizon.

Peters possessed a deep tan, the kind of tan only long hours in the sun can produce. His tan, along with his collar length dark-brown hair, allowed him to blend in with the local population when the need arose. Today, however, he looked like the typical American tourist: off-white shorts, a light-blue polo shirt, and dark sunglasses that concealed his hazel eyes. In his hand he carried a small, red nylon duffel bag, and around his waist was strapped a fanny pack. It was the contents of the duffel bag and fanny pack that distinguished him from most tourists. Fifty-thousand dollars in small denominations of U.S. currency was packed into the duffel bag. In the nylon pouch of the fanny pack was a 9mm Glock, round chambered, with the safety off. Sam would prefer to be carrying his Colt Commander but had decided to leave it on his boat. The all-plastic Glock was lighter and more compact than the .45, making it the best choice for today's activities. He hoped there would be no need for the weapon, but he lived by the Boy Scout motto: Always be prepared.

The ship had seen better days. Her sky-blue paint was peeling and her fittings rusted, but she appeared plenty able to make the short trip from Cancún to the island. Upon boarding the vessel Peters started taking a mental inventory of his surroundings. His life might depend on knowing who and what was on board. The ferry had two decks: a lower deck for vehicles and an upper deck for passengers. The bottom deck was currently filled with a half dozen cars and one old flatbed truck. A canvas tarp covered the truck's load. Three of the cars had passengers in them, and the driver of the flatbed truck was sitting behind the wheel. The only other people on the lower deck were a middle-aged Mexican woman with three young children and an old man with rheumy eyes holding a half-empty bottle of cheap tequila. He and the old man knew each other, but neither took notice of the other. The old man was part of his insurance policy. His bottle was not a prop; he was an alcoholic, but the old bastard knew how to shoot and wasn't afraid to take a life. The old man would rather face death than life without the juice.

Peters climbed the ship's metal stairway and walked out onto the upper deck. Immediately a dark-haired boy approached him holding a bottle of Superior Beer in one hand and a Coca-Cola in the other.

"*Señor, cerveza, coca?*"

Peters bought the Coke and moved to the back railing of the upper deck. From here he surveyed the area while sipping the soft drink. The top deck was just that, a deck with a railing around it. No seating accommodations were provided for passengers. There was a wheelhouse at the bow and the stern. Which end of the boat was the bow or stern depended upon which direction the boat was heading. There were close to twenty passengers on the upper deck, many of whom were standing along the railing soaking up the blue Caribbean waters. Most appeared to be locals, but there were a few tourists in the crowd. The car ferry was the cheapest way to travel to the island, thus it was the islanders favored mode of transportation.

A TOURIST IN THE YUCATÁN 9

Leaning against the railing at the front of the boat was a man Peters picked out as his contact: a short, skinny Mexican carrying a small red duffel bag. The man was dressed in white slacks, white shirt, and a white Panama hat. He also wore dark sunglasses, while under his pencil-thin moustache a skinny cigar was clamped between his narrow lips. Peters smiled to himself. The fellow looked like he just stepped out of a Quentin Tarentino movie. He could never understand why someone walking around with over fifty thousand dollars worth of blow would want to dress like a bantam rooster. It was like walking around shouting, "Hey, look at me! I'm a gangster!"

The deck vibrated as the ship's engines rumbled; he felt the forward motion as the ferry pulled away from the dock. It looked like the crossing would be rough this morning. Whitecaps could be seen out in the channel, as the earlier breeze had turned into a stiff wind.

To the southeast he saw a cabin cruiser out in the middle of the channel. It was his boat, and over the past two years he had used it to transport almost a ton of cocaine into the United States. At present, the craft appeared to be just another boat full of tourists fishing for barracuda, but in reality it was the other half of his insurance policy. On board were two men to whom Peters had entrusted his life. One of the men was a good friend, a friend who had kept him from going insane in the jungles of Nicaragua and who had carried his bullet punctured body for miles through those same jungles.

His contact, the "rooster," was now staring at him. Peters stared back. Their eyes locked for a moment, then the Mexican turned his head and looked back toward the sea. After taking a long drag on his cigar, the rooster flicked the butt over the railing then turned and sauntered over to the middle of the starboard railing.

Now at full speed, the ferry was a third of the way across the channel. The ship rocked easily through the small swells. Peters would wait until the halfway point before making contact. To the east, massive black thunder heads were rolling in off the sea. He watched as the island ahead disappeared into the rapidly approaching clouds. Powerful gusts of wind were blowing from the northeast. It appeared that he was going to get wet before this ride was over.

Deciding it was time, he strolled over to where the rooster stood and leaned against the deck railing. About four hundred yards off the starboard side of the ship he saw his cabin cruiser traveling in the same direction as the ferry. Keeping his eyes on the boat he said, "Doesn't look like a good day to be fishing."

"It depends what one is fishing for," replied the Mexican in heavily accented English.

Peters spoke flawless Spanish, but he concealed this attribute as much as possible. In the past he had gained useful information from the conversations of people who thought he was ignorant of the language.

The rooster looked down at the duffel bag Peters was carrying and then up to his face. Peters stared back into the dark eyes. He could see that the man's brown cheeks were deeply pitted, ravaged by acne sometime in his youth. The Mexican smiled, displaying a gold-capped tooth.

"Let us go downstairs to my car where we can talk in private," said the Mexican.

"No, I like it better up here. After all, we have nothing to hide," said Peters.

"I cannot do business with you until I am sure you have held up your end of the deal, and I don't think we want to display the contents of these bags here," replied the Mexican.

"You have the rest of the boat ride to take inventory, and I sure as hell can't go anywhere until we reach the island," explained Peters. "The people I work for do not deal in small quantities. The only reason I am here is that we were hoping for bigger things in the future, but this can only happen if both parties trust each other. Either we exchange here and now, or you can tell your people to go fuck themselves."

For a moment the smile left the man's face but immediately returned, again revealing the gold tooth. "Let us not be hasty. I just thought we might be more comfortable in my car. I thought you would like to get out of the weather."

Peters began to feel uncomfortable. Something was not right. The Mexican had given in too easily. He was trying to stay relaxed, but the hair on the back of his neck stood on end. Alarm bells sounded in his subconscious.

The wind settled down as fat rain drops began to fall. The large drops splattered on the deck, creating wet splotches that quickly multiplied. The ferry and the mountain of darkness were on a collision course. Soon the ship would be engulfed by the storm.

Out of the corner of his eye Peters saw a bright flash of light. He turned toward the flash, thinking it must be lightning, only to see the fishing boat—his boat—explode in a fury of fire and smoke. At this same moment he heard a spitting noise, and a heavy thump. The two noises were familiar. The first was the sound of a large caliber handgun being fired when it was equipped with a silencer, and the second was that of a bullet's impact on human flesh. The exploding fishing boat had saved Peters' life and cost the rooster his. When Peters turned toward the explosion, a bullet meant for him missed and struck the Mexican in the temple, blowing the back of the man's head into the sea below. Peters reacted within a half-second of hearing the shot. He dove for the deck as two more shots whizzed by, not taking time to look back at the rooster. He rolled his body toward the port side of the ship and the stairwell to the lower deck. Operating on pure instinct, he had no time to think, only to react.

The rain was now coming down in torrents, visibility near zero. Two bright flashes appeared in the doorway of the stern wheelhouse as he heard two bullets ricochet off the deck to his left. Peters continued rolling to his right, the red duffel bag flopping around him. His one thought was to make it to the stairwell, to safety.

An overweight man who was running for cover when the shooting started was now between Peters and the stern wheelhouse. As he rolled past the man he heard another shot. Lurching backwards, the man fell on his side, nearly landing on Peters. The man lay on the deck clutching his stomach, his blue-green Hawaiian shirt turning crimson.

Peters came to a stop lying on his stomach. The squirming fat man afforded him some cover, allowing him time to pull the Glock from his fanny pack. Two more slugs zinged past him. Leveling his weapon in the direction of the flashes, he fired three rounds into the wheelhouse. He heard the sound of glass shattering and then, through the rain, he saw a human form stumble out the door of the wheelhouse, fire a wild shot into the air, and crumple to the deck.

Peters scrambled to the stairwell for cover, still clutching the red duffel bag. For the first time he heard the screams of his fellow passengers. Only seconds had passed from when the fishing boat exploded. His mind was jumbled; life had shifted to fast forward. In less than thirty seconds he had seen at least five men killed. Two of the men he knew; one was a close friend. He had to get his thoughts together. He needed to think clearly.

Soaked by the rain, he crouched at the top of the stairway. Water was running off the deck and down the stairs. Along the starboard railing he could see the rooster, his head in a pool of bloody water. The fat man lay moaning in the middle of the deck. A woman was holding his head in her lap and crying hysterically. Looking down the stairway he saw the old drunk sprawled out on the lower deck, a bullet hole between his lifeless eyes. The old man's bottle lay next to him, its contents slowly pouring out on the deck. So much for insurance.

There was at least one person on the lower deck, and Peters was pretty sure this person would not be happy to see him. He had one advantage: whoever was down there thought he was dead.

Peters crawled down the first few steps head first and positioned himself so he could see most of the lower deck. The Mexican woman and the three children had taken refuge under a car. On the other side of the ferry, just within his view, he saw a man hastily removing the canvas tarp off the flatbed truck. A pistol was in the man's right hand. He wanted this man alive, at least for a while. He needed some questions answered.

Peters carefully took aim and shot the man in the right shoulder. The impact of the bullet spun the man around, and his pistol dropped from his hand as he fell to the deck. Peters got to his feet and rushed down the last few steps. At the bottom of the stairway he leaped over the old man's body. There was one car between him and the flatbed. The duffel bag in his left hand and the pistol in his right, he jumped up onto the hood of the car. On the other side of the car he could see the man lying on his stomach, his shirt soaked with blood in the area of his right shoulder. With his left hand the man was reaching for his gun. Peters stepped from the hood of the car and dropped down onto the wounded man, his foot crashing down on the man's left wrist. Screeching wildly, the man pulled his shattered wrist to his chest and rolled over onto his back, writhing in pain.

Leveling his weapon at the man's forehead, Peters said, "We can do this easy or hard, but either way you're going to tell me who set me up."

The man replied defiantly with a string of Spanish expletives concerning Peters' mother. Peters brought the butt of the pistol down hard on the man's face. Blood gushed from a broken nose as the man screamed. The eyes set in the bloody face glared with anger. As Peters glared back, he realized that he recognized this man. An uncontrollable fury rose up inside him. He had been set up. This man was an agent of the Mexican Federal Judiciary Police. A man who had been closer to him than a brother was now scattered across the Caribbean because of this man. Unable to contain his rage, Peters smashed the butt of his pistol savagely against the man's temple.

The first blow was enough but Peters was unable to stop himself. He beat at the man's face until it was unrecognizable. Finally, splattered with blood, Peters slumped onto the deck, breathing heavily. The man lay dead beside him.

Peters was overwhelmed, too much, too fast. As his rage subsided he became sickened by his own violence. Suddenly he felt tired; if only he could curl up and sleep. Concentrate, he had to concentrate. How would he get off the boat?

Looking up, he saw what was hidden underneath the tarp on the back of the flatbed. It was a small speed boat, his assassin's escape vehicle. Could he get the boat off the truck and into the water? It appeared to be his only way out.

He finished removing the tarp and unhitched the ropes that secured the boat to the truck's bed. The craft was a small custom-built model; it was more engine than boat. He could probably push it off the back of the truck, but he wasn't sure he could do this without damaging the boat. A shrill siren could now be heard above the din of the storm. Soon the island contingent of the Mexican Navy would be pulling alongside the ferry.

Peters knew what he had to do. He stuffed the red duffel bag into the back of the boat and then climbed into the cab of the flatbed and turned the ignition key. The starter groaned until the engine kicked over. He revved the accelerator a couple of times, then shifted the truck into reverse. The truck lurched backwards, jumped the raised back ramp of the ferry, and crashed into the ocean.

Peters jumped from the cab as soon as the truck hit the water. Without ceremony the machine quickly sank beneath the waves, but the speed boat was afloat. Dazed and disoriented, Peters tried to get his bearings. The boat was about twenty yards away, but in the rough sea it seemed more like twenty miles. He swam towards it but the ocean was not cooperating. Every time he got close a wave would knock him back. He was about played out, unsure how much fight he had left, when he felt the ocean swell and lift him forward. He hit the side of the small craft hard, momentarily knocking the wind out of him. Coughing and spitting up sea water, he hung onto the side of the boat with a death grip.

After a time, he managed to crawl aboard and get the engine started. The storm raged around him, pitching the small craft from side to side. Visibility was near zero, all was storm and sea. He had no idea which direction to head, but he had to make a choice. He prayed his navigational choice was toward land and not out to sea.

CHAPTER 2

The sun was low on the western horizon, a flaming orange light silhouetting the remnants of clouds left in the sky from the morning's storm. The light danced from far off the Caribbean waters until it reached the shore and was burst apart by the waves rolling onto the beach. Jack Phillips was mesmerized by the sun's light. It seemed to be traveling in a line across the sea that led straight to him. As he strolled down the beach the path of light followed him; or more likely, he thought, it followed the woman walking by his side.

The woman was his wife of five years, and even if they had not been strolling down a romantic beach at sunset he could honestly say he still loved her as intensely as he had when he first fell in love. With the passing of the years his love for her had matured, and now it was impossible for him to imagine her not being a part of his life.

At the moment his wife's dark shoulder-length curls were tied to the left side of her head, creating an exotic look that went well with her tanned body. Jo, short for Josephine, did not have classic cover girl good looks, but she did have an intangible quality that enchanted Jack and most other men who came into her presence. This quality was enhanced by a full yet firm figure that retained a certain athleticism. Jack pulled her to him and wrapped his arms around her. Looking into her dark-green eyes he smiled and said, "Woman, I think I still love you."

"You think?" Jo replied. "You better reword what you just said or you'll spend the last two weeks of our vacation alone."

He kissed her and said, "You're just looking for an excuse to run off with Gus and explore the ruins."

"Why do you think I planned this vacation? It was all so I could have a torrid jungle romance with the famous archeologist."

They both laughed at this as they continued their stroll down the beach. Jack was amused at the thought of his wife and Gus being romantically involved. Gus was not what Jack would consider handsome. His most distinguishing characteristics were his glasses, which were as thick as the bottom of a soda bottle, and a thin beard that never quite filled out. Jack was reminded of the guys who hung out in the computer lab at the university, eating Cheese Puffs and sucking down Cokes. Then again, he also remembered that Gus had never had any trouble meeting women. Jack had always attributed Gus's success with the opposite sex to his rebellious nature and his tales of adventure in foreign lands. Gus was an archaeologist, and his research had afforded him the chance to explore much of Mexico and Central America. Jack remembered more than one night when his wife and best friend had stayed up late discussing Gus's adventures. The archaeologist's work fascinated Jo.

Gus was the main reason they had chosen to vacation in the Yucatán. The last few years he had been deeply involved in research of the ancient Mayan cities. His stories of the Mayan culture and the ruin sites had so intrigued Jo that she had to come down here. Also, since Jo taught Spanish at the university it seemed appropriate they vacation in Mexico. She had traveled through most of Mexico as an exchange student but had never been to the Yucatán.

Initially Jack had not been particularly excited about vacationing in Mexico; he had visions of Tijuana slums. He considered Hawaii more his style. The week on this island had changed his mind though; it had been like a second honeymoon—carefree days spent lying on white sandy beaches, soaking up the tropical sun, with nothing more important to do than pick up a six pack of cervezas at the local tienda. There had been plenty of time to get to know each other again, to touch, to laugh, to just be together.

The last week had been in contrast to much of the last year, which they had spent in relationship hell. This was not to say that the path they traveled together had always been smooth. When he first met Jo she was a brash young coed with a smart-ass personality, and he was the handsome and eligible first-year history instructor. Her parents had died in a car accident when she was sixteen. The experience had left her a bitter person who felt the world was unjustly punishing her. Jack was the first man she had ever loved, but because of her past their relationship had a rocky beginning. Contrary to her public personality she was actually a loner who had known few men. She was afraid of falling in love with someone only to lose them. Over time Jack managed to break down the walls she was hiding behind and brought her back to the world of the living, a place she had not been since her parents passed away.

Their love had overcome these initial obstacles, but during the past year their relationship had slipped backwards. The year had started poorly when Jack's father died suddenly from a heart attack. It was the first time he had lost a close family member or friend, and Jack had a difficult time dealing with the loss and his own mortality. He had pulled inward, unable to share his feelings with Jo. To make matters worse, both of them had been too involved in their work to spend much quality time together. The times they were together they spent having petty arguments. They were separated by an emotional wall that neither of them was able to breach. Jo felt desperate and disconnected, while a grieving Jack had a difficult time understanding her feelings.

Last winter had been extremely tough. Jack was overcome with frustration and loneliness. On top of his marital problems and dealing with his father's death, he had an important research grant canceled and there were rumors that his department would be cutting back. Jack was not yet fully tenured. The career problems only increased the strain on the marriage. At the lowest point he even suspected that Jo had taken a lover, though he now felt certain that this had been wild speculation on his part.

Recently their life together had improved, though Jack was not exactly sure why. His job situation was now more secure, and he felt that he was finally coming to terms with his father's death. But there was something more, something he did not understand. Whatever the reasons he was pleased with the results. This vacation had also been a great tonic for their marriage. They seemed to be back in tune with each other, enjoying just being together.

The sun was now rapidly dropping below the horizon, leaving them in its dusky afterglow. In the dim light Jo thought her husband looked very sexy. His dark wavy hair was, as usual, in turmoil, and his normally clean shaven face now sported a three-day-old shadow. She thought he looked a bit rakish with his stubble and curls, at least for a conservative history professor.

"It will be nice to see Gus again. We haven't seen him for almost a year," stated Jack, interrupting Jo's thoughts.

"Ah, yes!" exclaimed Jo. "The time you two college buddies spent the night in the drunk tank for raising hell at McMurrey's. I could have killed you both. I spent half the night worrying about you. By the time I called the police I was sure both of you were spread across the highway somewhere."

"The only reason we were arrested was because Gus decided to relieve himself on the leg of a peace officer who had come to quiet us down. I still don't understand what that officer was doing there in the first place. All we were doing was singing," replied Jack.

"Your singing could be used as legitimate reason for reinstating capital punishment," cracked Josephine.

"Actually, I was lucky that incident didn't cost me my job. 'Small town college history professor thrown in jail for being drunk and disorderly.' Thankfully the administration was forgiving."

"I just hope you two can celebrate your reunion a little more conservatively this time. If you're thrown in jail here I might never see you again," said Jo.

"You don't have to worry about me. I have no plans on spending any time in a Mexican jail. Gus is the one we have to watch out for; sometimes I think that man has no fear."

"It is nice to hear you say that, but as soon as you get around Gus you revert back to your college days. I don't think you realize it but you're just as crazy as he is. I think I'll keep an empty beer bottle handy in case either of you get out of hand."

Hand in hand, they strolled down the beach without speaking. The sun had set, leaving a soft orange glow on the western horizon, while to the east stars were beginning to appear in the blackening sky. Night was swiftly approaching, enveloping them in darkness.

Jack looked to Josephine, and even through the darkness he could see a mischievous smile. She leaned into him, her warm body against his skin, her smell intoxicating. She pressed her lips softly against his. Jack was immediately aroused. He knew from experience that when his wife was in the mood there was no stopping her (not that he ever wanted to), but he was feeling a bit self-conscious about the possibility of making love on a public beach. Night had fallen, and the beach was deserted; still, someone might come along.

"Honey, we better not get carried away. I think they throw people in jail down here for doing it on a public beach."

"Doing what?" replied Jo with mock innocence, "kissing my husband?"

She sat down in the sand and then reached up for Jack's hand. She pulled him down to her. He feigned resistance but was soon lying beside her holding her in his arms. Her tongue tickled his lower lip as the fingers of her left hand slowly slid down his stomach and moved inside his swim trunks. Her fingers wrapped hungrily around his manhood. She definitely had more than kissing on her mind.

Jack's inhibitions were rapidly evaporating. He managed to pull down Jo's bikini top, exposing her plump breasts. With his tongue he began to trace wet circles around the swollen, upturned nipples. Jo let out a soft moan as Jack gently suckled her. She gripped him tighter.

He delighted in the smooth skin of her bosom until he felt her right hand guiding his head lower. His tongue was soon buried in her belly button, but he felt her urging him farther down. Slowly, he slipped her bikini bottom down past her knees as his lips and tongue teased the velvet-smooth skin of her inner thigh. Purposefully he stayed away from the one place she wanted him to concentrate, until she grabbed him by the hair and guided his lips to the spot. Her smell filled his head as her body quivered with his touch. She forced his head closer, burying it between her legs. A feeling of suffocation passed over him, but he remained in position. A series of small cries escaped her lips as spasms of pleasure rippled through her body. A sharp pain burned his scalp as she pulled at his hair.

"We better not get carried away," teased Jo once she had caught her breath.

"We're just getting started." Jack was so excited by this point that he had lost all feelings of inhibition.

She directed him to lie on his back and then began to return the pleasure he had just bestowed on her. Her mouth was warm and wet. He lay back staring up at the star-filled Caribbean sky, his arms outstretched, handfuls of sand gripped tightly in both hands. The pleasure was intense; he was about to lose control.

Sensing his condition, she stopped, then looked up at him and whispered, "Not yet, I want you inside of me."

She moved on top of him, her legs straddling his hips. Her hand guided him into her, then slowly she sank down onto his erection. Cupping a breast in each hand, he gently massaged her hard nipples. Moaning with pleasure, she began to rock back and forth, slowly at first but gradually increasing the tempo. With the rhythm of their bodies, the sound of the surf, and the smell of her perfume, at this moment Jack figured he had to be the luckiest man on earth.

*   *   *

Downtown Isla Mujeres sits on the northern tip of the small island of the same name. Its low sun-bleached buildings contrast with Cancún's beachfront high rises seen across the channel. The town's history also contrast's with its big brother on the mainland. While Cancún rose out of the jungle over the past few decades to become one of Mexico's most popular playgrounds, Isla Mujeres was occupied by man since the days of the ancient Mayans. A pirate named Mundaca once made the island his home. Still a legend among the locals, Mundaca retired on the island when the pirate business became unprofitable. He fell in love with one of the young island girls, who rejected his repeated advances. She eventually married another man, but for the rest of Mundaca's life he would build an ornate well dedicated to his love each time the young lady bore a child. The ruins of the pirate's estate, along with the monuments to his lost love, can still be found in the island's jungle.

The town was originally a fishing village, but over time the main economic resource had become tourism. The downtown businesses were mostly eating establishments and gift shops selling huaraches and blankets.

Feeling extremely hungry after their impetuous encounter on the beach, Jack and Jo decided to head to town for dinner. Their appetites had been ravenous the past two days, and tonight was no exception. They consumed a substantial meal at a small lobster house near the center of town. Their large appetites were, in part, a reaction to their first three days on the island when Montezuma took his revenge. They had not felt like eating, and what little they did consume slipped through their digestive systems much too fast, something of a problem when traveling in a country that does not place a high value on public restrooms.

From across the street floated the music of a *mariachi* band. It was about the hundredth time Jack had heard the song "La Bamba" since arriving on the island. The typical gringo seemed to request only one of three Mexican songs "La Bamba," "La Cucaracha," and "El Rancho Grande."

They finished their meal with coconut ice cream smothered in Khaluha and topped this off with an after dinner liqueur of Xabetune, a heavy anise flavored drink favored by the local Mayans. The Phillips sat enjoying their drinks and listening to the music. Neither of them said as much, but both wished they could stay like this forever. Tomorrow, though, they would leave the island to continue their vacation on the mainland.

They were still sipping Xabetune when an American couple entered the restaurant and sat down at the table next to them. The woman was very attractive for her age, which Jack estimated to be mid-forties. Her friend was quite handsome and quite young, twenty-five, give or take a couple of years. Jack could hear the woman's Texas twang when she ordered drinks for her friend and herself. He guessed she must be some rich oilman's wife who had brought her boyfriend down to the Yucatán for the weekend. Cancún and Cozumel were popular destinations for the Texas jet set crowd.

While the woman was waiting for the drinks to arrive, she looked over at the Phillips and twanged, "Is the food edible here?"

"We just had an excellent meal," Josephine replied. "I hope I still feel that way in the morning."

The woman laughed politely at Jo's attempt at humor. She did not appear to be enjoying herself; she was stressed, and it showed. The woman lit a long thin cigarette, blowing the smoke up above her head.

"Ya'll stuck on this dump of an island like the rest of us?" the woman asked. "Ya'll" was almost pronounced "you all;" she was definitely a refined Texan.

Jack was not sure what the lady was getting at, but he did not like her calling his island a dump. Though he had only been on the island for a week, he had become very attached to it.

"I don't know anything about being stuck. We spent the last seven days here enjoying good sun, good snorkeling, and great sex. We're leaving tomorrow, but I wish we could stay here another week," Jack replied calmly.

"Lord, you two must not have heard about the excitement on the car ferry. Where have you been all day? It's the only thing people have been talking about all afternoon. I am sick of hearing about it myself."

Jack still did not know what the woman was talking about, but he was getting a feeling that they had missed something. Hell, World War III could have started in the past week and they would not have noticed. Whatever had happened, he was sure they were about to be completely filled in.

"Some addict dope dealers blew up a fishing boat and had a shootout with the *Federales* on the car ferry this morning. Supposedly half a dozen people were killed, two of them were *Federales*."

The woman from Texas was momentarily interrupted when the waiter arrived with the drinks. Jack noticed that she paid for the drinks while the young man watched indifferently. The lady was definitely in charge.

"Anyway, one of the dopers somehow managed to escape off the ferry. The Mexicans have been going crazy looking for this guy; they even shut down all traffic between Isle Mujeres and Cancún until tomorrow morning. My friend and I came over for the day and are now trapped on this little paradise for the night. The El Presidente is all booked up so we can't even get a decent hotel room. This vacation sure turned into a pisser."

The woman took a last drag on her cigarette and snuffed it out in an ashtray.

"What a nightmare," said Jo. "It makes you wonder what's going on."

"Who knows?" the woman replied. "Whatever happened out there today has the Mexicans pretty stirred up. I don't think they like the idea of shootouts in their number one tourist resort; it could be bad for business. I know as soon as we get back to Cancún we're catching the next flight back to Houston and getting out of this back-ass, backward country."

The earlier romantic mood had been broken. After talking with the woman a while longer, Jack could see that she did not know anything more about the incident on the car ferry. Jack decided it was better to leave than to sit and listen to this lady whine about not being able to spend the night in a five-star hotel. He paid the dinner check, wished the couple luck on getting back to Houston, and then he and Josephine headed out onto the street.

As they walked down the narrow oyster-shell street between the small shops and restaurants they talked about what the lady from Texas had told them. It was not much fun having reality intrude on your vacation.

"Hell, honey, people get shot and killed every day on this crazy planet. I doubt there is anywhere you can go and be totally away from it," Jack said.

"I know you're right. I just wish it didn't have to happen here. This place is special; it should be a safe haven from the real world, " said Jo.

"Hey!" Jack exclaimed. "What are we doing? We have three more weeks of vacation! Let's get on with it. I want to know what our schedule is for tomorrow."

"We might as well get started early," answered Jo. "We'll catch the first ferry to Cancún and then find the bus station. I didn't plan on spending time in Cancún. According to Gus, the place didn't even exist until about twenty years ago. The whole city was built by the Mexican government to cater to tourists. Anyway, we travel by bus to Chichén Itzá. When we get to Chichén Itzá, we go to a hotel called the Dolores Alba. It's supposed to be about a mile and a half from the ruin site. The next morning . . . "

Jack was smiling at his wife. She was normally a semi-reserved college professor, but when she started talking about this trip she was anything but reserved.

Jo saw his knowing smile and knew he had stopped listening. Playfully she punched his side and said, "I'm getting carried away again, and you're not even listening to me."

"No, honey," Jack replied still smiling, "I was listening. It sounds great. I'm ready to do something besides sit on the beach." He kissed her on the cheek and then added, "But let's not take the car ferry tomorrow."

CHAPTER 3

"Why did Jo stay with the luggage?" Jack thought. Here he was at the ticket window in the Cancún bus station trying to buy two tickets to Chichén Itzá, while his wife—who spoke fluent Spanish—sat outside guarding their duffel bags. Unfamiliar with the Mexican transit system, Jack was not sure if he needed to buy tickets to Mérida now (their destination after Chichén Itzá), or to only purchase tickets to Chichén Itzá. He had a fear of going out into the jungle with no ticket back. The lady at the ticket window knew about as much English as he did Spanish, so she was no help in resolving his dilemma. The line to the ticket counter was backing up behind him with people in a hurry to catch a bus. For the first time in his life he was beginning to truly understand what it was like to be a foreigner, both culturally and linguistically. During their stay on the island Jack had never felt like he did now. The ticket lady was saying something in Spanish that he could not understand. Confused, he looked around the cramped, dingy terminal for help, but did not see any sympathetic faces in the crowd.

Frustrated, he was about to give up his place in line and send Jo in to buy the tickets, when from the other side of the crowded terminal he saw a man with blonde hair and blue eyes walking his way. Jack crossed his fingers and hoped the stranger knew both English and Spanish.

"You don't happen to *habla español*?" Jack asked the man as he passed by.

The man smiled and said, "A little. You need a translator?"

"That, or an explanation of how the bus service works down here. I need to buy tickets to Chichén Itzá, but should I also buy my tickets to Mérida now? I don't want to get stuck in the jungle with no way of getting out."

"This must be your first trip down here," the man replied. "Mexico's bus service is pretty extensive; it's how most of the population travels. As far as buying tickets is concerned, you buy them as you go. In fact, you can flag down a bus on most roads, and if the bus is not full the driver will usually stop and let you board. I wouldn't worry about getting stuck out in the middle of nowhere at Chichén Itzá; the place is more like Disneyland. By the way, when does the next bus leave for Chichén Itzâ?"

"As near as I can tell it was supposed to leave about ten minutes ago," Jack answered.

The man sighed and said, "Even if the bus is running on Mexican time I won't be able to get through this line fast enough to make the next departure."

"How many tickets do you need?" Jack asked.

"Just one," replied the stranger.

Jack quickly turned to the ticket lady and ordered three tickets. Just as quickly the woman handed Jack his tickets and his change, glad to see the confused gringo leave her window.

"Here, your ticket is on me," Jack said as he handed the man a ticket. The price of the bus ticket was approximately five U.S. dollars.

"You didn't have to do that, but thanks. It saves me from having to hang out here waiting for the next bus," said the man as he turned and began walking toward the boarding gate.

Separating his money from the tickets, Jack dropped one of the tickets. By the time he had reached down and snatched the ticket from the floor the stranger was gone. Jack was sorry to see him leave; it was nice to meet a fellow countryman. He hoped he would get a chance to talk to him on the bus. The fellow seemed to know his way around.

Outside the terminal he saw Jo in her flowered dress. She was standing in the doorway of the bus. From the look on the bus driver's face, Jack was certain she had spent the last ten minutes convincing the driver that he better not leave until her husband was on board.

"Jack! Where have you been? We were about to leave without you," Jo yelled as Jack climbed up the bus steps.

"You wouldn't be going anywhere without a ticket," replied Jack.

"Don't be so sure of yourself. The driver already told me I could ride for free if I would shut up and sit down."

Jack handed the tickets to the driver and then followed Jo to the back of the bus. The bus passengers were primarily Mexicans, though there were a few Anglos on board. The Anglos, for the most part, appeared to be young people traveling abroad, their backpacks bulging and *Mexico on Thirty Dollars a Day* books being avidly read.

In the next to the last seat to Jack's left sat the man whom he had met at the ticket window. The only two seats that were still empty were across the aisle from the stranger. Jack was pleased to see the empty seats next to this man. Jack and the blonde man nodded to each other, but said nothing. The stranger had been reading a book and immediately went back to his reading. Jack and Jo sat in the vacant seats, Jack taking the aisle seat.

Their seats were in the back of the bus, and not long after the bus pulled out of the station Jack was wishing he had been able to purchase the tickets faster so they could have secured better seats. Between the fumes and engine noise he was already feeling ill. Jo was reading a travel book. Every so often she would relay some useful or interesting piece of information. Watching her read did not make him feel any better. He had always been susceptible to motion sickness, but especially if he tried to read in a moving vehicle. Jo had always been the opposite. He was sure she could read *War and Peace* while riding a roller coaster.

Jack turned his attention to the world that was passing by outside, hoping it would distract his mind from the nausea in his stomach. He watched as the gray buildings of the city gave way to thatched huts, and the thatched huts gave way to a tropical forest. The two-lane highway cut a straight swath through an unending sea of jungle.

Gazing out the window at the green foliage and gray-black skies, Jack began to feel better. The weather did not look like it was going to improve. At least the rain kept the temperature relatively cool. If it had been hot, with the prevailing humidity, the bus ride would have been unbearable.

He was still hoping for a chance to talk with the blonde man. The man was still reading though, and Jack did not want to interrupt him. Jack hated being bothered when he wanted to be left alone.

The bus was entering a modest jungle village. Outside the window he could see a number of palm-thatched oval huts, or *naj* as the Mayans called them. The walls of these structures were made of vertical sticks tied together and then plastered. The basic design had remained unchanged for over a 1,000 years. Through the doorways of the *najs* he could see hammocks and blankets and old women. In one *naj* he thought he saw a television set. He wondered what the reception was like.

Chickens and pigs were numerous in the small village. Every yard the bus passed seemed to have a member of the swine family rooting around. Near one of the dwellings a Brahma steer was tied to a tree. The owner of this hut must have been prosperous; corrugated metal sheets made up the walls of his *naj* instead of the prevalent thatching.

One building, with an unpainted plywood exterior, appeared to be the local store. On the front of the building hung a Coca-Cola sign. A group of men stood near the doorway staring at the bus as it blasted past.

The village disappeared into the vegetation as quickly as it had materialized, leaving only the jungle and the occasional passing truck.

Jack heard the tap of rain drops on the roof of the bus. The rain beat out a slow rhythm that quickly grew in intensity. Soon the bus was in the middle of a torrential downpour. So intense was the rain that Jack wondered how the bus driver could see out the windshield. This was not a pleasant thought since the bus seemed to be traveling about ninety miles an hour.

"At least the road is straight," Jack thought to himself.

Entranced by the rain, Jack almost did not notice someone speaking to him, "You haven't seen it rain until you have seen rain in the tropics."

Jack was confused for a moment; who was talking? Between the engine noise and the rain pounding on the roof it was difficult to hear. He turned and realized it was the man from the ticket counter.

"Yeah, I was thinking the same thing," Jack shouted back. "Coming from Northern California I thought I knew what rain was, but I have never seen it rain as hard as it has down here."

"This isn't that bad. Wait until your first hurricane."

"Sounds like you're talking from experience."

"A hell of a lot more than I wish I had, but I guess one hurricane is enough in anybody's life," explained the man.

"I'll take your word on that and hope I never have to find out for myself. By the way, we haven't been properly introduced: Jack Phillips," said Jack holding out his hand.

"Pleased to meet you, Jack. Steve Potter," said the man, firmly shaking Jack's hand.

"I want to thank you again for helping me back at the ticket counter. It's actually pretty funny though; my wife is a Spanish teacher, so who goes to buy the tickets."

"No need to thank me," replied Potter. "I should be thanking you. If you hadn't bought my ticket back there, I would still be sitting in the bus station. You'll learn how to get around down here. It's not just the language but the culture and customs that are helpful to know. If you stay at the resorts and tourist areas it's not a problem, but if you go out into real Mexico, the back country, it does help to know the ways of the people. I wouldn't worry though; as long as you're halfway intelligent and respectful of the locals you'll do fine."

Potter's eyes were the color of the sky, his hair was the color of straw, while his crooked smile was genuine and easy. It was the type of smile that made women blush and men feel at ease. Potter also had a deep tan; the kind of tan that comes from long hours in the sun and not from a tanning salon. The shorts and flowered shirt he was wearing completed the picture of an aging surfer fresh off of a California beach.

Jack had already pegged Mr. Potter as a man who was well liked by the ladies. He did not exactly have glamour boy looks, but he did exude a certain confidence and charisma. Jack was sure that when Steve Potter entered a room filled with people most of the men would want to be his best friend and half the women would want to go to bed with him (the other half probably already had).

He wanted to ask Potter some questions. Who was he, what did he do for a living, and why did he appear to be traveling alone? Jack hesitated, feel it was not proper to ask such questions of a stranger.

As suddenly as it had started the rain stopped, and in spite of the rumble of the bus engine, it now seemed quiet. "Well, at least we can talk now without screaming," observed Potter.

"Yes, I am used to talking loud but that was a bit much," said Jack.

"Make a living with your vocal cords," stated Potter. "You must be one of three things: an actor, a politician, or a teacher. If you're an actor you're not a famous one, at least I've never heard of you. I sense you're an honest man so you can't be a politician. That leaves teacher. I would guess that you're a teacher."

"Very good. But to be more specific I'm a college professor. I wonder though, what makes you so sure of my honesty?" said Jack.

"I'm not," replied Potter, the crooked smile still on his face. "But I didn't think you would appreciate a stranger calling you dishonest."

"You're probably right," said Jack laughing.

"What college?" asked Steve.

"I teach American History at U.C. Davis. My specialty is Economic Development of the Industrialized Nations. It doesn't sound very exciting, but it's my little niche of expertise," explained Jack.

He felt Jo discreetly nudge him with her elbow. He knew this meant she wanted to be introduced. Jack had always been terrible at introductions; either he would not make introductions when he should or he would forget a lifelong friend's name when he was about to introduce them to someone. It was not that he was nervous or rude, he just had some of the qualities of an absent-minded professor. This problem had been a source of amusement for Jo and embarrassment for himself on more than one occasion.

"My wife also teaches at the university. Jo, this is Steve Potter. He helped me buy our bus tickets."

"Pleased to meet you, Steve," greeted Jo.

"Pleased to meet you, Mrs. Phillips," returned Potter.

"Well, Mr. Potter you know about us, now it's your turn. What do you do for a paycheck?" asked Jack.

"Please call me Steve," replied Potter. "I'm currently working for a small computer programming firm located in Salt Lake City. Most of our work is with small businesses; we tailor programs to fit individual needs. In fact this trip is a gift from the company. The firm's owner had built up enough frequent flyer miles for a free trip but he has to use the mileage before the first of the year. He wasn't going to be able to use it, so he gave the mileage to me."

"What a bonus! You must rate with the boss," said Jack.

"We're good friends. He wanted to make me a partner in the firm at one time, but I didn't want to get involved with the business end of the company. I'd rather work on my programs and not be bothered with making sales and keeping the books," explained Steve.

"I hope I'm not getting too personal, but how do you get such a great tan sitting in front of a computer terminal?" questioned Jo.

Potter laughed as a slight blush crossed his cheeks. "That's the great thing about my job: most of my work can be done at home. I can work my own hours. I ski about three days a week during the winter and during the summer I put a lot of miles in on my mountain bike and my sailboard. I work during the evening so I can play during the day."

"So, is this your first trip to Chichén Itzá?" Jo asked.

"No, I was there once before; about four years ago. I round-tripped the ruin site from Cancún in one day. I ended up having only a couple of hours to explore the site but saw enough to know that I had to come back when I could spend more time."

"We've been told the same story. We're planning on spending this afternoon and most of tomorrow exploring the ruin site, that is, if it stops raining," explained Jo.

"It sounds to me like you've done your homework. I was hoping I would be able to spend tomorrow morning at the ruins, but I probably should be leaving in the morning. I only have five days of vacation left. I would like to spend some time in Mérida and explore the ruin sites of Uxmal and Cobá."

"You're going to be traveling the same route we are, only we'll be doing it a little slower," said Jack.

The conversation lingered on as the bus rumbled down the highway. They found out that Steve had spent the last three days on Isla Mujeres. Jack wished they could have met him while they were on the island, for Steve was quite knowledgeable about Mexico and its culture. During the conversation Steve related some of his traveling adventures in Mexico and Central and South America. He also told them that he had spent nine months at a Mexican university in Monterrey as an exchange student.

Eventually the talk drifted to the shooting incident that had taken place on the car ferry. Steve had heard there was some trouble, but he really had not paid much attention to it. According to Steve, shootings related to Mexico's dope-supported underworld were not uncommon; however, they usually did not occur in the tourist areas. It was also rare for the *Federales* to be involved in the violence; they were usually paid handsomely to stay out of the way.

The Phillips' knowledge of the incident had not increased much from the night before. Jo had bought a newspaper when they were in

Cancún. According to an article in the paper, two Mexican *Federales* and a suspected drug runner were killed in the shootout; an American tourist had also been critically wounded. Three other men died in a nearby fishing boat explosion that occurred at approximately the same time as the shooting. It was suspected that the passengers on the fishing boat were in league with the drug smugglers, but so far no evidence had been found to link the two incidents. The article also reported that a manhunt was currently underway for a suspected drug runner who escaped off of the ferry after the shooting. Authorities did not have much to go on, only that the man apparently was an Anglo of medium build with dark hair. The article stressed that the man should be considered armed and dangerous.

Jack had taken an instant liking to Steve. Although they had met less than two hours ago, Jack already felt like the man was an old friend. Steve's age, intellect, charisma, and his knowledge of the country made him a perfect traveling companion. Jack could see that his wife was also intrigued. The only problem with this guy would be keeping his wife from falling in love with him.

Outside, a shaft of sunlight was shining through a crack in the cloud cover. The sun's rays shone down on what at first appeared to be a mountain of rock rising above the jungle canopy. Jack thought this was strange. For most of the last two hours, except for the occasional small town or village, the roof of the jungle had remained an unbroken sea of vegetation. Then Jack realized what he was looking at; he had been enjoying the conversation so much he did not realize they were almost to their destination. Above the top of the jungle he could see the ancient limestone shoulders of El Castillo illuminated in a brilliant yellow light that was pouring through a crack in the dark, storm-torn sky. Jack was immediately filled with a sense of reverence and wonder as he gazed at one of the world's great pyramids. He was still staring in awe at the top of El Castillo as the bus driver applied the brakes and turned the bus into Chichén Itzá's main entrance.

The parking lot at the main entrance was filled with buses, taxi cabs, rental cars, and people—lots of people. The entrance complex was made up of two long buildings that housed a museum, eating establishments, and gift shops. Rising behind the entrance complex could be seen the ancient stone city of Chichén Itzá. Here, for a few pesos, one could enter the *zona archelogica*, the archeological zone. Along one side of the parking lot the local merchants had set up shop selling everything from Chichén Itzá T-shirts to small plaster models of El Castillo. The place had the atmosphere of an amusement park. As the bus slowed to a stop, its brakes screeching, Jack looked at Steve and said, "You're right—Disneyland!"

CHAPTER 4

Three men sat at a round table in a small conference room. The room contained only the table and six chairs, which were surrounded by four empty walls, linoleum floor, and a ceiling that would have been bare if not for the fluorescent light fixtures. The room was soundproof and regularly swept for electronic listening devices. The men who sat at the table had neither pens nor pencils nor the yellow legal pads one would normally expect to see in this setting. In this room nothing would be written down or recorded except in the mind of each man.

Two of the men were currently in a heated discussion. Andrew Buck, a black man of medium height with the build and temperament of a Marine Corps drill sergeant, was employed by the Drug Enforcement Agency. The State Department's Ronald Allen was of Jewish descent. He stood five-foot seven-inches and was a few pounds short of obesity. A third man listened intently to the discourse between Buck and Allen.

"We are facing a decision none of us like," said Allen was. "As much as we don't want to admit it, the most likely scenario is that Peters has turned."

"Ron, I don't see it. I can't believe he would throw all our work away. The man is a pro," replied Buck emphatically.

"I know how you feel, Andy. Hell, I feel the same way. I've been on this project from the start. I hate the thought of Peters no longer being on our side, but I can't ignore the facts. Four people were killed on that car ferry, two of them Mexican federal agents. Eye witnesses, three of them Americans, reported seeing Peters pull a weapon on an unarmed man and blow his brains all over the Caribbean. He then proceeded to shoot and kill the two Mexican agents. While all of this was going on, Peters' boat carrying agents Foster and Cooper explodes. Only Sam knew that they would be on that boat. I hate to say it, but all the evidence leads to Peters," concluded Allen, exasperation showing on his round face.

"That's what I don't like about you so called State Department 'geniuses,'" replied Buck, his stern, dark eyes directed at Allen. "Sometimes you rely too much on evidence, facts, and intelligence. I just want you to balance all this evidence against Peters the man. We all know his service record by heart; it was the reason we selected him for this project. Now we're going to say he sold out, killing one of his best friends, a man who saved his life. That's too easy of a conclusion."

"You're reading me wrong, Andy, if you think I've given up on Sam, but you know we can't allow ourselves to get burned on this one. If the Mexicans find out it was one of our men who shot their agents this could turn into an international incident, not to mention the uproar that would arise in this country. I just wish Sam would make contact. If we could hear his side of the story things would be clearer."

Buck looked over at Senator Jason James Hightower. The man, even in his mid-fifties, still looked as if he could throw a football eighty yards. "J.J. you've been rather quiet. What are your thoughts on the situation?" asked Buck.

J.J. Hightower had been an All-American quarterback in college. A golden boy who, during his senior year at USC, led the Trojans to a national championship. Upon his graduation, the Los Angeles Rams made him their number one draft choice. Before he had played his first down of pro ball the media lauded him as a future Hall of Famer. It was not to be. Midway through his rookie season Hightower suffered a career-ending knee injury.

With football no longer a possibility, the young Hightower decided to try his hand at politics. He found that he could maneuver through the political world as easily as he had picked apart defenses in his college days. Running on a conservative line, with his handsome face and past football glories, he easily won his first election for a seat on the California State Assembly. From there his climb up the political ladder went mostly unimpeded, until currently he was a respected Senator who was committee chair on the Senate Select Subcommittee on Intelligence. The Senator was even considered to be a possible future presidential candidate.

"My first thought is, 'What in the hell am I doing here?' This whole thing is crazy. If the President hadn't asked me personally I would never have let myself get involved. He said he wanted me on this project to keep you guys in line, but as things have progressed we have gone farther and farther out on a limb until now I can hear it cracking under the weight of our lies and deceit. At this point I don't think there is a law on the books that we have not broken. I'm beginning to see the real reason the President wanted me on this project. He knew if I were involved, and things went sour, it would be difficult for the Chairman of the Senate Select Subcommittee on Intelligence to instigate an investigation against himself. Let's not concern ourselves with my dilemma though. It's nothing compared to what our man Peters may be facing.

"I don't think we can give up on this man who has given so much to his country," Hightower continued. "There is nothing in his record or his performance on this project to lead me to believe that he would sell out. On the other hand, greed is a powerful force. I think we owe it to Peters to try and establish contact before we pass judgment, even if it means sending our people in and bringing him back physically."

"You sound like you're ready to send in the Marines," replied Allen, a note of sarcasm in his voice.

Hightower and Allen went together like ice and fire. Allen did not have a high regard for the Senator's intellect, and Hightower did not care for Allen's superior attitude.

"No, I wasn't thinking of the Marines, but we do have people who could find the man. Don't we?" asked the Senator.

"Probably not," returned Allen. "If Peters has turned he is going to be awfully hard to find. He is one of the best at what he does, and he knows our Mexican operations better than anyone."

In a careful voice Buck spoke next, "There is one man who might have a chance. If he can't find Peters, no one can."

"Who is this man, Andrew?" questioned Hightower.

"I know who you're thinking of," interjected Allen. He then looked at Hightower and said, "Think, Senator: you have read Peters' service record, remember?"

"Yes, I've read his service record, and with what knowledge I have on the subject it seems that he has come in contact with just about everybody in the American intelligence community. How am I to pick out this special person from this voluminous file? I thought that was your job," said Hightower as he stared straight at Ron Allen. Allen's round face returned the stare as he tried to hold back a smirk.

"You're quite right, Senator," Buck cut in. "But if you will think about some of the men in Peters' special unit in Nicaragua, I think you will realize who Ron and I are considering."

The Senator laid his forefinger and thumb alongside his head in a moment of contemplation. He then nodded his head in recognition and said, "Travis Horn. Yes, that man did have what you would call special talents."

"Besides that, he and Peters are still good friends, which could work in our favor," added Buck.

"I hate to play the devil's advocate," said Allen, "but it could also work against us. Do you think Horn could carry out a beyond salvage situation if it arose?"

Buck went rigid at the mention of "beyond salvage ". He knew it was the real issue behind this meeting, but so far they had not discussed it in such blunt terms. As much as he did not like it, he knew it was a decision they would probably have to face.

"Good question," answered Buck slowly. "I think it would depend on what the situation is if and when he finds Peters. I do know this man would give us the true story, friend or not."

The three men were quiet for a moment, each reviewing the options. The silence was total.

"There is another item I think we need to discuss," said Allen finally. "If this does turn into a beyond salvage situation, we will need a cover story. We should develop a fake file on Peters, complete with photos. It would outline his criminal record, psychotic delusions, and violent past. This file we would make available to the Mexican authorities. With a positive photo I.D., the Mexicans would have a good chance of eliminating Peters for us, thus taking the problem out of our hands. Given Peters' cover for the past two years, the information won't be hard to assemble and should be quite convincing."

Buck slowly shook his head and said, "I can't believe it has come to this. Something stinks about this whole thing; I just can't put my finger on it. Here we are, planning the death of a man who has served his country for most of his adult life. Much of his work placed him in situations of grave danger. I need some time to think before we discuss final solutions."

"I agree with Andrew," said Hightower. "It does seem premature to be planning Peters' elimination. We could at least give him a few more hours to make contact."

"I don't think the decisions are going to be any easier tomorrow unless we hear from Peters, but I suppose we owe him a few more hours. Let's meet tomorrow morning at six," said Allen. "Before we leave today, do we want to initiate contact with Mr. Horn? That way we can start prepping him in case we have to send him after Peters."

Andrew Buck, hands clasped in front of his face, stared at the center of the table. His mind was in turmoil. He could not rid himself of the feeling that things were not what they appeared to be.

Buck came to a decision. He looked at Allen and said, "I think we should contact Travis immediately. He is the one man who can bring us the truth. The longer we wait to bring him in, the greater the chance that beyond salvage orders will have to be executed, and I don't want to have to be a part of that."

The Senator started shaking his head and said, "I don't think we should do anything until morning. A few more hours shouldn't make a big difference. Let's not give up on this project just yet. Once we start bringing others into this thing it could quickly grow beyond our control."

"Andy, I'm afraid this is one of the few times I have to agree with the Senator. If we're going to wait, we might as well wait," responded Allen.

"You two are probably right," Buck conceded. "I just want to make sure every effort is made to find out Peters' side of the story before any irreversible decisions are made."

The men were again silent for a moment, then the Senator spoke, "God help Peters . . . and us."

CHAPTER 5

The Jack, Jo and Steve Potter departed the bus at Chichén Itzá's main entrance and grabbed one of the many taxis competing for their pesos. Steve had not decided where he was staying for the night, so he decided to ride along with the Phillips and see what the accommodations were like at the Hotel Dolores Alba.

A mile and a half back down the main highway, the taxi dropped them off in front of a small hotel. Sitting alone in the jungle with only the highway for company, the Dolores Alba had a certain funky equatorial charm. The small rooms were not fancy, but they were clean, and the hotel did serve dinner and breakfast. A garden patio with a circular wading pool settled any doubts about where they were staying.

The storm had moved on and the sun was out, so after they checked into their rooms they asked the hotel manager to drive them back to the ruin site. Jack, Jo, Potter, and the manager squeezed into the hotel's beat-up Volkswagen bug.

After two miles of shimmying and shaking down the highway at sixty miles per hour, the dilapidated Volkswagen arrived at the rear entrance of the archeological zone. Jack climbed out of the back seat thankful to still be part of the living. He found that the rear entrance was not as elaborate as the main entrance. It consisted of a dirt parking lot, a chain link fence, and an old man selling tickets from a small wooden booth. As at the main entrance, locals had set up shop selling the same cheap trinkets.

The old man in the ticket booth took their money and stuck it in an old coffee can, then handed each of them a sheet of tickets. The current rate of inflation in Mexico was so high that ticket prices would rise before new tickets could be printed. Instead of constantly printing new tickets, the government sold each visitor the number of tickets that equaled the current entrance fee.

Upon entering the archeological zone they found themselves walking down a wide path. Both sides of the dusty red path were lined with trees. The overhanging branches provided some relief from the afternoon heat and humidity. Jack was filled with the anticipation of the curious, the promise of adventure lay ahead.

"This path was the ancient *sacbe* into the city," commented Potter as they walked along.

"*Sacbe?*" replied Jack, a quizzical expression on his face.

"Causeway, or road," explained Potter. "The function of the *sacbes* is somewhat mysterious. There is, of course, the obvious role of trade routes, but consider the thirty-foot wide *sacbe* that connected Cobá with Chichén Itzá. Constructed out of rock rubble, the causeway is over 60 miles long, elevated two to eight feet above ground, and covered with a smooth stucco facing. The Mayans had no wheeled vehicles or beasts of burden. Why did they need such a highly engineered road?"

Jack pondered the enigma of the *sacbe* as they continued down the jungle path. He was so preoccupied with his thoughts that at first he did not notice the forest had come to an abrupt end. He stood on the edge of a large clearing, in the middle of which loomed the giant El Castillo. The sudden appearance of such a gigantic, man-made geometric design out of the primeval forest was almost overpowering; the grand remnant of a lost civilization.

The terraces that formed the pyramid ascended toward the sky, the length of each terrace smaller than the one below it and thus forming a stair-step design. Occupying the uppermost terrace was a box-shaped temple with some type of jungle brush or grass struggling to grow on its roof. The solitary vegetation only added to the forlornness of the structure. On each face of the pyramid a wide stairway descended steeply from the temple. A pair of carved serpent heads guarded the lower steps of the north stairway. Time's passage had turned the limestone blocks a mottled gray, making the pyramid look as if it had been cut from a single block of granite. Jack stood in awe at the base of the ancient monolith, impressed not just by the sheer size but also with the intellect that had gone into the building of the structure.

"El Castillo was definitely built with the calendar in mind," Steve explained. "There are 364 stairs plus the temple platform which makes 365, equal to the number of days in a year. There are fifty-two panels on each face that represent the fifty-two year cycle of the Mayan calendar, and nine terraces on each side of the stairways, a total of eighteen terraces to represent the eighteen month Mayan solar calendar. If this isn't proof enough, come down here on March 21 for the spring equinox. When the sun goes down you will see the seven stairs of the northern stairway plus the serpent head carving at the base of the stairway touched with the last rays of the setting sun. In a little more than a half hour the serpent formed by this play of light appears to descend into the earth as the sun leaves each stair, going from top to bottom, ending with the serpent head. To the Mayans this was a fertility symbol: the golden sun has entered the earth, time to plant the corn."

"I'm impressed. You've done your reading," said Jack.

"I'm sorry, I didn't mean to give you a lecture. This place has always fascinated me, and I guess I get carried away sometimes."

"Not at all," declared Jo enthusiastically. "That was fantastic. You can lecture all you want. We'll pay you if we have to."

Jo snapped the customary photos. Then Jack asked, "Where to first?"

"How about if we check out the south section first, then circle back through the north section? We can end the day by climbing El Castillo," suggested Steve.

They all agreed to this plan, and started off for the south section also referred to as Maya Chichén. They strolled through the open grounds where the jungle had been cleared away to expose a jungle acropolis. Jack was struck by the massiveness of the place. Around every corner another stone edifice filled the space before him. Far off, the tops of distant structures poked their gray-white heads above the jungle canopy. The uppermost temples appeared to be hovering above the trees, as if some ancient levitation spell had been cast on the stone structures.

"The art and architecture of the south section are mostly of the Classic Mayan style and therefore generally considered to be older than the north section with its Toltec influences," explained Steve.

"Excuse my ignorance but what's the difference between Mayan and Toltec?" asked Jack.

"A simplified version of Chichén's history goes something like this: The Mayans, of course, were here first, but it's theorized that they were later conquered by the Toltecs, predecessors to the Aztecs. The Toltecs were from Tula, near present-day Mexico City. This theory of Toltec conquest is based on two facts: the myth of Quetzalcatl, the Mayan's Kulkulcán, and the amazing similarity between the Pyramid of Quetzalcatl at Tula and Chichén's Temple of the Warriors. The feathered serpent representation of Quetzalcatl is repeated many times in Chichén's north section. The early Spanish learned of the Myth of Quetzalcatl from the Aztecs. According to legend, Quetzalcatl once ruled Tula as a chaste king but was expelled after being tempted by the forbidden fruit. In one version of the myth the king sails off to the east, and archaeologists have interpreted this to mean he left for the Yucatán where he conquered Chichén Itzá. According to this theory Chichén's south section was extended north by the Toltecs, which explains the blend of Maya and Toltec styles found in the north section.

"More recently though, the established theories on Chichén Itzá's history have been challenged," Steve continued. "Archaeologists have found evidence that Toltec traits existed at Chichén before Tula was even founded. Some suggest that Tula may have been an outpost of Chichén, or even turn the old theory inside out by postulating that Tula was founded by exiles from Chichén Itzá. No one has yet been able to come up with a theory that fully explains the unique blend of Maya and Toltec art found here."

They had come to the base of a pyramid that had not been reconstructed. It looked more like a small grassy hill than a pyramid, only the feathered serpent columns of the original temple were still visible. Climbing to the top of Osario, also known as the High Priest's Grave, they were able to look down a shaft that cut through the middle of the pyramid. At the bottom of the shaft they could see steps leading down into a natural cave. Steve explained that a tomb had been discovered in the cave that contained human skeletons and offerings of jade, copper, crystals, and shells. Jack was fascinated as he peered down the shaft into the cool darkness of the cave. This was like something out of an old movie, he thought, a jungle tomb complete with skeletons and treasure, only this was the real thing, not a Hollywood set.

From the Osario they hiked over to the impressive El Caracol (The Snail), also known as the observatory. This structure was unique; its rambling architecture did not have the perfect symmetric design of the other pyramids and palaces. A circular tower sat askew upon two broad platforms and was accessed by a series of wide staircases. The upper portion of the tower was crumbling but retained its dome-like shape. Overall, the tower had the shape of a bowler hat set atop a round pedestal. The lower section of the tower had four doorways, each facing one of the cardinal points. A hooked nose mask of the rain god Chalk hung above each of the doors. Jack, Jo and Steve climbed the tower's small winding interior staircase to an upper chamber. There were three slit-like windows in the chamber's walls. From the north-facing window they could see the distant El Castillo rising above the jungle.

"El Caracol was an observatory for solar and planetary sightings, especially Venus," explained Steve. "Venus was important to the Maya as it was believed to be the reincarnation of Quetzalcatl. They believed that when the planet vanished from the sky it traveled for a time through an evil underworld. Venus rising from the underworld was a fearful event often marked by warfare."

They next explored the dank, dark rooms of the Nunnery, thick with the smell of bat guano. This large, rectangular palace structure, with its rows of small rooms separated by thick limestone walls, had evidently reminded the Spaniards of their convents back home. Alongside the

Nunnery was another Spanish-named building called The Church, a narrow, two-story structure with an ornate upper facade and roof comb. Rain god masks glared menacingly from the corners of the building's second story. The highlight of this structure was a large, anatomically correct penis that hung off a second story wall.

Jack asked Jo to take a picture of him standing under the phallic symbol. "This might be dedicated to one of my ancestors," explained Jack with mock seriousness.

"Too bad for me you didn't inherit their better traits," kidded Josephine.

Having thoroughly explored the south section, they started back north. Along the way they came to a small refreshment kiosk set back in the trees, with a selection of cold soft drinks and snacks. They rested and refueled their hot, sweaty bodies at the shady oasis, slaking their thirst with ice-cold Cokes.

Reinvigorated, they continued on, again passing under the giant El Castillo on their way to the Temple of the Warriors. This structure had a broad, three-terraced, pyramidal base. Upon this base sat a walled temple with no roof. In front of the structure were neatly lined rows of colonnades that at one time had supported a palm-thatched roof. The seven-foot-high columns had been carved in the image of warriors, an army of stone soldiers ready to march into battle.

They walked through the colonnades inspecting the life-size carvings and then climbed the steep stairway to the temple. On the upper platform, between two feathered serpent heads, a chacmool statue faced out toward the main plaza. The life-size reclining figure sat with its knees bent holding a large plate on its stomach.

"Chacmool sculptures are considered to be Toltec and were used in human sacrifice rituals. The stone receptacle on the chacmool's belly is where the priest would place the still-beating heart of the sacrificial victim," explained Steve.

Jack took a picture of Jo sitting on the sacrificial offering plate, draping her arm seductively around the figure's shoulder.

They left the Temple of the Warriors and headed to the Venus platform. As they walked through the main plaza Jack looked down at Jo and in a comical French accent said, "I take my love to the temple of love."

"Oui, oui, Monsieur," replied a giggling Jo.

"I hate to break this to you lovebirds, but the Venus Platform is not dedicated to the goddess of love," interjected a grinning Potter. "Remember, in Maya-Toltec lore Venus represents the feathered serpent god Quetzalcatl, not love."

The low-lying platform, situated at the base of El Castillo's north face, was not a thing of beauty. A carving of a feathered monster with a human head in its mouth decorated the platform.

From the Venus Platform they went north through the jungle. A dirt path led them to the edge of the Sacred *Cenote*, a giant natural well that was formed when the limestone plain collapsed into an underlying subterranean cave. The sink hole was a couple hundred feet in diameter. Steep limestone walls dropped approximately fifty feet into an inky black water that filled the bottom of the cavity. Thick jungle growth surrounded the ancient *cenote* and poured over its edge, giving the impression that the vegetation was floating on air.

"Chichén Itzá, roughly translated, means 'Well of the Itzá's.' This *cenote* may be how the city got its name," said Steve as they peered over the precipitous walls to the murky waters below.

"This is where they tossed the sacrificial virgins," said Jo.

"Actually the Mayans weren't that particular. They sacrificed men, women, and children, probably whoever was handy. A study of bones dredged up from the bottom indicates that many of the victims may have been diseased or feeble minded. This doesn't mean that they thought offerings to the well were unimportant, as a treasure in gold and jade has also been brought up," commented Potter.

Jack's legs were beginning to feel a bit weary as they hiked back to the main plaza. He looked up to see El Castillo and wondered why they saved the climb up the giant pyramid for last.

They were on their way to the Ball Court when they stopped for a moment to inspect the ominous *Tzompantli* or Wall of Skulls. Carved along the base of this platform was row upon row of human skulls. Also depicted were scenes of eagles tearing hearts out of human victims and warriors with writhing serpents projecting from their sides.

"I almost hate to ask what this place was used for," said Jo with a grimace.

"The heads of sacrificial victims were stuck on poles and displayed here," explained Steve. "When the Spanish arrived at Tenochtitlan they discovered similar Tzompantli, complete with real skulls of the recently deceased."

"So much for peaceful Native Americans living at one with nature," commented Jack.

"Wait until you see the Ball Court," replied Steve.

They entered the *Juego de Pelota*, or Main Ball Court, from the south end. The field was over 400 feet long and flanked by massive stone walls that ran its length. Hanging off each wall, about twenty-five feet above the playing field, was a stone ring. Gazing over the enormous arena Jack observed, "They must have had a hell of a Mayan Super Bowl here. Makes you wonder what the game was like."

"The actual rules of the game have been lost to time," Steve answered. "Most theories agree, though, that the game was played between two teams, and the object of the game was for one team to get a hard rubbery ball through one of the stone rings. This was supposedly done without the players using their hands."

Jack was most intrigued by what Steve said next. "If we walk over along the base of either wall we can see base reliefs depicting the sacrifice of team captains. The funny thing is no one has ever figured out if it was the captain of the losing or winning team who was sacrificed. You've already noticed that the Mayans were very much into sacrifice; it was an honor to sacrifice yourself to the gods. If it was an honor, why give the honor to the losing captain?"

"That must have made it tough on teams with long winning streaks," Jack quipped.

Fascinated by the repeated scenes along the base of the ball court wall, Jack paused to more closely inspect one of the carvings. Two opposing teams in full regalia were facing each other. One of the captains was down on one knee, his head missing. Above the kneeling man, the captain of the opposing team wielded an obsidian knife in one hand and the decapitated head of his opponent in the other. From the neck of the headless man sprouted six serpents and a flowering plant. Steve explained that the serpents symbolized blood and the plant symbolized fertility and renewal. The scene sent shivers down Jack's spine.

Presiding over the north end of the Ball Court was a structure appropriately named the North Temple. Compared to the grand scale of the Ball Court, it was somewhat unassuming. Steve wanted to show them something in the temple. He did not say what it was, but he convinced them to climb the steep steps. The temple afforded a magnificent view down the length of the Ball Court. Jack imagined a Mayan nobleman or priest watching a ball game from this vantage point.

Steve directed their attention to the back wall of the temple and asked, "Tell me what you see on the wall?"

Jack studied the wall. He could see indistinct carvings but could not make out any discernible shapes. Under her breath Jo muttered, "Oh wow! Do you see it, hon?"

"I guess not," replied Jack, still concentrating.

"Look here," said Jo, as her finger traced the wall carving.

Jack could now make out a profile of a man chiseled into the stone. What was so special about that? Most of the temples had similar carvings. But there was something different here, he suddenly realized. All the reliefs he had seen of the Mayans showed their prominent sloping foreheads. The ancient Mayans considered this a sign of nobility, so much so that they actually tied boards to their infants' foreheads to enhance the slope. The man depicted on the wall had no slope to his forehead. He also had a full beard and European features. Jack knew that facial hair was uncommon in the indigenous peoples of North America.

"'Oh, wow' is right!" Jack exclaimed. "Can they estimate the age of this carving?"

"I'm no expert on archeological dating techniques, but I think this temple has been estimated at least 600 years old," Steve answered.

"I wish we could go back in time and find out who this fellow was," said Jack, still staring at the carving.

"It does make one wonder," replied Steve. "But it's probably just a coincidence. The carving is somewhat indistinct, and the Toltecs were not into the sloped-forehead look. It could just be that natural weathering has deformed the original work. In either case I doubt we'll ever have an explanation for the Bearded Man, but it is an intriguing puzzle."

The three of them sat on the top step of the North Temple, resting their weary legs and enjoying the view of the Ball Court. Jack again imagined the Mayan priest watching the game below, but now at the priest's side sat a man with European features and a full beard.

"We better get moving if we're going to climb El Castillo before the site closes," stated Steve, interrupting Jack's contemplation.

"Why couldn't the Mayans have invented elevators?" commented Jo, as the three of them started down the temple steps.

CHAPTER 6

No matter how busy he was, Andrew Buck tried to reserve Friday evening to take his wife out to dinner. It had become a ritual since they moved to the Capital. It was the one time during the week when work was not allowed to interfere. For a few hours no one knew where they were and no telephones could bother them.

Tonight they had come to one of their favorite spots. In fact, lately they had been eating at this restaurant about every other week. It was a basic steak and potatoes place. The food was good and it did not attract any of the Washington social crowd, which was fine with Andrew.

From his seat at the cocktail lounge bar Andrew looked out to the restaurant entry, then glanced at his watch. Sharon was late as usual. "God, I love my wife," he thought to himself, "but is she ever going to be on time?" Tonight he was actually glad she was late. It gave him some time to think.

Andrew was perplexed by the Peters situation. He wasn't sure why, but he had the feeling they were walking into an ambush. Something was missing. These doubts had been with him ever since the afternoon meeting, and he had not been able to shake them. Maybe it was the "beyond salvage" talk. It was not something he was comfortable with. In Korea he had given orders that affected lives; he had seen men die carrying out orders he had issued. But that was different from this. In Korea he was in the field alongside his men; he shared in the danger and the fear. Now he sat in an air-conditioned room helping to decide whose life to put on the line, whose life to end.

For a moment he found himself longing for his days as a United States Marine. Things were simpler then; you obeyed orders and went by the book. If you followed the chain of command your ass was, for the most part, covered. But then the horrors of that ugly little war came back, reminding him of why he left the service: too much death with no purpose. For him Korea was a dark room, the door to which he would just as soon keep locked shut.

"Would you like another beer?" asked the bartender, interrupting Andrew's thoughts.

Buck saw that his glass was empty. "What the hell. It's Friday," he thought to himself as he ordered another Budweiser. The bartender, a Hispanic kid, looked a bit young to be jerking beer. Buck wondered where Charlie, the regular bartender, was, as the kid refilled his mug.

He sipped the fresh beer as he stared at his reflection in the mirror that filled the wall behind the bar. He wondered if this was the way he really wanted to live. Had his whole career led to this? Buck had gone to college on the G.I. bill. He majored in political science and had better than average grades, but after he graduated he found good jobs in the private sector hard to come by for a black man, even if he did have a college degree. Eventually he was hired by the Federal Bureau of Investigation. At the time, the FBI was being pressured to hire more blacks, as were all federal agencies. Buck was one of the lucky few.

He spent over twenty years with the Bureau. The path was not smooth, but slowly he moved up through the ranks—until he was one of the first black department heads of an FBI field office: special agent in charge of the Los Angeles field office. He would probably still be with the Bureau, but the Drug Enforcement Agency had been searching for a person to head their Special Projects unit. They came to Buck, offering him the position. He figured it would be a good way to finish his career, so he took the job and moved to Washington.

When Buck first arrived in Washington he was very proud of his new position. It was high stress and long hours, but he relished the power and the prestige. He felt it was the payoff for all the years of hard work. The last few days, however, made him wonder if it was all worth it. Had he climbed the ladder of success so he could decide when it was time for a man to be eliminated.

Buck had a hollow feeling in his soul and his temples throbbed. So far, the beer was not bringing relief. Questions filled his mind; they kept circling through the circuits inside his brain searching for an answer. The questions all led to Peters, but the available answers did not fit the man, at least not the man Buck had known. Something stank! What if Peters did not sell out? What did that mean? Had he been set up? Who would have been able to do this? All at once it was clear to him. The realization jolted him—like 110 volts jolt the kid who sticks his finger in the light socket. Buck had not felt gut-wrenching fear in a long time, probably not since Korea, but he was beginning to feel it now. He realized it was time to bring in outside help, and one name immediately came to mind. Buck asked the bartender where the nearest phone was.

* * *

Buck had found the phone and talked with the man he had wanted to talk with. Although still troubled, Buck did feel somewhat better.

He sat back down at the bar and started to order another beer when a sudden pain in his chest choked his words off. The pain was not unlike heartburn, and he had to think a moment, "What did I eat for lunch?"

He then remembered he had not eaten lunch; the only thing he had consumed all day was a dry piece of toast. The spasm subsided, and Buck felt some what better, but he decided against ordering another beer.

"Hi, honey. I'm sorry I'm late. I hope you haven't been waiting too long." It was Sharon as beautiful as ever. Buck had always been proud of the way his wife had kept up her good looks. She put a hand on his shoulder and kissed his cheek.

"Is our table ready yet?" she asked.

"It should be. Let me buy you a drink, and then I'll check to see if they're ready to seat us," said Buck.

After ordering a glass of wine for Sharon, he stood to go check on their table, but once on his feet the room started to spin. Buck grabbed the rolled leather edge of the bar to steady himself.

"Andrew, are you OK?" asked Sharon, concern in her voice.

His throat was suddenly dry, and the spasm had returned to his chest. He tried to answer his wife, but all he managed was a choking sound. Buck's left arm had become numb and his body was shaking. He looked into the mirror behind the bar, and what he saw scared him as much as the way he felt. His face was contorted, lips twisted, eyes bulging.

"Oh, lord! Andrew!" he heard his wife cry, the concern in her voice was turning to hysteria.

Buck's knees buckled, and he crashed to the floor, knocking over the bar stool he had been sitting on. Lying on his back, staring at the ceiling, it felt as if an elephant was standing on his chest. He thought his lungs were about to explode.

He could hear his wife screaming, "Somebody help me!"

"Is there a doctor here?" a man's voice yelled.

Buck could no longer see the ceiling. His world had gone dark, but at least the pain in his chest was relenting. A strange feeling of tranquility passed through him, and he felt as if he were floating. Briefly, he wondered what would happen to Sam Peters.

For a moment, he felt warmth in his right hand, another hand clutching it tightly. From far off he heard his wife's voice. "Andrew, I love you."

"I love you too," he thought to himself as the darkness engulfed him.

CHAPTER 7

"Lord, I could get used to this," Jack thought. He sat in the small circular wading pool at the Hotel Dolores Alba, his head leaning against the coping while he sipped a cold cerveza. It had been a day full of adventure, but at the moment he was pretty sure this was the best part.

Lifting his right leg out of the water, he inspected his big toe. The top half of the toenail was gone, and in its place was a bloody scab. He stared at the swollen and throbbing digit, wondering if it was broken.

One of the many things he learned today was that *huaraches* were not proper footwear for pyramid climbing. The limestone steps of Chichén Itzá's pyramids had been worn smooth from centuries of Mayans and more recently tourists clambering up their heights. Tire-soled sandals did not provide suitable traction on the polished stone. Half of his big toenail had been ripped off when he slipped on a slick step midway up El Castillo. Blood dribbling down his foot, Jack had sat halfway up the great pyramid trying to keep from falling down the steep stairway, while attempting to catch his breath and scream at the same time. The climb had been worth it, though, as the view of the stone city and surrounding jungle was spectacular.

Jack winced as he lowered his leg back into the pool. His legs ached from the day's climbing and the cool water stung his injured toe. The circular pool was about 15 feet in diameter and three feet deep. Jo and Steve Potter were also enjoying the water along with half-dozen of the hotel guests. After a long afternoon of pyramid climbing, the cool water was refreshing.

The air was heavy as the tropical afternoon slowly turned to evening. Conversation around the pool ranged from the day's adventures to the mysteries of the Mayan culture. Jack found it interesting that most of the hotel's guests, at least those in and around the pool, were not newcomers to Mexico's ruin sites. He found himself surrounded by amateur archaeologists, each with his or her own theories on the Mayan civilization.

Soaking in the last of the day's sun, the scent of jungle flowers in the air, Jack half listened to the talk as he drank his beer and reflected back on the day. A new world had opened up for him. He had not taken an active role in planning this trip; he had left that to Jo. Touring the ruin sites sounded interesting backhome, but what he had really been looking forward to was lying out on the beach, maybe some snorkeling or deep sea fishing. Today though, his priorities had been turned around. He had been overpowered by the massive structures, wondered at the haunting beauty of the art, and chilled by the scenes of brutality. The mystery surrounding the ancient Maya pulled at his curiosity, and he wanted to see more, learn more.

A shrill cry shattered the late afternoon serenity, shaking Jack from his reverie and almost causing him to drop his beer. It sounded like a cross between a blood-curdling scream and a rebel yell. He looked up to see, silhouetted in the sunlight, a human figure falling from the sky. As the body plunged toward the center of the pool, Jack saw looks of disbelief in the eyes of his fellow pool-mates. The man—Jack could now see the figure was a man—curled his body into the shape of a cannonball as he hit the water, sending liquid shockwaves throughout the small pool. Jack shot to his feet, despite his tired legs. The man remained submerged. The white panama hat he had been wearing floated on top of the water. Jack stood stunned, along with everyone else, and wondered what the hell was going on. Suddenly, the man rose up from beneath the water laughing hysterically. Jack could not believe who he was looking at, but there was Gus Wise, big as life, laughing his fool head off.

"Why you crazy son-of-a-bitch! I should have known it was you," exclaimed Jack, to his old friend.

"I heard there was a party going on in the neighborhood so I thought I'd drop in. First though, I think we all need a drink. My servant here will bring you people anything you would like to drink, as long as it's beer!" Gus said with bravado.

Gus's servant was actually a Mayan boy who worked at the hotel. He was already on his way to the pool with a tray full of Montejos and Leon Negras. Jack saw the irritated and confused expressions of the other guests turn to smiles as they were offered the free drinks. Gus knew how to make an entrance.

Water dripping down his thin beard and grinning like the Cheshire Cat, Gus stood in the center of the small pool. He removed his glasses and wiped off the water beads so he could see. Gus and the Phillipses exchanged hugs, and Jack introduced Gus to Steve Potter.

"What are you doing here? I thought we weren't going to see you until Mérida," Jack asked.

"I know, but things change. Starting day after tomorrow I was supposed to have four days off, but we've run into some problems at Cobá. Ends up that I'm going to be busy this week. I was able to get tonight and tomorrow off so I thought I'd come up and get drunk with you guys," explained Gus.

"Oh, no!" cried Jo. "You mean you're not going with us from Mérida to Cobá. We've been looking forward to traveling with you for the last three months."

"I know, I'm really sorry. I was looking forward to seeing you two just as much. This thing at Cobá is very important. I'll try and explain it to you over dinner tonight. I hope we can make it up on the end of your trip. When you get to Cobá, I should be able to get a few days off. We can go sit on the beach together for a couple of days. I'd actually enjoy that more than going to the ruin sites. Hell, I already spend all my time there now; I don't need to vacation at them," Gus said.

They spent the next hour bullshitting and drinking beer. Jack would start laughing whenever he looked at Gus sitting in the pool with a beer in his hand still wearing his Mexican peasant shirt and Panama hat. Every time the beers got low Gus would yell, "Garcon!" and the Mayan boy would come trotting out carrying another tray of *cervezas*.

Soon it was dark, and the hotel manager, who was also the chef, came out to tell the guests dinner would be served in a few minutes. By this time they were all pleasantly drunk. They decided it would be best to eat something before they passed out, so they left the pool to go dress for dinner.

*   *   *

With dinner finished, Jack, Gus, Jo, and Steve went out and sat by the pool. The evening was warm, and the bugs were not too voracious. Gus offered cigars to everyone. Jack and Steve both took one, but Jo held her nose and said, "No, thanks. I think I'll sit upwind from you men."

"Are you sure?" Gus asked. "These Havanas are smooth smokes, plus they help keep the mosquitos away."

"I'm sure. I think I'd rather have the bugs eat me alive than choke on one of your Havanas," replied Jo.

They sat under a full moon puffing their cigars (except for Jo who was busy squashing mosquitoes), talking about the days of the ancient Mayans. Jack was glad to see Gus and Steve hit it off so well. They had spent the whole dinner sharing tales of their travels over South and Central America. Steve was very interested in Gus's archeological work.

"This is a smooth smoke," agreed Jack, the cigar balanced between his lips. "I've never cared much for cigars but these could become addictive."

Gus leaned his head back blowing smoke rings into the air and then said, "Castro's best."

The mosquitoes were getting the best of Jo. She finally got up and moved her chair in between Jack and Gus, deciding their secondhand smoke was better than the bugs. Gus, wearing his best smart-ass smile, held the cigar he was smoking out for Jo. She pushed his hand away. "You smoke that thing. I moved over here so it would be easier to talk to you," she lied. "Earlier you said you were going to tell us about your problems at Cobá."

"Well, as I was telling you over dinner, the research at Cobá is being funded by a dual grant. Half the money is being put up by the Mexican government, the other half comes from the university. I'm second in command of the project behind a Mexican archeologist named Hector Flores. Hector is the whole reason for the project becoming a reality. His specialty is making sense of Mayan hieroglyphics. In the course of his research, Hector stumbled across some very interesting passages. What he found led him to believe that something very exciting may lay hidden at Cobá. What he is searching for, though, goes against established theories, and ideas of this nature can make it hard to get grants. Hector contacted me and asked if I was interested in getting involved, partly because we are old friends, but I was also part of his strategy. Hector organized the project under the guise of reconstructing some of Cobá's structures. I don't want to sound cocky, but I do have a modest reputation in the archeological world in the area of site restoration. Hector wanted me on the project to lend a degree of validity. This didn't bother me because Hector told me from the beginning what he was really after. He also knew I could get funding for the project through the university, another thing I am very good at.

"We've been on site now for six months, and to be truthful we have not accomplished much in the way of reconstructing Cobá's past glories, but we do think we're getting close to what Hector is searching for. The problem is that suddenly Carlos Cervantes, the director of the Mexican Federal Judiciary Police, who is currently running for president of Mexico, has made some statements that certain archeological projects are misusing government funds. Cervantes' statements have stirred up a mild controversy. He has put together a special task force that is reviewing all government-funded archeological sites in the country. This puts the Cobá project in a precarious situation; our finagling has backfired on us. In three days we are going to be audited and have a site inspection. Now, before you get too worried, this is not as bad as it sounds. We feel comfortable that we can cover ourselves, plus Hector's family is fairly powerful and can probably pull a few strings. But I definitely need to be on site the next few days."

"Why is this Cervantes fellow raising hell with you guys? With all of Mexico's serious economic problems, why make a big deal out of finding fraud at an archeological site?" Jack questioned.

"I've been reading about Cervantes," Jo interjected. "He's close but still trailing in the polls. Sounds like he is trying to find a cause to rally the people around. The Mexicans have a lot of pride in their culture and its history. They take their antiquities very seriously."

"Jo is basically right. Cervantes is trying to raise his standing in the polls, but I think there is more to it than that. I just hope we're not the ones he is looking for," said Gus, slowly shaking his head.

Steve had been shifting uneasily in his chair. Leaning forward he rested his elbows on his knees and said, "I try and keep up with Mexico's political scene as much as possible, and I seem to remember reading that one of Cervantes big supporters is a guy named Reyes, I think?"

"Ricardo Reyes! It would be more appropriate to say that Cervantes is Reyes's puppet," replied Gus sourly. "Cervantes was just a second-rate bureaucrat until he became involved with Reyes. It was Reyes' money and power that have given him the chance to become El Presidente."

"What I'm getting at is you said you hoped the Cobá project is not what Cervantes and Reyes are looking for. You said it like you may have an idea of what they are looking for," said Steve, a puzzled look on his face.

"I really don't know what Cervantes is up to. I just know that it must have a big payoff for them to be pushing the issue so close to the election. Reyes is one of Mexico's richest men; he has enough money to grease the right wheels. From what I've heard, he'd cut your nuts off if you cross him.

"I've heard rumors that Reyes deals in black market pre-Colombian artifacts, booty raided from Mayan temples still hidden in the jungle. Hector Flores fumes at the mention of Reyes. More recently the word has been that Señor Reyes is involved in cocaine trafficking, but like I said these are only rumors. Reyes is a member of one of Mexico's old wealthy families, which gives him a certain measure of respectability. Not so many years ago though, the family fortune wasn't much of a fortune. Reyes came back from college, USC, and quickly turned the family's financial situation around. At first everyone thought it was his great American education and financial genius, but now some people are beginning to question where all the money came from. How he did it doesn't really matter at this point. He is one wealthy and powerful son-of-a-bitch, and I wouldn't want to be in his way when he has a hard on."

"You seem to know a lot about this Reyes guy," said Jo.

"He has a big estate on the coast not far from Cobá, and the locals like to gossip about him. It's like living in the same neighborhood as Donald Trump," returned Gus.

"The current political situation is very interesting," said Jack. "But I want to hear more about what you and Hector are searching for at Cobá. What's the big secret?"

"I hate to have to be so mysterious, but I've already told you a lot more than I should have," replied Gus.

"Whatever it is, your work at Cobá sounds fascinating. Sometimes I wish I had pursued a career in archeology," Steve said wistfully.

"If you get a chance while you're down here, stop in and visit. I'll give you a tour of the site," offered Gus.

"Boy, that's an invitation that's hard to refuse, but I doubt I can fit it into my schedule," replied Steve.

"Hey! I just had a brainstorm," Jack exclaimed. "Why don't you travel with Jo and me to Cobá? We can catch an early bus to Mérida, from there we'll rent a car and drive to Cobá."

"I don't know. . . you two were planning on taking more time than I have to travel to Cobá. I'd hate to make you rush your trip," said Steve.

"Don't worry about it," Jack said. "We can be in Cobá in three days and still see most of the sights. Now that Gus isn't making the trip with us we won't have to stop at every *cantina* between here and the coast."

Steve leaned back in his chair rubbing his eyelids with his thumb and forefinger. The beer, the cigar and the warm evening appeared to be having an effect on him.

"Come on, Steve. We'd be lost without our guide," Jo coaxed.

Potter leaned forward and opened his eyes, "OK, you have me, for better or worse. Let's go to Cobá!"

CHAPTER 8

The drive to the secluded home overlooking Chesapeake Bay had been relaxing. Ron Allen had decided to push the Peters' situation from his thoughts. That would be dealt with in the morning; tonight was for Danielle.

Allen selected a bottle of wine from the wine rack, pulled the cork, and poured himself a glass of California Merlot. He checked his watch, nine thirty. Danielle would arrive soon. He wondered if anticipation was the best part. It had been three long weeks since he had last seen Danielle; sometimes she was all he could think of. For over a year they had been seeing each other, whenever he could get away for the night, which wasn't often enough.

Allen sat on the couch sipping his wine, wishing the assholes at the State Department could see him with her; they all thought he was gay. He would love to wipe the silly smirks off their faces. Most of them would never have a woman like Danielle. She was definitely worth the five hundred dollars a night.

A knock on the door startled him initially, then filled him with a rush of excitement. He jerked up from the couch and went to answer the door. It was Danielle.

"God, she is gorgeous," thought Allen as he stood in the doorway gawking at her.

"Hello, Ron. You look well tonight," Danielle said with a seductive smile.

"Not half as well as you look," said Allen his voice almost cracking. "Please, come in,"

She was wearing a black dress that clung to her body just enough to show off the curves. The plunging neckline revealed more than a hint of cleavage. Danielle was a looker. From her silky-soft auburn hair down to her well-shaped calves she had a body that men noticed. Her image, her scent, her very essence seemed to be pure sensuality. She had more than looks though; she also had an aura of class, the kind only an expensive call girl can have.

She entered the room and kissed Allen, her tongue darting between his lips. Allen had an immediate urge to rip off her dress and make love to her there on the tile foyer. He suppressed himself though. Danielle would have been willing, but he wanted to take his time. She had taught him the joys of long and adventurous foreplay.

"Would you like a glass of wine?" Allen asked as they entered the livingroom.

"Please," she replied. "The State Department must be keeping you busy. It has been three weeks since our last visit."

Allen returned from the kitchen and handed a glass of wine to Danielle, who had taken a seat on the couch. He sat beside her and said, "A couple of emergency situations did develop, but of course I can't discuss them."

"Especially with your whore," Danielle thought to herself. She knew Ron got a kick out of being on the inside, one of the select few privy to the secrets. It was probably what attracted him to his work, and what attracted him to her: his own secret whore. "You pompous geek," thought Danielle, keeping her smile from turning into a smirk.

For a while they sipped their wine and made small talk. Merely sitting and talking with Danielle excited Allen, especially with the sure knowledge that they would soon be in bed together.

She casually pulled the right strap of her dress down over her shoulder revealing a grapefruit-sized breast. "It's so nice to relax," she purred.

Allen's eyes were fixated on her exposed flesh. Danielle liked the attention; it gave her power. Power was the one thing that always turned her on and made it possible for her to make love to a man like Ron Allen. Of course, the money also helped.

Reaching out, she took his hand and brought it to her breast. He began to gently massage the soft, warm flesh. With his fingertips he lightly squeezed her hard nipple.

"I need to feel your tongue," whispered Danielle as she slipped off the left strap of her dress. She knew Ron liked her to be in charge, and she knew how to work him.

Both of her magnificent breasts were now before him. Allen did as he was told, his mouth enthusiastically exploring her bosom. She leaned back and enjoyed his attention, finding it hard to believe that she was getting paid good money for this.

Sensing that he was properly aroused, she stood up and let her dress fall about her ankles, uncovering her smooth skin and sensuous curves. She took his trembling hand and led him to the bedroom.

*   *   *

Allen lay at her side in a deep sleep brought on by the warm afterglow of their lovemaking. His breathing was slow and steady. Danielle slipped from under the covers and stood by the bed looking down at him.

"Tonight you had the best," she thought.

Silently she went to the bathroom where her purse sat on the white tile counter. Out of the purse she pulled a semiautomatic .22 caliber pistol. Staring at the black gun in her hand, she wondered if she had made the right decision. She quickly pushed the thought from her mind; this was no time to let her conscience interfere. The people who were paying her would not be pleased if she backed out now.

"What the hell," she thought. "For the half million they are paying me, the geek must have done something he deserves to die for."

Danielle pulled back the pistol's slide and released, thus inserting the first round into the firing chamber.

She crept back to the bed where Allen slept. He was lying on his stomach, his face half buried in a large pillow. She brought the pistol's muzzle within an inch of the back of his head. Before pulling the trigger she paused. It was kind of a shame she had to kill him, she thought. The geek was actually learning to be a pretty good lover.

Closing her eyes, Danielle turned her head away and pulled the trigger. Her ears filled with the pistol's report and the dull thud of the bullet passing through the back of Allen's head and out his mouth into the pillow. A high-pitched, gurgling moan floated up from the bed. Allen rolled violently over onto his back, his flailing arm brushing against her leg. She jumped back, swallowing a scream.

Allen lay on the bed trembling, bubbles of blood gurgling out his mouth and down his cheeks. His eyes stared into hers with a look of astonished terror, a look that burned into her brain.

"This should not be happening! He should be dead!" she thought wildly. They told her he would die instantly.

Her heart pounded in her head as panic overwhelmed her. Pointing the pistol at his forehead, she fired again, pulling the trigger repeatedly, not stopping until she heard the clicking sound of the firing pin releasing into an empty chamber.

Her body shaking, her breathing rapid and erratic, Danielle let the gun fall from her hand and onto the floor. Allen's body was now still, his right arm dangled lifelessly off the edge of the bed.

She looked down and saw that her stomach and thighs were splattered with blood. The room was slowly turning upside down, and she started to gag. Woozy and rubber-legged, she stumbled to the bathroom where she deposited that night's dinner into the commode.

Danielle sat naked on the bathroom floor, leaning against the wall by the toilet. She was trying to pull herself back together when she noticed the man standing in the doorway.

"What the hell are you doing here?" Danielle asked, an edge of fear in her voice.

"We had to be sure you'd complete the contract," replied the man.

"I did my job. He's dead," replied a trembling Danielle as she stared at him.

"Yes, he is. But you left something lying on the floor."

Stepping closer to her, he held her pistol out in front of him. She did not like him being so close. She felt trapped, and her fear grew. Suddenly she realized why he was here, and her fear turned to terror.

"You're not going to pay me my money, are you?" she sobbed.

A smirk formed on his lips as he fired a round into her forehead.

CHAPTER 9

J.J. Hightower's sixth floor apartment was modern and spacious, though modestly decorated. Hightower did not spend much time there, it functioned as a place to eat and sleep and little else. It was 7:03 AM and he had already shaved, showered, skimmed the *Washington Post*, and eaten a light breakfast. The day was going to be busy; the Peters' situation would require his full energy.

The Senator glanced at his watch; his chauffeur should be arriving soon to take him to his eight o'clock meeting. He decided to call his wife while he waited. He had not talked to Barbara in three days. She spent most of her time in their home state during the winter, partially because she preferred California winters to the Capitol's and also because of their two teenage children who were still in school. Instead of his wife, however, he got the answering machine and left a message.

Hightower had no sooner hung up when the phone rang. "J.J. Hightower," he answered.

"Jim Freeman," answered the voice on the other end of the line. "I'm your chauffeur. Armando could not make it to work today."

Armando Galvan had been the Senator's chauffeur for over a dozen years. "I hope Armando is all right," said the Senator.

"I would not know sir. All I was told is that I am to be your chauffeur for the day," replied Freeman.

"Yes, of course. I'll be right down," said Hightower.

The Senator grabbed his briefcase and was almost out the door when the phone rang again. He stood in the doorway a moment, contemplating leaving the phone unanswered, but he decided it might be something important.

"Hello."

"Hello, J.J., this is Stan. I'm afraid I have some bad news." Stan was one of the Senator's aides. "Andrew Buck and Ronald Allen are both dead."

"What! . . . How?" replied Hightower.

"It's weird. They both passed away in unrelated incidents. Buck had a coronary in the middle of his dinner. From what I've heard he went pretty fast, never made it off the floor of the restaurant. Allen was found in his bed this morning with half a dozen bullet holes in his brain."

"Jesus! Someone shot him!" gasped the Senator.

"The information on Allen's death has been skimpy. Nobody is saying much, but according to rumors the body of a woman was also found. Apparently she killed Allen and then shot herself."

"This is horrible. I can't believe what you're telling me," stammered Hightower.

"Yeah, it's a hell of a way to start the weekend. Makes you wonder who is next," said Stan. He did not know about his boss's connection with Allen and Buck, or Stan would have been more than wondering.

The Senator told Stan to keep updated on the two deaths, and that he would come by the office later in the morning.

Hightower hung up the phone and hurried out of his apartment and into the elevator at the end of the hall. The elevator dropped him to the basement parking garage. When the elevator doors slid open he saw his Lincoln parked in a nearby space. A man who appeared to be his chauffeur was leaning against the hood smoking a cigarette. On the far side of the garage, a man was loading a suitcase into the trunk of a car.

Seeing Hightower exit the elevator, the chauffeur flicked his cigarette to the concrete and crushed it out with the sole of his shoe. "Good morning, Senator Hightower," said the man as he moved to the back of the automobile and opened the right rear door.

"Good morning," replied the Senator. Except for the morning salutation he barely took notice of his driver as he stepped past him and took his seat.

The chauffeur had come around the car and sat down in the driver's seat when Hightower bellowed, "I forgot my damn overcoat. I have to go back and get it."

The driver started to get out of the car when the Senator told the man to sit back down. "I can let myself out of a car for once. Relax, I'll only be a few minutes."

Hightower let himself out of the car and headed for the elevator. Upon entering the elevator he pushed the round button marked "six". The doors slid shut. As he felt the floor rise beneath his feet, he checked his watch.

The sound of the explosion rumbled up from beneath the elevator, sending a chill through Hightower. He pressed the stop button, and the elevator jerked to a halt. He wavered a moment. He knew he should go back to his apartment and call the police, but he was also very curious. He pushed the button marked "G".

The elevator descended back to the parking garage. When the doors opened, Hightower immediately felt a rush of warm air wrap around him. The Lincoln was engulfed in an inferno, the flames rising up until they spread out against the concrete ceiling. The man who was earlier loading a suitcase into the trunk of his car now stood beside the Senator. He had a dazed expression on his face.

"Is anyone inside the car?" asked the man, a hysterical edge to his voice.

"My driver," replied the Senator.

The man could not hear the Senator's soft reply; his ears were still ringing from the blast that had reverberated off the concrete walls of the garage.

He stared at Hightower. He recognized the face but could not remember the name. Then something clicked in his mind. "You're Senator J.J. Hightower!" exclaimed the man, as if he had forgotten all about the Lincoln that was ablaze not fifty feet away.

Hightower nodded, his gaze still fixed on the burning car.

The stranger glanced at the flames, then back at Hightower. "Oh, shit!" said the man under his breath.

CHAPTER 10

Nelson Carlton was an undistinguished-looking fellow. His appearance was not unpleasant, but he did not stick out in a crowd, either. He was of average height and weight with average features and a head of close-cropped, gray-black hair. There was disgust in his hazel-green eyes, indicating a sour mood, as he walked down an interior hallway of the State Department building. Carlton did not consider himself to be the smartest man in the world, but he could smell garbage when it was being dumped on him. During his twenty-five years with the Central Intelligence Agency and two with the State Department, Carlton had smelled his share of garbage. He did not yet know why, but he was sure his new assignment was shit duty.

The morning had started poorly and then gone downhill. The ringing of his telephone had rudely awakened him from a deep alcohol-induced sleep. He tried ignoring the jangling phone, but, after a dozen rings, he decided he better answer. A voice on the phone said he was to meet the Secretary of State in the Secretary's office in one hour. Carlton mumbled, "Go to hell," and then hung up the phone. He was sure someone was jerking him around, and in his present condition he was not in the mood. A few seconds later the phone rang again. This time the caller managed to convince Carlton that it was not a joke, and that he better have his ass in the Secretary of State's office in one hour.

Carlton had managed to arrive in Secretary of State Goreman's office at the appointed hour. He sat on the other side of Lester Goreman's enormous desk trying to concentrate on what the Secretary of State was telling him. His head was pounding and he wished he had that shot of bourbon in his coffee that he had told himself he didn't need.

Carlton left Goreman's office more confused than when he had entered. Goreman informed him about the deaths of Andrew Buck and Ronald Allen, and the attempt on the Senator's life. He speculated that these incidents may be connected and could represent a breach in state security. The three men had been in charge of a highly classified operation with the code name Raven. Carlton's job was to conduct a special investigation to determine if there was a connection among the three incidents. The investigation was to be given top priority, and he would have the full cooperation of all U.S. governmental agencies.

To oversee an investigation such as the Secretary of State had outlined would be the highlight of many a career in the intelligence community, but Carlton felt more uneasy than honored. Goreman did not select Carlton for this job because of his brilliant intelligence briefs or his distinguished career. Carlton knew he was selected because it was the kind of job no one else wanted. The kind of job you gave to someone whose name was not used in the same sentence as "promotion," someone who was due to retire soon. In other words it was the kind of job for someone you could afford to sacrifice.

Carlton opened the door to a small conference room. Except for a table surrounded by chairs, the room was empty. In one of the chairs sat a man. The man was Senator Jason James Hightower.

Carlton's first impression of the Senator was his size. Even sitting down the man was an imposing figure, especially to Carlton, who was slender and not quite six feet. The two men exchanged salutations and shook hands. Carlton thought the Senator appeared to be shaken by the morning's events, not that he blamed the man. Watching your limo and chauffeur explode had to be a bit unnerving.

Carlton sat across the small table from the Senator, hoping the man did not notice his red-rimmed eyes or boozy odor. He was still groggy, and his throat was raw from the whiskey he had consumed the night before. He craved an unfiltered Camel, and his thoughts kept wandering to the pack in the top drawer of his office desk.

He cleared the phlegm from his throat, swallowed, and then spoke, "I would like to start, Senator, by telling you what I know and what my assignment is. Ron Allen of the State Department and Andrew Buck of the Drug Enforcement Agency both came to an untimely demise last night. This morning, an apparent attempt was made to end your life. Except for the fact that all three of you are—or were— very powerful and important people in this city, the three incidents seemed to be unrelated." Carlton paused. "That was until I met with Lester Goreman.

"According to the Secretary of State, there is reason to believe that the three incidents are related. The three of you composed a secret committee that was selected by the President. Goreman was not very helpful, though, in telling me the purpose of this committee. All he said was that it had something to do with trafficking drugs from Mexico into the United States.

"I'm supposed to find out what connection, if any, there is between the deaths of Buck and Allen and the attempt on your life, and how it all might be linked to Operation Raven."

Carlton always felt foolish using these silly code names. He wondered if there was some guy locked in a room deep within the bowels of the State Department whose job was to sit around all day and think up this shit.

"I can see this is all going to work very nicely," replied Hightower. "The President is already distancing himself from this mess, leaving old J.J. holding the bag of shit." Hightower no longer appeared shaken. The lines on his face were taut, and his blue eyes now had a spark to them.

"Look, Senator, I have no idea of what is going on here . . . "

"I know," interrupted Hightower, his face turning red as he spoke. "That is why you're here. I'm familiar with your past, Mr. Carlton. At one time you were one of the best field agents the agency ever had, but you let it all slip away when you stuck your head in a whiskey bottle. You're a drunk! You probably haven't had an original idea in the past year. Anyone with any sense would have resigned before accepting this assignment."

Carlton knew that the Senator was speaking the truth, but he still had to suppress a sudden urge to punch the man's teeth down his throat.

"Somehow they knew you would react this way," said Carlton, maintaining his composure. "According to Goreman, the President wants you to know that you're not being hung out to dry. The situation is to be contained, and you're to be protected. I'm supposed to make sure this happens, but I can't do my job unless you help me."

"'Contained,' hell!" boomed Hightower. "This project should have been contained in the very beginning by not even being started. I resent this whole deal. I resent secret committees; I resent secret meetings; I resent the President; I resent my car being bombed!"

Hightower took a deep breath. "I didn't want to become part of Operation Raven," He continued. "The President wanted me on board, though. He wanted me to keep the boys in line. He said it was the only way we were going to be able to slow the flow of drugs into the United States. He called in a few favors. Before I knew it, I was in it up to my eyeballs."

Though irritated, the Senator was starting to open up, and Carlton wanted to keep him talking. "Senator, I think I could get a better understanding of the situation if you could tell me the exact purpose of Operation Raven."

"I don't like this. I don't like being interrogated by a washed-up drunk. I will say no more until I speak with the President."

"I don't like this either, Senator!" replied Carlton, anger creeping into his voice. "I had planned to spend my Saturday afternoon roaring drunk, but you fucked that up. Now I have to spend it baby-sitting your precious ass. The problem you have is you are not going to get to meet the President; you're not going to meet anyone but me. I'm all you've got!"

Carlton let his words sink in. The set lines in Hightower's face softened, and his broad shoulders seemed to sag. Grudgingly, the Senator began to talk. "Operation Raven was initiated by DEA. I'm fairly sure it was Andrew Buck's brainchild. Somehow the DEA analysts figured out that a large percentage of the drugs trafficked through Mexico were being handled by one organization. The problem was they could not find out who was in control.

"One investigation after another failed to lead to the individuals in control. Every time DEA thought they were getting close, things would fall apart. It did not get serious, though, until DEA agents started to disappear. Somehow the bad guys were getting DEA intelligence information, and agents were getting killed.

"They tried tracing the leaks down a number of different ways but found only dead ends. The leaks were so numerous that it was beginning to look like someone high up must be involved or else there was a massive infiltration of DEA infrastructure.

"In the meantime, the President was stepping up his War on Drugs campaign. He wanted to toughen up his 'soft on crime' image, putting a lot of pressure on the DEA. He wanted to see some headline-grabbing busts.

"This is when the idea for the secret committee came up. As I said earlier, I think it was Buck. Anyway, he was the one who took the idea to the President. The President liked what he heard and gave the project the O.K."

Hightower paused a moment, as if collecting his thoughts. He then said, "I'm sorry if I'm not being specific enough on how this all came about, but I'm a politician, not a member of the intelligence community."

"No, Senator, this is very interesting. Please go on," urged Carlton.

The Senator took a breath then continued, "The plan was to select three men who were above reproach. They were to form a committee that would handpick a team of special agents and plan attack strategies. The target was the Mexican drug underworld. Operating outside the normal spheres of influence, the committee and its agents would avoid the leaks that plagued earlier investigations.

"The committee selected by the President was Buck, Allen and me. We were given carte blanche, all the President wanted was results. Our plan-of-attack was to send an agent undercover, 'deep cover' was the term Buck and Allen used. The agent was to pose as a successful drug trafficker."

"Why?" interrupted Carlton. "Seems like that would put your man in competition with the enemy—dangerous for him and not necessarily productive."

"That was my first thought, but Buck and Allen said that the organization we were after was strictly middle men. They don't actually grow the marijuana or process the coca plants, and they don't move the drugs across the border. They do, however, make sure the product gets from the producer to the trafficker. "The theory was, if our man could become a successful drug smuggler, these people would come looking for him and make him one of their outlets."

"Couldn't this get into a ticklish situation legally, I mean having one of our agents operating as a drug smuggler?" asked Carlton, a quizzical look on his face.

"You bet your ass it can. In fact, this is where the problems started, at least for me. You see, for the agent to be a drug smuggler he had to smuggle drugs, and for an extended period of time. The agent we sent in has been undercover for almost two years now, living every minute of his life as a criminal."

Carlton was now beginning to see why he was here. "You mean to tell me you have had an agent in deep cover for two years posing as a drug smuggler!"

"Don't put this all on my head! I never did like the strategy, but Buck and Allen did. It seemed like the only way," shot back Hightower.

The strain was beginning to tell in Hightower's voice, and Carlton thought the man was about to lose it. The Senator fiddled with a class ring on his right ring finger as he attempted to regain his composure. Carlton noted the raised letters on the front of the ring: USC 1962.

"I'm sorry," said Hightower, apologizing for his outburst. "I deserve some of the blame for this mess. I should never have allowed it to take place. Please understand, this thing gets worse, and I hate the fact that I was part of it." The Senator paused, he appeared to have regained his composure. "Our agent couldn't just pretend to be a smuggler," he continued. "He had to be a smuggler, and as I said, a very successful one."

"Are you saying the U.S. government staged drug trafficking operations?" asked a stunned Carlton.

"These people are not idiots. They would not have been fooled if we had tried to fake it. Drugs had to be delivered to dealers in the U.S. Buck and Allen considered it a short-term loss in order to realize a long term gain.

"Another benefit was to DEA public relations. Many of the drug shipments brought into the country by our agent were later targets of DEA drug busts. You see, since we brought the drugs into the country it was easy to keep track of the shipments. Many of the big DEA drug busts of the past year were nothing more than the confiscation of contraband originally brought into the country by our agent.

"I know this operation seems extreme, but the DEA intelligence analysts were certain that this one organization was responsible for a large percentage of the cocaine and marijuana entering this country. A giant hole would be created in the U.S. drug supplies if the Mexican middle men could be put out of business. The situation called for extreme measures."

Carlton was shocked. He had seen a lot of shit over the years, but he was having a hard time believing what he was hearing. If the press ever got hold of this it would make the Iran-Contra Affair look like a Boy Scout meeting. He could see the headlines: "Government Turns to Drug Smuggling to Reduce the National Debt."

Suddenly, Carlton realized that he now was one of the few people who knew what was happening. His ass was now on the line; they were grooming him to be the willing scapegoat.

He took a deep breath and spoke, "Let me get this straight. You, Buck, and Allen are selected by the President to form a committee. This committee operates in secrecy and answers to no one but the President. You handpick an agent to pose as a drug smuggler, hoping he will be able to infiltrate or at least make contact with this Mexican drug organization."

"Yes, that is basically correct," replied the Senator.

"The agent then was in a deep-cover situation. How did you contact him, or what was your control?" asked Carlton.

"The agent had a number of blind contacts in both Mexico and the U.S. These were people who had no idea who our agent was, but he could pass information through these contacts. Blind contacts were secondary though, used only in emergencies or unusual situations. Shadow agents were the main control. The shadows kept in contact with our deep-cover man."

"Was there anyone else, besides the committee members and the agents, who knew what was happening?" asked Carlton.

"No one else knew what we were doing. The President didn't even know exactly what we were up to, and this was one of his pet projects," answered Hightower.

Carlton scribbled on a note pad as he listened to the Senator. He wrote down three names: Andrew Buck, Ronald Allen, and Jason Hightower. He gazed at the list and then asked, "Could you give me the names of your agents?"

"The deep-cover man is Sam Peters, a DEA agent. The two shadow agents were Sean Cooper from DEA and Jim Foster from CIA. I say 'were' because both are now dead."

"Dead! How?" asked Carlton as he added the three names to his list.

"Did you hear about the shooting on the Mexican ferry?" inquired the Senator.

"Oh, shit!" replied Carlton, "It had something to do with your operation!"

"Cooper and Foster were both on the fishing boat that blew up. They were Peters' backup. It was Peters' boat. Peters was on board the ferry attempting to make a large purchase of cocaine from a man supposedly connected with the Mexican drug cartel.

"According to witnesses, Peters shot five people, including an American tourist. The information we had received as of yesterday was pretty sketchy. Supposedly Peters shot and killed the man he was to make contact with. The only problem was, there were two Federal Judicial Policemen on board the ferry at the time. Evidently, they attempted to apprehend Peters. Peters, though, managed to dispose of both men in a shootout. Two bystanders were also shot; one, a Mexican citizen, was killed and the other, an American tourist, was wounded and is in critical condition. Peters has not been heard from since this incident.

"He should have made contact within twenty-four hours of an event of this magnitude. According to Buck and Allen, he had more than one blind contact he could have reached in the Cancún area. Now forty-eight hours have passed since the incident on the ferry."

Carlton was beginning to wish he had stayed in bed. He knew what could happen when a man was undercover for extended periods in a stressful situation. Sam Peters would not be the first man to crack under such intense pressures.

"Do you think Peters has sold out?" asked Carlton

"I don't know. Buck, Allen and I were supposed to meet this morning and make a decision. Allen was ready to terminate Peters. He felt the risk was too great that Peters had been bought. Buck did not agree. He was sure there was a better explanation for what had happened; he just didn't know what it was."

Carlton could see the senator was confused; the man was out of his element. Carlton, however, was beginning to see things very clearly. Two men dead and a failed attempt on a third man. All three of the men were members of a secret committee that had sent agents undercover to break up a powerful drug ring. One agent had been living every minute of his life as a drug smuggler for almost two years. In the space of forty-eight hours almost everyone who was involved with the committee is dead except for Sam Peters and J.J. Hightower. Hightower would also be on the list of the deceased if he had not forgotten his overcoat. The equation was simple, but if Hightower had been killed, the numbers to the equation would have been lost.

"It seems very possible to me that the people you were pursuing decided that it was time to put your committee out of business," Carlton said. "Peters is the only man who could give them the information they would need to do this."

"I agree that there may be some connection between Buck and Allen's deaths and the attempt on my life, but how can you be sure Peters is the man responsible?" asked the Senator.

"I'm not sure. But from what you have told me, Peters has been out of contact for over forty-eight hours since the ferry incident. The man is a professional; he knows the rules. If he has not flipped out or sold out, he has at least been compromised. Any way you look at it the man has to be stopped."

The Senator's face turned red again as he listened to Carlton. "You damn spooks! You talk about taking a man's life like a banker talks about interest rates. You're all loony, but I'm crazier than any of you for getting involved in this masquerade!" said an exasperated Hightower.

Carlton normally kept his emotions well hidden, but his anger was rising. The combination of a massive hangover and the Senator's self-righteous bitching set him off.

"Quit your whining, Senator! You have been part of this from the very beginning. No one forced you to make the decisions you made. I've been 'a spook' for over twenty-five years and have had to make decisions on who lived and who died. I have taken lives with my own hands. I am not proud of my past, but I live with it, and I don't need you to tell me how I should feel about it. You're the man the people voted to represent them, but here you are involved in this shit. I may not have the most honorable profession, but at least I'm not a hypocrite."

The Senator sat up straighter in his chair and held his head up. "You're right, Mr. Carlton. I am wallowing a bit too much in my own self pity. I'm having a hard time handling this. I've never signed a man's death warrant before."

"If it makes you feel any better, I read that Peters left the ferry in a small boat in the middle of a tropical storm. There's a good chance he is already dead," said Carlton.

"Anything is possible, but neither Allen nor Buck thought it very likely. It seems Peters has a knack for avoiding death."

"Let's hope he wasn't so lucky this time; it would make my job much easier. This operation is 'Beyond Salvage.' I'm sending out termination orders to all U.S. agents. The Peters situation will be given top priority," said Carlton.

"You can do better than that," said Hightower. "Allen said we could use Peters' files against him. He has been deep for two years, building a criminal record. You wouldn't have to make up much, something about psychotic delusions, so if he is caught and starts talking it will already have been established that he is a dangerous nut case who gets his kicks running drugs. If you turn this information over to the Mexican authorities, complete with a recent photo of Peters, there's a good chance the Mexicans might get Peters for us."

"Sounds like a good idea to me. Keep our asses covered in case Peters lives," replied Carlton. "I never met the man, but everyone said Allen was sharp."

The Senator was making a great effort to maintain his composure, but Carlton could sense the man had endured enough for one day. "Senator, I have enough information to keep me busy for a while. I think you should get some rest. I've assigned two Secret Service agents to provide you with twenty-four hour security. If you like, they will escort you to your apartment, which has been swept by the FBI bomb squad. You should try and get some sleep."

Carlton almost laughed at the irony of what he had just said. How does a man get a good night's sleep when his home has to be searched for explosives?

CHAPTER 11

Whump, whump, whump . . . Jack awoke to the sound of the slowly revolving ceiling fan and the warm smell of her body. In the early morning, snuggled between the sheets, her scent reminded him of freshly baked bread. They lay together like spoons stacked in a drawer, but on their sides, Jo's back to Jack. He kissed the back of her neck as his hand gently caressed her inner thigh. She moaned softly, signifying she was also awake, but Jack did not know if it was a moan of pleasure or a "leave me alone; I want to go back to sleep" moan. He soon got his answer when he felt her hand fondling his groin. She rolled over to face him. Their lips met as their bodies pressed together: warm flesh; soft, wet tongues; blood rushing to erogenous zones. Sweaty bodies squirming between the cool sheets. Jack was on top of her, inside of her. Her legs wrapped around him pushing him deeper. She bit the flesh of his shoulder, creating an intense mixture of pain and pleasure. Consumed by passion their tempo increased and then peaked in a shattering climax. They fell back to sleep, the fan making circles above them. Whump, whump, whump . . .

*   *   *

Whump, whump, whump . . . The ceiling fan was still making lazy circles the second time Jack awoke. He looked at his watch and then jumped out of bed. "Hon, we better get moving. It is already after seven, and we're supposed to pick the rental car up at eight."

Jo moaned, and Jack easily identified this moan. It was the "I don't want to get up" moan. She pulled the sheets over her head and said, "Leave me alone."

Jack went to the bathroom and took a shower. He was glad to find the hot water was working, which had not been the case the previous morning at the hotel Dolores Alba.

He was drying himself off with the abrasive towel the hotel provided when Jo stumbled into the bathroom. Her eyes at half-mast, she kissed Jack on the cheek and said, "Did I say I liked tequila last night?"

"No, you said you loved tequila," replied Jack.

"Well, tequila doesn't love me," said Jo as she started up the shower.

Considering the amount of alcohol he had consumed last night, Jack was surprised how good he felt. The night had started rather innocently. Potter recommended they dine at Los Almendros, a modest restaurant that specializes in Yucatecan cuisine. They stuffed themselves on *sopa de lima*, a tangy lime soup made from chicken stock; *panuchos*, a tortilla fried open-faced and topped with beans; pickled onions; and strips of roasted pork; and *cochinita pibil*, pork marinated and then roasted. After dinner, their bellies full, they strolled along the *zócalo* enjoying the evening. They were headed back to the hotel when they decided to stop at a *cantina* and have a nightcap. The nightcap turned into playing backgammon for drinks with the locals. It was midnight before they staggered back to the hotel.

Jack dressed quickly, then shouted to Jo who was still in the shower, "Honey, I'm going down to the bakery. I'll bring back some breakfast."

"All right. Get some *bolillos* so we can make sandwiches for lunch," Jo yelled back over the sound of the rushing water.

Last night Potter had promised to make his famous "road trip" sandwiches: *bolillos*—bread rolls—filled with goat cheese and avocado, sprinkled with lime juice.

Before he left the hotel, Jack stopped at the room next door and knocked.

"Who's there?" came Potter's voice through the door.

"Just me," replied Jack. "I'm going down to the *panaderia*. Would you like anything special?"

"I could go for a cup of coffee, and if you wouldn't mind picking up some *bolillos*. Do you need some money?"

"No, the goodies are on me this morning. I'll see you in a bit."

Jack walked down the hallway toward the elevator, but instead of using the elevator, he turned and took the stairway. Their room was only on the second floor and waiting for the elevator usually took longer than taking the stairs. He bounded down the staircase taking the steps two at a time. Jack was excited; the day promised more adventure. The plan was to spend most of the day exploring the Uxmal ruin site. They also would now have a car, and Jack was looking forward to the freedom that would bring.

Outside, Mérida was beginning to wake up. Though early, the sidewalks were already filling with Mestizo men dressed in their chalk-white *guayaberas* and Mayan women wearing white *huipiles* embroidered with bright flowers. Jack found the morning bustle of the tropical city jarring. The city had been so romantic during the previous evening, people strolling around the tree-lined *zócalo*, while horse-drawn carriages carried lovers over the narrow streets.

As he walked down the sidewalk, Jack noticed the early morning sunlight brought out a hint of the city's original luster. Potter had told Jack that Mérida was known as the "White City," though in recent years the city's grand colonial buildings had turned various hues due to automobile exhaust.

Jack found a *panaderia*, went inside, and picked out some Mexican sweet rolls and *bolillos*. He stood in line at the cash register holding a metal tray of baked goods. Next to him was a man with a newspaper folded under his arm. A picture of a man on the paper's front page caught Jack's eye. The face looked familiar. When he turned his head sideways to get a better look at the photograph, he was astonished. Even with darker hair he recognized the face. Why was Steve Potter's face on the front page of a Mexican newspaper? Below the picture was the word *peligro*. Jack did not know much Spanish, but he understood the word meant danger.

Jack set the tray of *bolillos* and sweet rolls on the counter, and rushed from the bakery. He ran along the sidewalk searching for a newsstand. Finding a large corner stand, he stopped. Jack stared in disbelief at the rows of newspapers; on the front page of every paper was Potter's face. Again, his hair appeared darker and shorter but it was definitely Potter.

Jack began frantically searching for *The News* a Mexican newspaper printed in English. Every paper he looked at had the same photo of Potter on the front page, but they were all written in Spanish. Jack asked the vendor, "Do you have *The News*?"

"No *habla* English," replied the vendor.

Jack picked up a paper, pointed at it and said, "English."

"*Si!*" replied the man, his face lighting up as he realized what Jack was looking for. The man went to the back of the newsstand, pulled a newspaper off a stack and handed it to Jack. The paper was *The News* and Potter's face was on the front page. Jack read the article under the photo:

The man assumed to be responsible for the shootings on board the Punta Sam ferry has been identified. Samuel Peters, pictured above, is believed to be the man who shot and killed four people, two Mexican Federal officers and two Mexican citizens. A United States tourist was also injured in the incident.

Peters, who is known to use more than one alias, should be considered armed and dangerous. When last seen Peters had medium-length brown hair and hazel eyes, but he is known to be a master of disguise and may have already changed his hair and eye color.

A U.S. citizen, Peters has been under investigation by both Mexican and United States authorities as a suspected drug trafficker. It is believed that Peters is still in Mexico. . .

Jack was stunned; his mind scrambled. It was more than he could believe. They were traveling in a foreign country with a drug smuggler who was wanted for murder. The implications were terrifying. They had to get away from Potter. He and Jo had to leave town, leave the country. Jack dropped the paper and started sprinting back to the hotel.

*   *   *

Samuel Peters, alias Steve Potter, stood in front of the bathroom mirror concentrating on putting in his colored contact lenses. The contacts turned his hazel eyes blue, which went well with his currently blonde hair. He was having trouble getting the lens to set properly in his right eye. Peters hated wearing the damn things; they irritated his eyes. He had finally gotten the lens into place when there was a knock on the door.

He left the bathroom and pulled his 9mm Glock from a red duffle bag that set on the floor next to the door.

"Who's there?" asked Peters.

"Just me. I was wondering if you would like some company while we're waiting for Jack?"

He recognized Jo's voice. "Sure," he replied.

Peters placed the gun back on top of the fifty-thousand-dollars and zipped up the duffel bag. He then opened the door. Jo entered the room and said, "We're all packed up and ready to go as soon as Jack returns with breakfast."

"Good," replied Peters. "I'm almost ready. We should be able to get to the car rental agency by eight o'clock.

Jo sat in the lone chair in the room while Peters finished packing. "How are you feeling this morning, Mr. Potter?" she asked.

"Fine. Why do you ask?" replied Peters, with a questioning look.

"Why do I ask? God! I think we cut Mexico's tequila supply in half last night."

Peters started to laugh and chided, "Are we under the weather this morning?"

"That's an understatement. Actually, I don't feel so bad now, but it was ugly when I first got out of bed. How come you feel so good?"

"When it comes to drinking I have one rule: always know your limits. Although I have to admit, I occasionally forget this rule."

Jo watched Peters as he finished packing. He was dressed in a polo shirt, blue jeans, and white tennis shoes. She found his easygoing style and handsome face very attractive. Jo could not help thinking that if not for Jack, Steve would be hard to resist. "Steve, I want you to know how much we've enjoyed your company. Meeting you has been one of the highlights of our trip. It's been like traveling with an old friend."

"Thank you! I've enjoyed meeting both of you, and it's nice to know I haven't been a third wheel," said Peters as he walked toward the bathroom. The contact in his right eye still did not feel right.

"I don't want to be too mushy about it. I just want you to know how we feel," said Jo as she watched Peters disappear into the bathroom.

This was the moment she had been waiting for. Making convincing small talk had been difficult. It would soon be over with. She rose from her seat, moved silently over to the door and opened it. A large barrel-chested Mexican carrying a pistol entered the room. His features looked as if they were cut from stone. He wore a dark-brown suit that fit a little too tightly. Behind the big man followed a slight thin-faced Mexican, who was also carrying a gun. She knew the men would be there when she opened the door, but was still surprised by their swift ingress. Unnerved, Jo hoped this would be over quickly.

The men scanned the room, their guns held out in front of them. The big man looked at Josephine, his eyes questioning. Without speaking she motioned toward the bathroom. He nodded his head, then signaled for his accomplice to check the bathroom.

*   *   *

Sam Peters stood stock-still, his hands on the bathroom counter and all of his senses on alert. He had heard something, but what? Why was Josephine suddenly silent? She had seemed stiff, almost uncomfortable. He wanted to call out to her and be assured that everything was all right. The longer the silence lasted the more aware he became that something was wrong. He could not have explained how he knew, but he was certain there was someone else in the room besides Jo. Silently he cursed himself, for his weapon was in the other room and the bathroom had no back door. For the moment, he was trapped. Waiting seemed to be his best option; let them come to him. At least then he could gain some element of surprise. He hoped to God there was only one of them.

*   *   *

Josephine watched in tense silence as the smaller man crept closer to the open bathroom door. The man edged up against the door frame, careful to keep himself from Potter's view. Jo wanted to leave the tension-filled room, but was sure they would not allow this. She almost let out a shriek when a third man entered the room. It was the handsome one, the man with the dark eyes. He brought his finger to his lips indicating he wanted her to remain silent. She was not sure why, but his gaze caused her to shudder.

The thin man still stood by the bathroom door, his body tensed, coiled and ready to spring. In one swift movement, he swung into the open doorway with his arms extended, the gun in firing position.

*   *   *

Peters waited next to the door, his back against the wall. When the gun appeared, he grabbed for the thin man's wrists. His timing was perfect. The silenced handgun fired, shattering the mirror above the bathroom sink. Peters pulled the man into the room, simultaneously driving his right knee into the man's mid-section. The move had the desired effect. Flipping over Peters' leg, the attacker fell to the floor, his head colliding against the tile counter top on the way down.

Knocked senseless, the thin man lay in a crumpled heap. His gun lay on the floor beside him. Peters immediately reached for the pistol, but even as he did, he could see a second man in the doorway. A sudden force tore through his left shoulder, driving his body to the floor. A bullet ripped flesh and shattered bone.

Face down on the bathroom floor, he lay amongst the broken glass and puddles of blood. He felt a foot against his ribs, pushing him over. Figuring this might be his last chance, he grabbed at the foot with his right hand and tried to throw whoever was above him to the floor. The attempt was futile and was met with a boot to the face.

Peters swallowed a scream as he was rolled onto his back. The movement created a searing pain in his shoulder, almost causing him to black out. Lying on his back, he could now see that his left arm was almost detached from the rest of his body. Only a few strands of shredded muscle and sinew connected his arm with his shoulder. He was starting to feel light-headed from the loss of blood, blood that now soaked his shirt and flowed onto the floor.

Above him he could see two men staring down at him. Both held guns. One of the men was heavyset and stood farther back. Peters was fairly sure this was the man who had shot him. The other man stood directly above him, aiming a silenced hand gun at Peters' forehead. The man had a handsome Latin face that was marred by a line of pink scar tissue under his chin. It looked as if someone had attempted to slice his neck open and missed. The raised scar, however, was not the man's most distinguishing feature; his eyes were. They were the color of obsidian, cold and blank like a shark's, eyes that could look into hell and not blink.

Peters recognized the owner of these vacant eyes. He had not met the man before but he had looked at photographs. He also realized the muzzle of the man's gun would be the last thing he would ever see, and he was right.

*   *   *

Jack clambered up the hotel staircase, lungs burning, muscles aching, willing his legs to climb another step. Upon reaching the second floor he felt dizzy and swore at himself for not keeping in shape. Bent over, his hands on his knees, he rested long enough to suck some air into his oxygen-starved lungs. He relaxed slightly; he would soon be with her, and she would be safe.

Moving down the hall toward their room, he glanced at the closed door to Peters' room and cringed as he passed it. The cringe was equal parts fear and anger.

Stopping in front of the door to his room, Jack started to knock. He wanted to call out to Jo; he needed to hear her voice and know that she was all right. But he did neither. He did not want Steve Potter, or Sam Peters, or whatever the hell his name was, to know he was back. Reaching into his pocket, he pulled out his room key and used it to open the door as quietly as possible. The room was empty. Their two duffel bags sat neatly packed on the end of the bed.

Jack thought that Jo must be next door visiting with Peters. How would he get her out of there without arousing the criminal's suspicions? He feared Peters would look into his eyes and know the truth. He was sure the man would kill both of them if he found out that Jack knew his true identity.

Jack needed to collect his thoughts and catch his breath before he went next door. He went to the bathroom and washed the perspiration from his face. They had to separate themselves from Peters, but how? Could he get Peters to pick up the rental car by himself? That would give them a chance to get away. He considered calling the Mexican police, but that might cause more problems. It occurred to him that it would be difficult to explain why they had been traveling with a drug smuggler. He decided the best thing to do was to get away from Peters and leave the country.

Jack went next door and knocked, but there was no answer. Knocking again, he shouted, "Steve, are you there?"

There was no reply. His anxiety mounting, he tried the door knob; it was locked. Fear was again taking over. He had been sure Jo would be there, but no one answered him and the door was locked.

Jack kicked at the door, attempting to knock it down. The door did not budge. In a panic, he kicked at the door again, this time with enough force to send the door crashing into the room.

He entered the room through the splintered door jamb. The room was vacant. A half-packed carry-on bag sat on the dresser, and a small, red duffel bag was on the floor next to the door. His first thought was that he had overreacted. He pounded his head with his fist when he realized they had probably gone to get the rental car. How was he going to explain the broken door? He felt like Brier Rabbit trying to extricate himself from the tar baby; every move he made only exacerbated his situation.

Then Jack realized that his wife was probably walking the streets with a criminal whose face was on the front page of every paper in town. It would not be long before someone identified Peters, and Jo would be with him. Jack was about to run from the room when he saw part of a tennis shoe sticking out the bathroom door. He crept slowly toward the bathroom, his heart in his throat. As he got closer, he could see that a leg was attached to the shoe. Though terrified of what he would find, he moved closer.

When the body on the bathroom floor came into full view, Jack entered a reality he had never experienced, the reality of the dead. Steve's dull, glazed eyes stared at him, one blue eye and one hazel. A round bullet hole centered in Peter's forehead made his face look like a deflated basketball. The corpse lay in a pool of congealing blood, surrounded by shards of mirrored glass. Jack felt nausea, not just from the sight of the dead man, but also from the smell of death, with its mingling odors of drying blood, urine, and feces.

Backing away from the gruesome scene, Jack swallowed the bile that burned the back of his throat. He told himself that Jo must have gone for the rental car. "She is probably in the hotel lobby right now," thought Jack. He had to find her quickly, before Peters' body was discovered.

With shaking hands, he wedged the broken door shut and headed for the hotel lobby.

*   *   *

Thirty minutes had passed since he left Peters' room. Jack had searched the entire hotel and had not found Jo. Nor had the desk clerk nor the hotel manager seen her. He even questioned the hotel maids, though he doubted any of them understood a word of English. Jack cursed himself, how he could live with a Spanish teacher for five years and not know more than a dozen words of the language?

After searching the hotel, he had walked quickly around the block, then ran two blocks to the car rental agency. The man at the rental agency told him that no one had come for the car yet, and he had not seen anyone matching Jo's description.

Now back at the hotel, Jack climbed the stairs to the second floor, telling himself that he and Jo had, somehow, just missed each other and that she would be in their room waiting for him. She would probably tease him about being late again, and this time it would not bother him; he would just be glad to see her smiling face and hold her close.

When Jack entered the room his hopes were crushed for a final time. Not only was Jo gone, but this time Jack noticed something he had missed earlier. Jo's purse was sitting on the dresser. She would not have left the room for long without her purse. He had to face it; Jo was in trouble. Deep inside, he had known this the moment he first saw Peters' lifeless body, but he had hoped for some other explanation. But there was no reason for Jo to have gone anywhere; they had planned on leaving as soon as Jack got back from the *panaderia*.

Jack sat on the edge of the bed with his head in his hands. His mind was overloaded, his reality shattered. Their romantic vacation had suddenly turned into a dark nightmare. Images of blood flashed inside Jack's head, testing his sanity. He imagined Jo's body lying on the bathroom floor instead of Peter's. His unstable mind was soon convinced that his wife was next door, her body stuffed under the bed or in the shower stall. "She could be bleeding to death while I have been running all over town," thought Jack.

Gently he shoved open the door to Peters' room and once inside wedged it back shut. The room appeared as he had left it. Out of the corner of his eye he could see Peters' tennis shoe sticking out the door to the bathroom. Jake was trembling, afraid of what he might find.

There was really not much to search; the room was small with an open closet. The furnishings were sparse: dresser, bed, small table, and chair. The table and chair were against the wall, close to the door.

Finding nothing under the bed, he went to check the bathroom. Stepping over Peters' body, he looked into the shower stall. It was empty. Jack almost felt relieved. For the moment it was better not finding Jo than finding a cold, lifeless corpse. This feeling of relief did not last long, though; Jo was still missing. He realized whoever killed Peters probably had his wife, but what would they do with her?

Jack was about to leave the room when he noticed the red duffel bag that had been on the floor was gone! Between now and the first time he broke into the room, someone else had been here. He was trying to grasp what this might mean when he noticed a glint of light under the chair. Kneeling down by the small metal object to get a closer look, he saw it was a silver earring. He picked it up and gazed at the piece of silver in his hand. He felt like he had been punched in the gut when he recognized the earring as his wife's. She had bought it the previous day from an old Mayan woman on the street. He remembered it because he had teased her about already having bought enough jewelry.

Jack realized it was now time to go to the police. He had avoided it thus far only because of his fears concerning the Mexican justice system. Since he could not speak Spanish, he was somewhat unsure how to approach the authorities. He then remembered reading that Mérida had a United States Consulate. Possibly they would be able to help him. He slipped the earring into the pocket of his short's and then headed to his room.

Finding their tour book in Jo's purse, he flipped through the pages to the section on the city of Mérida. A map showed that the consulate was on the edge of the city, about two miles from the hotel. He also found a phone number. He decided he would call the consulate. The room did not have a phone, but there was one in the hotel lobby for guest's use.

The phone sat on the edge of the reception desk. Jack gave the desk clerk the consulate number. All local calls were free, but the clerk had to dial the number. After entering the number, the clerk handed the receiver to Jack.

After two rings an efficient-sounding voice came on the line, "U.S. Consulate, Mérida. Joan Brannon speaking."

Jack stood there at the reception desk, holding the receiver, unsure of what to say.

"Hello?" questioned the same efficient voice.

Jack swallowed hard and said, "Hello. I'm not sure where to start, but I need some help."

"How about with your name?" asked Joan Brannon.

"My name is Jack Phillips," he sputtered. "I'm an American citizen, and I have a problem." Jack was having trouble getting the words out. His throat was dry and tight, his heart beat accelerated.

"I think my wife has been kidnaped."

CHAPTER 12

The morning sun turned the city into a steam bath. Over the last few days, the rains that kept the tropical climate hospitable had waned and then stopped altogether. Jack did not mind the heat as much as the humidity. It felt as if his body was wrapped in cellophane. At least he was standing on the east side of the street, where the city buildings blocked enough of the morning sun to allow for some shade.

All around him the city morning was in full swing. The narrow streets were choked with cars, trucks, and buses that seemed to be getting nowhere fast. Irritated drivers honked horns, while taxi drivers boldly maneuvered through the traffic. The sidewalk was crowded with people trying to get their business done before the afternoon siesta. He wondered how these people functioned at such a busy pace in the sweltering heat.

Jack felt somewhat better since his talk with Joan Brannon. Feelings of dread and emptiness were still with him, but he had regained his composure. On the phone he had become very emotional, but he had managed to tell his story to Ms. Brannon, who listened without interrupting. She said that the situation sounded serious and that she would send a driver over to take him to the consulate.

After their conversation, Jack went back to his room. Out of Jo's purse he grabbed both of their passports and tourist cards. He then headed back downstairs, leaving the remainder of their luggage in the room.

Jack was concentrating on the traffic, hoping to spot his ride. He did not notice a group of uniformed men approaching the hotel. Before he realized what was happening the men had maneuvered through the crowded sidewalk and had him surrounded.

A Mexican wearing a dark-colored T-shirt and jeans stepped forward, shouting in Spanish. The man grabbed Jack by the shirt collar and thrust him face first against the hotel building. Still screaming, the man shoved a large pistol into the back of his head. Jack tensed, waiting for the explosion that would end his life, but it did not happen. Instead, he was jolted by a blow to his lower back. The precisely executed kidney punch sent ripples of pain throughout his body as he dropped to his knees. The man forced Jack to the concrete and cuffed his hands behind his back.

Jack lay face down on the blistering sidewalk. Above him, he could see his attacker wearing a black cap with the letters M.F.J.P. stenciled above the brim. He knew the initials stood for Mexican Federal Judicial Police. The police had to be looking for Peters, but Jack wondered how they had found him. It did not take him long to figure it out. Peters' photograph was only on the front page of every newspaper in town. Probably one of the hotel employees had recognized Peters. Evidently, they also identified Jack as an associate of Peters'. He also knew it would not take the police long to discover Peters' body.

From where Jack lay on the sidewalk, he could not see the entrance to the hotel, but he could see more uniformed men heading toward the hotel and hear their excited Spanish. The man in the dark T-shirt went to the hotel, leaving two uniformed policemen to stand over Jack, presumably to prevent him from leaving. In spite of his situation, Jack almost laughed at the thought of the guards. His hands were cuffed and he was still dizzy from the blow to his kidney. For the moment he was not going anywhere under his own power. His humor quickly evaporated, though, when he thought of Jo. How would he ever find her from a Mexican jail cell?

A kind of urgent calm settled over Jack. Part of him wanted to scream at the policemen to find his wife, but another part of him overruled this urge. He figured if he were going to convince the Mexican authorities of his story, he would have to calmly and coherently explain what had happened. Yelling and screaming while lying face down on the sidewalk, would get him nowhere.

The man in the M.F.J.P. cap returned and said something to the guards, who nodded their heads. They pulled Jack to his feet. It felt good to be off of the hot sidewalk, but the blood rushing from his head almost caused him to pass out.

The two policemen led Jack to a waiting patrol car, shoved him into the back seat, and slammed the door shut. He could now see the hotel entrance. A group of uniformed officers was keeping a large crowd of gawkers out of the way and allowing only certain important-looking people to pass through into the hotel. Jack watched the excitement blankly as the patrol car moved forward into the traffic, headed he knew not where.

*   *   *

The long morning was moving toward afternoon. A few short hours ago, in what seemed like another life, Jack had been in bed making love to his wife. He now sat alone in a small dingy room of the Mérida police station with his hands cuffed behind his back. The room had one entrance and no windows. A lone light bulb hanging from the ceiling was the only light source, and a wooden table and two wooden chairs were the only furnishings. This was not a happy place.

For almost thirty minutes he had been alone, but to Jack it seemed like hours. The minutes passed uneasily, not because he was worried about himself but because he was worried for Jo. When he arrived at the station, he had tried to explain to the police about his wife, but no one seemed to understand English. He was searched and his wallet, money, passport and tourist papers were confiscated. They even took Jo's earring he had found on the floor of Peters' room. But no one would listen to his story.

After he was processed, two policemen escorted Jack to the room where he now sat. Before the men left the room, Jack pleaded with them to listen. In halting English, one of the men told Jack that he would soon be questioned by an English-speaking officer.

Jack waited quietly, but his anxieties were beginning to eat away at his self control. While he sat alone in this room, whoever had Jo was getting farther away. Unable to wait any longer, he got to his feet and started toward the door. He was going to demand to speak to someone in charge. Before he reached it, the door opened and a man entered the room.

"Sit, please," commanded the man, it was not a suggestion.

The man was dressed in a dark-blue suit with a matching striped tie, and in his hands he carried a manila folder. He was of average height with a stocky build. A slight bulge around the man's waist indicated that he ate well, while his copper-colored skin hinted of Indian ancestry. In the middle of his round face was a bushy black moustache. The man's sad eyes had a hard look about them, a look that told Jack this was a man who did not like to be jerked around. Jack returned to his chair.

Setting the folder on the small table, the Mexican took a seat. He opened the folder and arranged the papers inside it. Among the papers Jack could see both his and Jo's passports and tourist cards.

"I am Inspector José Ortiz of the Federal Judicial Police. Are you Jack Phillips, United States citizen?" asked the man in heavily accented, though correct, English.

"Yes! Inspector Ortiz you have got to help . . . "

"Please wait," interrupted Ortiz. "Before beginning the questioning, I want you to understand your situation. You have been detained for questioning. You have not yet been placed under arrest. For the moment, you are being treated as a witness, but if charges are brought against you what you say here can be used against you in a Mexican court of law.

"I want you to understand, this is serious. Mexico is very hard on drug traffickers, especially ones who kill our agents. You are not in some small town jail on false charges. You cannot buy your freedom, but we will deal with you fairly. If you are innocent you have nothing to fear. We do not want to jail U.S. citizens unjustly."

As Ortiz spoke, he pulled a roll of antacid tablets out of his coat pocket. He unwrapped one, popped it in his mouth and continued speaking, "First, I would like you to tell me what your relationship is with Samuel Peters?"

Ortiz had a hard edge to his voice but his words had an honest ring to them. This gave Jack new hope. If the man was telling the truth about treating him fairly, maybe he wouldn't have to spend the rest of his life in a Mexican jail cell. Maybe he would help him find Jo.

"I met Sam Peters for the first time three days ago," Jack began. "We had no idea who he was. This morning, when I saw his picture in the paper, I couldn't believe it. I ran back to the hotel. I just wanted to get my wife and get away from the man, but when I got back to the room he was dead and my wife was gone. You have got to find her!" He spoke rapidly, words tumbling over one another.

"Please try and talk slower, Mr. Phillips," instructed the Inspector. "My English is not as good as you may think. Start from when you first met Mr. Peters, and in as much detail as possible, tell me what has occurred."

"There is no time! The men who killed Peters have my wife," pleaded Jack. "While we sit here, they're getting farther away! You have got to start looking for her."

"I cannot help you until I have a better understanding of the situation. So far all I know is your name and that you have been traveling with a man suspected of drug trafficking and murder. I cannot find your wife until you help me," explained Ortiz in a firm voice.

Jack could see it was useless arguing with Ortiz, so he took a deep breath and started telling how he met Peters in the Cancún bus station. The Inspector listened intently, writing down notes as Jack explained the events leading up to Jo's disappearance and Peters' death.

"He was just someone to travel with. He seemed like a nice guy. We had no idea who he was. Now these people, whoever they are, have my wife." Jack could feel his eyes filling with tears. He fought them back, though, not allowing them to spill down his face. "Inspector, you have got to find her!"

Ortiz laid down his pencil and leaned back in his chair. He stared at Jack and said, "Jack Phillips, you are either the best liar I have ever met or you are telling the truth. I think you are telling the truth."

The Inspector's words took Jack by surprise. He had not expected a favorable reaction.

Leaning forward, Ortiz rested his elbows on the small, wooden table. The hardness in his voice was replaced by more compassionate tones. "I do not want to mislead you; if the men who killed Peters have your wife, she is in much danger. Once they find she is of no use to them, they will most likely kill her. There is a chance, though, that we can find her. The Federal Judiciary Police and the army are presently coordinating road blocks on all roads leading in and out of Mérida. You see, we also want these people very much.

"The man Peters killed on the Punta Sam ferry was a courier for a large drug ring that I have been investigating for the past three years. I am fairly sure Peters was murdered in retaliation for the Punta Sam incident. If we can catch the men who killed Peters, they may lead us to the people in control of the drug ring. Knowing that the killers have your wife should make it easier to identify them."

Jack felt a measure of relief. The odds were long, but at least Ortiz believed his story, and the police would start searching for his wife. "What happens now?" asked Jack.

"If your story is true, you have broken no Mexican law; you have just had bad luck," answered Ortiz. "Until we are sure of your innocence, though, we will have to hold you. I hope you understand that your word alone is not enough. When we catch these men who have your wife, then we should know the truth."

"I don't care what you do to me, just find my wife," said Jack.

Ortiz shuffled his paperwork together, placed it in the folder and said, "I want to talk with you again this afternoon. I have more questions but I need to get this information out immediately. You will be taken downstairs to a holding cell. The cell will be private, and the jailers will be told to treat you as a guest."

"Inspector, may I be allowed a telephone call? I would like to call the friend we were going to see today. He will be worried when we don't show up."

"Is this the same friend who met you at Chichén Itzá?" asked Ortiz, a puzzled look on his face.

"Yes," replied Jack.

"This was a question I was going to ask you later, but now that you have brought it up, who is this friend of yours?" asked Ortiz.

"His name is Gus Wise, he's an archeologist . . . "

"August Wise! The U.S. archeologist working at Cobá?" interrupted Ortiz.

"Yes, but how do you know Gus?" inquired a surprised Jack.

Ignoring the question, Ortiz continued, "How long have you known Mr. Wise?"

"Years. We were roommates in college. What does this have to do with anything?" asked Jack, perplexed by the Inspector's interest in Gus.

His hard edge had returned as Ortiz said, "I am afraid you have a lot more explaining to do. August Wise is currently under investigation by my department. He is suspected of transporting illegal drugs across Mexico's borders."

"What the hell are you talking about? Gus is an archeologist!" replied Jack.

"Yes, at least that is what we are supposed to think, but his job would make a good cover for other activities. A week ago a special investigation that was looking into supposed mismanagement of funds at government-supported archeological sites stumbled upon Mr. Wise's other occupation. It appears he has been using his position as a cover to move drugs through Mexico. Now you tell me Wise and Peters spent the night at the same hotel. This would appear to be more than coincidence."

Jack was confused. Gus would never get involved with drug smuggling, but he had shown up unexpectedly at Chichén Itzá, and Peters was there.

"Gus is an archeologist. He is my friend," explained Jack, agitation creeping into his voice. "He had just come to visit my wife and me. Peters was there but it was a chance meeting. If he had not been with us, Peters would never have met Gus."

"Come now, Mr. Phillips. You expect me to believe this was a chance meeting," returned Ortiz, condescendingly. "Looking at you and listening to your story, I do not think you are the type who would normally get involved in something like this. Maybe, though, you have financial difficulties. You find you will not be able to make the mortgage payments on your nice home. Your good friend Mr. Wise tells you of a way to make a lot of money fast. The idea does not appeal to you, but you need the money. So you come down to sunny Mexico for a vacation, visit your good friend Mr. Wise and pick up a package. Everything probably would have worked out fine, but you came down right when my investigation was closing in on Mr. Wise and Mr. Peters."

"No!" shouted Jack.

"Maybe it is another way," Ortiz continued. "Maybe you had no idea what was going on. Tell me, are you and your wife happily married?"

"What the hell are you getting at?" asked Jack, his agitation turning to anger.

"Maybe your wife is tired of you. Maybe she wants to be rich. She and your friend, Mr. Wise, may have a plan to make some quick money and then run away together. Maybe your wife shot Mr. Peters."

Jack's mind was reeling. "You're crazy! My wife loves me, she loves her work, and Gus is one of my best friends. What you're saying could never happen," said Jack, trying hard not to sound hysterical.

Ortiz looked down at the wooden tabletop and sadly shook his head. "We can be much easier on you if you tell us the truth, Mr. Phillips. Even if you have committed a crime, if you will help me find the men behind all of this, I would be willing to make a deal for your freedom. You must also try and be receptive to other ideas; you would not be the first man jilted by what he thought was a loving wife."

"You don't know me, my wife, or my friend. You sit here telling me this shit while the real criminals are escaping with my wife!" Spittle danced off of Jack's lips as he shouted at the Inspector. Something had cracked inside of Jack, and a flood of hopelessness, frustration, and anger was released.

His rage was cut short when Ortiz reached up and grabbed a handful of Jack's hair and slammed his head down on the table top. Ortiz did this with a quick, almost unconscious motion, the way most people would swat a fly. The blow stunned Jack more than hurt him. The ease with which Ortiz had taken control led Jack to believe the man could have sent his face through the tabletop if he had wanted.

"You need to learn to respect officers of the law," said Ortiz. "This is Mexico, not the United States. If you do not show the proper respect for the law here, you go to jail and never come out. But you do not have to worry about this because you will help us and then go back to the States, to your nice home.

"For now, though, I think you need to rest and think about what you want to tell me. I will see you later this afternoon. Maybe then your memory will be better. Please do not worry about your wife. We will search for her; after all, she is a suspect." Ortiz collected his papers and left the room.

Jack was shell shocked; the light at the end of the tunnel had been an oncoming train. He realized that the Inspector had been baiting him during the entire interrogation, saying enough of what Jack wanted to hear to keep him talking. Ortiz had no intention of releasing Jack, and if they found Jo, she would also face a Mexican jail cell.

Confused, Jack found himself wondering if Jo could be involved in something like this. He thought of the many late nights Jo and Gus had spent talking about Gus's adventures. They had plenty of time to plan something. Jack and Jo's last year of married life had been rocky, and it was her idea to come to Mexico in the first place. Then Jack caught himself. "What the hell am I thinking?!" Jack screamed to the empty room.

He realized he would go mad if he had to sit alone with these thoughts in his head. This had to be part of Ortiz's plan; push Jack to the edge of his sanity, soften him up so he would talk more freely. The only problem was Jack had no idea what was going on. He had already told the Inspector everything he knew.

Not long after Ortiz left, two uniformed men entered the room. In halting English one of the men ordered Jack to stand. In a daze from the interrogation, his will to resist low, he did as he was told. The men stood on either side of him. Each gripped one of Jack's arms just above the elbow. Jack's hands were still cuffed behind his back as the guards guided him from the room and down a hallway.

The hallway led back to the police station's main entrance, with which Jack was already familiar. Approximately 30 by 50 feet, the main entrance hall had two large glass doors at one end that allowed entry from the street, and at the opposite end was a large reception desk that was almost as long as the hall's width. Behind the desk was the first place Jack had been taken upon entering the police station. It was here they fingerprinted him and took his picture. Down the length of the hall was a row of chairs against the wall. They were the molded plastic type, each chair welded to the chair on either side of it, like those found in bus stations and airports. The hallway that Jack and his guards were traveling through intersected the main hallway about halfway between the glass doors and the reception desk.

Jack was still in a stupor. He did not notice the people who sat in the plastic chairs nor the elderly woman who was speaking with one of the two uniformed men behind the reception desk. If he had, he would have seen a man across the hall sitting in the last chair nearest the reception desk. The man had dark-brown hair and bronze skin. In spite of his hair and skin color, the man did not appear to be Mestizo or Mayan. He was substantially larger than most of the local population and was dressed in a white shirt, no tie, and a gray sports coat. This man was one of three people who were watching Jack and his two guards as they approached the main hallway.

Two other men sat together about halfway down the row of chairs and directly across from the hallway Jack and his guards were exiting. Both men were Mexican and dressed in cheap-looking dark suits. One of the men had a thin face and long neck with a pronounced Adam's apple. He stood up when Jack and his guards reached the main hallway and started walking toward the smaller hallway, seeming to pay no attention to Jack or the guards. The thin-faced man was within ten feet of them when he slipped his hand inside his coat.

Jack felt the two guards release their hold on his arms and looked up to see the thin-faced man pull a black pistol from under his coat. Staring straight at Jack, the gunman's eyes were filled with a vacant intensity as he aimed the barrel of the weapon at Jack's forehead. Jack had never seen eyes like this before; these were the eyes of an executioner. Their eye contact lasted less than a second, but it was a second Jack would not forget. One moment he was looking into the face of the reaper, and the next, the side of the killer's face exploded, splattering blood across Jack's face. The hallway filled with the report of a gunshot as the thin-faced man dropped to the floor still holding his unfired gun.

Jack now saw the man in the gray sports coat standing near the reception desk . He was holding a gun and appeared to be pointing it at Jack. Jack froze, his mind overloaded. It was not from fear—there was no time for fear—it was just that everything was moving so fast.

The other Mexican in a dark suit was now on his feet with a gun in his hand. This man was shorter than his thin-faced compadre and had puffy cheeks that made him look like a chipmunk.

The guard on Jack's right had instinctively reached for his sidearm when he saw the thin face man pull out his weapon, only his revolver was not there. As is the custom in most jails, the guards were not allowed to wear sidearms when inside the holding areas. Chipmunk Face saw the guard reaching for his empty holster and reacted on instinct, firing two .38 slugs into the guard's mid-section.

The blasts of the second two gunshots shook Jack from his trance. He turned and ran back down the hallway he had just come through. The skin between his shoulder blades twitched when he heard two more shots fired, but the expected bullets never came. He did not see the man in the gray sports coat deposit two rounds into the second gunman's chest.

Jack ran down the empty hallway as best he could with his hands still cuffed behind his back, which limited his running motion. In spite of the handicap, he was moving at a good clip, putting some distance between himself and the small war that had erupted. Jack kept his legs pumping as he approached the first corner. Rounding the corner, he collided with something moving in the opposite direction and was knocked from his feet. He dropped to the floor like a sack of cement.

His circuits scrambled, the world went fuzzy. Had he run into a wall? Shaking his head to clear the fog, he looked up to see that the wall was actually Inspector Ortiz. Ortiz stood above him, a pistol in his hand and a big grin on his face, glad to see his prisoner was still in one piece. The Inspector started to say something to Jack when a fist suddenly crashed into the man's face. Jack winced; the blow sounded like a watermelon being dropped on a concrete sidewalk. For a brief moment Ortiz stayed on his feet, seemingly unaffected by the punch. Jack thought the man must be made of granite. Ortiz was human, though. His eyes crossed and he slowly dropped to his knees and then fell over on his side.

The man who had delivered the punch lifted Jack to his feet. It was the big dark haired man wearing the gray sports coat. Bending over Ortiz, the man took the badge clipped to the unconscious man's jacket pocket. He then clipped the badge to the pocket of his own coat and said, "Do exactly as I say or you're dead."

Jack nodded his head, affirming that he understood. He also noticed that the man had what sounded like a Midwest accent.

Grabbing Jack by the arm, the mysterious stranger led him farther down the hallway, away from the station's main entrance. Two uniformed men came running toward them with their revolvers drawn. One of the men Jack recognized from his arrest in front of the hotel. The man in the gray sports coat shouted to them in Spanish as they approached. Both officers nodded in understanding and continued down the hall toward the main entrance.

Jack was impressed; the man appeared to speak Spanish as well as English. The stranger's English had convinced Jack the man was from the United States, but now he was not so sure; after all, the man spoke Spanish well enough for the two officers to believe he was a Mexican cop.

Reaching the end of the hall they came to a door marked *Salida*. The man pushed Jack face-first against the wall. The sudden movement caused Jack, who was still dizzy from the collision with Ortiz, to lose his balance. He would have fallen had the stranger not pinned him against the wall.

"We may have to move fast, so I'm taking the cuffs off. But please don't try anything. I don't miss," said the stranger as he pulled back his coat just enough to reveal the 9mm automag tucked into his shoulder holster.

Jack looked from the gun up to the man's serious, brown eyes. He believed what the man said.

The stranger motioned for Jack to lead the way. Jack opened the door marked *Salida* and walked out into the harsh sunlight. They found themselves in a small parking lot behind the police station. An unmarked sedan, two patrol cars, and a paddy wagon were the only vehicles present.

"This might be our ticket for a quick exit out of town," said the stranger as he surveyed the patrol cars. He tried the doors on both patrol cars, but they were locked. Undeterred, he took off his sports coat and wrapped it around his right hand. He then took a martial arts stance and drove his fist through the driver's side window. Reaching through the shattered glass, the stranger unlocked and then opened the door. He motioned to Jack, who then entered through the driver's side door and slid across to the passenger's seat. The stranger followed Jack into the car, then quickly dismantled the ignition. He touched two wires together, and the engine turned over and roared to life. From the moment he broke the window until the car was started, less than sixty seconds had passed.

As he drove out of the lot and onto the street, the stranger rolled down the broken driver-side window. The act of stealing the police car appeared to amuse him. The speed with which he had done it convinced Jack that this was not the first car he had stolen.

"Don't you think we will stand out driving around town in a stolen police car?" deadpanned Jack.

The man glanced at Jack. He appeared to be surprised by the sound of Jack's voice. "Hell no!" he said. "The Mexicans probably won't realize it's stolen until sometime next week. For now, this car gives me the freedom to go where I want without being hassled by roadblocks or curious *Federales*."

He flashed the badge clipped to his coat pocket toward Jack, "Besides, I've got the badge, I might as well have the car."

Jack did not know what to make of the stranger. For the moment he was just glad to have escaped the Mexican jail.

They had traveled less than three blocks when the man pulled up to the curb. Jack wondered why they were stopping so close to the police station. He was anxious; he wanted some miles between himself and Mérida.

"Wait here," the man told Jack as he got out of the car.

Jack watched him unlock and open the hatchback of a Volkswagen Golf that was parked along the curb. The urge to run was strong. Ortiz and his men could come around the corner at any moment and spot him. Also, he did not know what the stranger wanted from him and was not sure he wanted to find out. As if he sensed what Jack was thinking, the stranger turned around and shot Jack a glance that took away any thoughts of escape.

From the trunk of the car, the man pulled a red duffel bag. Anxiety turned to panic when Jack recognized the duffel bag. It was Peters', the one that had vanished from the hotel room. The man brought the duffel back and tossed it onto the patrol car's rear seat. Jack's mind was racing. What did the red duffel bag mean? Was this the man who had killed Peters? If he were, what had he done to Jo? Filled with a sudden rage, Jack was prepared to beat the shit out of the man in order to find out. "What have you done with her?" screamed Jack, as he lunged for the stranger's throat.

Jack was no match for the dark-haired man, who quickly deflected the attack and contained Jack with a headlock. He twisted and jerked Jack's neck, causing a loud popping noise. Jack's entire body began to tingle. The man released Jack, who then slumped back into the passenger seat, his body numb. Jack was unable to move. He wondered if his neck were broken. The stranger quickly wrapped a rubber hose around Jack's left arm. He watched in horror as the stranger used a syringe equipped with a hypodermic needle to inject something into his swollen vein. Jack wanted to pull his arm away, but the message did not make it from his brain to his arm, all the lines were scrambled. Gradually, the tingling numbness was replaced by a warm glow, and soon Jack felt like he was floating in a warm sea. His thoughts went fuzzy. He looked out the window as the darkness smothered him. The street was packed with cars, trucks, and buses all loaded with human cargo. The sidewalks were full with a crush of humanity. "Can't anyone see what is happening?" was Jack's last thought as he slipped into unconsciousness.

CHAPTER 13

Nelson Carlton's office should have been declared a disaster area. Paperwork was scattered across his desk and piled on the floor. Any remaining space was occupied by empty doughnut boxes, fast food wrappers, and soda cans filled with cigarette butts. The office was small, with enough room for Carlton and his desk. "Office! Hell, there's not enough room for squirrels to fuck," were Carlton's words two years ago when he first saw the tiny room.

Carlton sat at his desk nursing a cup of hot black coffee as he read a file that lay open on his desk. Normal operating procedure called for a splash of Old Number Seven in his coffee. This usually loosened him up and removed any ill effects of the previous night's imbibing. He considered the whiskey, but decided to keep his head clear. With his new responsibilities he never knew when he might be called into Lester Goreman's office. He thought it best not to appear at the Secretary of State's office half drunk, leastwise not before noon. There was another reason for not spiking his coffee this morning; this was the second morning in a row he had awakened hangover free. The investigation was occupying him to the point of interfering with his drinking time. Without the pain of a hangover, he discovered his urge for a morning boost was not insurmountable, and he found that he sort of enjoyed spending his mornings sober.

Carlton was now fully immersed in the investigation, although he had no idea where it was leading him. There was still no evidence to link the deaths of Buck and Allen or the attempt on Senator Hightower's life. The FBI was conducting separate investigations into the three incidents, but so far the information received by Carlton was meager. So much for "top priority" and "full cooperation." He could see that the boys over at Buzzard Point were going to be parsimonious in their exchange of information.

For now, Carlton was not concerned with the speed at which the FBI operated, as he already had plenty to keep him busy. Yesterday, Sam Peters finally checked in through one of his blind contacts. The message had traveled through the Drug Enforcement Agency intelligence network and was directed to Andrew Buck. Carlton was receiving copies of all the late director's intelligence communications. The short message indicated that Peters was going underground and would be unavailable for an undetermined amount of time. Carlton was unsure of what this might mean. It did raise questions about whether the termination order was warranted. Peters had made contact, though late. If he had switched sides, why bother sending a message? At this point it would be difficult to reverse the order, plus the Mexican authorities had already been alerted. The doctored information on Peters, along with a physical description and photographs, had been delivered.

Carlton could not afford to play this one close. He had to assume Peters had turned, been compromised, or had cracked from the stress of living two years under deep-cover. If he had decided to join the bad guys, he may have been using the contact in an attempt to hide his true intentions. This did not make sense though, for Peters would have to assume that the cat was out of the bag after the ferry incident and the murders in Washington. Why leave a trail, however faint, as to his whereabouts?

If Peters had been compromised, the message could be a goodbye note. But if this were the case, why not say so in the message? At least then his superiors could account for his disappearance. The final consideration was that Peters may have flipped out. If this were the situation, there could be a million reasons why the message was sent, all of them only to be understood by an unbalanced mind.

The message contained one other piece of unexplained information. It was a name: Ricardo Reyes. The name meant nothing to Carlton, but some research turned up a State Department file on a Mexican citizen named Ricardo Reyes. Carlton was currently examining this file.

The dossier was about an inch thick and contained in a manila folder with "top secret" stamped in red on the outside. Carlton smiled. He doubted there was anything in the file worthy of the screaming red letters. Most of the State Department files concerning foreign citizens were filled with nothing but newspaper articles clipped from foreign newspapers. He noted that this file had been originated by the Customs Department.

According to the information in the file, Reyes had been born into money, his family a member of Mexico's elite upper class. He was brought up with all the comforts of the privileged: expensive cars, fancy clothes, and private schools. He attended the University of Southern California in the early 1960s. After graduating, he came home to find that much of the family fortune had been squandered by his inept, if not unscrupulous, uncle. An ugly legal battle ensued, but Reyes must have eventually realized that the amount of money remaining was not worth fighting over. Reyes went about making his own fortune, and over the next twenty years he was fabulously successful, becoming one of Mexico's richest men.

He was heavily invested in legitimate businesses, but how he came up with his initial capital was somewhat murky. During the seventies, Reyes was the subject of a Customs Department investigation. Customs suspected Reyes was involved in the black market sale of pre-Colombian artifacts but was never able to build a good case. It was rumored that Reyes had a substantial collection of ancient Mayan art housed at his Yucatán estate. According to the file, Reyes spent most of his time on this secluded estate located on the Caribbean coast.

The most recent information on the man, and the reason for the State Department file, had to do with his support of Carlos Cervantes, a candidate in Mexico's upcoming presidential election. Reyes was funneling large amounts of cash into his candidate's campaign coffers. Initially, Cervantes appeared to have little chance of beating the incumbent, but the race had tightened. As the Director of the Mexican Federal Judicial Police, Cervantes was running a law and order campaign.

Carlton lit up a Camel and leaned back in his chair. He blew streams of smoke toward the ceiling as his mind sorted through what he had learned. Why did Peters send Buck the name Ricardo Reyes? Was Reyes the middleman Operation Raven had been searching for? There was nothing in the file to indicate that the man was involved in the drug trade. Then again, they were looking for a mystery man; it was the reason they were trying something as extreme as Operation Raven.

Carlton began to construct a possible scenario in his mind. One thing that had bothered him was that Peters' service record indicated that the man was a special individual. He had been in a number of deep-cover operations and had survived, both physically and mentally. Peters appeared to have a strong understanding of his own limitations. An overdeveloped ego was deadly in this business. This did not disprove he sold out or lost his marbles. Carlton had seen too much to rule out either of these possibilities. But assuming Peters had not defected or become defective, what were the possibilities? Suppose the incident on the Punta Sam ferry was an attempt to eliminate Peters, but he manages to escape his attackers. Somehow, he discovers that Ricardo Reyes is the man for whom Operation Raven has been searching. Peters' network has broken down, his shadow agents killed. A highly classified operation has been compromised. Peters is left out in the cold. He can trust no one without putting himself in danger. His only choice is to disappear until things can be sorted out. Before he goes underground, he sends a final message that names Ricardo Reyes in the hope that his one trusted superior can put the pieces together.

For some unknown reason, he is afraid to give too much information, possibly because he suspects Operation Raven has been infiltrated.

Carlton decided it was a workable theory. The only problem was, he had nothing that linked Reyes to any of this, other than a message from an apparent renegade agent.

Carlton felt a headache coming on and decided a walk and a bite to eat might help clear his head. He was almost out of the office when the phone rang. It was Lester Goreman. As he listened to the Secretary of State, the intensity of his headache increased. There would be no bite to eat, he was to report to Goreman's office immediately. Samuel Peters' body had been found in a Mérida hotel room.

CHAPTER 14

Whump, whump, whump . . . floating in a fog for hours, days, or was it only seconds? Dreams had filled his head, but he could not remember what they were about. His mind was heavy with the fog, in a state between somnolence and consciousness. The early morning battle between sleep and wakefulness was being fought. Through the fog he was able to see the white blades of a ceiling fan slowly revolving above his head. Whump, whump, whump . . .

His thoughts were moving like honey on a cold morning. He wanted to roll over and wrap his body around hers, feel her warmth. He did not move though. It was as if his brain had been separated from his body. Questions rolled through his mind as he stared at the revolving ceiling fan. Where am I? How did I get here? Bits and pieces of dream flashed into his thoughts, a drive in a car. Questions, someone asking him questions. Whump, whump, whump . . .

Gradually, he became aware of the tropical air, thick and sticky with a heavy odor that was more than just the smell of his sweating body. The memory banks were stimulated and kicked out a little information: Mexico, vacation, Josephine. His eyes remained transfixed on the slowly rotating fan as he tried to put his thoughts together and recall where he was. Whump, whump, whump . . .

Then it hit him like a sledgehammer between the eyes. Jo was gone! They had taken her, and he had to find her. He tried to sit up, but both of his arms were constricted above his head. Wildly, he pulled and jerked his arms, trying to free his wrists from whatever had enclosed them. Looking to his wrists, he saw that they were cuffed to the bed's iron headboard. The handcuffs were securely attached to both the headboard and his wrists.

Jack lay on his back, his hands cuffed above his head, and took stock of his surroundings. It appeared that he was being held prisoner in a low-budget Mexican hotel. The walls needed a coat of paint, and now that he was fully awake he could feel a mattress spring poking his lower back. A dingy curtain covered the room's only window. The little bit of light that did sneak around the worn fabric told Jack that the sun was up, but he could only guess at the time of day. Across the room an open doorway appeared to lead to a bathroom. Through the doorway he saw what looked to be the edge of a sink. He decided the hotel could not be too low budget; it did have a private bath.

Jack also saw there was another bed in the room, its covers mussed and tumbled. Someone had slept in this other bed, but who?

For the moment he forgot about trying to free himself and concentrated on remembering how he had gotten here. Jack was still not operating at full speed, but he was awake enough to suspect that he was suffering from the effects of heavy sedation. It was not unlike a couple of massive hangovers he had experienced, the kind where you wake in the morning and cannot remember the night before.

Jack rummaged through his memory, his head throbbing, trying to find his last conscious thoughts. He was having difficulty placing himself in time and space. He remembered Jo's disappearance, the bullet hole in the middle of Sam Peters' forehead, and the interrogation by Inspector Ortiz. He also remembered the horror of the police station shootout; his terror turning to revulsion as he watched his would-be assassin's face explode, and then expecting a bullet in his back as he ran from the madness. After this, his memory was garbled. The fog was rolling back into his brain and his stomach burned. It was a cross between hunger and nausea. How long had he been asleep? When did he last eat? The questions were tormenting him. Looking back at the empty bed, he wondered: who had slept there?

Jack fought the fog, attempting to concentrate, straining to remember. He thought he was going crazy when finally another door to his memory opened. It was like someone turned a light on. Suddenly, he remembered the man stealing the police car. They drove off in the car, but what happened next was lost in the fuzz. Something happened, but he could not pull the memory out of the recesses of his mind. Who was this dark-haired stranger, and where had they gone in the police car? It seemed like every time he remembered something it only added to his confusion and fear.

Where did they go in the police car? He had a vague recollection of a feeling of motion, as if he had been trying to sleep in a moving vehicle. There was also a faint memory of questions, someone asking him lots of question. He was not even sure if these were things that had actually happened or if he had only dreamed them. The only thing he was sure of was that he had a terrible hangover.

His eyes kept drifting back to the empty bed. Who had slept there? Was it the stranger or someone else? More importantly, what were the intentions of whoever was holding him hostage? He remembered going along with the man without putting up resistance or asking question.

Of course, at the time he did not have much choice. Ortiz seemed ready to railroad him into jail for life and someone else wanted him dead badly enough to hire two men to gun him down in the middle of a police station. Considering the situation, the stranger appeared like a guardian angel. Why, though, did his guardian angel need to sedate him and keep him handcuffed to the bed?

When would the confusion end? Maybe this was all a bad dream. Maybe he would wake up in his own bed holding Josephine in his arms. It was not a dream, though, and the reality of it tormented him. How would he ever find Jo? And even if he did, how would they ever get out of the country? The Mexican authorities knew who he was and they would be searching for him at all airports and border crossings.

Jack was startled from his thoughts when he heard the noise of a key being inserted into the room's door lock. He jerked his head around so he could see the door. His heart thumped wildly in his chest as he watched the knob turn and the door swing into the room. The room filled with sunlight. Blinded by the sudden increase in light, Jack was unable to make out who was coming through the door. Gripped by fear, he was sure he looked like a trapped rat to whoever was entering the room.

"Good morning! It's good to see you're awake."

He knew the voice. The man shut the door, and the room was plunged back into a gloomy gray. Again able to see, Jack immediately recognized the dark-haired stranger. The man had a light-bronze cast to the skin of his handsome yet hard face, with eyes that could go from twinkling to killer and back again in a matter of seconds. In his hands he held a brown paper bag and two Styrofoam cups. Jack could smell the coffee as the man set the cups on a small dresser.

"Sorry about the cuffs, but I didn't know what your mental state would be when you woke up."

The man fished around in his pants pocket and pulled out a key that he used to remove the cuffs from Jack's wrists. Jack sat up slowly, massaging his wrists, unsure of how he should react.

"I know you're probably a little disoriented and that you have some questions," said the man. "I want you to understand you have nothing to fear from me."

Jack sat on the edge of the bed and nodded.

"I thought you might be hungry," continued the man. "So I brought back some pastries from the *panadería*. I also brought some coffee."

The mention of food reminded Jack of the burning ache in his stomach. He grabbed the paper bag the man offered. Inside he found three bread rolls with sugar sprinkled on top. He took one of the rolls out of the bag and wolfed it down, barely taking time to chew.

"You are hungry," said the man as he took one of the steaming cups of coffee off of the dresser and handed it to Jack.

Jack accepted the coffee and said, "Thank you."

"Well, at least we know you can still speak," said the man.

Sitting on the small dresser, he sipped coffee and watched Jack devour his small breakfast. Both men remained silent.

Jack finished the last of the sugared rolls and washed them down with the coffee. Though he would have liked something a little more substantial, the coffee and rolls did take the edge off of his appetite. The meal, the coffee especially, helped remove the fog in his head. Feeling somewhat fortified, Jack looked up at the man and asked, "Who are you?"

"For the moment I seem to be the only friend you've got," he answered

"This is nice to know, but maybe you have a name?" queried Jack, a trace of bitter sarcasm in his voice.

The stranger luaghed and said, "Yes, I do. You can call me Travis."

Jack stared at the man, perplexed that any humor could be found in the current situation. "Is that Travis as in Travis or is it Travis as in Tim, Tom or maybe Terry?" he retorted.

"Look, I'm sorry. I really shouldn't be laughing. In my line of work you have to keep your sense of humor. I've laughed my way through some pretty sad and crazy situations. I think I have some explaining to do so you'll understand what's going on."

"You sure as hell do!" replied Jack. "Like where am I, and why do you have to keep me chained to a bed?" he was now fully awake and quickly becoming angry.

"I cuffed you because I didn't know what you might do if you woke. I knew you would be disoriented. You probably don't realize it, but you are currently one of the most wanted men in Mexico. Your mug is on the front page of every paper in town. If you go out on the streets, it wouldn't be long before you'd be spotted, especially if you start flashing your name around. As for where you are, you're in the city of Campeche. I brought you here yesterday."

"Campeche? That's on the Gulf Coast," said Jack, a quizzical look on his face.

"Yes," confirmed Travis, "about 100 miles southwest of Mérida. I assume you realize that you have been under heavy sedation. I'm sorry, but after you attacked me you didn't leave me much choice. I did not know who you were or your intentions. There was also no reason for you to trust me, so for expedience, I kept you asleep for a while."

Jack was confused, he had no memory of his attack. "You trust me now?" he asked skeptically.

"Yes, I know who you are now: Jack Phillips, a history professor. You came to Mexico for a vacation with your wife. Yesterday you find the man you were traveling with has been shot in the head and your wife has vanished. You have no idea what is going on, and you're scared shitless."

"You seem to know a lot about me, Travis. May I ask where you get your information?" questioned Jack.

"Actually, you were the source of my information," replied Travis. "I had a long discussion with you while you were sleeping."

Under normal circumstances Jack would have been furious to find out he had been interrogated while under the influence of drugs, his innermost thoughts laid open to some stranger, but at the moment he felt only emptiness. Too much had happened too fast for him to comprehend the significance of it all. His world was spinning and gyrating around wildly in a universe gone out of control. His mind had been raped and his emotions were spent, but he could feel no anger. Jack stared at the floor and slowly shook his head.

"It's not a good feeling. Believe me, I know. But it was the only way I could verify your identity," explained Travis.

"So you trust me, but why should I trust you?" asked Jack in a defeated tone.

"I don't see that you have much of a choice. Besides, I know who you are and at this point you are only a liability to me. In spite of this, I'm going to arrange your passage back to the United States. If I were really your enemy you'd be dead."

"Arrange passage? What about my wife?" questioned Jack.

"I'm down here for a reason, and it's not to save your ass. The reason I am here involves the same people who probably have your wife. If she can be found, I'll find her."

"If you think I am going home without my wife, you're out of your mind," stated Jack.

"You do not understand, Mr. Phillips. It's not just the *Federales* who want you. Who do you think those men were who tried to shoot you at the police station? If you stay in Mexico you would not only have to avoid the *Federales* but also these assassins. Through no fault of your own you have a lot of people thinking you are something you are not. Despite what you told me when you were drugged, I almost don't believe it. You were traveling through Mexico with a suspected drug runner who gets his brains blown out, and at the same time your good friend, Gus Wise, is wanted by the Judicial Police for drug trafficking.

You have definitely been hanging out with the wrong people. Someone now wants to see you eliminated. You're a wild card; they don't know what you're up to or what you will do next."

The mention of Gus stung Jack. He had forgotten about Gus's trouble. What had Gus done? It was another unsettling question for which Jack did not have an answer.

"Who are you, some kind of CIA spy?" asked Jack.

"As far as you're concerned it doesn't matter who I am," said Travis. "The less you know, the better. You will just have to believe me when I tell you that I have your best interests in mind. You also need to realize it will not be easy getting you back to the U.S., but I think I have found a fisherman, who, for the right amount of money, is willing to try and float you across the Gulf."

Jack was unsure of what to say. He wished there was someone he could trust. Travis gave every indication that he was telling the truth, but Jack also got the feeling that the man was hiding something. He also sensed that Travis was not a man he wanted to go against. Travis was attempting to not make him feel like a hostage, but Jack was certain the man would not allow him to leave the hotel. Part of Jack wanted to surrender, let Travis take care of things, get out of this country and back to the United States. But then he thought of Josephine; he could not leave without Jo.

"I thank you for all you have done for me," said Jack in a controlled voice. "But I will not leave Mexico without my wife. I'll go back to the Mexican authorities if I have to. If I turn myself in, maybe that will convince them of my innocence. Whatever the situation turns out to be, I am not leaving."

Travis ran his fingers through his dark hair, a look of exasperation passing over his face. He then said, "I was hoping I could sidestep this issue, but I can see that you are adamant. You will never see your wife again, Mr. Phillips. One of two things has happened. One, she was involved in the killing of Peters. Possibly she and Mr. Wise were partners; they kill Peters and take off with the drug money. She's your wife, you should have a better idea than I do as to how plausible this theory is."

"No way! You are talking about my wife and best friend!" exclaimed Jack, the emotion evident in his voice.

"OK, I believe you," said Travis, though the look on his face indicated he was not so sure. "The only other possibility is that your wife was kidnaped by the man or men who shot Peters. They will try and get information out of her, but once they find out who she is and that she knows nothing, they will kill her."

Jack started to tremble as he listened to Travis. "We have to find her! We're wasting time! We can't let them kill her!" he pleaded, his voice high and tight.

"There is nothing we can do. It is already too late," replied Travis.

Tears began rolling down Jack's face. Travis was speaking the truth, a truth Jack had feared since finding Peters' lifeless body. All along, in the back of his mind, he had known he would never see Jo again. The salty tears tumbled down his cheeks and nose and dropped to the floor. His body shook as he gasped for air between sobs. He did not try to wipe back the tears or swallow his cries; the loss was too great.

As he wept, he noticed he was still wearing the same shorts and shirt as yesterday. When he put these clothes on Jo had been taking a shower; she had been alive, enjoying the warm water on her skin. His clothes were now filthy, and he wondered where he would get something clean to wear. He also wondered what made him think of such a thing in the middle of his grief. At this point what did clothes matter?

CHAPTER 15

Nelson Carlton sat with his feet propped up on his desk and a half-smoked Camel between his lips. The clutter of his office surrounded him. He was watching a small portable television that sat on his desk. The T.V. was about all he had from his days with the Central Intelligence Agency; it had been part of a hidden camera setup used in surveillance work. The visage of Senator Jason James Hightower filled the puny screen. Over the last few days, the Senator had become something of a national hero as word leaked to the media about the bombing of his limo. The Senator was delivering a speech informing the nation that the terrorists of the world would not deter him. He would continue the fight for all things good, righteous, and American. It occurred to Carlton that he might be watching a future President of the United States.

"Senator Hightower is a profile in courage," gushed the newsman at the end of Hightower's speech.

"You should have seen him shitting in his pants a few days ago," said Carlton to the small television.

Tired of hearing what an inspiration Jason James Hightower was to the nation, he tapped the on-off button with the toe of his shoe, turning off the television. Carlton reached for the copy of *Screw Up Your Life* magazine lying on his desk. He had filched the magazine off of a secretary's desk earlier in the morning. On the cover were the faces of Andrew Buck, Ronald Allen, and Senator Hightower. In bold letters across the bottom the question was asked, "Is there a connection?"

"Why should I care?" said Carlton as he tossed the rag back on his desk.

He had already read the articles: nothing new. According to the magazine, the two deaths and the attempt on the Senator's life were separate unrelated incidents. The only relationship among the three events was time; they all took place within a twelve-hour period. One of the writers went so far as to bring up the old cliche about things happening in threes.

The articles were stuffed with information straight from the State Department's PR men. Andrew Buck was dead from a weak heart.

Ron Allen was killed by a call girl he had promised to marry; supposedly Allen changed his mind, so the hooker blew his brains out and then swallowed a bullet herself. It was an ugly little mess, but the only reputation it destroyed was Allen's, and he was dead. A terrorist group Carlton had never heard of was being held responsible for the attempt on Hightower's life.

Carlton was sure someone had the editors by the balls. This was a publication that usually found controversy where none existed, and here they were passing up real controversy. Everything was wrapped up in a neat little package and everyone was happy, everyone but Carlton. He did not like neat little packages.

He knew the cover up would happen, the powers-that-be always have to have their asses protected. He also knew that whoever ordered the murders of Buck and Allen was getting away with them. Peters was dead, but he did not organize this whole deal himself; at most he was just a pawn on someone else's chess board. No one was even concerned with a character named Ricardo Reyes.

It was not just the cover up that was bothering Carlton; this morning he had been informed his services would no longer be needed. The investigation of Operation Raven was terminated, and he was to forget everything he had learned since his first meeting with Secretary of State Lester Goreman. Carlton felt used. He had been set up to play the fall guy from the start. If the press had found out what was going on, he and Hightower would have been the sacrificial lambs. Now that Peters was eliminated, everyone felt safe. They wanted Carlton to crawl back into his hole of an office and be forgotten.

He knew that he should be grateful. If it had gone another way he may have found himself spending his retirement in a federal penitentiary. But Carlton was not grateful; he was restless. There were too many unanswered questions. He was confident the deaths of Andrew Buck and Ronald Allen and the attempt on Hightower's life were all related. The problem was he did not have a shred of evidence that connected the three incidents.

The FBI investigations of the two murders and the attempt on the Senator's life had moved at glacial speed. Information from one investigation was not allowed to be shared with agents working on another investigation. Each case was kept separate to the point of ridiculousness. At first, Carlton thought this was being done to prevent leaks to the media about possible connections among the three incidents. He figured each investigation would report to him, and it would be his job to find any links. The only problem was that Peters was killed and Carlton was ordered to cease his investigation, while at the same time the FBI closed the book on the Allen murder and claimed that Andrew Buck died of natural causes.

It now seemed that no one cared if the three incidents were related. And Carlton knew why: damage control. If what Buck, Allen, and Hightower were up to became public knowledge, the shit would hit the fan. And if it were known that the President had approved the project, it would be the same as saying the President of the United States deals drugs. The President had to get the situation controlled quickly. That meant Peters eliminated and the Buck, Allen, and Hightower cases solved and closed. This had to be why the Bureau went to such great lengths to keep the investigations separate. The President could not afford connections being made among the three cases or soon the investigators would uncover Operation Raven, and, once the digging started, even the best kept secrets would be hard to hide.

What worried Carlton the most, actually terrified him, was not the cover up and all that it entailed—that crap went on all the time—but the fact that a crime organization from a foreign country had infiltrated the U.S. government at such a high level. The bad guys had assassinated two highly placed government officials, attempted to take the life of a third, and bought off or compromised a deep-cover agent, and did it in such a way that the President and his men had no choice but to cover up the incidents.

"Fuck it," Carlton said to himself. It was time to forget; he had done it before in the name of national security. This was just like two years ago, except this time he would keep his mouth shut.

It was only midmorning, but Carlton craved a bourbon over ice. The past few days he had cut back on his drinking. The Peters' situation had kept him busy, and gave him something to do besides get drunk. He did not have the ice, but there was a bottle of Jack Daniel's in his bottom desk drawer. He pulled the whiskey out and set it on his desk.

Carlton stared at the bottle as if transfixed by its contents. It occurred to him that two years of his life had passed since the first time he had walked into this office. Where had the time gone? Most of the last two years he could not remember; it had been spent in an alcoholic haze. As he stared at the bottle, he realized what a failure at life he had become. His job was a joke, and he had no close family or friends. It seemed like the only thing left for him to accomplish was dying. Being sober brought the full pain of his situation to bear on him; the unremitting pain of loneliness and grief that can seem worse than death itself.

He had considered suicide on more than one occasion, but he had come to the conclusion that he did not have the guts to kill himself. He would have to live with his pain and loneliness, and the only way he could do that was to keep his brain soaked in booze. "Stay numb and dumb, and nothing can hurt you," had been Carlton's motto.

The whiskey, the gin, and the vodka had allowed him to hide from reality: I'm an alcoholic, so I can't help myself. Now that he was sober he had to face up to what he had known all along. He was not a true alcoholic; it was not his body that needed the sauce, it was his soul.

Carlton grabbed the bottle of whiskey off his desk and flung it across the small office. The bottle shattered against the wall. Leaning forward, his elbows resting on the desk top, he held his head in his hands. A long, low moan escaped his lips as a tear trickled down his cheek. Carlton started sobbing and could not stop. A flood of emotions that had been held back for two years were suddenly released. This was the first time he had cried since the day his wife passed away.

CHAPTER 16

The morning had slowly turned into late afternoon with Jack still in the cheap hotel room. He was lying on his back on a lumpy mattress, wearing the shorts and T-shirt Travis had loaned him, watching the white blades of the ceiling fan slowly spinning above his head. He had been like this for hours, barely moving and not showing any sign of emotion. She was gone. One part of him understood this, but another part could not comprehend it. Jack had suffered grief and depression before in his life. When his father passed away he had suffered deeply, but he had never experienced anything like this. It was a struggle between what he knew to be true and what he was willing to accept. He felt like an empty vessel, able to travel on in life, but with no direction or reason to go.

Travis had gone to finalize a deal with the fisherman. Jack would soon be heading home in a small fishing skiff. If he had been in a more stable emotional state, he might have severely questioned crossing the Gulf of Mexico in such a small craft. Jack was in a kind of stupor, though. He no longer had any control of what happened around him; he had given himself over to Travis. Travis says go back to the United States and Jack goes back to the United States.

The need to relieve his swollen bladder forced Jack off the bed and into the bathroom. After urinating he stood in front of the small cracked mirror hanging over the sink and stared at his reflection. His dark hair was now blonde. Travis had insisted that Jack change his hair color to help hide his identity. This show of concern by Travis had reinforced Jack's feeling that the man could be trusted and would take care of him. He thought of Peters, remembering the photo of him in the newspaper and his dark hair. The man had also had to change his hair color. Jack wondered what Peters had really been like? He had been such a good traveling companion. Even after all he had been through, Jack found it hard to believe the man was a criminal. Peters had demonstrated such a knowledge and love of the Mayan culture, he could not have faked that. As these thoughts passed through Jack's mind, he suddenly remembered Peter's red duffel bag! More importantly he remembered Travis pulling the duffel bag from the trunk of his car. This was what he had been trying to recall when he first awoke. Until now his mind had not been able to pull this information out of his memory banks.

The pumping of his heart began to accelerate as he wondered how Travis had gotten hold of Peters' duffel bag. Was it Travis who shot Peters? And if he did, what had he done to Josephine? A sense of urgency came over Jack; maybe he had been too trusting. Maybe he had given up on Jo too easily. This thought made him feel guilty. He suddenly felt the need to get away from Travis, away from this stranger. He decided it was time to take control of his circumstances. He also decided he would not leave Mexico without discovering what happened to his wife.

Jack left the bathroom and started to go through Travis's things. He Found a pair of slacks and a shirt that he put on over the shorts and T-shirt he was already wearing. Travis's clothes were a bit loose on Jack but with a belt to keep the pants up they would be serviceable. Jack also borrowed some clean socks before he put on his tennis shoes.

He wanted to leave immediately. Travis could come back at any moment. How long had he been gone? One hour? Two hours? Jack had lost all track of time. But before leaving he had to try and find the red duffel bag. The contents of the bag might answer some questions.

Jack searched the room and soon found the duffel bag under Travis's bed. He lifted the bag onto the bed and pulled open the zipper. Inside he found a 9 mm Glock and more money than he had ever seen in one place before. It occurred to Jack that this was why Peters was murdered; Travis had killed the man for his money and, if this were true, it probably also meant that he had killed Josephine. Why had he not killed Jack, though? Of course, the fisherman might be instructed to dump Jack overboard once they were out at sea. He was confused. The contents of the bag had not helped him understand anything except for the need to get away from this Travis and sort things out.

Jack counted out $5,000 in one hundred dollar bills and set it on the bed. Then he picked up the gun and thought for a moment before placing it back in the duffel bag. The pistol would probably get him into more trouble than it would get him out of. Jack did not have much experience with firearms and could see himself blowing his foot off. He put the red duffel bag back where he found it. He then took the paper bag that Travis had brought the sugared rolls in and stuffed the $5,000 into the bag. Jack then left the room with nothing but the clothes on his back and his bag of money. He had no idea where he was going.

Outside he found that his room was on the second floor and looked out over an interior courtyard. The exterior of the hotel looked as depressed as the interior. The place had a 1950s stucco and cement, modern look that was neither modern nor quaint forty years later. The exterior paint was faded and peeling and the tropical plants in the planter boxes were mostly dead. Jack walked down the hotel's strange curving hallway that was open to the courtyard on the first floor and then descended a circular stairway. He wondered how Travis had managed to get his unconscious body to the second floor room without raising suspicions. Jack had a vision of himself draped over Travis's shoulder and Travis telling the hotel's night clerk, "My friend here had too much tequila." He could even hear the clerk chuckling at his condition. Jack's mind did a double take at this thought; it was as if he remembered it really happening. Déjà vu? Shaking his head, he continued down the stairs.

In the hotel's drab lobby a Mexican woman with a young girl by her side stood at the check in desk talking with the clerk. The clerk was a white-haired old man with a pair of bifocal glasses perched on the end of his nose. Neither the woman nor the clerk appeared to take notice of Jack, but the girl stared at him as he walked out the hotel's front entrance.

A sense of relief swept over him as he stepped out onto the sidewalk. The fresh sea breeze and sunshine were delicious, and he felt lucky to have escaped the hotel. He then remembered what happened in front of the hotel in Merida. Thoughts of his arrest pushed him farther down the street, away from the hotel.

The first thing he noticed about Campeche was the relaxed atmosphere; it was in sharp contrast to the bustle of Mérida. Jack felt as if he had stepped back into the sixteenth century. He was surrounded by buildings of the Mexican Colonial style with histories dating back to the year 1540. The mostly two-story stone block buildings sat close to the street. Narrow wrought iron balconies decorated the second story on most of the buildings, but they appeared to be more ornamentation than to actually serve a useful purpose. Through the windows and large doorways, Jack could see into the colonial past: the high-beamed ceilings, the Moorish arches, and the interior courtyards.

As he walked down the narrow cobblestone street, Jack remembered that Jo and he had originally planned on visiting Campeche. He recalled reading about this "fortress" city on the edge of the sea. During the 16th and 17th centuries Campeche had flourished as the major port on the Yucatán peninsula, exporting timber, dye, woods, and chicle to Europe. Marauding pirates with names like "Pegleg" and "Diego the Mulatto" were attracted by Campeche's wealth and were soon making regular trips to the city to burn, loot, and plunder. The Campechanos eventually tired of the depredations and constructed a wall, complete with bulwarks, around the entire city to protect it from the pirates. At one point, Campeche was considered the most heavily fortified city in the New World.

Jack did not have time to contemplate the city's history as he decided on a course of action. He had no idea of where to go or what to do. When he came to the first intersection, he stopped, unsure of the direction he wanted to travel. Across the street, towering above the intersection, a large church was sandwiched between the buildings on either side of it. More of a cathedral than a church, its spires dominated the sky. Blue and white tile work decorated the facade of the church from around the large entryway to the inspiring roof line. The bright tile work created a sharp contrast to the dull brown-gray stone work of the remainder of the exterior. Jack wondered what actually separated a cathedral from an everyday church; he also wondered if the church would grant him sanctuary.

The question of direction was answered for Jack when he saw a policeman strolling toward him on the intersecting street. The cop was on the opposite side of the street to Jack's left. He started to feel queasy as he remembered what Travis had said about every cop in Mexico being on the look out for him. Jack crossed the street he had been traveling and started down the intersecting street in the same direction, but ahead of the cop. Jack tried to look nonchalant; he was sure the cop was closely watching him. He wanted to look back and check if the cop was following him, but he also did not want to reveal his face. He prayed that his change in hair color had sufficiently changed his appearance.

Jack was about twenty feet from the next intersecting street when an oncoming taxi passed by. His eyes locked with those of the passenger in the back seat—Travis. Jack's first thought was that the man would kill him when he found out about the money. Breaking into a run, Jack turned right onto the intersecting street. Behind him he heard the squeal of the taxi's brakes. Jack ran approximately half of a block before he looked back to see how close Travis was behind him. Surprised to find neither Travis nor the taxi, he slowed to a stop and tried to figure out why the man was not in pursuit. He noted that he was traveling down a one-way street in the opposite direction of the traffic flow. This explained why the taxi was not following him, but why had Travis not taken up the chase on foot? This question was soon answered when he saw the taxi ahead of him, turning onto the street he was traveling. The taxi had circled around the block in an attempt to cut Jack off at the next intersection. He had been running his heart out while Travis took a ride around the block.

The taxi was rapidly approaching. He needed to think of something quick. With fresh legs, Travis would easily be able to run him down. He then saw the alleyway, and wasted little time escaping into its shadows.

The alley was narrow, with enough room for a pedestrian but too small for a car. It was open to the street one block over. His feet pounded furiously on the cobblestone surface as he raced down the passageway. He prayed Travis had not seen him enter the alley and that he could reach the opposite end before the taxi pulled up to the alley entrance, for there was nowhere to hide in the alley.

Jack rushed out of the alley and onto the sidewalk one block over, almost running over an old Mexican woman. Gasping for breath, he could not excuse himself. The woman cursed him in Spanish and then continued on her way, glancing over her shoulder every so often, making sure the crazy gringo was not following.

His breath exploded out of his burning lungs in rapid gasps. Stooped over, his hands on his knees, Jack again wished he had kept himself in better shape. His heart, which was beating furiously, skipped a beat when he saw the cop he had passed earlier strolling down the sidewalk on the opposite side of the street. Jack's fear quickly abated as the cop appeared to take no notice of him.

Jack cautiously peered around the corner of the building he was leaning against to look back down the alley. At the opposite end he could see the back half of a taxi. The rear window was down and he could see a man's face staring down the alleyway. Jack instinctively pulled his head back from the opening of the alley, though there was little chance Travis would be able to identify him at this distance.

The second time Jack peered back down the alley the cab was gone. Re-entering the alley, he began jogging back the direction he had just traveled. Jack was still unsure what he hoped to accomplish, but for the moment he was happy to have outsmarted Travis. Keeping up his current pace would be impossible; between the heavy sedation and emotional roller coaster, his metabolism was screwed up and the physical exertion was not improving his condition. He was suffering from a splitting headache, and wobbly legs, and was starting to spit up blood from his overworked and under-conditioned lungs. Avoiding Travis and finding somewhere to rest was imperative.

Reaching the end of the alley, he checked the street to make sure Travis and his taxi had moved on before leaving the cover of the alley. Taking a right onto the sidewalk, he continued in the direction he had been traveling before he had ducked into the alley. Slowing his pace down to a quick walk, his eyes searched for Travis. Neither Travis nor his taxi appeared, which allowed Jack to continue at a walk and bring his respiration back to normal.

The walls of the city had pulled back and Jack realized he had wandered up to Campeche's *zócalo*. The *zócalo's* manicured lawn and regal shade trees were surrounded by an ornate wrought iron fence. In the center of the square was a hexagon-shaped bandstand. A cathedral dominated the far side of the *zócalo*, its twin bell towers rising four stories into the sky. Refracted light from the setting sun colored the upper half of the bell towers a burnt orange.

A taxi parked alongside the *zócalo* caught Jack's eye. His stomach churned as he wondered where Travis was. Then he realized it was not Travis's taxi. The empty taxi gave Jack an idea. He now knew where he wanted to go, even though he was not sure why. Jack trotted over to the driver's window. Inside sat a huge fellow, his enormous belly wedged between the seat and the steering wheel. Jack wondered how the man managed to steer the car. "*Habla usted Ingles?*" Jack asked the driver.

"No much," replied the driver as he pulled a finger out of his nose.

Jack was hoping to find a driver who understood English, but under the circumstances he could not afford to be to choosy. "Can you take me to Cobá?" he asked.

The driver inspected the green substance on the end of his index finger, then looked at Jack, a confused expression on his fat face. The cabbie shook his head as he flicked the crusty token out the window. Jack decided his situation was not that bad; he could find another taxi.

Twenty feet up the street another taxi was parked. He was about to move toward it when he saw Travis's taxi cruising down the street. Crouching down, he concealed himself behind the fat man's vehicle. Gordo poked his head out the driver's window to see what Jack was up to. Travis's taxi rolled on by without stopping. A relieved Jack stood and walked briskly toward the other taxi, only looking back once to make sure Travis was still traveling in the opposite direction.

"*Habla usted Ingles?*" Jack asked the driver.

"I understand good, I speak not so good," answered the driver in a heavy accent. A thin small man, the cabbie had a big smile that displayed lots of teeth. It was as if the man was trying to make up for what he lacked in stature with his smile.

"How much for you to take me to Cobá?" asked Jack. He felt foolish, for he was speaking with an accent as if that would make it easier for the man to understand.

"Cobá very far . . . I no take you there."

"I will pay whatever you want. Tell me your price." urged Jack.

The man looked at Jack with a pained expression; it was obvious he did not want to drive the over three hundred miles to Cobá. He quoted a price in pesos that was roughly equivalent to three hundred U.S. dollars, a price that the driver was sure would discourage the gringo.

"Good! Then you will take me to Cobá. I will pay you three hundred dollars now and another three hundred dollars when we arrive at the archeological zone," said Jack as he opened the rear door of the taxi and took a seat.

The driver was shocked. The crazy gringo was going to pay twice his already ridiculously high price! "*Si, señor,*" replied the driver as he happily took Jack's money.

Jack reclined back in his seat as the driver shifted the taxi into gear. The initial relief of avoiding Travis quickly faded as his thoughts turned to what he hoped to accomplish or find at Cobá. Hopefully, Gus would still be there; he could use his friend's help. He had nowhere else to turn. The taxi pulled onto Avenida Circuito Baluartes, the street that paralleled the old fortified walls of the city. Jack did not notice the crumbling ramparts and bulwarks as they passed by; his mind was elsewhere. For a brief moment he was able to catch a glimpse of the Gulf. The sun was dipping below the horizon, giving one last light show for the day. As the taxi sped out of town, Jack thought of Josephine. He had never felt so alone.

CHAPTER 17

Carlton was on edge as he walked down the city sidewalk, unsure what he hoped to accomplish. It was as if an unknown force pushed him on. He had been tailing Donald Schovich all afternoon, waiting for the right moment to approach the man. Schovich liked to knock back a few when he got the chance, which was usually anytime he was not working. Carlton was hoping he could corner the man in one of his favorite drinking establishments and share a few cocktails. Hopefully, the liquor would loosen Schovich's tongue and maybe he would share some of his thoughts with Carlton.

He first met Donald Schovich about ten years ago. At the time, Carlton was tracking suspected Soviet spies. The FBI was also investigating Soviet espionage on the domestic scene, and Schovich was involved in the investigation. When it was discovered they were after the same people, the Bureau and the Agency decided to combine their efforts. The only spy they were able to catch was an economics professor from Georgetown University who was copying government technical manuals and sending them to the Kremlin. He had no real connections to the KGB; he was just a few bricks short of a load. The incident did give Carlton and Schovich a chance to get to know each other. Over the next couple of years the two men crossed tracks a few times and on occasion shared a round of drinks. Carlton liked keeping in touch with the FBI man because the contact could come in handy someday, and he was sure the same thought had occurred to Schovich.

One night, in an inebriated state, Schovich's wife ran her car under a semi-truck trailer, neatly removing the roof of her Mercedes along with her head. For three years Carlton did not see Schovich. Then one evening a few days after Carlton lost his wife, Schovich showed up at the door with a bottle of scotch. The man was one of the few people whose sympathy had seemed sincere. Carlton still did not consider Schovich to be his bosom buddy—who was?—but he was a friend.

In spite of their friendship, Carlton did not want to just walk up to Don and start quizzing him; the man would get suspicious. Carlton wanted information, but he did not want anyone to know he was getting it. If he could make it appear that on sheer coincidence he had run into Schovich in a bar, then buy him a few drinks, maybe he could get him talking without raising suspicions. Over the years Carlton had gathered more intelligence through alcohol and a relaxed atmosphere than with fancy listening devices and phone taps.

Carlton saw he was going to get his chance as he watched Schovich enter a tavern. A sign over the door identified the place as "The Senate." Carlton, who had been following from the opposite sidewalk, crossed the street and entered the small bar. The Senate had a comfortable atmosphere, especially for the sports fan. The walls were covered with sports memorabilia, pennants, and photos of famous sportsmen. The Washington Redskins were well represented. Three televisions were strategically placed around the bar so that every seat afforded a good view of at least one screen. It was a little after six on a Thursday evening and the bar was half-full of patrons relaxing with an after-work drink. At the far end of the bar he picked out Schovich sitting alone with a highball in his hand.

Donald Schovich was a tall man with a lean face. He was fifty-three years old, but looked ten years younger. The gray was just beginning to creep into his sandy-blonde hair.

"I've really let myself slip if I'm drinking in bars that appeal to Don Schovich!" stated Carlton as he sat on a stool next to the FBI agent.

"Shit," replied Schovich. "This used to be a nice place until they started letting all the riffraff in."

The smiles on their faces indicated their true feelings.

"How the fuck are you?" continued Schovich. "You know, I was thinking about you the other day, wondering what the hell you were up to."

Carlton lit a cigarette and replied, "I'm OK. still working the salt mines over at the State Department. How are you doing?"

"Can't complain. They keep passing me over for promotion. I guess if you're still pounding the pavement at my age you're bound to pound it into retirement," said Schovich.

"Hell, you'd probably be director by now if you had ever learned to control your mouth," Carlton replied. There was some truth in Carlton's words. More than one of Schovich's superiors were not impressed with the man's use of the English language.

"So, what brings you to this part of town? I've never seen you in here before," quizzed Schovich.

"I had an early dinner date with this lady real estate agent, but she stood me up at the last minute. Some big sale she was closing," lied Carlton. "I saw this place and figured I'd come inside and drown my sorrows. You know me, never found a bar I didn't like."

After awhile the conversation drifted to football and centered on whether the Redskins would ever find a quarterback who could lead them back to the Super Bowl.

"Maybe they could get J.J. Hightower to Q.B. He seems to be having a run of luck lately," cracked Carlton in an attempt to direct the conversation.

"He couldn't do any worse than that bum they've got in there now," replied Schovich. "Hell, you've been sitting here all this time without me offering to buy you a drink. What'll you have?"

"I've been off the hard stuff lately, but I'd go for a beer."

He had casually laid out the bait but Schovich was not biting. He had to be careful; Schovich was probably already wondering what was up. The wheels inside Carlton's head were turning; he wanted to stay on the subject of Hightower, but he had to do it without raising suspicions. The bartender set a mug of beer in front of Carlton, who picked it up and took a swallow.

"What is the scuttlebutt over at State on the Hightower situation?" asked Schovich.

"Bingo!" thought Carlton to himself. Schovich had opened the door, now if Carlton could keep it open he might be able to learn something.

"I'm not sure what is going on, but in my opinion something is not kosher. I was involved superficially with the State Department's end of the investigation," Carlton lied. "Looking into state security, making sure the deaths or the attempt on Hightower were not connected or related to influences outside of the United States. Personally, I don't know of any connections among the three incidents, but all the higher-ups have become very closed mouth. No one wants to talk about what happened."

"Same thing over at the Bureau," stated Schovich. "I was on the investigation of the Allen murder. We had turned up some pretty interesting stuff. No telling where it would have led, but it needed to be looked into. All of a sudden, though, we're told the case is closed. Allen was murdered by the whore, who then shot herself, and we're not to discuss any aspects of the case—that is if we want to keep our jobs."

Carlton felt the adrenalin rush through his body, he was onto something. He had to keep Schovich talking. To do this he would have to give a little to get a little. The man would not give out free information. But Carlton did not have any information he could afford to give Schovich. He decided to gamble. The gamble required Carlton to make assumptions about what was really found during the FBI investigations and what Schovich knew about those investigations. He would have to move slowly and carefully.

"What you're saying is very interesting. Before they shut us down over at State, I was told by the FBI agent heading up the investigation of Andrew Buck's death that Buck's death might not have been a simple heart attack," lied Carlton.

He had no idea if the Bureau had reason to question the cause of Buck's death. But if what Carlton suspected were true, Buck did not die of natural causes; he was murdered. Carlton also knew there were drugs that could cause or simulate a heart attack and that some of these drugs were almost undetectable after the fact. If the FBI had evidence indicating Buck's death was caused by foul play, then Schovich might have heard rumors. Secrets were a difficult thing to keep in any organization; rumors both true and untrue travel fast. Carlton's lie was a good one for it was not specific as to why Buck's death might not be simple. If Schovich had already heard rumors, a statement like Carlton's might go far in confirming the rumor in his mind, thus leading Schovich to believe he had just received some important information.

"There was similar talk, hell, more of a whisper, around the Bureau. Once the cases were closed, the talk stopped. I heard they had found traces of a drug in his blood stream that caused his heart attack," stated Schovich, though the look on his face indicated he wanted confirmation.

Carlton was scoring big. He now knew that both FBI investigations into the murder of Allen and the death of Andrew Buck had discovered suspicions of foul play.

"I heard the same thing. It's a drug that was developed over at the Agency, a tasteless powder that dissolves in liquid. A small amount of this stuff in your drink and we're talking massive coronary," Carlton continued to lie, but the lie was surrounded by truth; the CIA had developed such a drug.

Schovich had a contemplative look on his face. "Seems like I've heard about that shit before, but I can't remember where."

"There is a reason you don't remember much about it; it's ultra top secret stuff. In fact, there are only a handful of people who know what it is. It's a great way to eliminate people and make it appear their deaths were from natural causes. I hear it is so difficult to detect that only the guys who developed this stuff can find it in a stiff."

Carlton swallowed the last of his beer and then ordered another round, a beer for himself and a scotch for Schovich. He had fed Schovich enough bullshit that hopefully the man would now reciprocate with what he knew about Allen's death. Schovich had already downed two highballs and was working on a third, his tongue should be plenty loose.

"This is crazy shit, someone is trying to hide something," said Schovich. "I mean, I suspected something was up, but now you confirm all this crap I heard about Buck. You see, I know the hooker didn't kill herself. I thought maybe they put the lid on this case to fool whoever the third party was and cut down on the media developing conspiracy theories. But now I'm wondering if there isn't a connection, and someone—or a number of someones—is trying to cover up."

The man was starting to ramble; Carlton would have to keep Schovich focused. Lighting another unfiltered Camel, he sucked the nicotine-laden smoke deep into his lungs, and then said, "So, what the fuck? Buck may have been murdered, but why are you so sure Allen wasn't killed by the whore?"

Schovich finished off his third scotch in one long gulp and then set the tumbler back on the bar as he ordered another.

"At first everything indicated that the whore shot Allen, then plugged herself. It all fit; we had even lifted her fingerprints off the empty shell casings. Then the coroner's report comes back with some shit about an odd bullet entry in the whore's head. The bullet that killed her had entered the top of her forehead and traveled downward to the center of her brain. To shoot herself this way, she would have to hold the pistol above her head with the barrel pointed down. Not an impossible feat but extremely weird. I bet you didn't know it, but 99 percent of all suicides using a gun either aim at their temple or stick the barrel in their mouth."

"I didn't know that," replied Carlton, as he recalled the times he had sucked on the barrel of his pistol and contemplated pulling the trigger.

"Well, neither did I until a few days ago. Hell, I'm a G-man. I don't deal much with suicide. Any big city detective would have been suspicious the minute he saw the body.

"Anyway, now the investigation is starting to heat up; the whore may have been shot by a third party. I end up getting the pleasure of interviewing one of the deceased's few friends, and she gave me the impression that our call girl was one independent bitch. Not someone to go gaga over a man like Ron Allen and certainly not someone with suicidal tendencies. I come back to the office thinking I'm in the middle of a big murder investigation only to find the case has been closed. Word came down from the top: Allen was shot by the whore, who then took her own life. This was the gospel, and no Bureau man would question it."

"So, you think someone else killed Allen?" asked Carlton. It was more of a statement than a question.

"Danielle—that was the whore's name—may have killed Allen," replied Schovich. "I'm not going to say she didn't. Hell, there were powder traces on her hands; but I'm positive she didn't kill herself."

"I hope someone knows what is going on," said Carlton. "I would hate to think that people like Buck and Allen can be knocked off and no one is doing anything about it."

"Personally, I don't give a fuck," replied Schovich. "I've seen too much shit go down in this town. It'll never change. In two years I can retire on full benefits. I'm going to sell my house, buy one of those recreational vehicles, and drive it across the country."

Carlton had one last beer as they talked about places worth visiting in the United States. By the time they got to the Grand Canyon, Carlton had finished his beer. He told Schovich that he had to get going, but that they should get together more often.

Carlton left the bar and stepped out onto the sidewalk. The sun, which was setting when he entered the tavern, was now gone from the sky, replaced by a crescent moon. It was early October, and the cool air carried the first hint of fall. Carlton walked down the sidewalk, going over what he had learned from Schovich. His suspicions were proving to be true. He still had no hard evidence or direct links between the deaths of Buck and Allen and the attempted hit on Hightower, except for the fact they were all part of Operation Raven. But he now knew there were rumors that Buck may not have died of natural causes, and that Allen's hooker probably did not commit suicide. He still could not say what he hoped to accomplish or why he even cared. Not being able to answer these questions only depressed him. He thought of what Schovich said about "not giving a fuck." No one had asked him to do what he was doing; he had no backing or support. The only reason he could think of was that he had nothing better to do.

CHAPTER 18

The smell of the Caribbean was thick; a mixture of salt, fish, and water cooked by the tropical sun into nature's stew. Along with the pungent smell of the sea was the sound of waves gently rolling onto a sandy beach. His mind was fuzzy. His senses told him he was near the ocean, he just wished he could remember which ocean. He lay on the concrete floor of a small, enclosed *palapa*; four plaster walls, a bamboo door, and a palm-thatched roof surrounded him. One bare light bulb hung from the ceiling, but it was turned off. The only light in the room was that which snuck under the eaves of the thatched roof and through the bamboo door. Rolling over on his side, he spat a wad of semi-congealed blood into a dark red pool that was forming on the concrete. His head was heavy and the rich taste of blood was thick in his mouth. Gus Wise had experienced better mornings.

Gently, he ran his tongue along his jagged upper gum line. His front teeth between both canines were gone. He thought he remembered spitting out some teeth during the previous night's festivities. Looking down at his left hand he saw that all four fingers were dislocated at the second knuckle. The swollen digits stuck out of his hand at grotesque angles. With his right hand, which had been spared abuse, he tenderly inspected his face and found a smashed nose and bulging lips. If Gus Wise was a wrecked car, the insurance company would have declared him "totaled" and written the owner a check. Living had taken on a surreal quality, as if he had become a spectator of his own life. The previous night had been spent enduring moments of intense physical pain, searing pain that had made Gus light headed and nauseous. Presently, his body was one big, dull ache, painful, but nothing like he experienced the night before. It was as if his body could stand only so much pain and, after a certain threshold, the sensory systems had shut down.

The last twenty-four hours had passed by in a violent haze. Yesterday morning he realized they were coming for him. Gus had hoped beyond hope that the investigation of the ruin sites was for the stated purpose, even though deep down he had sensed this was not true. He could have avoided the *Federales* and left the country, but he figured he would be able to bullshit his way out of any real trouble. What could the Judicial Police know? Not much, he had hoped. He was wrong on all accounts except one: The *Federales* did come to Cobá.

They arrested Gus and put him in the back of one of their cars, his hands cuffed behind his back. He became concerned with their intentions when they blindfolded him. After what he guessed to be an hour drive, they arrived at this current location. He did not know where he was, for all he had been allowed to see was the interior of the *palapa*; at least that was all he could remember seeing. The only thing he was sure of was that he was near the ocean; all was quiet except for the sound of the surf.

Not long after the *Federales* imprisoned him in the *palapa*, two men showed up and began a brutal interrogation that lasted deep into the night. Gus sensed that neither man was a regular *Federale*; in fact, he was fairly certain they were not formal employees of any part of the Mexican government. One of the men was heavyset and wore a tight-fitting, dark-brown suit. This bull of a man appeared to have only one reason for being present and that was to hold Gus up off the concrete so his compadre could more easily inflict his punishments. Gus did not recall the "bull" speaking. Except for his size, Gus could not remember much about the big man.

The face of the other interrogator was burned into Gus's brain; he would never forget that face. Approximately six feet tall, the man was lean, but solidly built. It was the face, though, not the dimensions, that were unforgettable. The handsome, angular face was olive in color, hinting of his Spanish and Indian ancestors, and his well-groomed jet black hair did nothing to disclaim this. A line of pink scar tissue marred the smooth skin under the man's chin. His most arresting feature, though, was his eyes. Gus had never seen human eyes like this before, coal black, seemingly lifeless. When the man stared at him it felt as if he gazed freely upon Gus's soul. Throughout the questioning the man spoke Spanish, in soft, almost soothing tones. His voice never rose, it was always under control, but when the man got an answer he did not like he dislocated another finger or moved Gus's nose to the other side of his face. The pain had been excruciating, causing him to drift in and out of consciousness with the man's soft voice continually questioning. It was a nightmare world where wrong answers were rewarded with broken bones.

One question kept recurring, almost torturing Gus: Why had they not used drugs on him? There were drugs that could get information from a man quickly and painlessly. Why couldn't these people have used these drugs? Why did they have to beat the crap out of him?

Gus began to cough violently until he hacked up a large glob of bloody phlegm. He spat the crimson mass into the ever-widening pool of blood on the concrete floor. Though he lay bloody and broken, there was something that bothered him more than the physical pain; it was the mental torment at the thought of what they would do to Josephine. They had her; that was the only explanation for some of the questions they had asked. He also felt that he had betrayed Jack. If they did not have Jack yet, they soon would. How could he have involved them in his twisted world?

It did not stop with Jack and Josephine, though. He also had falsely represented himself to his friend Hector Flores. All he had ever wanted to be was an archeologist, but he thought it might be nice to be a rich archeologist. It was going to be a one time deal—bring a little coke home, make a little money. How stupid he had been. Now he would miss out on one of the most important archeological finds of the 20th Century.

Gus decided that he should at least attempt to escape. He knew his chances were slim; he was not even sure he could stand up. If he could get to the right people, though, and tell them what was happening, maybe he could help his friends. He owed them that much. Plus, Gus would rather die trying to escape than face more torture.

The bamboo door at the entrance to the *palapa* did not appear to represent much of a barrier, but he had a feeling there would be someone standing guard on the other side. Struggling to his feet, he was surprised to find he could stand. Though lightheaded and needing the wall to lean against, he was upright. During his struggle to stand, he experienced a shooting pain on the right side of his torso, probably a busted rib. Something was also wrong with his right foot; he felt a tingling, throbbing sensation. At the moment, he did not have the courage to inspect it more closely. Besides, the foot was swollen so tightly inside his tennis shoe he doubted he could remove the shoe. He tested the injured foot and, despite the pain, he found it could carry weight. Taking off his shirt, he wrapped it around his mangled left hand, forming it—as best he could—into the shape of a fist. If the need arose, he could now use his left arm as a club.

Gus attempted the three steps to the door of the *palapa* and, in spite of almost toppling over, he made it to the door. Dizzy and nauseated, he leaned against the wall trying to catch his breath. Resting a moment, he concentrated on keeping his stomach below his throat and modulating his breathing. He had to keep his respiration under control as his broken rib made each breath a painful experience and puncturing a lung was a real fear.

"Why the hell couldn't I have been an accountant?" Gus thought.

Somewhat collected, Gus reached for the doorknob. Surprisingly, the knob turned, and the door moved outward. He pushed the door open a couple of inches, enabling him to view what was on the other side. He could now see why the door was unlocked; a guard sat in a chair just outside the door. Gus's luck had not run out yet; the guard, a shotgun cradled in his arms, appeared to be asleep. Cautiously, Gus opened the door wide enough to slip through. He sneaked past the sleeping guard, his heart in his throat, expecting the man to wake at any moment and put a bullet in his back. No bullet came though, and he hobbled forward through the sand.

Gus found himself on a brilliantly white, sandy beach, with the clear blue waters of the Caribbean in front of him. From the angle of the sun he figured it to be somewhere between 7:00 and 8:00 in the morning. He stopped for a moment to get his bearings and catch his breath. His right lung ached, each breath pure agony. The rest also gave his eyes a chance to adjust to the early morning light. When his eyes were able to focus on his surroundings, he was stunned. Set back from the beach, not more than a hundred yards to the south, was what looked to be an ancient Mayan palace.

Stretched along the beachfront, the long, low building had a commanding presence. Gus was forced to squint as the morning light reflected brutally off the stark, white building. The structure had a flat roof supported by stone pillars. Gus quickly realized this was not a remnant of an ancient civilization, because in between the pillars were large glass windows that looked out toward the surf. In front of the windows stretched a large stone terrace upon which sat some expensive-looking patio furniture. From the terrace, an elongated stairway descended to the sand. The width of the stairway was almost equal to the building's length. Both sides of the stairway were bordered by a stone balustrade in the form of large serpents that appeared to be descending to the sea, their fearsome, feathered heads resting on the sand guarding the bottom steps against intruders. A chacmool statue graced the top of the stairs. Centered on the terrace's length, the reclining figure stared out to sea, holding the sacrificial plate on its belly. The weathered look of the statue led Gus to believe it to be the real thing. Compared to the chacmool, the rest of the building appeared to be made out of freshly cut stone. This was not an ancient Mayan palace, but someone's modern beach estate.

As Gus took in the magnificent yet solitary structure, it suddenly occurred to him where he was. The Indian laborers at Cobá had talked of this place. It was the estate of Ricardo Reyes. Gus was not surprised at Reyes' involvement; he had sensed it for some time, but the chilling reality of the truth still caused him to shudder. This new knowledge increased his desire to escape.

Considering the condition of his foot, Gus did not figure to be walking out of here. He had heard the estate was surrounded by miles of jungle and desolate coastline, and he saw nothing to convince him differently. To the south, the shoreline became what looked to be miles of rocky cliff, the dense jungle growing up to the edge and even spilling over in places. To the north, the jungle and ocean were separated by a line of white sand which faded into a rocky peninsula. The peninsula jutted out into the sea, creating what appeared to be an impassable barrier. He had been brought here in a car, so there had to be a road into this place. Possibly he could steal a car and drive out of here. Men with guns, though, would probably be guarding the house and the road. Gus was becoming extremely anxious; he had to think of something quickly. At any moment the sleeping guard could wake up and sound the alarm.

When he noticed the boat, Gus began to think that maybe his escape was destined to happen: first the unlocked door, then the sleeping guard, and now a perfectly good boat. Moored just offshore, the boat was held in place by an anchor line off the stern and a bow line secured to the beach. The fifteen-foot fiberglass skiff was the type favored by Yucatán fishing and diving guides. Gus limped toward the craft, filled with a sense of hope that made it easier to ignore the myriad of aches currently afflicting his body. Grabbing onto the line connecting the bow of the boat to the shore, he waded into the surf. He used the line as a hand rail to help him keep his balance. The line rose and fell as the boat rocked in the gentle swells. He almost lost his hold on the line when a large swell lifted the bow of the boat out of the water, jerking the mooring line high above his head. Gus held on in spite of the pain caused by the sudden motion.

Alongside the skiff, he found the water belly deep. His good hand clung to the gunwale as he tried to catch his breath and figure out a way to get his damaged body up into the craft. After studying the situation, he lifted his left leg out of the water and hooked it over the side of the boat. This action put most of his weight on his injured right foot, causing excruciating pain, but at least his body was buoyed somewhat by the surrounding seawater. Gus's next motion, using his good hand and good leg, was to pull himself up and over the gunwale. This ended up being easier than he thought it would be, as his weight caused the boat to tip toward him, thus lowering the side of the boat he was trying to climb over. Gus rolled over the side, his back hitting the bottom of the boat with a thud. Immediately, he was paralyzed by a pain emanating from his rib cage. He wanted to scream but kept silent, his mind swimming in a red heat. A dark fog drifted over his consciousness, threatening to take control. He fought back the darkness as he waited for the pain to subside, willing himself to remain conscious .

*   *   *

Gus was unsure of how much time had passed since he climbed into the boat: five minutes, ten minutes, an hour? He had not passed out, but for some amount of time he had been on the fringe of consciousness. Looking over the side of the boat, he saw no sign of life on the estate of Ricardo Reyes. Gus was able to sit himself up and clamber to the stern where the boat's outboard motor hung over the side. Staring at the motor, he wished he had developed some rudimentary mechanical skills. He would not be able to escape anywhere if he could not start the outboard. Gus fumbled around until by pure chance he found the ignition switch. The motor turned over but then sputtered out. It was at this point he heard the sound of shouting voices. With no time to look over his shoulder, he concentrated on starting the motor. He tried the ignition again, but this time there was only a grinding noise. His pursuers were getting closer. In desperation he tried the starter three more times as he played with the choke, but the engine would not turn over.

"What the fuck is the matter with this thing?!" Gus yelled at himself.

Then he saw the problem, and it was really very simple. "I can't believe it," he cried. "Jesus fucking Christ! I don't have any fuel!"

He slumped against the side of the boat realizing it was over, all hopes of escape evaporated. Numb and weary, he felt he could sleep right where he sat. Two of Reyes' men had already made it to the water and were crashing through the surf. Halfway between the big house and the water a third man ran toward the boat. Still two more men could be seen walking briskly down the steps of the patio. As the two men in the water approached the boat, one yelled in Spanish for Gus to leave the boat and come ashore. "Fuck you," replied Gus as he sat unmoving in the bow of the boat.

The men waded alongside the boat, and the same man again asked Gus to leave the boat. Gus was silent this time but held up a fist displaying his crooked middle finger. This did not please his questioner, who reached over the side of the boat and grabbed Gus around the neck. The man rudely pulled the archeologist out of the boat and into the sea. Gus's right rib cage was again on fire. The two men pulled Gus's inert body through the waves and up onto the beach. They dropped him on the sand.

Three men walked up to where Gus lay. He looked up and saw "Scarface," the interrogator, and his fat buddy. Scarface looked quite dapper this morning; his hair was slicked-back and he was wearing a pair of white slacks with a white cotton shirt. The guard who had fallen asleep was explaining to Scarface how he had been tricked by the gringo. Scarface listened to the guard's story, then asked the man for his gun. Grudgingly, the man relinquished his weapon. Scarface flicked the safety off and without a trace of emotion shot the guard in the head. The man was dead before he hit the sand, his face frozen in an expression of shock.

Even in his current state of mind, Gus was repulsed by this brutal disrespect for human life. An anger that had been burning deep inside him flared up. Gus had never been a pacifist; he had been in a few fights, and more often than not he had the crap beaten out of him, but he could honestly say he had never hated a man enough to kill him. This was no longer true. Given the opportunity, Gus Wise would gladly take the life of Scarface. He took some strength from his rage, and raised himself up on his knees. Gus stared at Scarface, the fury evident in his eyes.

"This is no way to treat a guest," said Scarface, his voice low and even.

For a moment, Gus was overtaken by a coughing jag. The men, except for Scarface, laughed at Gus and his misery. He hacked up a mass of bloody phlegm and rolled it around in his mouth. In what he knew to be his last act of defiance, he spat the bloody mass at Scarface. "Fuck you," said Gus, who then tilted his head back and started to laugh uncontrollably.

The bloody projectile splattered onto Scarface's right cheek. The main wad of crimson phlegm rolled off his face and onto his clean white shirt. Scarface was good; he attempted not to show his emotions, but Gus could see the anger in the man's eyes.

The two guards grabbed Gus and held his arms back while Scarface wiped the blood from his face. He then took an object handed to him by his fat buddy. A shiny thin blade popped out with an audible click.

"You do get angry, you sadistic son-of-a-bitch!" cried Gus as he continued to laugh.

Sunlight glinted off the polished steel as Scarface approached. The knife slashed at Gus's belly. The laughing stopped abruptly as blood and entrails spilled onto the sand.

CHAPTER 19

José Ortiz chewed on an antacid tablet as he turned his car off Highway 307 and onto a small one-lane road. The narrow lane could easily be missed from the main highway if one was not familiar with it. On his right, Ortiz saw a large "No Trespassing" sign written in both Spanish and English. He followed the pavement through a green tunnel of vegetation that filtered the equatorial sunlight. After traveling about a mile, he came upon a large iron gate. From a small building to the left of the gate stepped a man in a nondescript gray uniform. The man held an automatic rifle in his hands and had a pistol strapped to his side. Ortiz stopped his car, rolled down the window, and said in Spanish, "José Ortiz. I have an appointment to see Señor Reyes."

The man nodded and went back in the building. Ortiz knew the man was calling to order the gate open. It was controlled from Ricardo Reyes' estate two miles farther down the road. Ortiz looked at the video camera mounted on the gate, knowing someone was studying his image on a monitor, making sure of his identity. The gate opened slowly, and Ortiz drove through.

As he drove down the road, he fished around in his glove compartment for a bottle of aspirin. He found the bottle and popped three tablets into his mouth. His head still throbbed from the blow he had received two days ago. He would love to run into that big bastard again, only he did not know what the man looked like. At least the swelling in his left eye had reduced to the point where he could see out of it again. For the first twenty-four hours, his eye had been swollen shut.

The jungle soon thinned out, and the estate of Ricardo Reyes came into view. Reyes' private piece of paradise was situated on a magnificent stretch of white sand and aquamarine water. The midmorning sun reflecting off the low white buildings caused Ortiz to squint. This was not his first trip to the home of Ricardo Reyes, but he was still impressed. Cut out of five square miles of jungle and coastline, Reyes' estate included tennis courts, stables, and a swimming pool, all the amenities of a first-class resort. Ortiz had a hard time conceiving that one man owned all of this.

Ortiz had come from the lower portion of Mexican society. His family had been hill people of the Sierra Madre, poor dirt-farmers. His father died when José was very young, leaving his mother with two children and a few worthless acres. With little hope left on their farm, his mother decided to move the family to Mexico City. Her sister lived there and had a job as a maid for a wealthy politician. The politician needed more domestic help, and Ortiz's mother was able to get a job working for the man.

Moving to the city was a turning point in Ortiz's young life. The wealthy politician, Javier Francisco Vasquez, was a very generous employer. He held education in high esteem; all of his employees' children went to school. Vasquez did not allow any of the children under sixteen to work or beg in the streets. Vasquez took a liking to the young Ortiz, and told the boy he would pay for his education if José could qualify for admission to a college. It was a chance for Ortiz to climb above his social class, something most Mexicans never dreamed of. Ortiz made the most of this opportunity, managing to get accepted to a small but well respected agricultural college. He wanted to study veterinary medicine. He had always liked working with animals; it was what he missed most about life on the farm. Halfway through his freshmen year, tragedy struck when a car bomb destroyed Javier Vasquez's new Mercedes with Vasquez in the back seat. The politician had been a pseudo father figure to Ortiz, who was crushed by the man's death. To further José's, pain no one was ever apprehended in connection with the assassination. The Vasquez family agreed to continue paying for José's education, but he now decided to change directions. He chose to study law enforcement and spend his life putting away criminals like the scum who had killed Javier Vasquez.

The shining ideals of his youth had been battered by the Mexican legal system. Inspector Ortiz often wondered if it was all worth it. He was tired of having to kiss the ass of bastards like Reyes.

Ortiz parked his car outside the main house and stuck another antacid tablet into his mouth. This would not be easy; first his men screw up on the ferry and then Phillips escapes from the Mérida police station in broad daylight. However, it was not Peters or Phillips that worried him. Peters was dead, and Ortiz was almost certain that Phillips just happened to be in the wrong place at the wrong time. Phillips knew nothing. It was the cause of his headache that concerned him, the big man who helped Phillips escape. The unknown was what worried the Inspector.

He climbed the stairs to the entrance of Reyes' home and pressed the doorbell. A young but full-figured Mexican girl, dressed in a maid's uniform, answered the door. She could not have been much more than eighteen years old. It was well known that Reyes loved the women, and that he had what amounted to a personal harem.

"José Ortiz. I'm here to see Señor Reyes."

The girl motioned him inside and said, "One moment, please."

She left him standing in the large tile foyer. As she walked away Ortiz admired her form.

Against the wall, opposite the foyer's entry, was a pedestal upon which sat a beautiful limestone sculpture of the head of a Mayan nobleman. The sculpted head displayed the classic Mayan features: oval eyes; elongated, triangular-shaped nose; thin lips; and a sloping forehead on top of which sat a gaudy headdress of quetzal feathers. Ortiz was no expert in Mayan art work, but he was sure this was an original. Reyes' home was decorated with Mayan artifacts, and it would be unlike the man to have anything but the real thing. Ortiz had often speculated on how Reyes had come by his collection, which was more extensive than many museums.

The sculpture reminded Ortiz of Javier Vasquez. He recalled how the politician was especially fascinated by the Mayan culture. Vasquez had championed protecting and preserving Mexico's antiquities. Many of his political fights involved appropriating more money for the exploration and restoration of important archeological sites. Ortiz had often wondered if Vasquez had been murdered for his beliefs in preserving Mexico's ancient heritage. During the early 1970s, Mexico's archeological sites were being plundered at an alarming rate. High prices for black-market artifacts and an impoverished Mexican economy combined to create an epidemic of thievery. Most of Mexico's citizens condemned the looting, especially the native Indians who still revered the ancient sites. But it is hard to convince a hungry man of the worth of his culture. A week before he died, Vasquez claimed to have evidence that a large and well-organized black-marketing ring—dealing in antiquities—was operating in Mexico. Vasquez was killed, though, and his evidence died with him. Ortiz still had a dream, though a faded one, that one day he would deliver justice to the killers of Javier Francisco Vasquez.

"Señor Reyes will see you now," said the girl who had reappeared.

Ortiz lumbered down the hallway behind the girl into Reyes' living room. The room was spacious and decorated in off-white colors, with a few items of Mayan artwork tastefully spread about. The focal point of the room was the view through the giant windows, across a large patio to the beach and the Caribbean beyond. Every meeting he had ever had with Reyes had taken place in this room. Ortiz figured Reyes liked the relaxed atmosphere, or maybe Reyes wanted him to feel like one of the family.

"Señor Reyes will be with you shortly," said the girl before leaving.

Ortiz ambled over to the window to take in the view. He immediately noted the ragged figure of a man crumpled on the beach.

It could have been a drunk sleeping one off, but even at this distance Ortiz could smell death.

"Good morning, Inspector," chimed a cheerful Ricardo Reyes.

"Good morning," returned Ortiz as he turned from the window to see Reyes stride confidently into the room.

Reyes was a short delicate man. His pencil-thin moustache and receding hairline combined to give his round face a look of refinement. At first glance he appeared to be the mild-mannered sort; it was the steely glint in his eyes that announced his inner fires.

"Would you like a drink or something to eat, perhaps?" Offered Reyes.

"No, thank you."

The same offer was made every time he met with Reyes, and Ortiz always declined.

"Please, have a seat," said Reyes as he gestured toward a couch facing the window. "What happened to your eye? It looks awful," asked Reyes as he sat down.

"Ran into a door," Ortiz lied.

"You must be more careful," said Reyes, his voice full of concern.

"Nice to know you care," dead-panned Ortiz.

"Inspector, you like to get right to business," stated Reyes.

"Yes, I do"

He usually did not give it much thought, but at the moment Ortiz realized how much he did not care for Ricardo Reyes.

"Very well. I am concerned with this Jack Phillips. We know nothing about him, and he may know too much about my business."

In all of their talks, Reyes never said what his business actually was, but Ortiz did not need it explained.

"Señor Reyes," Ortiz interrupted, "I do not think you need to worry about Phillips. As you may know, I interrogated the man before his escape. The poor bastard had no idea of what was going on. He was scared and confused. His wife and this Gus Wise may be up to something, but if they are, I'm certain Phillips is ignorant."

Reyes listened to the Inspector, then with cool sarcasm said, "I also remember you saying you were certain you could eliminate Sam Peters. Instead, your agents shot one of my men and got themselves killed."

Ortiz ground his teeth together as his stomach churned. He desperately wanted one of the antacid tablets he had left on the front seat of the car. He knew Reyes would bring up the incident on the ferry, but that did not make this any easier.

"I am not saying we should ignore Phillips, but I think we should be more concerned with his wife and Mr. Wise," said Ortiz.

"Gus Wise and Mrs. Phillips have already been attended to. The only unknown is Mr. Phillips," stated Reyes.

Through the window Ortiz watched two men on the beach drag the limp body that had been lying in the sand out to a waiting boat.

"Is that Mr. Wise going out for a day of fishing?" asked Ortiz, as he nodded his head toward the window.

"You should learn to control your curiosity; there are things you are better off not knowing," replied Reyes.

Reyes' words irritated, partially because they were true, but also because Reyes had the prerogative to say them. The man expected to be treated with the highest respect; he was lord and master. Ortiz's smart-ass remarks could cost him dearly; however, kissing Reyes' ass made him want to puke.

"You are correct. I meant no disrespect," apologized Ortiz trying not to choke on his words.

Reyes smiled and then said, "I do not understand how a man could have the ability to escape from jail and not be considered dangerous? Maybe you could enlighten me, Inspector."

Ortiz needed to choose his words very carefully; he did not want to tell more than was necessary. He was not sure if it was Reyes who had engineered Phillips' escape in order to kidnap the man. This did not make sense, though, for Phillips was under Ortiz's control. It was more likely that Reyes ordered Phillips to be eliminated. The surviving guard claimed that the two men were trying to kill Phillips, and that the third man shot them down before they could accomplish this task. During the shooting, things became confusing; all the witnesses gave different accounts as to what happened and no one was able to give a decent description of the third man (the one who had knocked Ortiz senseless). Ortiz did not want to tell Reyes about this third man unless he had to; it would only upset him, and Ortiz wanted to get this bastard on his own.

"His escape was dumb luck, not ingenuity. The lobby was a shooting gallery; an officer was down and people were running in all directions. I imagine Phillips was terrified and started to run. In the confusion, it was a while before he was missed. I realize it is hard to believe that a man in handcuffs, running through the streets of Mérida, would be hard to apprehend, but strange things happen. Maybe he made it to the U.S. Consulate? If they took him in, then there is not much I can do."

Both men were silent for a moment as Reyes digested the Inspector's words and Ortiz hoped they rang true.

"Inspector, what you say is very discouraging, because I think you are not telling the truth. I have heard from another source that Phillips had an accomplice in his escape and that this accomplice knocked you unconscious, took your badge, and then stole a police car that still has not been recovered."

Ortiz was stunned. The rug had been pulled out from under him. He thought he had controlled the situation at the police station, but evidently his own men were informing on him. His emotions were a mixture of fear and anger: anger because Reyes was making him look like a fool, and fear because he had been caught in a lie. How would he explain his way out of this?

"Evidently, Phillips knew how to get this other man to help him escape custody," continued Reyes. "But you tell me nothing of this accomplice; you tell me not to worry about Phillips. I am starting to think you no longer respect me. First, your men bungle with Peters, then you let Phillips escape, and now you lie to me. Maybe you think Ricardo Reyes is a fool?"

Reyes' voice had stayed calm, but his words were sharp. Ortiz sat still as a statue, though inside he was squirming. He felt like a child about to be reprimanded for playing hooky. The difference was, his punishment could be much more severe.

Reyes silently stared at Ortiz waiting for an explanation. Ortiz was cornered; he could not afford to jerk Reyes around any longer. He decided the truth was his best hope.

"I do not think you are a fool," said a contrite Ortiz. "I am the fool. I let a suspect escape after I had him in my custody. I failed. I did not want to tell you about the accomplice because my pride was hurt. I wanted to find this man on my own. I stand by what I said about Phillips, though. The man knows nothing. It is the one who helped him escape who is dangerous. The problem is I do not have a good description of the man."

Reyes slowly shook his head and then said, "The Latin machismo causes normally intelligent men to act like fools. Over the past two years I have paid you very well and have asked for little in return—a little information, a favor or two—and now you treat me like this. But I am going to give you a chance to redeem yourself, only because I believe your mistakes were errors in judgment and not attacks on me. I want you to bring me Phillips and his accomplice. You are to make this your number one priority. If they leave the country, bring them back or do not come back. I would prefer you deliver these men alive, but I will not be too upset if all I get are their heads."

*   *   *

In the hallway leading to the livingroom stood a dark-haired man with a scar under his chin. From his hiding place he had listened to the conversation in the other room. He had heard enough. Reyes had not signaled for him. He slid the safety of the pistol he held in his hand into the safe position, then turned and walked silently back down the hallway.

CHAPTER 20

From Cancún, on the northern tip of the Yucatán Peninsula, to Chetumal, on Mexico's southern border with Belize, runs Mexico's Highway 307. Paralleling the Caribbean coast, this two-lane jungle highway is the main artery of the Mexican state of Quintana Roo. Jack's taxi, which was heading north on Highway 307, slowed and made a left turn onto the paved road to Cobá. A few minutes earlier, a blue Ford sedan driven by José Ortiz had sped past the slower-moving taxi; neither Jack nor Ortiz would ever know they had passed each other.

It was midmorning and Jack could not stand the smell of himself. The water had not been working at the motel, so he had not been able to shower. He decided that it probably did not matter as he had only one set of clothes, and they were already soaked with yesterday's sweat.

Jack sat in the back seat gazing out the window. He noted that the jungle here was more lush and a deeper green than that which surrounded Chichén Itzá.

Last night had been spent in the village of Ticul. Jack had wanted to drive straight to Cobá, but the taxi driver, Fernando, had refused to drive in the dark.

"The holes in the road will swallow my little auto," Fernando had protested.

Jack found it hard to disagree; the sizes of the potholes were sometimes amazing. Besides, it did not make sense to arrive at Cobá in the middle of the night without a place to stay. Gus had described the place as being remote.

They found a small motel on the outskirts of Ticul. The inhabitants of the village all seemed to ride around on large three- wheeled bicycles. From the road the motel did not appear very attractive, but on closer inspection Jack found the place to be livable. The sheets were clean, and there was a patio restaurant. Upon entering the restaurant, Jack and Fernando had found the drunken motel manager sitting at a table with a bottle of tequila. The smiling manager, who was also the owner, immediately wanted to buy drinks for Jack and Fernando. Fernando gladly accepted the free tequila, but Jack refused. The mouth-watering scents emanating from the kitchen made Jack realize how hungry he was, and tequila was the last thing he wanted to put in an empty stomach. He devoured two plates of roasted pork wrapped in tortillas and washed it down with a Leon Negra. It was the first decent meal he had eaten in the last thirty-six hours. The motel owner, who seemed insulted by Jack's refusal to drink, was somewhat mollified by Jack's apparent pleasure with his establishment's cuisine. With the meal concluded, the drunken owner again offered Jack a drink, and this time he accepted. Jack had purchased separate rooms for Fernando and himself. After finishing his drink, Jack retired, leaving Fernando to get drunk with their host.

Jack was exhausted, but sleep did not come easily; Josephine haunted him. Memories of the love they shared were juxtaposed with tormenting thoughts of her final hours. Alone in the darkness he could only see the futility of life, that in the end there is only despair. This despair he now understood with brutal clarity. It was the cold black nothingness of infinity. For the first time in his life he understood how a man could put the barrel of a gun to his head and pull the trigger, or at least he thought he could.

As he stared out the window of the taxi Jack contemplated his dark thoughts of last night. In the light of day his despair was not so clear. The feelings of loss and hopelessness were still with him, but the cold, black emptiness of the previous night seemed more like a bad dream, something that never really existed. Someplace deep inside he knew this blackness endured, and like a cancer it would reappear to feed on his grief.

The early morning drive had given Jack time to think. He still was not sure what he hoped to find at Cobá. By now, Gus had probably been arrested or fled the country, but Jack felt he needed answers; his life had been destroyed and he wanted to know why. He understood what he was doing would—at best—earn him life in a Mexican prison, and—at worst—cost him his life. At this point he did not fear these things; in fact, death might be a welcome relief.

Jack was pulled from his thoughts when he noticed the jungle had given way to a small settlement consisting of a few forlorn *najs*. Fernando slowed the taxi as they passed a small store selling soft drinks and souvenirs. A monkey chained to the front porch screeched at the passing automobile. Just past and below the souvenir shop a brown-colored lake stretched out into the jungle. It was the first lake Jack had seen since arriving on the Yucatán peninsula. Usually the limestone shelf that makes up the peninsula quickly sucks up all surface water, leaving the terrain virtually barren of lakes and streams.

The road came to an end next to what looked like a patio restaurant with a palm-thatched roof. Dense jungle surrounded a parking area and the small restaurant. Jack did not realize where he was until he saw the sign, *zona archelogica Cobá*

Fernando parked the taxi and killed the engine. Jack remained seated long after the engine died. Fernando looked over his shoulder and said, "Cobá, Señor. You are here."

Jack stepped slowly out of the taxi carrying his paper bag full of money. Except for the sign, there was no indication that this was the entrance to a ruin site. Unlike Chichén Itzá, there were no crowds of tourists or manicured grounds and, at least from this vantage point, no lofty ancient structures rising above the trees. Of course, the surrounding vegetation severely limited the view.

Jack took in everything as he slowly walked to the restaurant. Fernando left the taxi and followed, not because he was interested in what the crazy gringo was up to, but 300 dollars was 300 dollars.

A portion of the restaurant was actually a souvenir shop selling everything from reproductions of ancient Mayan art to silk-screened T-shirts that would declare the wearer a member of the Cobá Beach Club (despite the fact that the only beach for miles around was down by the lake, and its muddy shores did not look very inviting). The only human presence was a short, middle-aged man wearing a soiled white apron. The man, who was Mayan, sat at one of the empty tables smoking a cigarette. He nodded his head as Jack and Fernando walked into the restaurant.

"*Hola*," said Jack as he returned the nod.

"*Buenos días*," said the man.

"*Habla usted inglés?*" asked Jack.

"*No lo entiendo muy bien inglés*," replied the man.

"Where can I find Señor Gus Wise?" tried Jack anyway.

At the mention of Gus's name the man appeared to tense, his eyes inspecting Jack more closely.

"Señor Wise is my amigo," continued Jack as he pointed his index finger at his chest.

The man stared at Jack, saying nothing. Jack asked Fernando to question the man in Spanish. The man replied to Fernando, who then translated to Jack. "The *Federales* came and took Señor Wise, but he does not know why."

This was not a surprise. Jack suspected that Gus had either been arrested or fled the country. He instructed Fernando to ask the man where Hector Flores could be found. The man did not reply to Fernando's inquiry; instead his eyes shifted back and forth as he studied both Jack and Fernando. Jack suddenly became uncomfortable under the man's scrutinizing gaze. Unkempt as he was and holding his brown paper bag, Jack was sure he looked like a suspicious character. He became even more unsettled when it occurred to him that his picture was probably in all the newspapers, identifying him as a wanted man. Had this man realized who he was?

Without a word, the man rose to his feet and went to the back of the *palapa*. For a brief moment Jack considered hightailing it out of there.

"Roberto!" the man yelled into the jungle.

Soon, a smiling, barefooted boy came running into the restaurant. The boy, whom Jack took to be the man's son, appeared to be about ten years old. The man spoke rapidly to the boy. Jack heard Flores' name mentioned, but could not decipher the rest. The man next spoke to Fernando who in turn said to Jack, "His son will take you to where Señor Flores works."

"*Muchas gracias,*" Jack thanked the man.

Jack was following the boy out of the restaurant when an anxious Fernando said, "Señor, I must return to Campeche . . ."

"Of course," interrupted Jack, embarrassed that he had forgotten to pay his cab fare.

Jack pulled three one-hundred-dollar-bills out of his paper bag and handed them to Fernando. Fernando thanked him for the money, then got in his cab and drove away. Jack watched as his only mode of transportation disappeared around the bend. Except for the boy, Jack stood alone in the empty Cobá parking lot.

Signaling for Jack to follow, the boy started down a path leading into the *selva*. The day was heating up, and even in the shade of the jungle canopy the air was oppressive. Beads of perspiration dribbled down the side of his face, and his sweat-soaked shirt clung to his back. The combination of exercise and sweltering climate made Jack lightheaded. He was unsure if he could keep up with the boy, who was moving quickly down the tract, seemingly unaffected by the heat and humidity.

Jack found Cobá very different from Chichén Itzá. Here the thick vegetation had not been tamed to make room for giant lawns that allowed the ancient monoliths to be viewed from afar. Also, there were no crowds here. The gift shop and restaurant at the entrance attested to the fact that visitors do come to Cobá, but so far Jack had not seen a tourist. At first, Jack saw little to indicate this was the site of an ancient city. The monotony of the jungle was interrupted only by a few indistinct small hills or mounds. After a while, Jack noted that there were right angle blocks visible amongst the dense vegetation. He suddenly realized these mounds were the rubble of ancient buildings that had been taken over by the jungle. Chichén Itzá must have looked like this upon its discovery. He wondered how archaeologists were ever able to reassemble the ancient cities out of such disorder.

Through a break in the foliage Jack was able to get a glimpse of a tall, graceful pyramid. It had a delicate, almost ethereal appearance. Later he would find out he was looking at Cobá's own El Castillo, at 120 feet the tallest and arguably the most beautiful, pyramid on the Yucatán.

Jack stopped when he noticed a rectangular stone slab standing upright a few feet from the trail. He moved closer to the stele so he could inspect the carvings engraved into the limestone monument. The stele was approximately five feet tall and depicted a human figure holding some type of bar above its head while standing on the backs of two prone figures. Mayan hieroglyphics bordered the scene. Jack became so engrossed with the stele that he almost lost track of the boy, who was still marching steadily down the trail. He was forced to move on. They passed more stelae, though none were as well preserved as the first one Jack had seen. Some were so badly weathered only the faintest traces of hieroglyphics were visible.

Jack found himself entranced by this ancient city hidden in the jungle. Chichén Itzá had also intrigued him, but there was something different about Cobá. It had an almost magical quality that would have been hard for Jack to describe. It was as if he half-expected to see the ghost of an ancient Mayan nobleman come drifting down the path. His heart ached when he thought of Josephine; she would have loved this place.

Jack had been following the dark-haired boy for more than twenty minutes and with each step the trail became narrower and more indistinct. While climbing around a downed tree, Jack almost became entangled in a huge spider web, in the middle of which sat an enormous black and yellow striped spider. The arachnid looked like it could suck him dry in a matter of minutes.

He was ready to inform the boy that he needed a rest when he heard the sound of male voices. Figuring they were close to their destination he continued on and soon reached a clearing in the jungle. In the center of the cleared area was a mound approximately 50 feet high. Men were busy pushing wheelbarrows full of rock away from the mound. Jack stopped at the sight of the workers; this had to be Flores' archeological dig. The boy gleefully galloped toward the working men, quickly leaving Jack behind.

Jack had started forward again when he noted another stele standing about thirty feet to his left. Curious, he moved toward it to get a closer look. This stele was extremely well preserved; the profile of a man was carved into its face. Jack was stunned when he saw the figure on the stele had European features and a beard. It appeared to be a depiction of the same man whose likeness was carved into the North temple at Chichén Itzá. He was enthralled by the ancient relief; it was the first time in the last three days his mind was not on his own troubles.

Jack pulled himself away from the carved stone and walked to the work area. The half-dozen laborers stopped their industry to watch his approach, their brown eyes staring at him from expressionless dark faces. They were all Mayan Indians with short, sturdy bodies. Their compact frames had a defined musculature developed from hard work. The brown faces showed not a trace of perspiration, which was in contrast to Jack who was dripping with sweat. They all wore hats, mostly ball caps or panamas, but one fellow had a felt cowboy hat. Footwear ranged from rubber boots to leather sandals. Their dress was not much different from the Mexican field workers of California. Jack wondered how many California field workers had Yucatánian roots.

He was close enough now to see that the mound was actually a pyramid. From the side of the pyramid an entry had been excavated, and the workers had been hauling wheelbarrows full of rock from inside. Jack smiled at the men, unsure of what to say, his eyes searching the area for someone who might be named Hector Flores.

From the dark entry strode a tall lean man dressed in khaki pants and a white cotton work shirt. Upon seeing Jack the man stopped, his eyes appraising. Jack stared back, sure he was about to meet Hector Flores. The man had a long handsome face framed by shoulder-length brown hair. His tanned skin told of long hours in the sun. Jacked guessed the man to be in his late thirties. His face was expressionless, and for a moment Jack thought the man was going to tell him to get the hell out. Instead, in flawless English, the man said, "I'm Hector Flores. Can I help you?"

"Jack Phillips. I'm a friend of Gus Wise," replied Jack

The face lit up with recognition, and the man said, "Yes, Gus said you might show up."

Flores wiped his hand with a rag he was holding and then extended his hand toward Jack. Firm handshakes were exchanged.

"What happened to Gus?" asked Jack.

The smile left Hector's face. "The *Federales* arrested him yesterday morning."

"Where did they take him?"

"Mérida, I would guess. I have not been able to confirm this yet. Don't worry, though. My family is fairly influential in Mexico's political circles. I have powerful friends who are looking into Gus's situation. The problem is, there are no phones here at Cobá. I have to drive to Tulum to make calls and receive messages. I spent most of yesterday afternoon in Tulum on the phone, but I could not get any information on Gus."

Flores spoke of Gus's arrest as if it were an ordinary problem, but Jack sensed the man was more concerned than he was letting on.

There was an awkward moment of silence as neither man knew what to say. Hector looked over his shoulder, back at the dark hole leading into the pyramid, and an expression of longing passing over his face. Jack thought the man was about to run back down the hole when he turned and said, "We need to talk. We could have an early lunch and then drive to Tulum to see if there is any new information on Gus's situation."

Flores shouted some orders to his men and then led Jack through the jungle a short distance to a narrow dirt road where a Land Rover was parked. They climbed into the vehicle, and Flores drove them down a bumpy road to a small collection of *palapas* and *najs*. Flores informed Jack that this was the base camp for the dig. A half-dozen *najs* surrounded one large central *palapa* that had no walls, only a palm-thatched roof under which was a number of tables and chairs. Around the eaves of the central *palapa* were rolls of mosquito netting that could be let down when the bugs got bad.

"Take a seat if you like," said Flores as he gestured toward the tables.

Jack sat while Flores entered a nearby *naj*. He came back with two bottles of beer, handing one to Jack as he sat down. The beer was cold. Jack rolled the icy bottle along his forehead before he took his first sip.

"Gus said you were traveling with your wife; did she come to Cobá with you?" asked Flores.

Except for Travis, who had already known the situation, Jack had not yet had to explain losing Josephine to anyone. His throat tightened; he was not sure he could make the words. He had been struggling with his pain, trying to find a place to store it that would allow him to keep functioning. Telling his story would only keep the pain alive.

"Murdered, most probably," stated Jack. He was surprised at how easily the words actually came.

Hector closed his eyes and winced as if he had been stung by Jack's words. "Gus said something like this might happen, but I did not believe him," replied Flores.

Jack was puzzled by what Flores said; how could Gus have suspected the danger? "Gus told me of the problems you were having with Cervantes and his task force, but I don't think his arrest has anything to do with that. In fact, you can probably blame me for Gus's arrest."

Jack recounted the last few days to Flores, how they befriended Steve Potter, and of the morning in Mérida when he discovered that

Steve was actually Sam Peters—the man responsible for the murders on the Punta Sam ferry. He described his mad dash back to the hotel only to find Josephine missing and Peters dead, his arrest on the sidewalk, and the interrogation by Inspector Ortiz. Purposely, he left out Ortiz's suspicion that Gus and Josephine had something to do with Peters' death; the theory was too far-fetched for Jack to give it any credence. He also related how the stranger had saved his life in the Mérida police station, only to drug him and spirit him away to Campeche.

The telling of his story was difficult, but Flores seemed to be a sympathetic listener and soon the words flowed easily. As Jack talked, the weight of his hardships seemed to become more bearable. Involved in his narrative, he hardly noticed the Mayan woman dressed in a white *huipile* bring plates of roasted pork, tortillas, pickled onions and green chili salsa to the table. The table was set and the food served by the time Jack had finished telling Flores about the red duffel bag full of money and his escape from Travis.

"I'm just an archeologist. I'm as unsure as you are as to what is going on, but Gus may be more involved in your problems than you think," said Flores as he filled a tortilla with roasted pork. "Somehow Gus knew the *Federales* were coming. Before they arrived he pulled me aside to talk. My friend had secrets that he kept from both of us."

Flores stopped talking long enough to take a bite of his lunch, chew and swallow. Jack started to fill his own plate as he waited for Flores to continue.

"Gus asked me to relate his story to you if you arrived at Cobá," Flores began, "About five years ago Gus was flying back to the United States from Guatemala, where he had been involved in a reconstruction project at Tikal. Before he left, one of the locals asked Gus to deliver a package to a friend in the U.S. Gus was told that he would be paid handsomely upon delivery of the package. He knew the package probably contained drugs, but Gus was young and needed money. He had just finished his doctorate and had student loans to pay off—most archaeologists do not make great salaries. It looked like easy money. On his previous trips abroad his luggage had never been searched. He was confident he could pass through Customs, and even if he were caught, he figured he could talk his way out of any real trouble. His thinking was that since he really did not know what was in the package how could they find him at fault?"

Flores took another bite of his tortilla and washed it down with beer. "It is hard to believe such an intelligent man could be so stupid."

"Gus always thought he could talk his way out of anything," affirmed Jack as he stared at the pork-filled tortilla in his hand.

"Of course, Customs found the package, and they were not as understanding as Gus hoped they would be," continued Flores. "'They had me by the balls,' were Gus's exact words. He was facing prison until someone at the United States Drug Enforcement Agency heard about his plight. They saw that Gus's research caused him to spend a lot of time in Mexico and Central America. They could also see that Gus was not a major drug trafficker; the amount he had brought in was hardly worth the risk. Your *Federales* gave Gus a choice: he could go to prison for a couple of years, or he could go to work for the DEA. Gus was not to have any specific duties, just be on call. The DEA even wanted him to continue his research, preferably spending as much time in Mexico and Central America as possible. The only catch was he had to be available any time they needed local help. Gus really had no choice. He went to work for the DEA."

The tone of Flores' voice indicated the man was repulsed by what he was saying, and Jack wondered why. For a short moment the two men stared at each other in silence.

Flores noted the confusion on Jack's face and said, "I'm not blaming Gus. It was his error in judgment that got him into the situation, but it was the United States government that arranged the situation. I do not believe the United States has the right to interfere with the internal affairs of other countries without first being invited. My feelings aside, I actually benefitted from Gus's problem. It was partly DEA money that financed this project. The DEA wanted Gus down here, so they made sure he received funding for his research. My peers always tried to get Gus Wise interested in their projects because he could get the funding. Now I know where the money came from."

Jack was having a difficult time putting all this information into perspective; he no longer knew what to believe. "I don't understand. What could Gus do for the DEA?" he asked.

"According to Gus, he was seldom asked to do much of anything and when he was, it was usually some minor task such as delivering a message or a package or maybe giving someone shelter for a few days. He was never told the purpose behind his appointed duties. They would ask him to do something, and he would do it."

"But how is this connected to Gus's arrest?" interrupted Jack.

"I'm getting to that," replied Hector. "As the years passed, Gus began to wonder if he would spend his entire life at the mercy of his government. He wanted out, but the DEA was not quite ready to let him go; they had one more project for him. They made him a deal; if he would do this one last assignment, they would release him from their service. Gus would not tell me what this assignment is. He claimed I was better off ignorant, but he did say that it involved Ricardo Reyes, and that the *Federales* were coming specifically for him.

"I told Gus that he was overreacting. If the *Federales* did come, it was because Cervantes' task force was trying to put a scare into us. Cervantes is just a struggling politician trying to get elected. I was more worried about my research. The *Federales* did come, though, and they arrested Gus."

Flores dropped his half-eaten tortilla onto his plate, he no longer had an appetite.

Jack did not know what to say or do. He had come to Cobá with the hope that he could start to unravel the mystery that had shrouded his life the past few days, maybe even find Gus. The confusion had only increased, and his resolve was crumbling. He was a wanted man in a foreign country; his wife had vanished and was presumed dead; and his best friend had been arrested. A part of Jack wished he were back home in California—if Jo is dead, what could he do here? He did not want to leave Mexico before finding out what happened to her, but he was beginning to realize that he might never know the truth.

"I do not know what your plans are, but you can stay here as long as you like," offered Flores. "I might be able to help you find out what became of your wife, and when you are ready, I'm sure I can arrange your passage back to the United States."

Jack was silent, but nodded his head in understanding.

CHAPTER 21

For a man who was supposedly cutting down on his drinking, Carlton found himself spending a lot of time in bars. He was keeping to beer, though, no hard stuff. Not that he wouldn't love to knock back a couple of highballs. He was sitting at the bar in the cocktail lounge of the Prime Cut restaurant. It was late afternoon, and the place was empty, too late for the lunch crowd and too early for the dinner crowd.

Carlton conversed with the barkeep while he nursed his beer. The man was solidly built and of above average height, with a bushy mustache that matched his bushy eyebrows. His open and friendly manner must have served him well in his chosen profession.

In the process of completing his tasks, the barkeep left the bar for a moment, leaving Carlton with only the television for entertainment. The face of J.J. Hightower filled the screen of the television hanging above the bar. It seemed Carlton could no longer look at a television screen without seeing the Senator's face. Hightower had become the nation's number one political personality, and with an election year coming up, the Senator's name was being bandied about as a possible vice presidential candidate. The President was going to be up for reelection next year, but his popularity was extremely low. It was rumored that the current vice president might decline to run for a second term. Many political insiders thought that if Hightower were added to the ticket, his current popularity would give the President's campaign the added push it needed, and in Hightower the party would have another strong Presidential candidate for down the road. If all went well, the party could look forward to controlling the executive office well into the next century. All of this apparently pleased Hightower, as he had been keeping a very high public profile.

Carlton had to give Hightower credit for guts, though his intelligence was questionable. Someone had attempted to kill him just a few short days ago, and, so far, no suspects had been apprehended. You would think a person in Hightower's position would lay low for a while, keep his pretty face out of the cross hairs of high-powered rifles.

"That Hightower is one tough customer. He doesn't take any crap from those terrorists," said the bartender as he walked back behind the bar. "You know, they're starting to talk about him as a vice presidential candidate. Hell, I think he ought to run for President."

"He has made a name for himself in the last week," replied Carlton.

"I tell you, when those bastards start trying to knock off our representatives, they've gone too far. It's time we taught them a lesson, and I bet J.J. Hightower is the man for the job," lectured the bartender.

Carlton wanted to ask him: Who exactly was to be taught this lesson, since at this point, information on the supposed terrorist group was nonexistent. But he decided he was better off not trying to play devil's advocate with the man.

"This town had enough sorrow this past week. Hightower surviving that attack was the one bright spot. Kind of keeps people from losing faith," concluded the barkeep.

Carlton lit a cigarette and then said, "It was a pretty depressing week; first Ron Allen is murdered and then that DEA guy has a heart attack in the middle of his dinner."

The bartender looked at Carlton with a confused expression. "Where are you from?" he asked.

"Omaha. I'm here on business. It's my first time in D.C.," lied Carlton.

The barkeep nodded his head and said, "So, you don't know where you are?"

"What do you mean? Where am I?" replied Carlton, a bewildered look on his face.

"You are sitting on the bar stool where Andrew Buck spent the last moments of his life," answered the bartender, trying to sound nonchalant, but it was easy to see that the man took pleasure in informing Carlton of his ignorance.

Carlton gave the bartender a wide-eyed expression of disbelief. "You mean this is the bar where the guy died?"

"I mean you are sitting on the actual stool," replied the man.

"This is unbelievable! I had no idea this was the place he croaked," gushed Carlton in his best Midwest accent. "So, were you here when it happened?"

"I sure was. I did miss the first part because I had gone to the back room to get some cocktail napkins. When I came back he was lying on the floor. I thought maybe he was choking. This kid I had hired to help tend bar that night was kneeling over the guy screaming for a doctor. Massive heart attack. Buck was dead before the ambulance arrived."

"Must have been kind of rough on this kid." asked Carlton his interest pricked by the mention of this kid.

"Guess so. He only worked for me that one night and never even collected his paycheck. That whole deal was pretty weird," explained the barkeep.

"Oh yeah?" coaxed Carlton. He could see the man was on a roll and just wanted to let him keep talking.

"My regular help that day, Charlie Wilson, calls in about an hour before work and tells me he can't make it. A couple of guys had broken into Charlie's apartment while he was still home. They beat the crap out of him and took off, leaving Charlie with a busted rib and me with no help. Well, I was sweating pretty good, Friday is our busiest night, and with such short notice I couldn't find any backup help. Then this Mexican fellow shows up looking for work; he says he's a bartender. I hired him on the spot; two hours later he's standing over Mr. Buck screaming his head off. The whole thing must have been pretty hard on the kid; I told him he had a job, but he never came back."

The bartender stroked his moustache in silence, his thoughts evidently on the kid.

"So, was the Mexican serving drinks to Buck?" asked Carton. Immediately after uttering these words, Carlton wanted to bite his tongue off; he was pushing too hard.

"Who are you?" demanded the barkeep. The friendly tone in his voice had hardened.

Carlton put a confused and ignorant expression on his face and said, "What do you mean? I'm Ted Rogers from Omaha."

"Yeah maybe, but you're starting to ask questions like a cop," replied the barkeep.

Carlton chuckled and said, "You're right. I guess I've read too many murder mysteries."

"Sure," said the unconvinced barkeep.

Not wanting to raise the man's suspicions further, Carlton ordered another beer and talked nothing but baseball, playing the part of the Midwest business traveler until he felt the barkeep's suspicions were diminished. He even had dinner in the restaurant, just another traveling salesman looking for a few drinks and a good meal. Carlton soon understood why Buck ate here, as his steak was excellent. The dinner also gave him a chance to assimilate this new information.

Learning about the Mexican bartender who appeared immediately before Buck's death and then disappeared immediately afterwards, solidified in Carlton's mind that the death of Andrew Buck was not what the FBI made it out to be. He was now certain that Buck was murdered. If he looked deeper into the mugging of Charlie the bartender, he would not be surprised to learn that the attackers were

Mexican. He was also sure that if he had pushed a little harder he would have found out the Mexican kid served Buck his drinks. All these items would have to be thoroughly researched if this were a criminal investigation to build a case that would hold up in court. This was not his aim. Carlton was performing this investigation for himself, though what he hoped to accomplish was unclear.

Carlton was now positive that both Buck and Allen were murdered for reasons related to their involvement in Operation Raven. He was also fairly certain that their deaths had been orchestrated by someone or some group of people involved in the Mexican drug underworld, but he had no hard evidence to prove any of this. It also appeared to Carlton that people high up in the U.S. government were covering up these murders for political reasons.

Carlton could not hope to go against this cover up, he may not even want to. There could be legitimate national security reasons for it, and they surely were not going to inform an old lush like himself what these reasons were. More importantly, the people involved were powerful; they could squash him like a bug. Still, there was this tickling in the back of his mind. Something was not right, and his instincts were trying to alert him. When he was a field operative he had learned to trust his instincts; he found that most of the time they led him to do the right thing. The problem was he had fallen out of touch with his instincts the last couple of years. Could he still trust them?

CHAPTER 22

Jack had finally hit bottom, and he knew it. His emotional free-fall was over. The pain and confusion were still with him and probably would be for a long time to come, but he could fall no further. The fabric of his life had been shredded, his heart shattered. Death might be a welcome relief. In a strange way it gave him a kind of peace of mind.

Jack sat on the edge of a bed in a small *naj* holding a hand-written letter between his fingers. The *naj* was Gus's sleeping quarters at the Cobá base camp. Flores had told Jack to bunk here, as it did not appear Gus would be back any time soon. It would also give Jack a chance to go through Gus's things. Both Flores and Jack agreed that some answers to the mystery surrounding Gus might be found among his personal effects.

They had arrived back at Cobá after dark, and at first Jack thought he might wait until morning to search through Gus's personal effects. It had been a long day; the afternoon was spent in Tulum, with Flores attempting to trace Gus's whereabouts. Flores made and received countless phone calls but could not get any information concerning Gus. Not one of Flores' contacts could find any record of Gus being arrested, or even of a warrant being issued for his arrest. As far as Mexican law enforcement agencies were concerned, Gus Wise did not exist. Frustrated and depressed, the two men left Tulum knowing no more than when they arrived. Earlier, Flores had not seemed overly worried about Gus's arrest. His attitude, though, had been tempered by the trip to Tulum. Flores tried to hide his heightened anxiety, but Jack had already sensed the change. The trip back to Cobá was made in silence. Flores drove, while Jack stared out the window watching the fireflies winking off and on in the dark. By the time Jack had reached Gus's *naj* his body ached for sleep, but his curiosity would not let him rest. He decided that if he could not sleep, he might as well take a look through Gus's things.

The search did not take long. There was not much to search: a small battered chest of drawers, two cardboard boxes filled with books and papers, and a frameless backpack were the only items in the *naj*, except for the bed. He started with the boxes and found them to be full of research journals and books on archeology. The boxes seemed to hold no clues, so he went on to the backpack, but made a mental note to do a more thorough search of the boxes later. The backpack was also of no help, holding just a few articles of clothing and a map of the Yucatán Peninsula. Jack searched the dilapidated dresser last. In the top drawer he found an old cigar box buried among Gus's underwear. He removed the box from the drawer and sat on the edge of the bed. Inside he found mementoes and trinkets from Gus's life. There was everything from two cat's-eye marbles to a college acceptance notice. Jack smiled at a ticket stub from a 1978 Eagles concert; he and Gus had attended that concert together. He also found a photo of Gus, Josephine and himself. Packs were strapped to their backs with the rugged Yosemite backcountry behind them. The box appeared to be something kept from childhood, and Jack felt peculiar rummaging through these keepsakes. This was a personal catalog not intended for the eyes of others. His need to understand what was happening, though, overrode his uneasiness about snooping.

At the bottom of the box was an envelope containing a letter. The handwritten postscript caught Jack's attention, for it was his wife's handwriting. Jack wondered how a letter from Jo could have earned a place in Gus's box of personal mementoes? He noted from the post mark that the letter had been mailed a little over a year ago. A shiver of apprehension passed through Jack and settled in his stomach as his trembling fingers pulled the letter from the envelope. The handwritten words on the lined stationary crumbled Jack's heart. It also brought the incidents that had transpired over the past year into a new perspective. He now realized he would have to consider all possibilities if he were ever going to understand what had happened to Josephine and Gus.

Jack read the letter one more time, wishing the meaning of the words would change:

Dear Gus,

I hope everything is going well with your new project. It is hard to believe you're living in an ancient city in the Yucatán jungle while I live out my life in such a monotonous manner. It seems like your life is one big adventure, and there are times I wish I could be part of that adventure. I never pictured my life turning out this way.

My marriage is rapidly deteriorating. This morning we had a terrible fight. Jack left the house saying he never wanted to see me again. I spent the remainder of the day in tears. What should we do? He won't talk, and I'm a royal bitch. I don't know if it is worth the effort anymore. I just want to be happy.

Last week I came really close to buying a plane ticket to Cancún, like we joked about before you left. I might never come back though, and I believe

Jack—whatever his faults—deserves better treatment than that. I keep wondering if I am expecting too much? In spite of our problems he tells me he still loves me (although this morning his words were not so tender). He doesn't fool around, and we share the same interests, but the spark I used to feel whenever I was around him is gone. I cannot live the rest of my life without those special feelings.

At times I feel like I'm being pulled in three different directions: one moment I think Jack and I can work things out, the next I think about being with you, but then I envision Jack alone and the guilt drags me down. I also cannot bear to think of Jack and your friendship being destroyed. More and more I feel like chucking everything and finding a new place to start my life over, someplace where nobody knows the old me.

I can't believe I'm writing such a whimpering letter. I am sorry if it makes you uncomfortable. You are one of my few confidants and the only person who knows the truth of my current situation. I hope what happened between us has not changed this. Right now I need you as a friend more than I need you as a lover.

This letter is so disjointed, I can't think straight anymore. I just wanted you to know that I miss you, but I need to get my life in order before I make any long-term decisions. Please write if you get the time (in care of my office!).

Love,   Josephine

The letter slipped from his hand and dropped to the floor as Jack reclined on the bed. He stared at the light bulb that hung from the ceiling as if hypnotized by the electric glow. Stunned by Jo's words, a lost and lonesome feeling settled in his stomach. He had hit bottom.

CHAPTER 23

Nelson Carlton sat on a stone bench overlooking the resting place of his wife. He pulled his overcoat tightly around his body in an effort to ward off the early morning chill. The sun was slowly climbing above the maple trees bordering the east end of the cemetery, its light just reaching the roses that Carlton had placed on the grave moments earlier. His breath turned to fog in the cold air as he tried to remember the last time he had sat on this bench. The first year after Elizabeth was murdered he had come to the cemetery every Sunday. It was a place to sit and think . . . remember. As time went on his visits became more sporadic, and now he could not remember when he had last been here. So much of the last two years had been lost to the booze. He now realized that he might as well have been dead. She would be angry with him if she knew he had become a drunkard.

Carlton had come here to sit and think, to try and sort out what he had learned about the deaths of Buck and Allen and how they might be tied in with the attempt on Senator Hightower's life. But Elizabeth's memory was strong this morning, and his guilt weighed heavily upon him, clouding his thoughts. He wished, as he had many times over the last two years, that he could turn back the clock to that fateful night and trade his life for hers. In his mind she deserved to live and he did not.

Their marriage had not been idyllic, but for the most part they had enjoyed their time together. The only major difficulties the marriage suffered were the times apart, which were many. Carlton's employment with the CIA had meant many long nights at the office and sometimes extended trips abroad. Elizabeth handled the separations well enough, but Nelson did not. His problem was an inability to avoid involving himself with other women. He was fairly certain that Elizabeth had never known the full extent of his philandering, for when he was with her it was never a problem. Only when they were separated for long periods would his heart start to wander. He had truly loved his wife and had felt terrible the first few times he had cheated, swearing to himself that he would never do it again. But as his dalliances mounted he saw that his oaths of fidelity were useless. Eventually, he decided it was part of the job, part of the way he was. Carlton tried to ignore it, but the guilt stayed with him. He did not realize the full measure of his shame until she was killed by a bullet meant for him. Elizabeth had been gone for over two years, and he had not shared a bed or desired a woman in all that time. Sometimes he blamed it on his age or his drinking, but he knew the truth; his years of unfaithfulness had mired him in guilt.

Carlton closed his eyes, as if this might block the painful memories, and tilted his head toward the sun, letting his face soak in the early morning rays. The sunlight warmed his skin causing a glow that helped to clear his head. It was time to make some decisions concerning his present situation. It now appeared very likely that both Buck and Allen were murdered, and that these murders were connected with the attempt on Senator Hightower's life. He also had the name of a man who may have ordered these attacks: Ricardo Reyes. But what should he do with this information? The reason he had been brought in on this in the first place was because he was considered incompetent and expendable. The men at the top had been sure Nelson Carlton would never put the truth together, and, if the situation got out of control, he would make the perfect fall guy. That crap really did not matter now, though. What worried Carlton was that the upper echelon of the United States government was ignoring the connections between the murders of Buck and Allen and the attempt on Hightower's life in order to cover up Operation Raven and protect the President's ass. In this process, it appeared Ricardo Reyes possible involvement was going to go unchallenged.

Carlton wanted to believe that his government was doing something to correct this situation. There was no reason officials would inform him of what other investigations were going on; he was not considered reliable. But if this were true, why were they allowing Senator Hightower to keep such a high profile? The man was a walking target. Reyes, or whoever ordered the assassinations, still wanted to see the Senator assume room temperature. If Hightower were eliminated, there would be no one left with first-hand knowledge of Operation Raven. The only answer Carlton could find was that this was what everybody wanted. If Hightower were dead, then the whole ugly episode would be dead; no way to link the murders to Ricardo Reyes, and no one to say that the U.S. government, by order of the President, trafficked drugs into the country.

He was beginning to comprehend the tickling in the back of his head, as the situation became startlingly clear. It was the way the murders were committed. The murders and the attempt on Hightower were professional in almost every way, with enough "face value" evidence to make them appear to be unrelated incidents. On closer inspection, however, there were inconsistencies that did not fit in with the overall professionalism of the murders: bullet angles that did not make sense, the call girl not being the suicidal type, rumors that Buck's heart attack had been artificially induced, and the Latin bartender who disappeared as suddenly as he had appeared. It was as if the murders had been staged in such a way as to warn off further investigation, an arrogant warning to play along or take the fall. Reyes' message to the U.S. President was becoming clear, "Don't fuck with me, or I will take you down."

The U.S. government was being blackmailed, and the President and his men had to remain quiet or risk being exposed. They were probably hoping Reyes would finish off Hightower, thus removing the only man who could fully expose the operation. Carlton shuddered at what he was thinking. If he were right, Hightower was a marked man, and the President or men close to the President were doing nothing to protect the Senator.

Reaching into his coat pocket, he pulled out a pack of Camels. Extracting one of the unfiltered cigarettes from the pack, he lit up his first of the day, inhaling the smoke deep into his lungs as he pondered the situation. The scenario he had developed was based on a lot of supposition; there was no solid evidence that Reyes was involved in any of this, or that the murders were connected. He thought of taking his suspicions to Secretary of State Lester Goreman, but that would mean admitting he had continued his inquiries after being ordered to terminate the investigation. Technically, he could be tried for treason against the United States government, and that did not sound like a party he wanted to attend. If only he could forget, pretend he had never been involved. What did he owe anyone? If it were his ass on the line, no one would give a shit.

Carlton could not shake the feeling that something was very wrong and no one was doing anything about it. He saw only one way to solve his dilemma and that was to inform the Senator of what he had learned. Hightower could decide what to do. The man should have enough power in Washington to protect himself, especially if he knew from which direction the danger was coming. This would also lift any feelings of responsibility from Carlton. He could walk away with a clean conscience.

Carlton crushed out his cigarette on the side of the stone bench and stuffed the butt into his coat pocket. Standing up, he shoved his hands into the pockets of his overcoat. For a moment he gazed at the roses. "She always loved roses," he thought to himself. He then turned and strode away across the manicured lawn.

CHAPTER 24

It was hot, the air heavy with the smell of rotting vegetation. Jack sucked on a large bottle of water, beads of sweat rolling down his face and neck onto his soaked shirt. He sat in the shade at the entrance to the pyramid. Over the last four days he had become very familiar with the fifty feet between where he presently sat and the rubble at the end of the dark passage. Nearby, Flores and his laborers sat under the lunch tarp eating beans and tortillas. Today there would be no siesta; Flores was certain they were near the end of the tunnel.

He had been at Cobá for four days, working alongside Hector Flores and his men. It was hard labor in stifling heat and humidity, but the work did act as a catharsis for his troubled mind. At least it gave him something to do other than dwell on his loss. The rational part of his brain had accepted that Jo was gone, but he could not decide where to go from here. With the work to keep him busy, it was easy to procrastinate on a decision. It also allowed him to lock up his feelings and not deal with them. Jack was unsure if he could handle his present situation without the work to occupy him.

Last night the dream had come again. It was the same dream he had experienced for the last three nights. He feared sleep, and even when awake the dream haunted him. It rolled around in his head never far from his thoughts. The dream started out pleasantly; he was back in California wandering through his ranch-style home. Feeling safe and comfortable, he walked through the familiar rooms. In the dream Mexico did not exist. Eventually, he would find himself seated on the living room sofa talking baseball with his deceased father. A general aura of serenity pervaded, but this did not last. In the surreal way dreams mutate, Jack was suddenly alone in the living room, gripped by an inexplicable fear. He began to frantically search the house, looking for something, though not really understanding his urgency. At first he thought he might be looking for his father, but he soon realized it was something else. Opening the door to the master bedroom, he discovered his wife lying naked on the bed, her lips curled in a provocative smirk. Jack's heart would begin to pump wildly. No words were spoken, but the meaning was evident in her expression. His mouth attempted to form words, but no sounds came; he was frozen, unable to move. Then a naked man appeared and climbed on top of Josephine, inserting himself inside her. Their bodies moved together in a primal, rhythmic motion; the ecstasy on her face seeming to mock Jack. He watched in horror, unable to stop them or look away. Still implanted in Josephine the man would turn and look at Jack. It was the smiling face of Gus Wise. Jack wanted to scream, to run, but his voice was silent and his legs paralyzed. He would awake in a cold sweat, the sound of their laughter still in his ears. Even now as he recalled the dream, his heart accelerated and a sick feeling settled in the pit of his stomach.

Sitting alone with his thoughts and the memory of the dream, Jack felt the tentacles of depression wrap around him. It was a feeling of hopelessness mixed with rejection that threatened to overwhelm him. It was only a dream, but he could not stop asking himself the question: "How could my wife and best friend do this to me?" The dream mixed with the reality of Jo's letter, making it difficult for Jack to separate the two. The bitter seeds of resentment and anger were sprouting within his soul.

Jack ate his lunch while watching Flores and his men laugh and joke under the shade of the lunch tarp. Flores wore a broad easy smile that showed off a set of straight white teeth. While working, Flores kept a sober demeanor, but during lunch break or after work he seemed to enjoy bantering with his men. The workers also appeared to genuinely enjoy the company of their employer. Jack wished he could understand the language and take part in the camaraderie.

He had taken an immediate liking to Hector Flores. Though consumed by his work, the man remained affable and quick to share his knowledge of the ancient Mayan civilization. Over the past few days Jack had learned much about Flores' work at Cobá. Two years ago, while researching some obscure hieroglyphics at Chichén Itzá, Flores discovered a passage that referred to a man "who had come from the sea." He was intrigued by the passage and wondered who this visitor might have been. The stele on which this event was recorded was partially damaged, preventing full translation of the text, but Flores was able to decipher a line alluding to a tomb at Cobá. This did not mean it was the tomb of the "Man From the Sea," though information on any single stele was usually related.

With nothing more than a few broken passages, Flores began to research all of the hieroglyphical text that had been cataloged at Cobá. He discovered a few more references to the Man From the Sea, but the new material did not add any substantial information about whom the man was. At this point, Flores was not even sure if the Man From the Sea had been an actual human being or was some sort of mythical deity, as Mayan writings often mixed historical events with mythology. With nothing more to go on, Flores put his interest in this information aside as he had other important projects to finish.

Flores had almost forgotten about the Man From the Sea when an associate sent him a pottery shard unearthed at the Kabah ruin site. A painting on the shard was well preserved; it depicted the visage of a man with a full black beard. The facial features of the painted face were European with white skin color. This was in contrast to a second portrait on the same shard of a man with a sloped forehead and copper skin color. The contrast in features made this a startling find. The Mayan had the classic Mayan profile, while the bearded face could have been drawn in ancient Greece. The estimated age of the shard was approximately 1,000 years, 600 years before Christopher Columbus sailed onto the Caribbean. On viewing the shard, Flores' mind had filled with questions: Who was this man? Where did he come from? And how did he come to be on the Yucatán hundreds of years before the first European explorers? Flores remembered the stele at Chichén Itzá. If the man depicted on the pottery was a European, he would have had to cross the Atlantic Ocean and, from the Mayans' perspective, would have come from the sea.

Flores was still unsure of what to do with this information when he recalled the fabled Bearded Man on the North temple of Chichén Itzá's main ball court. Flores had always been skeptical of the Bearded Man carving, attributing the image to some trick of weathering. He retrieved some photos and artist-enhanced sketches of the Bearded Man, which he had in his files. When he compared the likeness on the pottery shard to that on the back wall of the North Temple, a chill slipped down his spine and goose bumps formed on his skin. The similarities between the two images were astonishing. Flores found himself consumed with a desire to solve the mystery behind the Bearded Man and the Man From the Sea. Though he had no hard evidence, he suspected the two were the same man. The only connections he had were the similarities between the two images, and that the estimated age of the pottery shard was close to two dates he had discovered on the Man From the Sea stele.

Flores decided to organize a research project at Cobá to try and uncover more information on the Bearded Man and maybe even unearth his tomb. He operated on two assumptions: one was that the Man From the Sea and the Bearded Man were the same person, and two, that the tomb mentioned on the stele at Chichén Itzá was the tomb of the Bearded Man. These were chancy assumptions but worth the risks for the possible payoff. Even if both assumptions proved to be faulty, much could be learned during the exploration.

Flores had heard that Gus Wise was attempting to organize a reconstruction project at Cobá. He informed his old friend of his findings and convinced Gus to join his research team. They agreed to use Gus's original reconstruction project as a cover for their true purposes. Flores explained to Jack that for decades one crackpot after another had tried to prove theories that ancient Mexican civilization was imported by everything from Egyptian Pharaohs to ancient astronauts. Time after time these theories had been proven insupportable by reputable archaeologists. One of the basic tenets all of these theories shared is that the Mayan peoples were not sophisticated or intelligent enough to be fully responsible for their advancement in such fields as architecture and astronomy. These theories concluded that without some form of outside help the ancient Mexican civilizations could not have developed to such a high degree. The archeological profession had become so jaded by such ridiculous and racist theories that most serious archaeologists steered clear of research that might contribute viability to cross-cultural influences. Both Flores and Gus knew that if word of their research leaked to the archeological community, their credibility could be greatly diminished. For this reason they hid their true purpose behind the reconstruction project.

Flores would have liked to perform a systematic search of the entire Cobá site for all references to the Bearded Man, but Cobá was a large city, much of it still hidden beneath the jungle vegetation. They did not have the time, manpower, or money for such an extensive search, so they began by collecting and analyzing all previous research and exploration pertaining to Cobá. Flores and Gus spent months coordinating all the available data and then used this information to select areas of the city where they would do intensive on-site exploration and research. This way, they had hoped to concentrate their efforts to areas most likely to yield results. But after six months of intensive research and on-site exploration, Flores was no closer to solving the mystery of the Bearded Man than when he first gazed at the pottery shard.

They had just about decided to close down the Cobá project when Gus literally stumbled over the break they had been searching for. As Flores recalled to Jack, Gus was making a reconnaissance in a little-explored section of the ruin site that was accessed by a poorly maintained tract. Gus had lost the trail and was struggling through the thick vegetation when he tripped and fell over a large object hidden in the thick undergrowth. On closer inspection he discovered that the object was a large limestone stele that had toppled over sometime during the last few centuries. Gus realized immediately that this could be an important find as the stele lay face down, protecting its carved front from the climatic elements that damaged stelae left standing or that happened to fall face up. He marked the area of his discovery and made his way back to the base camp.

With the news of Gus's find Flores canceled the next day's dig and organized the labor force for an attempt to upright Gus's stele. Flores had just about given up on learning anything more about the Bearded Man, but finding a well-preserved stele could be an important find; after all, an archeologist has to produce or research funds become scarce. Exciting finds help keep an archeologist in the minds of grantors.

The next morning Gus led the work crew to his find and the work of clearing the area began. Uprighting the thousand-pound stone block was not a simple process, as great care had to be taken not to damage the carved face. It was not until late in the afternoon that the stone was raised and Flores and Gus gazed at the profile of the Bearded Man etched into the stone. This was the same stele Jack had stumbled upon his first day at Cobá.

The discovery was more than Flores could have hoped for. Hieroglyphic text on the stele identified the profile to be that of the Man From the Sea. He finally had conclusive evidence that the Bearded Man and the Man From the Sea were the same person. The text also suggested that the final resting place of the Bearded Man was nearby.

The pyramid below which Jack currently sat was discovered not far from the stele. Once the pyramid and the area around it were cleared of vegetation, a corbeled arch entry was found at ground level on the north side of the pyramid. A stone block wall filled the entrance. The archway and the stone blocks that sealed it were in surprisingly good condition compared to the rest of the structure, which looked more like a small rocky hill than a work of man. Jungle growth had taken over most of the structure, the green vegetation concealing the rubble below. Bits and pieces of hieroglyphics were recovered on and around the pyramid, and Flores was able to interpret text referring to the Man From the Sea. They had gone from what appeared to be certain failure to what could be extraordinary success.

The stone wall at the entry to the pyramid was carefully removed only to find a passage on the other side filled from floor to ceiling with rock rubble. Some fifty feet of the six feet high by three feet wide passage had been cleared over the past few months. The work was painfully slow. Day after day Flores, Gus, and their small band of Mayan laborers excavated rock from the passage. Each piece of rubble was inspected, removed, and sorted in order to make a permanent record of the site. Over the past few days Jack had learned how difficult this work was. Tropical heat and humidity combined with sweating bodies made for a miserable environment in the dark narrow passage. It was back-breaking labor, but it gave Jack a sense of purpose, plus he was fascinated by the prospects of what might lie at the end of the passage.

Jack's thoughts were interrupted when he noted that Flores and his small work force were on their feet and headed back to the tunnel. Usually the middle of the day was reserved for siesta, three to four hours of sleep in a hammock, which avoided strenuous activity during the hottest portion of the day. Today, however, it looked as if they would reach the end of the passage; right before lunch the outline of a block wall was visible through the remaining rubble. Flores figured that they could gain access to whatever was behind this wall before dark if they worked through the afternoon. He promised the workers a paid day off tomorrow if this goal was reached. Jack took one last slug of water from his bottle and joined the men.

Full bellies and the steam bath conditions made for a sluggish start to the afternoon labors. The only one unaffected by this malaise was Flores, who appeared energized by the possibility of finally reaching his goal.

They worked through the sweltering afternoon removing the remaining rubble from the passage. Wheelbarrows were filled with rock, then pushed outside where the rock was dumped into separate piles, each pile containing two feet of excavated tunnel. Twenty-five piles of rubble were now lined up outside the pyramid. The reason for the separation was to keep a record of which rocks had come from which part of the passage. Flores had explained that any archaeological dig was actually destroying the site, meaning that the site could never be put back as it existed before the dig commenced. He illustrated this with a story of how an early French archaeologist had used dynamite on the nunnery at Chichén Itzá in order to expose the building's infrastructure. The Frenchman was able to get a good look at how the structure was constructed, but he also destroyed much of the building in the process.

"This story may sound funny when compared to today's standards," Flores had replied to Jack's laughter. "But do not forget they might be laughing at our techniques one hundred years from now."

Flores' point was that no matter how careful the archaeologist was at a site, portions of the record would be destroyed and lost forever; it was an understood cost of excavating a site. Because of this problem, it was considered proper technique to leave a portion of a site untouched so that it could be available for study under improved archaeological technologies that might be developed in the future. It was also important to catalog, as much as possible, the relationship of objects moved at the site; in this case even the rock rubble.

Soaked with sweat, eyes burning from the perspiration rolling into their eyes, they labored on. The atmosphere was stifling inside the pyramid, the air heavy with the smell of working men and a musty odor that seemed to be part of the ancient stonework. The only light was that emanating from the fluorescent lanterns.

Before the last of the rubble was cleared, Flores started on the chore of removing the wall blocking the rear of the passage. The wall was made up of one foot square limestone blocks that had been cut to an exacting fit. Flores found it difficult to extract the blocks without causing damage. Jack was impressed by how the archaeologist performed the tedious task in the dim light and stuffy atmosphere and still managed to keep his cool manner. Jack wished they had some of the Frenchman's dynamite.

It occurred to Jack that maybe this was all there was to the passage, a dead end. What if there was just more stonework behind the wall? Though no words were spoken, Jack was sure the same thought had occurred to Flores. All thoughts of failure quickly vanished when the first block was removed to reveal dark open space on the other side of the wall. The tension was high, aching muscles, heat, and humidity were ignored. Three more blocks were removed, making a space wide enough for a man to crawl through.

Jack saw the anticipation in Flores' eyes as he handed him a lantern. He also noted that the Mayans had backed away a few feet. They appeared to be uneasy, as if maybe they were having second thoughts about disturbing the final resting place of one of their ancestors. For a moment, it was like a scene out of a 1930s horror film, the one where the natives' eyes grow to the size of saucers and they run screaming, as the brave but stupid archaeologists enter the pharaoh's tomb.

Without a word, Flores wormed his way through the hole with Jack following close behind. The opening was at the top of the wall, so they had to climb up into it and then drop down head first on the other side. Once inside, they stood up holding their lanterns in front of them, both silent. They were the first men to enter this place in a millennium. A twelve-foot by twelve-foot chamber was illuminated by the fluorescent light. A stifling musty smell filled the chamber, but the temperature was relatively cool. Jack did not have to be a trained archaeologist to realize this was not what Flores had expected. The chamber was empty, only four stone walls. Six months of work only to find an empty room.

CHAPTER 25

Nelson Carlton glanced at his watch; he had been waiting in the underground garage for over an hour. He had arrived twenty minutes early, but Senator Hightower was now forty minutes late. It appeared that the Senator was going to pull a no-show. When Carlton phoned Hightower to set up this meeting, the man had not been warm to the idea of having a powwow. His interest had increased when Carlton hinted he had evidence that the deaths of Buck and Allen may have gone down differently than explained by the FBI. When Carlton explained that this information was too sensitive to travel via Ma Bell, Hightower invited him to his office. Carlton nixed that idea, informing the Senator it would be best if their meeting were kept secret. He asked Hightower to meet him on the basement level of a downtown parking garage at 7:30 p.m., and to tell no one about the meeting.

Maybe the Senator had changed his mind. Had the cloak and dagger stuff scared the politician away? Carlton was not sure, but if the man did not show up soon he was going to walk. It was too damned cold to spend the night in a basement garage. After all, he had come here out of pure charity; he did not have to do this.

He took one last drag on his Camel, dropped the smoldering butt to the concrete, and crushed it out with the sole of his shoe. Blowing the last of the heavy smoke from his lungs, he started toward the stairs that would lead him back to the street. Charity could only be stretched so far. J.J. Hightower would have to make his own way; Carlton was through with this business.

He had taken two steps when he saw twin beams of light moving along the preformed concrete wall of the garage indicating that a car was entering from the street above. A Lincoln Town car, from which the twin beams of light emanated, came rolling out of the darkness. The car turned toward Carlton and slowed to a stop not more than ten feet from where he stood. The headlights blinded him. An uneasy moment passed; this might not be Hightower. Washington was not always a friendly place after dark. Hearing a motorized whirring noise, he realized that the driver's side window was being lowered. This was followed by a slightly accented voice. "The Senator is waiting. Please enter through the right rear door."

"The Senator is waiting. What the hell have I been doing for the past hour?" thought Carlton, somewhat perturbed by the driver's tone of voice.

He moved around to the right-hand side of the vehicle and entered the rear door. There in the back seat was the nation's current media darling, J.J. Hightower, the man who had heroically thwarted a terrorist attack on his life by forgetting his overcoat. Hightower's narrow escape from the jaws of death had been sensationalized by the national media, especially on television shows like "20/20" and "Dateline." The Senator, who was already well known, became a national celebrity overnight. For the moment, the press was in love with him. They did not make fun of him in political cartoons or tear him apart in editorials.

When Carlton opened the car door, the cab light came on and stayed on until he closed the door behind him. In this brief period of time he made a quick and unobtrusive visual inspection of the vehicle's interior. The only occupants were the Senator and his driver. The man seated behind the wheel stared straight ahead, keeping the back of his head to Carlton. He was able to get a glimpse of the driver's profile: full cheeks, thick but not quite bushy mustache, light brown skin, and dark hair. Though the man was seated, Carlton estimated the driver would be pushing six feet with an athletic build. He assumed the man was Armando Galvan, Senator Hightower's personal driver. Carlton recalled how he originally suspected Galvan of being involved with the bombing. After all, the man had managed to miss work on the one day his boss's car was vaporized.

Galvan was dismissed as a possible suspect for two reasons. The first was that the night before the bombing he had been badly beat up by two burglars he had surprised in his apartment, a very good reason for missing a day of work. The second reason was that he had been the Senator's driver for over ten years. Hightower vouched for the man, claiming Galvan was like a family member.

Carlton had forgotten about Galvan's beating. It now flashed through his mind that this incident was remarkably similar to what had happened to Charlie Wilson, the bartender at the Prime Cut restaurant, who had his face rearranged the afternoon prior to Buck's death. Carlton let the flash fizzle, though; after tonight he was going to forget all about this. No more investigating, no more postulating; it was not his problem. Were not hundreds of people victimized by violent crimes every day in this city? There was no need to suspect some kind of connection between every person who had been thumped in the last week, even if it did cause certain people to be conveniently absent from their normal routines.

As Carlton settled in the seat, he noted the driver's probing eyes reflected in the rearview mirror. They were hard eyes that carried a simple message, "Fuck with the passenger, and I fuck with you."

The Senator sat on the rear seat with his hands on his lap. He wore a light brown overcoat that covered most of the perfunctory dark-blue power suit and red striped tie. He did not look at Carlton. The interior of the car was warm, and if nothing else, Carlton was glad to be out of the frosty night air.

"Do we sit here, or are we going somewhere?" were Hightower's first words.

"Pull out of the garage and take a right, then take a left at the first intersection. Continue straight until I say otherwise," replied Carlton, more to the driver than to Hightower.

The driver did not put the Lincoln into gear until the Senator nodded for him to go ahead. The point was made.

"I'm sorry about the cloak-and-dagger routine, Senator, but I think you will understand once you hear my story," explained Carlton.

"You intimated on the phone that you had information I would consider very important, information you could not relate over the phone. I had promised myself to stay away from the 'cloak and dagger' as you call it. I'm sure you understood how I felt about it by the conclusion of our first meeting, but you are not the type of man to exaggerate. If you say we need to meet, I will meet with you. There better be a good reason, though, why we can't meet during regular business hours," replied Hightower as the Lincoln pulled out of the garage and into traffic.

"It would not be wise for either of us to be seen in each other's company," Carlton replied. "I was ordered to cease my investigation into the deaths of Buck and Allen and the attempt on your life. All documentation was to be shredded, and I was informed it would be best if I forgot what I had learned. Technically, my meeting with you could be construed as a treasonous act. You, Senator, have a much better reason for keeping a low profile. Someone wants to put you in a body bag, and I think there are some highly placed people in the U.S. government who know this but are looking the other way."

"I don't need this crap! You better not be jerking me around," exclaimed a red-faced Hightower.

"Can we shut this?" asked Carlton as he motioned to a sliding Plexiglass window mounted across the front seat.

Hightower nodded affirmatively. As Carlton slid the partition shut, his eyes met the stone-cold stare of the driver reflected in the rearview mirror. He smiled and winked at Galvan through the Plexiglass, hoping for a reaction, but the hard stare remained unchanged.

"Senator, I'm here to inform, that is all. What you do with the information is not my concern. If you are wondering what my motives are, I can't tell you, because I'm not sure myself. Maybe I just don't like to see people get shit on. If you think you do not need to hear what I have to say, then tell your driver to drop me off."

Carlton's statement hung in the silence, and for a moment he thought Hightower was going to signal the driver to stop. Instead, the Senator apologized and asked Carlton to continue.

He began by telling the Senator about his suspicions when the State Department shut down his investigation and the FBI closed both the Buck and Allen cases. He told the Senator about the final enigmatic message that identified Ricardo Reyes received from Sam Peters only twenty-four hours prior to the man being found dead in a Mérida hotel room. Without identifying Schovich, Carlton related their conversation, how there were rumors around the Bureau that Buck's heart failure had been induced, and that the hooker who killed Allen may not have committed suicide. He also explained the situation at the Prime Cut restaurant, how the Mexican bartender conveniently showed up the afternoon of Buck's death after the regular bartender had the crap beaten out of him.

"I realize this is all very circumstantial, but when you put it all together it has to make you wonder. I'm on the outside now, so I don't know if anyone is still looking into these matters. Maybe they are. I probably should have consoled myself with this, but you were keeping such a high profile for a man possibly at the top of someone's hit list. It then occurred to me, with Buck, Allen, and Peters dead, you are the only one left alive who was directly involved in Operation Raven. Reyes pops you and he has a clean sweep. The President and his men are staying on the sidelines because they don't want to take a chance on Operation Raven becoming public knowledge. It would be the same as announcing the President of the United States is a drug dealer. They may even be hoping that you are eliminated; then there would be no one left to tell tales. They could close the book on Operation Raven."

Both men were silent while Hightower digested the information that had been imparted to him. The Lincoln was currently stopped at a busy intersection, and the nearby streetlights illuminated the interior of the car. Carlton saw that Hightower was fiddling with the class ring on his right ring finger as he had the day of their first meeting. In the dim light he could again read the raised letters on the face of the ring, USC 1962. But this time he also noted the Greek letters ΣΑΓ on the side of the ring. Carlton knew the letters stood for Sigma Alpha Gama, a Greek college fraternity. Evidently, Hightower had been a member.

"I'm wondering, assuming your 'theories' were correct, why you do not considered yourself a target?" quizzed the Senator.

Carlton noted that Hightower already spoke of his "theories" in the past tense.

"Reyes probably has no way of knowing about me and as far as the President and his men are concerned, I am not a problem. To them I'm a drunken idiot who has a hard enough time figuring out how to get out of bed in the morning, let alone put something like this together. If I ever went public, they could have me written off as some kind of inebriated lunatic. What would I have? Only a wild story with no evidence."

"But I'm supposed to believe an inebriated lunatic over what I have been told by the FBI?" shot back Hightower. "You might be a disgruntled State Department employee who is trying to strike back at the system that has dumped you on your drunken ass."

"Look, Senator, I have my problems. They selected me for this investigation because of my problems. A seldom sober, friendless man who no one would give a shit about when he was hung out to dry. Since the killings, it has all been damage control. I don't think anyone really wanted to know the truth. I know I don't, not anymore. The only reason I came to you is that it appeared they were leaving you exposed. I'm giving you this information free of charge. What you do with it is your business."

"I'm sorry, Mr. Carlton. I did not mean to personally attack you. I am sure you understand that I have more to consider than just how these events affect either you or me. Your theory is very interesting, but as you said yourself, it is based on very circumstantial evidence," the Senator calmly replied.

As he listened to the Senator, Carlton recalled how high strung the man had been during their first meeting. Though he had tried to hide it then, Hightower had appeared very worried about his future. This was in contrast to the cool and collected individual who currently confronted him.

The Senator continued. "You must also realize that I may have knowledge you are unaware of. This is not to say that I do not value your information, but it may be important for reasons that do not concern you." Hightower paused to let the meaning of his words sink in. He then asked, "Is there anything else that would give credence to your theories?"

Carlton was thrown off balance by Hightower's suggestion that "he already had explanations" that Carlton was not, and never would be, privy to.

"No. There is nothing else," replied a sullen Carlton. "I have said my piece, and you evidently have things under control. I am now going

to try and forget this mess and get on with my life." Carlton felt the
blood rush to his face as he spoke. He was flustered, sure his face had
turned crimson. Blushing was not his normal style, but the Senator had
made him feel foolish. He suddenly saw himself as a caricature of the
man he used to be.

"Tell your driver to take a left on Maple. It's about three more
blocks. Then take another left onto Elm. If no one follows us, I will
leave you there."

The Senator slid the Plexiglass partition open and informed the
driver of the directions. He then leaned back in his seat and said, "Mr.
Carlton, you are right. There is a lot more going on here. Your
information may be useful, but in ways that I must keep to myself. Any
more information you can relate to me in the future would be
appreciated. I agree with what you said, though. It probably would be
in your best interest to forget about this mess."

The Senator's tone was condescending, which did not make Carlton
feel any better. Pick up your toys and go home, little boy.

The road they were traveling was lined with mini marts, gas stations,
and fast food joints. But as the Lincoln turned onto Maple Street, the
corporate service sector immediately gave way to a tree-lined street of
three bedroom, two bath homes. Three blocks passed, and the Lincoln
turned onto Elm Street. When he was certain they were not being
followed, Carlton asked the driver to pull over.

"Thank you for your attention, Senator. I hope I haven't wasted
your time," apologized Carlton.

"Nonsense. I appreciate the information and your concern," replied
the Senator as Carlton climbed out of the car.

"Nelson."

Carlton stood on the sidewalk holding the car door open, surprised
to hear the Senator use his first name.

"Stay off the booze. You're killing yourself. I read your file soon
after our first meeting. You were one of the best minds the CIA ever
had; they couldn't keep you out of the field, though."

Both men stared at each other. Hightower seemed to be collecting
his thoughts while Carlton wondered why this jerk had to start
preaching to him.

"You have to let her go; it wasn't your fault," concluded the Senator.

"I'm trying, but it's easier said than done," replied Carlton, not trying
to hide the sarcasm in his voice.

He shut the car door and watched the Lincoln move off down the
street. It was cold, but he was glad to be out of the car. Fishing his
Camels out of his coat pocket, he lit up a smoke and started walking

toward the nearest bus stop. The residential street was empty. The eerie blue-gray glow of television light spilled out of family room windows. A dog barked. It was a clear night; he could see the stars. It was cold, but still a good night for a walk.

He had expected a sense of relief after unloading his worries on the Senator, but it had not gone as he expected. Instead of relief he found confusion and humiliation. His speculations had proven faulty, and he now felt like a fool. There was a time, not that long ago, he had been a rising star of the Central Intelligence Agency. A top field agent whose insights into the KGB had been considered brilliant. He had the ear of powerful people; now these same people would not give him the time of day. It was time to forget, and he knew where there was a bottle of Kentucky whiskey to help him do just that.

CHAPTER 26

It was well after dark by the time Jack and Flores had finished dinner. The evening meal had been a somber affair. "Pass the tortillas," were the only words the archaeologist spoke during the entire meal. In fact, Flores had not said much of anything since entering the empty chamber. Jack could understand the disappointment but was beginning to wonder if the man was taking this too hard, when Flores brought out a bottle of Commemerativo. With a wry grin on his face, he handed the open bottle of tequila to Jack and said, "As you gringos say, you can't win them all."

They sat under the dining canopy with the mosquito netting pulled down and passed the bottle back and forth, letting the tequila wash away their wasted efforts. The smooth liquor went down easily, enveloping Jack in a warm glow. The conversation was comfortable, and the periods of silence were not awkward. A circle of light emanated from the lantern, attracting a congregation of large black beetles. In a futile attempt to reach the light, the strange-looking insects repeatedly smacked against the mosquito netting, beating out an incessant thump-bump rhythm. In between slugs of tequila, Jack watched the fireflies blink off and on in the surrounding darkness. Somehow everything seemed right in this moment. Jack had not felt this relaxed since before Mérida.

"I had hoped we would find something more dramatic than an empty chamber," said a resigned Flores.

"You still made some important discoveries. You now have evidence that the Man From the Sea and the Bearded Man were the same person, and it seems to me that there is still a lot of jungle out there to search," replied Jack.

"Yes, I have that, but there can be no more research until I raise more money. The project is broke. A dramatic find would have made it much easier to raise funding. I tried not to think about it, but I really thought we were onto an amazing find. I could not stop comparing the similarities between this site and the Temple of the Inscriptions at Palenque."

Flores had related these similarities in earlier conversations, fascinating Jack with the story of the ancient city of Palenque. Nestled in the tropical rain forest in the foothills of the Sierra Madre de Chiapas, the ruins of Palenque overlook the savannah that stretches to the Gulf Coast. The city reached its zenith under the reign of Lord Pacal, who ruled for almost seventy years (he was only twelve when he first ascended the throne). To honor the great ruler, the Temple of the Inscriptions was constructed on top of a 75-foot high pyramid. The temple was named after the extensive hieroglyphic texts found inside the portico that recorded Pacal's ancestry and rise to power. The similarity between the Cobá site and the Temple of the Inscriptions was not what was inside the temple, but what was found underneath it.

In 1949, archaeologist Alberto Ruz L'Huiller noticed that the temple walls continued beyond the floor and that one of the temple's floor slabs had holes along its edges. Upon lifting the slab, Ruz discovered an arched ceiling and a stairwell filled with rock rubble. It took four seasons of back-breaking work to clear the rubble from the stairwell, but Ruz's efforts were rewarded in 1952 when the tomb of Lord Pacal was uncovered deep inside the base of the pyramid. This was the first tomb found in a Mayan pyramid. Up to this point, archaeologists did not believe the pyramids were utilized for burials. Even Ruz initially thought he had discovered an altar or sacred chapel, until the five-ton sarcophagus lid was lifted to reveal the jade-adorned skeleton of Pacal. The tomb was an awesome find. Fantastic wall carvings represented the nine lords of the Mayan underworld and depicted the lords marching around the walls of the tomb. The crypt was sealed with an exquisitely carved sarcophagus lid. It was this carving that pseudo-archeologist Eric Von Dainken claimed was a depiction of an ancient astronaut inside a space craft. Most credible archaeologists agree that the carving represents Pacal in death falling to the underworld. Inside the crypt, beautiful jade jewelry and other ornaments graced the bones of the dead leader. The most spectacular of these pieces was a jade death mask.

"Someday I would like to go to Palenque and see Pacal's tomb," mused Jack between sips of tequila.

"It is a worthwhile trip," replied Flores.

"Do they have Pacal's death mask on display?" questioned Jack.

"The death mask is not on display anywhere. It was stolen from Mexico City's National Museum of Anthropology. It probably sits in some rich bastard's display case hidden from the rest of the world."

"How did that happen?" asked Jack.

"It was Christmas Eve, 1985. I don't think the authorities ever figured exactly how the thieves operated, but it was evident that they were well-informed professionals. They knew exactly what they wanted, where it was, and how to get it."

For a moment both men were quiet, each with his own thoughts. Jack wondered where Pacal's death mask had ended up, while Flores pondered future research possibilities. The only sound was that of the large black beetles bouncing off the mosquito netting in their vain attempt to reach the lantern light. The silence was finally broken by Flores. "We sit here discussing my problems when they are nothing compared to yours. I do not know your plans, my friend, but you are welcome to come with me to Mexico City. I know some people who could help you get out of the country."

Flores waited a beat, giving Jack a chance to interject, but Jack remained silent. Flores continued. "From what you have told me it appears you are in deep trouble with the Judicial Police. They will not stop searching for you. We are isolated here; no newspapers or television, no one knows who you are, but if you start traveling around you are going to be seen, and someone will identify you. Photographs of you have probably been on television and in the newspapers. If you were to return to the United States, they could not reach you; you would be free to tell your story. Maybe something could be arranged. I assure you that I will do everything I can to find out what happened to your wife and to Gus, but I think you should leave Mexico before it is too late."

Jack remained silent, not knowing what to say. Since his discovery of Josephine's letter to Gus (which he had not shared with Flores) he had avoided thinking about what he would do when it came time to leave Cobá. Jo was gone, and part of Jack accepted this, but he knew the full impact would not be felt until he arrived back home to an empty house; a house filled with memories. Also, he still did not like the thought of leaving the country without learning the truth about his wife.

After an uncomfortable period of silence Jack finally spoke, "To be truthful, I have not considered what I will do next. Staying here at Cobá and working with you has allowed me to insulate myself from my problems. Not knowing what to do has been an excuse to do nothing. I appreciate your offer and will give it strong consideration, but I'm in no condition to make a decision tonight."

Jack felt his face flush as a feeling of embarrassment twisted his gut. The liquor was playing hell on his emotions. He wanted control where there was none to be had.

"I understand, my friend," replied Flores. "Tonight was probably not the best time to discuss this."

"Don't worry about it, Hector. I know I have to face my problems. Tonight, though, I just want to bullshit and drink tequila."

They stayed up telling stories until the light from the lantern had dimmed to a dull yellow. The night ended with the tequila bottle empty and both men laughing uproariously at the plight of humanity.

"You learn to laugh in the archaeological business, because if you do not, the disappointments will kill you," claimed Flores as they stumbled back to their *najs*.

"That's life, not archaeology," replied Jack.

CHAPTER 27

The early morning light was creeping into Gus's *naj* when Jack awoke with a dull pounding in his head and a mouth full of cotton. His slumber had been deep and dreamless, uninterrupted by the nightmares that had plagued him on previous nights. This morning, however, the "tequila blues" were taking their toll. He would have stayed in bed, but a strong urge to relieve himself pushed him from the cot, and then a strong thirst took him to the kitchen for a bottle of water.

Once up, Jack decided that an early morning walk might help clear the cobwebs. Nursing a cup of coffee, he headed out in no particular direction. The sun was low on the horizon, its light blocked by the surrounding jungle. The motionless morning air was warm and held the promise of a sultry afternoon. A pair of toucans flew through the trees above Jack. He found himself walking the same track they drove down every morning. He thought about going in a different direction to see something new, but he found himself drawn to the pyramid. He was intrigued by the empty chamber that had been sealed for a thousand years.

Jack started to feel human again as the coffee and the walk slowly washed away the effects of last night's imbibing. Usually by this time of day they were already hard at work in the passage. It was nice to spend a morning in a more leisurely manner.

Eventually, Jack made his way to the pyramid's entrance and found a fluorescent lantern that had been left behind. Normally, all the equipment was brought back to the base camp at the end of the day to prevent it from walking off the work site during the night. The Mayan workers were generally honest men who looked down on thievery, but one lantern could be sold for more money than most of them made in a week.

Jack set his empty coffee mug down and picked up the lantern. He switched it on; the light was strong, indicating the batteries still had plenty of juice. Keeping his head down to avoid smacking it on the low ceiling, he cautiously entered the pyramid. The place felt different this morning. At first he did not understand it; after all, over the last few days he had spent most of his waking hours hauling a ton of rock out of this hole. From his first day on the site he had been captivated by this pyramid and the mysterious rubble-filled passage, but this morning the feeling of intrigue was mixed with trepidation. He then realized that he had never been here alone. Without the camaraderie of the other men, the mystery of this place seemed more powerful, even forbidding. The urge to go back to the base camp was strong. A grim smile formed on his lips; after what he had been through recently, how could he fear this place? Did he expect the ghost of a Mayan priest to come strolling out of the dark, ready to rip out his heart for a sacrifice to the gods? Then again, this wasn't Kansas.

A part of Jack found his fear reassuring. It proved to him that he still wanted to go forward with his life. If he had truly given up, there would be no fear. Swallowing his apprehension, he continued down the narrow passage, the fluorescent lantern illuminating the darkness. Slowly his anxieties transformed into an exhilaration that reminded him of how he felt as a child the first time his parents had gone out for the night and left him home alone. There was the excitement of having the entire house to himself. He could watch what he wanted on television and eat a second bowl of ice cream without adult intervention, but as darkness descended there were the sounds of the night to contend with. Freedom always comes with the price of the unknown.

Jack made his way into the small chamber only to find it as empty as it was the day before. No ancient ghost materialized. His pounding heart slowed, and he laughed at his unreasonable fears.

He set the lantern down in the middle of the chamber; its fluorescent light cast an eerie glow on the barren block walls. What was so important about this empty room that a thousand years ago the Mayans had gone to such trouble to seal it off from the outside world? Maybe the ancients had entombed one of their chieftains here, but the years had turned his remains to dust. This thought sent the proverbial chill up Jack's spine. He decided to not let his thoughts tarry too long on this subject. Besides, it made no sense. Flores had informed him that the Mayans liked to send the dead off in a big way, at least the very important dead (Jack thought of them as the VID, kind of like being a VIP but without being there to enjoy it). Lords like Pacal went to the hereafter with plenty of gold and jade in ornately carved tombs that depicted the life of the deceased and their relationship with the gods. The organic remains might decompose to the elements, but gold and jade would last through the ages.

He considered the possibility that they may have stuffed the remains of some unpopular "Very Important Dead" person in the chamber; a tyrannical king the people were glad to see go. The subjects of this ancient despot may have kept the king's treasures and then sealed the body inside the pyramid to make sure the deceased's evil spirit could not escape. Jack mulled this theory over for a while then discarded it for one that involved the Bearded Man. After all, they suspected this pyramid had been built for him.

What if the Bearded Man was a European? The Mayans might have thought he was some kind of god. (No telling what this European would have thought of the Mayans.) A white man with a full beard would have been a strange sight to the brown, smooth-skinned locals—even more so if he was a blonde. Having somehow crossed the Pacific Ocean 500 years before Columbus, this European would have been unable to bring along many personal effects. The Mayans, though, might have been in awe of this stranger and built him a grand final resting place; he just did not have much in the way of personal effects to take with him on his journey to the underworld, thus the empty chamber. Jack decided this did not make sense either. The Bearded Man was evidently on the Yucatán for some amount of time, as there were records of him visiting at least two other cities. Such an honored guest would surely have received plenty of gifts on his travels (Jack assumed the stranger would have been an honored guest. Why else would the Mayans have built him such a grand memorial?)

This was all wild speculation on Jack's part. Flores had no hard evidence that this pyramid was built for the Bearded Man or that it even held a tomb. Jack had learned that most Mayan pyramids do not contain tombs; Pacal's was the exception, not the rule.

Still musing over the mystery of the empty chamber, Jack picked up the lantern and walked to the wall opposite the entrance to the chamber. He sat down with his back against the wall and his legs extended in front of him, the lantern sat between his legs. From the pocket of his shorts he pulled a photograph. It was the picture he had found in the cigar box: Gus, Jo, and himself on a backpacking trip. He stared at the smiling faces framed by the Yosemite backcountry. It had been a great trip; he had never caught so many trout. How had he gone from there to here? What had happened? Jack wanted his life back.

He switched off the lantern and the room slipped into total darkness except for a small amount of morning light drifting in at the entrance to the passage. Minutes passed and he remained unmoving, trance-like, his mind preciously unoccupied. Time stopped; there was only the cool darkness and the musty smell of the chamber. It felt good to just sit and be. It was quiet here, and for some reason, maybe the stone walls, he felt protected.

He had to make a decision about Flores' offer to arrange his passage back to the United States. When Jack first arrived at Cobá, he could not imagine leaving Mexico without finding out what became of his wife, but things were different now. For one, at the time of his arrival he was in an extreme emotional state, unwilling to accept what had occurred. Now that some time had passed, he was beginning to see the futility of his situation. Another difference was the letter that indicated that his wife and best friend were having an affair. Both Gus and Jo had vanished and were probably dead, or maybe Ortiz was right in speculating that the two of them had plotted this scheme so they could run away together. But what was their scheme? To kill Peters for the red duffel bag full of cash? That was plausible; the bag appeared to contain a small fortune. But how did the money end up in the possession of the stranger who called himself Travis? Had Travis killed Jo and Gus for the money? How much cash was in the bag? Was it really enough to kill for? There was also the strange story Gus had related to Flores. Was Gus really some kind of agent for the DEA?

The questions circulated through his mind with few possible answers. The more he considered the situation, the more confusing it became. Above all the questions and confusion, one thing remained, casting a shadow on all other considerations: the letter. Along with the recurring dream, the letter had put him in a state of dark melancholy. Not only was he lost and lonely, but rejected. His crippled ego made it difficult for him to make a decision. He thought he still loved his wife, but there was also a part of him that did not want to see her again; a part that despised her for what she had done.

Why was he tormenting himself? Deep down he knew he would leave with Flores. There was no other choice. His wife was either dead or had run off with another man; neither situation warranted his staying in Mexico. Jack relaxed as he realized his decision to go had been made.

The inky blackness was replaced by dark, dull grayness as his eyes gradually adjusted to the lack of light. He could barely make out the block walls surrounding him, or at least imagined he could. While his thoughts had been occupied by his troubles, the fingers of his right hand had been fiddling in the dirt on the floor of the chamber. His fingers had discovered a stone block floor beneath the dusty dirt. He would trace the outline of one block, then move on to trace the outline of an adjoining block. Moving out from the wall, each line of blocks was offset a half-block from the previous line of blocks. The outlines of the precisely cut blocks followed a predictable path until his fingers had moved four blocks out from the wall. At this point they came up against one large block, the border of which ran parallel to the wall. The border remained unbroken for as far as he could reach from his sitting position.

His conscious mind had barely been aware of his doodling fingers, but when the pattern of the stone work was broken, he became curious about the structure of the floor. The previous evening they had taken no notice of the floor structure. He turned the lantern back on, flooding the chamber with light. Now on his hands and knees, he began scraping away the soil that covered the chamber floor. His eyes confirmed what his fingers had discovered. Approximately three feet from the base of the wall, the stone blockwork came up against one giant stone block. He could not tell how large the block was; he had uncovered three feet of the edge parallel to the wall and still had not come to a corner.

For the next ten minutes Jack scraped the soil off of the larger block. First he worked with his hands, but when his back started to cramp he stood up and scraped with his feet. Dust filled the air and stuck to the beads of perspiration that had formed along his brow. His labor eventually revealed a six foot by three foot slab of limestone set in the center of the floor. The length of the slab was perpendicular to the passage leading into the chamber. He stood in the hazy light waiting for the dust to settle, contemplating his find. In spite of all he had learned over the last few days he was still ignorant of Mayan architecture. This could be standard floor design, but he had a feeling it was something more. His feeling was confirmed when he noticed an irregularity along the edge of the slab closest to the chamber entrance. He knelt down to get a closer look, and after brushing the remaining dirt away he discovered a three-inch diameter hole on the seam between the slab and the remaining stone work. Jack's heart began to race as he immediately thought of the fake floor in the Temple of the Inscriptions and the hidden passageway that led to Pacal's tomb. Electrified, Jack grabbed the lantern and started back to camp.

*   *   *

Hector Flores was down on his hands and knees inspecting the limestone slab that dominated the center of the chamber's floor. He was concentrating on the seam created between the slab and the remainder of the floor. In his right hand he held a small brush that he used to sweep away dirt and dust from the area he was inspecting. His long dark hair hung down in front of his expressionless face. The man's power of concentration and self-constraint impressed Jack. Jack wanted to crack the stone slab out of the floor, but Flores followed archaeological procedures that were slow and meticulous.

The archaeologist worked his way around the entire slab, and although his face remained expressionless, his eyes were alive, piercing. They had not been so alive when Jack first arrived in camp with news of his find. Flores appeared to have just risen from slumber, with morning face and a five o'clock shadow. His eyes were like cherry tomatoes; his hair tangled and sticking out in all directions—the stereotypical caricature of a man with a screaming hangover. Hector was clumsily tucking his shirt into his pants as Jack rushed up to him. He had stared at Jack groggily, squinting through one eye as he listened to the words tumble out of Jack's mouth.

"I think there is something under the floor of the chamber. It's like the false floor in the Temple of the Inscriptions."

Flores' eyes opened a bit wider, but they also held a glint of disbelief. "What makes you think this?" quizzed the wobbly archaeologist.

"I was down at the site this morning. Under the layer of dirt on the chamber's floor I discovered a stone block floor. In the center of the floor . . . "

Flores held up his hands indicating he wanted Jack to stop. "Let's go to the dining area where we can sit while you explain this to me, and more importantly, I can have a cup of coffee," croaked the archaeologist.

The two men sat in the dining area while Jack related his discovery. Flores interrupted with a few questions, but mostly listened while he sucked down two cups of industrial-strength coffee. Jack's discovery and the caffeine had an immediate effect on Flores' condition. He appeared to shrug off the effects of the hangover and started planning an excavation of the chamber floor. They were soon loading tools and equipment into the Land Rover.

Pax Chi was the only laborer available as Flores had given his Mayan workers the day off. Pax was quartered at the base camp because his mother was the camp cook; the rest of the workers resided in the nearby village. Flores could have rounded up more help, but he figured the three of them could handle the situation. The men needed the rest, and if their efforts were required later, they could be summoned.

According to Flores, the Mayan definition of "Pax Chi" was any small musical instrument. Pax's Mother had given him this name because she had heard the sounds of a flute while giving birth to her son. Pax was the only worker with whom Jack had any identity. This was partly because Pax lived at the base camp, so Jack spent more time with him than the others; but also because Pax, like Jack, was a new addition to the work force. Pax had been hired the day Jack arrived at Cobá. He had been working on the coast, but after losing his job he came to Cobá seeking employment. Flores did not need the help, but he hired the young man as a favor to Pax's mother. Laborers were easy to come by, but not good cooks. Jack estimated the young man's age to be in the late teens. A good foot shorter than Jack, Pax had straight jet-black hair and a pair of twinkling brown eyes set in an oval-shaped face. An infectious smile was usually spread across his face, and he was about the only person who could get a smile out of Jack. Though neither spoke the other's language, Jack felt that he and Pax understood each other.

Jack and Pax now stood watching Flores inspect the limestone slab imbedded in the floor, Pax smoking while Jack chewed his thumbnail. Flores had circumnavigated the entire block and had uncovered another three-inch diameter hole in addition to the one Jack had discovered earlier. The holes were approximately two feet apart and centered along the slab's lengthwise seam closest to the chamber's entry. Jack wanted to hear the archaeologist's explanation as to the meaning of the two holes but stayed quiet as he watched Flores clean the dirt from the cavities.

After what seemed like an eternity to Jack, Flores stood, stretched his arms, and arched his cramped back. "You have found something here, my friend, but I am not sure what," he said with a faraway look in his eyes that indicated to Jack the man was sizing up the mystery even as he spoke. "I do believe this block was designed so that it could be removed from the floor. As to what lies beneath it . . ." Flores hunched his shoulders and held his palms up in a gesture of ignorance.

He got down on one knee next to one of the holes on the slab's seam and motioned for Jack to come closer. "The two holes appear to penetrate the depth of the block. I have removed the soil out of the holes until I reached a solid bottom. The holes are approximately 15 centimeters deep."

Jack did some quick calculating and estimated that the holes were about a six-inches deep.

"It appears that the purpose of the holes is to enable the removal of the block from the floor. Poles could be inserted into the holes and then used to pry the block from the floor."

"It must weigh a ton!" interrupted Jack. Until this moment he had not considered how heavy the slab might be.

"Actually, I do not think it is quite that heavy, probably more like five hundred to a thousand pounds. The key to removing the block is leverage. Two men, each with a pole, should be able to raise the block far enough out of the floor so a third man can place wedges under the raised block in order to prevent it from dropping back into place. Once the block is propped up and secured, three men might be able to manhandle the stone onto its side. The question now is, what are the ancients hiding?" Flores pointed at the block.

"It sure seems similar to the Temple of the Inscriptions and its false floor hiding the passage to Pacal's tomb," suggested Jack.

"Yes, there are similarities," answered Flores, "but you must remember Pacal's tomb was the exception, not the rule. In general,

Mayan pyramids and temples—especially on the Yucatán—have not been found to contain tombs."

"But I thought the reason we are excavating this passage was in hope of finding the tomb of the Bearded Man. What are we busting our butts for if not in search of a tomb?" asked Jack in exasperation.

"You are confusing temples and tombs with things even I cannot explain. The Mayans existed here for thousands of years before the Europeans arrived. Their culture was not static. It changed from century to century and from region to region. You cannot necessarily compare what took place at Palanque to what happened at Cobá a few hundred years later. For example, compare New York City of the 1700s to the present city, or today's New York to one of your small Midwestern communities. I think you would agree that the differences are numerous. I am not only talking about technological advances: what kind of reception would New Yorkers of the 1700s give to a homosexual political action group? It has been the same throughout time; cultures change over the centuries, and what is accepted in one region is taboo in another.

"The purpose of this project is not to find the remains of the Bearded Man, although that would be exciting, but hopefully to find a temple dedicated to the Bearded Man; a place where his history in Mayan culture would be documented. What form this would take is difficult to say. We still know so little about the ancient Mayans."

Flores stared at the stone block for a moment, then looked up at Jack, a smile on his lips and a whimsical glint in his eyes. "Enough of my professional opinion. As you gringos say, 'It's all bullshit anyway.' It's time we pull this rock out of the floor."

Both Flores and Jack laughed while Pax smiled uneasily, not understanding their humor.

*   *   *

Flores and Jack sat in the shade at the pyramid's entrance, waiting for Pax to return with two pry-bars. Both men were silent in their anticipation. They soon saw Pax, pry-bar on his shoulder, making his way back from the Land Rover. He was not alone. Following behind was another man also carrying a pry-bar. At first Jack thought it might be one of the regular workers who found out they were working today. When there was work available most of the laborers could not afford not to work. As the fellow came closer, Jack could see this was not the case; the man was a stranger.

Flores and Jack both stood as Pax and the stranger arrived at the entrance. Pax spoke first, but Jack could not understand the rapid Spanish. He watched as the young man articulated and gestured toward the stranger. Flores spoke to the man, who then answered back. Jack assumed the man was looking for work. Since Jack arrived at Cobá other men had shown up at the work site asking about employment. Flores routinely turned these men away as he already had a full complement of workers he could, for the most part, trust. At least he knew their faults. A stranger on the work site always had to be watched closely. Besides, just about every one of his regular workers had a brother, uncle, or son ready to work, so there was no reason to bring a total stranger onto the site. As Flores continued to question the stranger, Jack wished they could get on with the work. The increasing heat and humidity were beginning to sap his energies, and the hangover, which he thought had vanished, was making a comeback.

Jack was surprised when Flores turned and said, "He's searching for work. The extra hands could be useful so I hired him for the day."

Smiling, Jack extended his hand to the man and said, "*Buenos días.*"

With an uncertain smile on his face the man shook Jack's hand and nodded his head in acknowledgment of Jack's greeting. He was a small man with a thin frame. His face had sharp features and a peach fuzz mustache above narrow lips. He appeared nervous but glad to have found employment.

Pointing his finger at his own chest, Jack said, "My name is Jack."

The man stared at Jack with a puzzled expression.

"Jack," repeated Jack, still pointing at his chest.

Pax spoke to the stranger in Spanish, and a look of understanding came over the man's face as he nodded his head.

"Jesus," said the stranger as he pointed his finger at his chest.

The four of them walked back to the chamber. Jack was thankful to get out of the sun. The chamber was stuffy but at least cooler than the exterior temperatures.

Flores immediately started explaining to Pax and Jesus how the slab was to be removed and what each of their responsibilities would be. Jack sat down, his back against the stone wall, and watched Flores lecture. He could not understand the Spanish but was able to decipher many of the very careful instructions by watching the archaeologist's gestures. Jack's concentration was not strong, and his thoughts soon drifted to Josephine.

For a few hours her memory had left him alone. The discovery of the false floor had allowed him to forget about his earlier decision, but a longing was now creeping into his being, a longing that filled his chest and turned his heart to stone. It was a mixture of desire and despair that took on an edge of rage as a vision of his dream came back to him. Gus and Jo wrapped up together, in Jack's own bed, smirks on their faces.

His stone heart dropped to his stomach, leaving him with a hollow queasy feeling. Would his conflicting emotions drive him insane? One moment his heart was cracking at the thought of never having her love again, and the next he was filled with disgust. If only he could know what had happened to his wife. Maybe then it would be easier to work out his emotion. Should he love, hate, or mourn her? The letter to Gus tormented him; it said little but implied much. What was the extent of their affair? Was it even an affair? The letter was ambiguous, leaving too much to his imagination. If only he could know the truth.

Jack was shaken from his thoughts by the sound of Flores' voice. "Jack, are you listening to me?"

He looked up at Flores with a mixture of confusion and embarrassment.

"Are you all right?" asked a concerned Flores.

"Yeah, I'm sorry. I guess I drifted off," answered Jack.

Flores did not comment, but the look on his face said that he understood. He explained to Jack the plan for lifting the slab from the floor. "You and I will work the pry-bars, as we are the heaviest. The two of us should be able to pry the slab from the floor. Once we have it raised, Pax and Jesus will place the wooden blocks under the stone to keep it jacked up. If you and I are unable to lift the slab then Pax can help us work the pry-bars. Jesus will then place the wooden blocks by himself. If the three of us are unable to lift the slab, then we are in trouble since we need one man free to set the blocks. Once we have the stone tilted out of the floor we should be able to muscle it onto its side."

Flores was silent for a moment, then added, "Any questions?"

"Sounds simple enough," replied Jack as he got to his feet.

Jack's spirits rose somewhat as he buried his thoughts of Josephine and focused on the adventure at hand. Flores and Jack inserted the pry-bars into the two holes on the slab's seam while Pax and Jesus stood ready with the wooden blocks. Jack noted for the first time how the placement of the holes allowed for the arc of the pry-bars to follow into the chamber's entrance. If the holes had been placed on one of the three remaining sides of the slab, the close proximity of the chamber's walls would not have allowed enough arc for the pry-bars to lever the slab from the floor.

Both Flores and Jack were at the ready when the archaeologist looked to Jack and said, "On *tres*."

Jack gripped the iron bar as Flores counted, "*Uno, dos, tres!*"

Jack pulled down hard on the bar, but nothing happened, no movement. The bar jerked back from Jack, and he almost lost his grip.

He suspected that Flores had grossly underestimated the weight of the block. They might as well have been trying to pry the Empire State Building from its foundations.

"Put all your weight into it, Jack. Remember this rock has been stuck in the floor for over a thousand years," urged Flores.

Jack pulled again, straining against the iron bar until he had practically lifted himself from the floor. Unexpectedly, the bar inched toward him and a muffled grinding noise rose from the floor. The seal was broken; the stone had risen about an inch. Flores and Jack were both surprised by the slab's sudden movement and lost their momentum. The block dropped back into place with a solid thump.

With renewed vigor they made another attempt. Jack heaved at the bar with his entire weight. The bar came toward him as the slab slowly rose from the floor with a low grinding noise that reverberated off the chamber's stone walls. Through much exertion, both Jack and Flores pushed the ends of the pry-bars down to waist level. By holding their arms straight down with their elbows locked, they were able to balance the tilted slab with their body weight. This allowed them to catch their breath before making the final pull. The lower edge of the slab was not yet high enough to place the wooden blocks. If they were to need Pax's help, it would be in the next few inches, as the higher they lifted the slab the more weight they would be pulling.

Flores nodded at Jack and asked, "Ready?"

Jack nodded and pushed down on the bar, forcing it toward the floor. With every inch of downward movement the weight on the end of the bar increased. They both struggled against the increasing weight until the ends of the pry-bars were about a foot off the floor. Jack was about played out, his arms shaking while beads of sweat stung his eyes. Flores was in nearly the same condition. The bottom edge of the slab was now about an inch above the floor, not quite enough to get the wooden blocks underneath.

"Get your foot onto the bar and stand on it," grunted Flores, "The full weight of our bodies might be enough. We only need a bit more."

Jack did not like the idea of standing on the bar. He had a vision of his foot slipping and the bar shooting up between his legs. It was not the kind of injury he wanted to contemplate, but they were too close to quit now. Carefully, he placed his right foot onto the bar and slowly shifted his weight until he was standing on the bar. Flores went through the same procedure. The ends of the pry-bars were now on the floor and the bottom edge of the slab was approximately four inches above floor level. Pax and Jesus were just able to wedge the wooden blocks into place. Jack and Flores stepped off the bars, and the slab remained tilted out of the floor resting on the wooden blocks. The door was ajar.

Jack stood doubled over, his hands on his knees, trying to catch his breath. Flores was also panting, but immediately grabbed a flashlight and went to the opening they had created in the floor. The archaeologist was down on his knees, his face stuck in the crack, shining the flashlight into the darkness.

"Well, boss, what did we find?" asked Jack in between deep breaths.

Flores replied with an unintelligible grunt, his face still under the slab.

Curious, Jack shuffled over to the slab and peered into the opening. His surprised eyes saw a set of narrow stone steps dropping down into a black hole. "The bastards went subterranean on us!" he exclaimed.

"Yes," replied Flores. "This is very unusual."

Jack noted a cool draft coming up out of the hole. It felt delicious on his perspiring face, like sticking his head in a refrigerator on a hot day.

"I wonder where it goes?" questioned Jack, more to himself than to Flores.

"We will not know until we finish moving this rock," stated Flores as he stood up.

Jack could see the man was ready to go again. He would not have minded a few minutes rest, but Flores was on a roll. The man was doing what he loved best, consumed by what might be a big find. Jack figured Flores's soul must be on fire, something like when Beethoven wrote the Fifth, or Einstein first calculated the theory of relativity.

"You still think the four of us can lift this thing out of the floor?" asked Jack as he watched Flores stare at the stone.

"We will find out," answered the archaeologist.

Flores lined the four of them up along the jacked-up side of the block and instructed them to lift with their knees, not their backs. "All you need now is a hernia," quipped Flores to Jack.

"Thanks," replied Jack as he rolled his eyes.

Flores instructed Pax and Jesus in Spanish and then said to Jack, "On *tres*."

They crouched along the opening, their hands gripping the underside of the slab.

"*Uno, dos, tres!*"

In unison the four men thrust their bodies up into the stone, legs driving and arms pushing. The slab gradually rose from the floor, propelled by straining muscles. Grunting and gasping, faces red, they pushed the stone up onto its side where it was able to stand on its own.

Jack took a step back as a sudden dizzy spell passed over him, and for a moment he thought he might black out. The exertion and heat were taking a toll. He sat down on the edge of the opening, his feet hanging down into the stairwell, enjoying the cool air flowing up from the darkness.

Flores grabbed a plastic water jug and sat beside Jack, while Pax and Jesus sat down against the chamber's wall, both lighting cigarettes. Jack wondered how they could suck smoke into their lungs while he was still gasping for air. Flores gulped water from the jug, then handed it to Jack. The water was warm, but it quenched his dry throat.

"You know, I am almost afraid to go down those steps. I might lose it if we find another rock-filled passage or stone door," stated Jack.

"If we do, you may convince me to break out the dynamite," returned Flores, a crooked smile on his lips.

Hector slugged down another mouthful of water, then stood up. Pax and Jesus started to rise, but Flores said something in Spanish, and the two men slumped back against the wall. Flores gathered two of the four lanterns that were lighting the chamber and gave one to Jack.

"I told them to rest. You and I can make this first exploration on our own. I'll go down first, and you can follow when I call."

Hector started down the steep narrow stairway holding the lantern in front of him. Jack watched from above as Flores' lantern illuminated the darkness below. The stone steps had no more than a six-inch tread with a one foot drop between each step. Jack imagined that if one were to stumble and fall, one might not stop until hitting bottom, wherever that was. The stairwell was approximately two and a half feet wide with a five and a half foot ceiling. Flores had to lean back and tilt his head to the side as he descended in order to avoid hitting his head on the ceiling. The archaeologist slowly dropped out of Jack's sight until only the lantern light filtered up from below, and then even the light faded.

After a few anxious minutes, he heard Flores' voice echoing up from the blackness, instructing Jack to follow. As he gazed down the constricted stairwell, Jack was struck by a distant childhood memory of his older brother locking him in a small closet. He recalled the terror of being trapped in the darkness, the unreasonable fear that had ripped at his psyche until he went into a rage. Though only a small boy, he had managed to kick a hole in the closet door. His father had taken a belt to both his brother and him, but the whipping had been nothing compared to the terror of the dark closet.

Jack controlled his fear and started down the thin steep steps. The stone slab that had hidden the stairwell crossed his mind. Just how stable was the slab? What if it fell back into place? Pax Chi and Jesus would be unable lift the slab by themselves. He tried to push this unpleasant thought from his mind.

After dropping about twenty feet, the stairway ended. The man-made square-cut stone blocks gave way to nature's limestone walls. Jack quickly realized that he had come to some kind of natural cavern. The height of the cave was a little over six feet, the width not more than three feet. Damp with the smell of wet limestone, the cavern was deliciously cool; Jack almost shivered.

He followed a rocky path between the narrow stone walls trying not to think about the surrounding darkness. Declining slightly, the path led him deeper into the subterranean night. Gradually, the height and width of the cavern increased, helping to relieve his feelings of claustrophobia. The walls were now approximately six feet apart, and the ceiling was five to eight feet above his head. Small stalactites hung from the rocky ceiling, the lantern light illuminating the opaque white, icicle-shaped formations. He stopped for a moment to admire a curtain of calcite that had formed along a joint plane in the cavern's ceiling, a mineralized wing iridescent in the fluorescent light. One end of the wing hung down over six feet. The undulating sheet was frozen in time, a billowing wisp of porcelain that Jack thought might shatter at his mere presence.

He made his way through this weird, dank, dark world, until up ahead he saw another light shimmering off a group of white pillars. Jack marveled at the perfectly shaped one to two-foot diameter columns that connected the ceiling to the floor. Clustered close together, the columns filled one side of the cavern. He wondered how the ancients had constructed these shimmering objects until he realized they were not man-made. The columns had formed when stalactites and stalagmites grew together forming pillars that stretched from floor to ceiling.

He could not yet see Hector or his lantern, but the light illuminating the colonnade appeared to emanate from the left side of the cavern. As Jack moved closer, a grotto opened up to his left. It was here where he caught up with Hector. Flores was standing over what appeared to be a large stone table, inspecting its surface. Jack took little notice of the archaeologist; his attention immediately focused on the life-size figure of a man carved into the cavern wall behind Flores. Detailed and with good proportion, the carving was an exceptional work of art. A shiver passed through Jack as he recognized the figure as that of the Bearded Man.

The chiseled head was in profile, with hair down to the shoulders and a bushy beard under a Roman nose. A cape hung off the figure's shoulder, and the right hand held what appeared to be a sword. The sword was brandished above the head as if ready to strike down an aggressor. On both sides of the carving were rows of block-like hieroglyphic text. Jack stood in awed silence, his mouth hanging open.

"Come and see this," said Flores, his eyes still locked on top of the stone table.

Jack walked over to where Flores stood and studied what he had first taken to be a table. Set on a base of limestone blocks, the stone slab was about three feet off the floor. Approximately six feet long by three feet wide with a thickness of six inches, the slab overhung the base by about three inches on all sides.

"Here is your tomb, Jack," stated Flores. "From what I can interpret off the sarcophagus lid, it appears to be the final resting place of the Bearded Man."

Jack gazed down on the top of the slab, which had rows of hieroglyphic figures carved into it. The glyphs were just meaningless scribbles to Jack, but Flores studied them like they held the meaning of life. Across one end of the sarcophagus's lid lay a long piece of rusted metal. At first Jack thought it was a section of iron pipe and wondered how the hell it had gotten down here. The metal was so oxidized that orange rust stains had formed on the stone around where the object lay. Whatever it was, the cavern's moisture had not been kind to it.

Jack moved over to the object to take a closer look when Flores snapped at him, "Do not touch anything!"

He was startled by Flores's sudden stern tone.

"Excuse my abruptness. I do not mean to offend, but this is an undisturbed site. I do not want to lose anything. We must be very careful," explained Flores.

Jack nodded to Hector, indicating he understood, and turned back to the rusting object.

"It's a sword," remarked the Flores, his eyes still studying the glyphs.

Jack could now make out the shape of a double-edged broad sword in the decaying object. He glanced back at the carving on the wall. The rusting sword looked similar to the one held by the figure on the wall. Jack understood that the pre-Colombian Mayans were not supposed to have had highly developed metallurgy skills. He stood in silent awe, not knowing what to think. Apparently, they were the first to enter this place, an ancient burial site, in over a thousand years. But it was even more significant than that, for, according to recorded history and current archaeological theories, the metal sword and the man depicted on the cavern wall should not have been present on the Yucatán Peninsula one thousand years ago.

"Well, we found him," stated Jack as he pointed to the carving on the wall." But where did he come from and how did he get here?"

"How he came here we may never know," replied Flores. "Hopefully, the glyphs on the lid and on the wall will give us something.

From the lid I have already deciphered a birthdate that would be approximately one thousand years ago. The date of death is recorded as occurring two years later. Unless that wall carving is a poor likeness, I think the Bearded Man was much older than two years when he died. Probably the birthdate is actually the date when the fellow first came in contact with the Mayans. You have to be somewhat careful with Mayan dates. According to dates found on Pacal's tomb, the ruler had lived into his late 70s, but a study of the bones found in the tomb indicated he was a much younger man.

"Anyway, the dates on the lid match closely with other Mayan dates I have found in reference to the Bearded Man. I think we can assume he lived among the Mayans for a couple of years approximately one thousand years ago. Knowing when he arrived on the Yucatán could be very important in figuring out how he came here.

"The other part of your question, 'where did he come from?' I think I can answer. Come over here. I want to show you something."

Flores motioned Jack over to the cavern wall immediately behind the tomb. On the floor, beneath the carving of the Bearded Man, was a row of half a dozen earthenware bowls, jugs, and jars. Most of the pottery was decorated with painted scenes depicting Mayan life. Jack was unable to inspect the pottery as Flores was directing his attention to a stone tablet leaning against the cavern wall. Carved into the tablet were rows of straight lines arranged singly and in combinations. It appeared to be some kind of written language, and even Jack's untrained eyes could tell that it was very different from the Mayan Hieroglyphics.

"What is it?" asked Jack.

"I think it maybe a message from our friend over there," replied Flores as he pointed at the tomb.

Jack glanced at the tomb and then back to the tablet, a puzzled expression on his face.

"I think the characters on the tablet are runes that make up an ancient Germanic language that is the basis of today's Scandinavian languages," informed Flores.

"Are you trying to tell me there is a Viking resting in the tomb?" exclaimed an unbelieving Jack.

"I cannot say for certain. I'm not an expert in ancient Germanic languages, but the sword, the facial features, and the dress of the man depicted in the carving all suggest a Nordic origin. The Vikings were at the height of their conquests approximately one thousand years ago. They were competent sailors who terrorized the coastal towns of Europe. It has even been proven that the Vikings crossed the Atlantic to North America."

"I understand basic Scandinavian history," replied Jack. "But it is a long way from Newfoundland to the Yucatán Peninsula, and I don't recall any Viking fairy tales about tropical lands with balmy breezes."

"That is not surprising, as our friend evidently never made it back north to tell any tales," responded Flores.

It was difficult for Jack to accept what the archaeologist was saying so matter-of-factly, but he could not find a more reasonable explanation for what they had discovered.

"Whatever the situation turns out to be, we may finally have enough evidence to nail down the identity of the Bearded Man," said Flores. "We now need to secure this site. Our first job will be to make a photographic record of the site before we disturb anything.

"I am going to be busy here for quite some time. Not only is there the cataloging of the immediate site, but there may be more caverns to explore. It appears that the cave continues on past the columns over there," continued Flores as he pointed toward the mineralized colonnade glimmering in the fluorescent light.

Both men stood in almost reverential silence, taking in what they had found one more time before starting back to work. For a full minute no words were spoken. There was only the tomb, illuminated by their lanterns, surrounded by the cool darkness of the cavern.

"Enough sightseeing. It is time to head back up top and get the photographic equipment in order," stated Flores, ending the moment of silence.

Jack followed Flores back through the cavern and up into the stairwell leading to the pyramid chamber. Flores was at the top of the stairs when he suddenly stopped, his head and shoulders the only portion of his body above the floor level of the chamber. Jack's head bumped into the posterior of the unmoving Flores.

"What's up?" shouted Jack.

The archaeologist did not answer or move. Jack did not like the narrow confines of the stairwell. Frustrated, he swallowed back an urge to shove Flores up the final few steps. Jack forgot about his claustrophobia when he heard a strange voice shouting out orders in the chamber above. Although he could not understand the Spanish, he sensed that things were not right.

Without a word, Flores climbed the final steps into the chamber. Jack could see the archaeologist standing above him framed in the opening of the stairwell. The voice shouted more orders in Spanish, and Jack watched as Flores placed his hands behind his head. He was now certain that things were not right. It crossed his mind that he should run, but to where? Into the dark, seemingly endless, cavern?

Jack's dilemma did not last long as Flores moved out of his view and Jesus appeared holding a pistol. Jesus motioned with the gun, indicating he wanted Jack to climb up into the chamber. The expression on Jesus's face was serious, as was the large gun in his hand. Jack obeyed the directions.

Once in the chamber, he saw both Flores and Pax Chi were lying face down on the stone floor their hands behind their heads, an expression of smoldering anger slowly burned across the face of the archaeologist. Jesus directed some gruff sounding Spanish at Jack. He did not understand the words, but he knew what was expected of him. Jack lay face down on the floor and placed his hands behind his head.

*   *   *

Ortiz lowered the field glasses, then wiped the sweat from his brow with a soggy handkerchief. The sun was straight up, blistering the jungle, the air thick and muggy. It was the time of day sane people spent stretched out in a shade-covered hammock. He hardly noticed the steam bath conditions. The hunter was closing in; the prey too close at hand for him to be bothered by the heat and humidity. Voices coming over the wireless informed him that his men were almost in position. Once the site was surrounded they would move in. It was difficult to wait, but he wanted to make sure that Phillips did not escape. He could not afford another screw up.

Ortiz and his agents had spent the last week chasing ghosts. With all of his men and resources, the Inspector had been unable to find a trace of the two gringos who had vanished in Mérida. The most maddening thing was that the big bastard had stolen his badge and then a police car. Both the badge and the car were still missing. Chances of finding the gringos appeared grim until yesterday morning when an agent in Campeche came up with a break.

The agent had found a hotel clerk who recognized Phillips. The old man told an interesting story about two gringos who had spent the night in his run-down establishment. A big man had walked in looking for a room, carrying an unconscious man over his shoulder. The clerk was able to identify the unconscious man as Phillips. In broken and slurred Spanish the big man had explained to the clerk that his friend had enjoyed too much tequila. The clerk did not find this unusual as he had seen many a drunken *tourista* passed out on a Campeche sidewalk puking up stone crab. The next morning the big gringo was in and out of the hotel, but the clerk did not see Phillips again until late that afternoon when he left the hotel alone. Sometime later that evening the big gringo showed up and checked out of the hotel.

Ortiz and a dozen agents were in Campeche by mid-afternoon, and by that evening they had found a cab driver named Fernando Gonzales. Gonzales identified Phillips as a strange gringo he had driven to Cobá. According to the cabby, Phillips was alone and in a hurry to leave Campeche.

Ortiz was practically giddy with this new information. He now had a good idea of what had transpired since Mérida and a strong lead as to where Phillips was hiding. It appeared that Phillips might have been held captive by the big gringo, whom he had somehow managed to escape. The big gringo had brought Phillips to the hotel unconscious; Phillips was not seen again until late the following afternoon when he left the hotel alone, and then hired a taxi to take him to Cobá. Ortiz thought it was strange that Phillips would head for Cobá. The man knew Wise was wanted by the *Federales*. What could he hope to find at Cobá? Then Ortiz realized that there was nowhere else for the man to go. He was still certain that Phillips was an innocent who had no idea of what was happening around him. It made sense that he would go to the one place he had a friend, even if that friend was no longer there.

No trace of the big gringo had been found; the man had vanished again. This did not surprise Ortiz. He had guessed this man was a professional and did not expect to see him again.

Ortiz and his agents left Campeche early in the morning headed for Cobá. Before leaving, he contacted one of his agents in Tulum and ordered him to Cobá. The agent was to see about finding employment as a laborer at the ruin site. If he did get hired, he was to bide his time until backup help arrived. He was not to apprehend the suspect unless an easy opportunity presented itself or Phillips attempted to leave Cobá. If the agent did not get hired—the more likely scenario—he was to reconnoiter the situation at the ruin site and hopefully identify Phillips.

When Ortiz and his agents arrived at Cobá, there was no sign of the agent from Tulum. The base camp was unoccupied except for an old woman who claimed to be the camp cook. She said a man had come looking for work this morning, and she had sent him to see Señor Flores. The woman was somewhat suspicious, but with a little persuasion she informed Ortiz how to find the pyramid.

Ortiz was feeling confident that the situation was almost under control. They had found the Land Rover at the end of the jungle track and the pyramid soon after. He had not yet seen his quarry, but they had to be inside the pyramid.

Reaching into his pocket, the Inspector pulled out a half-used roll of antacid tablets. He started to pull off a tablet but had second thoughts and tossed the roll into the brush. He had to stop living on the things; they were turning his shit a funny color.

"Why should I worry? The situation is under control. . .well, almost," thought Ortiz as he glanced back at the two thugs behind him. They were two of Reyes' men who had shown up this morning. Ortiz had suspected it for some time but was now sure that his agent in Tulum was on Reyes' payroll. The fat one he could not remember having ever met, but the dark one he had met once before. It was a very brief meeting about a year ago on Reyes' estate.

The dark one. Ortiz wondered why this was his impression of the man. He did have jet black hair, but his complexion was lighter than most Mexicans. Ortiz decided it was the man's eyes. He had never seen darker eyes. The dark one had a handsome face, but the smooth skin below his chin was marred by a line of raised pink scar tissue that told of an extremely close call.

Ortiz did not like the presence of Reyes' goons. He would let them observe, but if they got in his way, he would put the bastards in their place. After all, he was an officer of the government, not a gangster.

Out of the corner of his eye, the Inspector noted movement in front of the pyramid. He raised the field glasses to his eyes in time to see the figure of a man ambling into the entrance of the pyramid. Ortiz flushed with anger as he wondered which of his men was making a grandstand play. His anger quickly shifted to disbelief when he realized it was not one of his men, but someone else, someone he thought he recognized. He had only seen the man once before, and only for a brief moment; so he could not be sure. But a certain feeling in the pit of his stomach was starting to pump the adrenalin. Trying to sound calm he began sending orders over the wireless.

*   *   *

Jack lay face down on the stone floor, his hands behind his head, his chin resting on the stone. His neck was cramped and the grit on the floor ground into his chin. He had tried to take the pressure off of his chin by resting his head on his left cheek, but Jesus had grabbed him by the hair and forced Jack's head to rest on his chin. Unable to understand the Spanish, he had no idea what was happening. Jesus had the gun, so for now there was nothing to do but wait.

Out of the corner of his eye, Jack could see Flores. The archaeologist lay alongside Jack, his face glowering in silent indignation. He sensed the man's emotions were boiling. The situation had changed quickly for the archaeologist. Hector had gone from a major archaeological find to being held hostage. Jack noted that his own emotions were relatively calm, with none of the unbridled fear he had experienced on the Mérida sidewalk. Was he becoming an old hand at this? Maybe he just did not care anymore.

Jack estimated they had been lying on the floor for about twenty minutes, though it felt longer. Their faces were pointed to the back wall of the chamber, the wall opposite the entry. Jesus was behind them, out of their vision. Jack's curiosity finally overcame his fears of a boot to the face; he cocked his head and glanced over his shoulder. Their captor, still holding the gun, was gazing down the passageway. Jack turned his head back to the stone wall.

The minutes stretched on until Jack became aware of a voice echoing down the passage. It was a male voice speaking Spanish. Jack cursed himself again for not learning the language. He glanced at Flores, hoping to interpret some kind of meaning of what was being said from the archaeologist's expression. The smoldering look remained unchanged. The voice became clearer. Whoever it was had entered the chamber. It occurred to Jack that the voice was familiar, but he could not connect the voice with a face. Again his curiosity overruled his fear as he turned his head around to see to whom the voice belonged. He was stunned by what he saw. His fear forgotten, his hands came down from behind his head and rested on the floor. It was the stranger who had abducted him from the Mérida police station, the man who called himself Travis.

The stranger was dressed for comfort in the jungle: lightweight hiking boots, khaki pants, and a loose-fitting long-sleeved cotton shirt. A blue baseball cap covered his dark hair. To the pocket of his shirt was pinned the badge of Inspector Ortiz. Travis appeared to be giving orders to a wary Jesus, who was looking closely at Travis's badge. Glancing back at his prisoners, Jesus saw Jack staring back at him. He started to shout a reprimand when a large fist slammed into his left temple. The pistol dropped harmlessly from the little man's hand as his eyes rolled back in his head and his body crumpled to the floor.

Jack lay frozen, staring back at Travis, not knowing what to do or say. He was amazed at the big man's strength and quickness. With one blow he had reduced their captor to a pile of immobile flesh. He watched as Travis picked Jesus's gun up off the floor.

"Hello, Jack," greeted Travis. "It's good to see you again. You left Campeche without saying goodbye."

"Sorry, but I was kind of in a hurry," answered Jack as he started to come out of his shock. Jack was tentative, unsure of what to make of the stranger's reappearance. When he left Campeche, Jack had thought of it as an escape. Travis was not to be trusted; the man had stolen Peters' drug money. Jack had run from this man, and Travis had pursued him. The hunter and the prey, but the hunter had just eliminated their captor.

"Are you going to introduce me to your friend, Jack?" asked Flores, who was now up on his knees staring in disbelief at Travis.

"Hector Flores, meet Travis Horn, the mysterious stranger who kidnaped me and took me to Campeche, the one who shot me to the moon then raped my mind. I'm not sure you would call him my friend," replied Jack.

"Jack, you misread my intentions," said Travis. "Is this the thanks I get for saving your life a second time? Excuse Jack's rudeness, Dr. Flores. I am pleased to meet you."

"And I'm pleased to meet you, I think," returned Flores. The archaeologist was unsure of what to think of Travis, but at least the man was not pointing a gun at him.

"Now that the introductions are over, will one of you tell me what is going on here?" asked a perplexed Jack.

"Actually, we don't have much time to chat," said Travis. "Inspector Ortiz and about a dozen Judicial police agents are surrounding us right now. It seems this little fellow is with the Judicial Police." Travis pointed at the unconscious man. "He apparently was holding you until Ortiz and his men arrived."

Jack looked at Flores for confirmation of the stranger's story.

"I do not know about Inspector Ortiz, but the little bastard had placed us under arrest," said Flores. "When Travis walked in, he announced himself as a federal agent. He congratulated Jesus on apprehending us, then informed him that Inspector Ortiz wanted to see him outside. You saw the rest."

"We can discuss this later," stated Travis. "Ortiz and his agents could close in on us at any moment. If you're coming with me, you're leaving now. Either of you have any experience with a handgun?"

Jack shook his head, but Flores replied, "I have done some target shooting, and I used to hunt wild pigs when I was younger, but I've never shot a man."

"Same idea, except now the pigs will be shooting back," said Travis as he handed Jesus's weapon to the archaeologist.

They were all on their feet now, including Pax Chi who had a wide-eyed expression on his face. Flores spoke to the young man, and Pax nodded his head in understanding. Flores, Jack, and Pax followed Travis down the narrow tunnel toward the entrance to the pyramid.

In low tones, Travis informed them about their situation as they moved along. "When I made my way in here, Ortiz and his agents were in the process of securing the area. I don't have much of a plan, but I don't think they'll be expecting us to make a run for it. If we surprise them, we might make it into the jungle where at least we will have a chance. The shortest distance into the bush will be to our immediate right as we leave the pyramid. I will lead out, taking down anyone that gets in our way. The rest of you follow, with Hector in the rear. Hector, if you see anybody, drop 'em."

Jack was incredulous. He could not believe what he was hearing. "This is fucking crazy," he muttered loud enough for all to hear.

"Do you have a better idea, Jack?" replied Travis coolly.

Jack was not sure if Travis was being sarcastic or if he actually expected Jack to have a better idea.

They were now close enough to the entrance to get a good view outside. Travis motioned for the others to wait. Keeping close to the wall, Travis crept up to the entrance where he could get the best possible view of the outside without exposing himself to whoever was out there. After scanning the area he moved back to the others with a grim expression on his face.

"It doesn't look good out there. I can make out at least three different men in position along the edge of the clearing. They could make their move at any moment. If you have any second thoughts about going with me, this is your last chance to change your mind."

Jack wanted to sit down; his legs were jelly and he suddenly felt faint. The full impact of the situation was now crystal clear. There were men outside with guns, men who would shoot to kill, and this crazy bastard wanted to play John Wayne. Jack wished he could think of a way out, but all he wanted to do was puke.

*   *   *

A feeling of pride, mixed with anticipation, swelled within Ortiz as he watched his men secure the area around the pyramid. With machine-like efficiency they had come around from the rear of the pyramid while the men in front held cover in case any of the suspects tried to escape. Two men armed with machine pistols were now in place, one on each side of the pyramid entrance. The chance of escape had been eliminated.

One of the men positioned near the entrance shouted out orders, first in Spanish, then in English, for anyone inside to come out with their hands on top of their heads. The seconds passed without a reply; the order was repeated. Finally, Ortiz gave the signal to use the tear gas. One of the agents crept up to the entrance and tossed a spewing canister into the dark passage. The minutes passed with the white gas pouring out of the entrance, but there was no sign of the suspects.

Ortiz was feeling uneasy; something was not right. The tear gas should have flushed them out. He reached into his pocket for his antacid tablets, forgetting he had tossed them. He thought about rummaging through the brush in hopes of finding the tablets but realized he would look foolish.

Two of the men at the entrance donned gas masks and cautiously entered the pyramid. Ortiz left his post in the trees and started making his way across the clearing. Something had gone wrong, but what? The feelings of pride and anticipation were quickly replaced by confusion and anger. By the time he had made it to the entrance, the men with the gas masks were returning from their interior inspection. They reported that the interior of the pyramid was empty.

Ortiz's body shook with anger. How could they have escaped? His own eyes had witnessed the big man entering the pyramid. He grabbed a gas mask and flashlight from one of the agents and entered the pyramid for his own inspection. He had to see for himself. He made his way down the narrow passage. Some of the tear gas managed to get through the mask, burning his nostrils and stinging his eyes. A tear tickled his skin as it slowly rolled down his cheek, but because of the mask he could not wipe it away. The Inspector was soon standing in the same spot Hector Flores had stood the day before, with feelings not much different from those experienced by the archaeologist. The chamber was empty, four stone walls, a ceiling, and a floor. Where the hell did they go?

CHAPTER 28

They stood before the tomb of the Bearded Man: Jack, Flores, Pax, Travis, and a wobbly Jesus. The lantern light bounced off the grotto's limestone walls illuminating the sarcophagus and the wall carving. Jack could see the amazement in Travis's eyes.

"This is incredible!" exclaimed Travis.

"Yes, it is, but I fear what will happen if the idiots up above get their hands on it. Much could be lost," stated a bitter Flores.

"I wouldn't bet on it," said Jack. "Look how long it took trained archaeologists to discover the false floor in the Temple of the Inscriptions."

"This is true, but they will not accept the fact that we just vanished. They will inspect the chamber over and over until they find our escape route," replied Flores.

"Not necessarily," opined Travis. "I'm not sure Ortiz or any of his men actually saw you enter the pyramid; he probably assumed it was where you were. Once he finds an empty chamber he may start to question himself. I wouldn't be surprised if he already has his men frantically searching the jungle." Travis thought a moment, then added, "The only problem is, there's a good chance they saw me enter the pyramid. At the very least, they are wondering how I disappeared."

"Whatever the situation, unless they brought along a couple of stout pry-bars they will not be lifting the block any time soon," stated Jack.

Of course, if they could not find another way out of this hole Jack would be praying for Ortiz and his men to lift the block from the floor. Jack was surprised that he had even conceived of this method of escape. The concept had seemed sound enough when faced with Ortiz's agents and their automatic weapons. Jack's plan came to him in a last ditch-effort to avoid following Travis into a hail of bullets. He recalled the rush of cool air that had streamed into the chamber when the slab was lifted from the floor. According to the laws of thermodynamics, the cooler cavern air should not have risen into the chamber's warmer air without some other force coming into play. It occurred to Jack that there must be another opening into the cavern and that this opening was somehow forming a draft into the chamber. If there was another opening, this could be their escape route. He had quickly explained his theory to the others. Flores immediately accepted the idea; he had been in other caverns on the Yucatán and many of them had more than one entrance. Travis did not seem so sure; Jack imagined the man would rather face the situation with his guns blazing than run down a hole like a rabbit.

"What are the odds that this cave has more than one entrance?" Travis had quizzed Flores.

"I would say that it almost certainly does have another opening. Jack is correct about the draft. The question is whether the opening will be large enough for us to pass through and be located in a place that we can access. Even if a second entrance exists, finding it could be a whole other problem. The cavern could be a honeycomb of passages, a maze we might not find our way out of."

"Sounds like fun," Travis had replied. "But I guess it's our best option. I figure if we go out the front door, the best case scenario is that two of us make it to the trees. At worst, and probably most likely, we all become jungle mulch."

The decision made, the four of them moved back down the passage and into the chamber. Pry-bars, lanterns, everything in the chamber, including Jesus, was moved down the steps and into the cavern. No trace of their occupation was left behind. Dropping the slab back into place was the final act. This was difficult due to the stone's weight and the small constraints of the stairway. They worried that the slab might not fall directly back into the slot and be left cantilevered out of the chamber floor. They had only one chance at this, for the slab was too heavy to lift from below. If the stone was not set back into the slot, Ortiz and his men would have no trouble re-excavating it from the floor. The slab was lowered the last few feet by Travis and Pax Chi alone, as there was only enough room in the stairwell for the two men. They did not lower the slab as much as guide the falling object into place. In order to keep from being crushed, they were forced to move down the stairs as they lowered the stone into place. The slab landed with a thud as it slipped back into the position it had held for the last thousand years. Literally, their fates were sealed.

Now that Jack was surrounded by the dark dampness of the cavern, he wondered if this had been such a bright idea. He had little time to ponder this question as Travis was starting to organize.

"We have four lanterns, and one already appears to be dimmer than the rest," stated Travis as he pointed to the lantern Jack held.

"How many hours of light will the batteries provide?" he asked Flores.

"Once the light begins to dim they go pretty fast. I doubt Jack's lantern has more than thirty minutes left."

"Turn off your lantern Jack," interrupted Travis.

Jack did as he was told. Flores continued, "I generally get from five to six hours out of each set of batteries. Sometimes less. I put new batteries in all of these lanterns this morning, and they now have about two hours of use; but you can see that Jack's lantern is about done. If the batteries in the other three lanterns are not duds, we can expect three to four hours of light out of each one."

"That means if we burn them one at a time, we have ten to twelve hours of light, assuming no more duds," calculated Travis. "Unless circumstances demand otherwise, we keep only one lantern burning at a time. Señor Flores, you seem to be our cave expert so you can lead the way carrying the 'on' lantern. Jack and Pax follow behind Flores, and I will bring up the rear with our friend here," ordered Travis as he pulled the shirt off of a still groggy Jesus.

Travis ripped the shirt into strips of cloth that he then used to secure Jesus's hands behind his back. "To keep you out of trouble, my friend," said Travis as he bound the man's hands.

"Why bring him with us?" asked Flores as he motioned toward Jesus.

"If we leave him here, he could make enough noise to alert Ortiz to our whereabouts; plus, he may become useful if we make it out of this hole," explained Travis.

Flores nodded his head in understanding.

Jack was not comfortable with the way Travis had assumed command of the situation. Who put him in charge? He wanted to say something but stayed silent partially because he was not sure he wanted to confront Travis, but also because Flores seemed to accept Travis's authority.

The only way out, besides heading back to the pyramid, was through the natural colonnade that filled one side of the grotto. Flores led the party through the mineralized forest. The columns were spaced two to three feet apart, and Jack imagined them to be pillars of ice or the teeth of some giant beast. He could not resist the temptation to touch the milky iridescent surface. The cool wetness of the columns had the texture of a melting ice cube, though not as cold.

They had traveled about a hundred feet when the distance between the pillars began to increase while at the same time the total area of the passage shrank. Soon they had moved out of the mineralized columns, but the walls of the passage were now only four feet apart and the ceiling was so low that everyone except Pax Chi and Jesus had to walk stooped over. Jack was starting to feel squeezed.

Flores brought the group to a halt as he studied the situation. The ceiling was now tilted and ran from the floor to the opposite wall, thus the cavern had a triangular shape. In front of them, the area of the passage continued to shrink, and in another thirty feet they would be crawling on hands and knees in order to pass. Though no one said as much, they all feared they had come to the end. There had been no other possible routes; if this was a dead end they were trapped.

"Why don't you hold here while I check out this passage. I don't like the thought of you guys stacked behind me if I come to a dead end," explained Flores.

Flores went forward, stooped over, until the narrowing confines forced him onto his hands and knees. Travis turned on his lantern as the archeologist disappeared into the darkness.

As they waited for Flores, Jack noted that Jesus appeared to be recovering his senses. His eyes, no longer glazed, were darting back and forth. Travis also noted the change and directed a scowl at his prisoner who lowered his head in resignation.

A few minutes had passed when Flores' voice floated back through the darkness, "Come along. It's tight for about twenty feet then it opens up again."

"'Tight for about twenty feet.' What the hell does that mean?" thought Jack to himself. A feeling of claustrophobia was wrapping around him. He was not sure he could bring himself to crawl into the black hole before him. He swallowed hard, then looked to Pax and said, "you first," as he pointed into the dark passage.

Jack took a deep breath as he watched Pax crawl forward.

"You OK, Jack?" asked Travis.

"I guess. Just feeling a little closed in," replied Jack.

"After all you've been through, how can this shit scare you? Hell, even if we make it out of this hole, I doubt you'll leave Mexico alive," joked Travis.

"Thanks for putting things into perspective," cracked Jack. He took a couple of deep breaths, mumbled, "Oh, fuck it!" and started forward into the narrow fissure.

"I'm going to have to untie our friend so he can crawl through. Make sure Flores has his gun ready," warned Travis.

Jack crawled through the rocky passage on his hands and knees, the lantern handle gripped between his teeth. The distance between the ceiling and the floor soon diminished to the point where he was forced to slither along on his belly and push the lantern in front of him. The rough floor of the passage was damp and slimy, the wetness soaking through his pants and shirt. He concentrated on moving forward, blocking thoughts of the darkness and the surrounding rock that threatened to grab hold and not let go.

Twenty feet seemed to have turned into twenty miles. His elbows and knees were scraped and bruised and, in his haste, he cracked his head on a knob of limestone that projected out of the ceiling. Stinging shooters of pain electrified his scalp. Wild thoughts began to circulate as he massaged the swelling knot forming just above his forehead. He decided that Flores was crazy; the bastard was going to get them all stuck in this fucking hole! Filled with urgent dread he began to hyperventilate. Jack could feel himself slipping; he knew it was no good but could not control the fear that was engulfing him. He wanted to stand up and scream.

Paralyzed with fear, he was about to go over the edge of sanity when he noted a faint light up ahead. Concentrating on the light while controlling his breathing, he forced himself forward; if he could just make it to the light he would be all right. The passage gradually widened to where Jack was back on his hands and knees; then suddenly he came out into an open area where Flores and Pax stood.

Jack stood up panting, beads of sweat on his brow, his clothes soaked and soiled, his head throbbing, but he felt as if he had just stepped out into the sunshine. Flores had not been joking when he said the cavern would open up. Jack found himself in a huge underground cathedral. The walls were now one hundred feet apart, and the ceiling climbed ten, twenty, even thirty feet above the cavern floor. The ceiling was covered with an inverted forest of giant stalactites. Some of these frozen shapes hung down over fifteen feet. On both sides of this subterranean ballroom, Jack could see lesser anterooms, while the far end was lost in darkness.

Jesus was not far behind Jack and was welcomed by the muzzle of Flores' pistol. After Travis arrived, he secured the prisoner and the group moved on. They now had to decide which direction to travel since there was a myriad of smaller passages leading off from the main hall. They decided to keep to the main chamber, but after traveling a couple hundred feet, the cavern began to close back in around them. For the next two hours they tramped through a maze of smaller passages, the directional choices seemed endless. More than once they found themselves backtracking from a dead end or circling back to a place they had passed earlier. To make matters worse, Flores' lantern was noticeably dimmer than it had been moments earlier. They decided to take a break. The archeologist turned off the lantern and they rested in the darkness.

"Your lantern is running out of juice after only two hours. We may have less light than we originally calculated," commented Travis.

"If the other two lanterns have no more power than the first two, we may have less than fours of light left, " added Flores.

Jack did not like the thought of being down here without a light source. They had already passed a couple of vertical shafts in the cavern that would have been easy to wander into in the dark. Also, without light it would be impossible to mark the passing of certain points; they could travel in circles for days. Jack shivered at the thought of spending his final moments in the subterranean darkness.

"I hate to bring this up, but since we started it seems we have dropped further underground," said Jack.

"We have," replied Flores, "but we have not had much of a choice."

Flores asked Pax to turn his lantern on. The light from this lantern illuminated the cavern more brightly than had Flores' lantern. Flores traded his lantern for Pax's, and the group started moving again.

For the next hour they moved through a passage that more or less kept them traveling in a straight line. There were no side passages in this section of the cavern so no time was wasted selecting alternate routes. They were brought to a halt when they came to a vertical shaft that filled the space in front of them. The hole was about forty feet in circumference with shear side walls that plunged into an eternal night. Jack picked up a rock that lay at his feet and tossed it into the abyss. The stone tumbled through the air and disappeared into the void below. They heard the faint echo of the stone smacking off rock and then a splash as the stone landed in an unseen body of water.

"It looks like we just wasted two hours of light," stated Travis.

"Not necessarily. Look over there to the right," said Flores as he pointed to the opposite side of the cavity. On the far side there appeared to be a passage leading away from the vertical shaft.

"I think we can traverse around the right-hand side of the shaft," continued Flores. "We may have to do a little hand over hand climbing, but I think we can make it without too much difficulty. We should at least make an inspection."

It was decided that Flores and Pax would attempt to traverse around the right side of the shaft and then make a reconnaissance of the passage on the opposite side. Jack and Travis watched in silence as Flores and Pax picked their way across the edge of the chasm. The traverse went more easily than expected. There was only one spot, about half way across, that was somewhat tricky. To pass this point, they had to move out onto a small ledge, then pull themselves up a six-foot face to a rocky shelf. It was not that difficult a maneuver, but one slip meant a long fall into the abyss below. Once up on the shelf, it was only a short scramble to the potential passage. The two men disappeared from view as they made their way into the passage.

After a few minutes, Flores reappeared on the opposite side of the shaft and shouted across to the others, "This route appears to be our best chance. It continues on, and better yet, it's ascending toward the surface. What do you think?"

"Well?" said Travis as he turned and looked at Jack.

"What do I know?" said Jack. "I'll go along with whatever you guys think is best, but there is something we should consider. If we go much farther, and don't find an exit, we may not have enough light to find our way back to the pyramid."

"Jack you're a bright guy, but I don't think you are clear on the concept here. If the *Federales* get their hands on you, you're a dead man."

"Point taken. I'm just not used to being on a hit list," quipped Jack.

Travis turned and shouted across the void, "It's your decision, scout."

"I say we keep moving forward," answered Flores.

"We're on our way," returned Travis.

Both men turned on their lanterns to have plenty of light for the traverse. Travis untied Jesus and said something to the man in Spanish.

"What did you tell him?" asked Jack.

"I told him that if he caused any trouble, I'd toss him into the pit," answered Travis.

The three of them made their way around the giant hole, Jack in the lead and Travis in the rear. They came to the six-foot face and Jack edged out onto the small ledge. Fortunately, he had no fear of heights comparable to his fear of small places, for below him was nothing but inky blackness. He wedged his dimly burning lantern between two rocks on the upper shelf then pulled himself up onto the safety of the shelf. He sat on a rock and watched as Jesus started up the face next. Jesus gripped the upper shelf and appeared to be bracing himself for the pull up when he suddenly kicked out behind himself, smashing his foot into Travis's groin. Jack watched in frozen horror as Travis was pushed out, toward oblivion. Dropping the lantern, Travis reached for the foot of his attacker. The lantern spun crazily into the darkness, its light illuminating the stone cliffs as it fell. Travis got hold of Jesus's foot and managed to hold on long enough to pull himself back into the wall, where he was able to get a handhold on the lower ledge. Travis hung by his fingertips, below him the maw beckoned. Jesus immediately began stomping his foot on Travis's left hand. The hand was soon dislodged, leaving Travis dangling by a single handhold. Jack watched in stunned silence, frozen, unable to move as Jesus booted Travis on the face. Blood running from his nose, Travis stubbornly hung on.

"Jack! I would appreciate a hand here!" shouted Travis in between blows to his head.

Travis's words brought Jack out of his paralysis; he had no time to think, only react. From his seated position he kicked out with both feet aiming at Jesus's head. His left foot connected solidly with the side of the man's neck. The force of the kick alone probably was not enough to dislodge the man, but Jesus saw the kick coming out of the corner of his eye. In a reflex action he released his handhold in an attempt to block the kick. This movement, along with the force of the blow, was enough. Jesus was now off balance, his arms waved crazily, and Jack could see a wild look in the man's eyes. The Mexican made a final attempt at saving himself by reaching for Jack's legs, but the attempt was futile. Jesus tumbled backwards into the chasm, his screams echoing off the limestone walls as he fell.

"Hold on!" yelled a frantic Jack as he climbed down to where Travis still clung to the ledge.

He helped Travis up onto the small ledge. They sat on the ledge, their feet dangling over the brink, trying to catch their breath.

"For a while there I thought you were going to let the bastard drop me," remarked Travis in between gasps.

"I would have done something sooner, but I thought you had the situation under control," remarked Jack, a smile on his face.

The world exploded in light as Flores appeared on the shelf above holding his lantern. "Are you all right?" he shouted.

"Two of us are, but thanks to Jack, Jesus took an unscheduled flight," answered Travis.

They moved up to a safer location, away from the sheer sides of the cavity, where they rested and reorganized. Now they were down to one good lantern, and it had already been burning for over three hours. The other two lanterns only had a few minutes of power left in their batteries.

"At most we have two hours of power left in the batteries and maybe less than an hour. We better find our way out of here soon, or we're going to be stumbling around in the dark," said Travis.

"There is another factor we need to consider. It is almost five o'clock. In a couple of hours it will be dark up top. Once the sun goes down, it will be more difficult to find our way out. Without sunlight to lead the way we could pass by possible exits," explained Flores.

"I guess we better get moving then," stated Travis as he got to his feet.

Their march continued through a narrow passage that forced them to travel single file, Flores in the lead, then Pax, Jack, and Travis. The passage had started out ascending toward the surface but soon leveled off. At least the ceiling stayed two to three feet above their heads, which allowed them to walk upright.

As they plodded on through the darkness searching for daylight, Travis spoke to Jack. "I want to thank you for what you did back there. If that bastard had gone at me any longer, I would have met the devil a little sooner than I had planned; at least I wouldn't have had far to go."

"I would like to say I did it to pay you back. After all, you've saved my skin a couple of times. The thing is, all I did was react, and I almost didn't react fast enough. If you had not yelled at me, you might have traded places with Jesus," replied Jack.

Both men were silent for a moment, then Jack added, "I've never taken a man's life before. I'll never forget the look in his eyes as he fell."

"You didn't have much choice. It was either him or me. I'm just glad you chose me," stated Travis.

"If you really want to thank me, tell me who you are and why you've been following me across the Yucatán?" asked Jack.

"I don't think you have a need to know," answered Travis.

"What are you protecting me from? It's your opinion that I probably won't make it out of Mexico alive. Hell, the way it looks we might not even make it out of this damned hole. If I'm going to die, I would at least like to have some idea as to why," returned Jack.

"Who said I'm protecting you?" parried Travis.

Jack was not sure how to answer this. He was silent for a few minutes while he thought the situation over. He then tried a different tack. "You know, we might be able to help each other. I've learned some things since we last met, and I'm certain you know more than you let on."

"You make a good point, but I think you'd be surprised to find out how little I do know," replied Travis.

Jack and Travis were brought to a stop by Flores, who had turned around and was now facing them. The archeologist looked at Travis as he spoke. "I'm afraid I have to agree with Jack, Mr. Horn. I appreciate your efforts in extracting us from our prior predicament, but I think you owe us an explanation, especially since we now are all fugitives of the law."

Flores stood his ground, blocking the passage as if he intended to let no one pass until his questions were answered. Jack was taken aback by the archaeologist's sudden intractability, and he watched with trepidation as Travis stared back at Flores, seeming to size up the man.

"OK, you guys win. I'll tell you what I can, but can we keep moving while I spill my guts?" said Travis, breaking the tension.

Flores nodded his head, then turned and continued walking. Jack was relieved that Travis had acquiesced. For a moment he thought the two men might come to blows over the matter, and he could not imagine his friend Flores coming out the better.

"I work for the U.S. government but not any agency or department you've ever heard of," explained Travis, as he followed behind Jack. "You've heard of those government grants to fund research on such things as the sex habits of the Antarctic swamp rat. Let's just say that some of those funds pay my salary. Don't ask for any more information on my employer. Who I work for doesn't matter anyway; I'm in Mexico on personal business. Sam Peters, alias Steve Potter to you, Jack, was a friend of mine. Sam wasn't a drug smuggler. He was a DEA agent working undercover."

Travis explained how he had received a strange phone call from an old acquaintance. He did not mention Andrew Buck by name but related the conversation he had with the man.

"My friend told me that both he and Sam were part of a highly classified operation that was attempting to uncover a large drug-smuggling enterprise based on the Yucatán Peninsula. The enterprise was acting as a middleman between the Colombian drug cartels and the U.S. markets. Apparently the DEA could not infiltrate this organization, nor could it track down its leaders. Sam was acting as a successful smuggler in an attempt to infiltrate the Mexican operation. After two years they finally thought they were going to get their first big break. Sam had arranged a drug purchase with someone he thought might be connected with the Mexican organization. Something went wrong on the Punta Sam ferry, though I'm not sure what. Apparently, Sam killed two *Federales*, and two of Sam's backups were killed when that fishing boat exploded. One of the men was a close friend of both Sam and me. Sam's superiors back in Washington began to get nervous, especially when Sam stayed out of contact. They began speculating on whether he had turned and even contemplated having Sam terminated."

"You mean kill him?" interrupted Jack.

"Something like that," replied Travis, who then continued with his narrative. "My friend did not like the termination talk. He was not convinced that Sam had turned and began to wonder if Sam had been set up. If it was a set up, then the operation had been compromised from the Washington end. Feeling he could no longer trust anyone inside the operation, he called me to see if I would go to Mexico and bring Peters back before the situation got any further out of control. A couple of hours later I was on a plane to Cancún, and my friend was dead from a heart attack."

Travis went on to tell how he found the Mérida hotel where Peters and the Phillipses were staying but arrived only to find the broken door and Peters' body.

"If I had been twenty minutes earlier, Sam might still be alive," related Travis, a trace of anger evident in his voice. "It was then that I came into possession of the red duffel bag, Jack."

Jack had been reliving the events of that day as he listened to Travis, when it suddenly came back to him. He remembered seeing the red duffel bag in Peters' room when he first discovered the body, but the duffel bag was gone when he entered the room the second time. This memory corroborated Travis's account of that day. Travis could not have killed Peters' for the duffel bag, as Peters was already dead.

"From the hotel, I went directly to the consulate. When I arrived there, Joan Brannon had just gotten off the phone with Jack and was looking for a driver to pick him up. Joan already knew me from a meeting I had with her the day before, where I had represented myself as a DEA agent who was hunting Sam. I volunteered to pick you up, Jack, but when I arrived at the hotel, the police already had you on the sidewalk. I needed to find out who you were. I hadn't gone to the police station with plans of a jailbreak, but when the attempt was made on your life, I didn't have much of a choice. I had just found the body of a good friend with his brains splattered on the floor. I wanted to find who was responsible, and you seemed to be my only lead. You know what happened next. I'm sorry about the drugs, but I had to find out who you were.

"As far as my arrival at Cobá, that was more luck than anything. I had run out of leads. I came here hoping that Señor Flores could shine some light on the situation. I also had a feeling that this is where you had run to, Jack. I spent the morning observing your movements and getting the lay of the land. I was interrupted when Ortiz showed up and was forced to take action."

Jack had listened skeptically to Travis's story, searching for inconsistencies but not finding anything that did not fit with what he already knew. He was surprised to learn that Peters was actually an undercover agent. Jack was somehow more comfortable with this image of the man than that of a ruthless drug smuggler.

"If you came to Mexico in search of your friend, what keeps you here now that you know he is dead?" asked Flores.

"Call me vindictive, but I want to meet the man responsible for Sam's death. Not necessarily the bastard who did the actual killing, though that would be a pleasant diversion, but the traitor who framed Sam. You see this is a war between the U.S. government and the smugglers, a war the government is losing, by the way. As long as there are people who want drugs, there will be people who will be willing to supply them for a price. We may or may not agree with the government's current policy on illegal drugs, but I think we can all agree that there is a war going on. Sam understood this was a war, and he knew what the enemy would do to him if they caught him. But Sam wasn't taken down by the enemy alone. Sam was set up by one of his own people, betrayed by someone he trusted, and this is the man I want to meet. Sam was close; he may have even discovered who was behind the Mexican organization. That is why they took him out. If I can discover what Sam learned, I may be able to use that information to track down the slime who framed him."

Travis's last statement suddenly brought everything into focus for Jack. The fog had lifted, and Jack's worst fears were realized. His wife and best friend were responsible for murdering Peters. They had both the motive and the means. Jack was left with a sick feeling, no longer sure he wanted to leave the cavern.

"I've shared. Now it's your turn, Jack," said Travis.

"I have something to say, but first Hector should tell you what he learned from Gus the day Gus was arrested," said Jack.

Flores told of Gus's short career as a cocaine smuggler and how it led to an association with the DEA, of a mysterious last assignment for the DEA, and how Gus was arrested only to vanish into the Mexican law enforcement bureaucracy. Finally, he told of Gus's reference to Ricardo Reyes.

Travis listened intently to the archeologist and then said, "I was informed by a source within the Drug Enforcement Agency that Peters made one last contact after the ferry incident. The message indicated that Sam was going underground. It also named Ricardo Reyes. I was not able to confirm this information, but if we assume that Gus was one of Sam's contacts, it could explain much of what has transpired. Jack, it may not have been pure luck that you happened to meet up with Sam; it might have been arranged by Gus. What better cover for Sam than traveling with two unsuspecting tourists."

"I don't believe it was luck," agreed Jack. "There is something else to add into this mix. I'm fairly certain my wife and best friend were lovers."

Flores stopped and turned to face the others, stunned by what Jack had said. Jack himself was surprised by his own words and the ease with which they had rolled off his tongue. He explained about the letter he had found in Gus's *naj*. Somehow, talking about it was not as bad as he had imagined.

"You sound pretty certain that Peters was set up by one of his own people," said Jack to Travis. "I think that person may have been Gus. I assume the bad guys would pay very well for this information, enough money that Gus could escape from the DEA and start a new life with Jo. It seems he would have both the motive and the means."

"Hold on, Sherlock," interrupted Travis. "Let's not jump to conclusions. The amount we don't know still outweighs what we do know. Just because your wife and best friend may have performed together in a midnight rodeo doesn't mean they committed murder. I could come up with a hundred different scenarios to explain what has happened."

"I've known Gus a long time, and he may have made some mistakes, but I don't see him stealing a friend's wife or being capable of cold-blooded murder," added Flores.

A week ago Jack would have agreed with Flores. Gus had been Jack's closest friend since his freshmen year at college, but so much had happened over the last few days. He did not know what to believe anymore. Jack suddenly felt very tired.

They started out again in silence, each man ruminating over what had been learned. As they marched on, the one good lantern began to dim. No one commented; they all knew what it meant. The sense of urgency that had descended on the group was slowly replaced by a gloomy realization that they would soon be in the dark.

Jack trudged behind the others until his attention was captured by something on the cavern wall. He stopped to inspect, not really understanding what he was looking at. It was the outline of three small hand prints painted on the stone. It appeared as if someone had placed their hand on the wall and then spray painted over it with a can of black spray paint.

Flores was immediately excited by Jack's find. "Similar hand prints have been found in other caves on the Yucatán," explained the archeologist. "In fact, they have been found in caves and on rock surfaces around the world. Making hand prints seem to be a shared trait of most Stone Age cultures. These prints were made by blowing paint out of the mouth over the hand and onto the stone, thus making a painted outline of the hand. The meaning of the prints is unknown, but they were probably just a simple way for a man to leave his mark, no different from someone carving their initials on a tree or writing graffiti on a bathroom wall. Whatever their original meaning, their meaning to us is that there must be another entrance to the cavern. Mayan artifacts have been found fairly deep in the caverns at Loutune, but I doubt that with only primitive torches the Mayans would have traveled underground as far as we have. The people who made these prints must have entered the cavern from another point."

In spite of the dim lantern light, they moved forward with renewed hope. They heard the distant screech of a bird before they noticed the gradual increase of light. Soon the light around them was stronger than that of the lantern. They followed the light until it exploded above them as they entered a large chamber. The ceiling of the chamber had collapsed sometime during the last few thousand years, opening up the interior to the sunlight above. Just out of reach, the opening in the roof floated above them like an inverted island. The jungle above poured down through the ragged gap, the roots and vines draping down searching for something solid. The floor was littered with rock rubble that at one time formed the ceiling. Oval shaped, the chamber was approximately sixty feet long by thirty feet wide. They could find no other entry into the chamber other than the way they had entered, and the stone walls were too steep to negotiate.

"It looks like were going to have to make like Tarzan if we're going to get out of here," stated Travis.

He climbed a large rock centered under the opening and reached for a tree root that hung down from above. "I might as well go first since I'm heaviest. If this root can hold me, the rest of you should have no problem."

Travis gripped the root and pulled himself up. He hung for a moment, testing the root's strength. The root held, and he began pulling himself hand over hand toward the surface. The rock around the opening did not appear stable, and Jack watched with crossed fingers. Making it to the top, Travis swung himself over the lip of the opening. He sat on the edge of the hole with his legs dangling down.

"Come on up; the weather's great up here," he smiled.

Flores went next. He was a bit slower than Travis, but eventually made it to the top where Travis helped him over the lip. Jack followed Flores and found the climbing more arduous than either Travis or Flores had made it look. He struggled on though; nothing was going to keep him from reaching the surface.

He was halfway up when a portion of the roof gave way and the root jerked down two feet. Jack struggled to maintain his grip as a pumpkin-sized boulder whizzed past his head. The root held, and Jack continued climbing, his heart in his throat.

Busy with his own problems, Jack did not notice that Pax Chi was almost crushed by the falling rock. He had to dive out of the way to avoid being pulverized. As Pax lay on his side and looked back up at Jack, he saw a piece of paper slip from Jack's pocket and spiral down toward him. He picked up the paper from where it landed and saw that it was a photograph. The photo was of two men and a woman; granite peaks fringed with snow filled the background. Pax Chi immediately recognized one of the men as Jack Phillips. The woman and the other man also looked familiar, but he could not remember where he had seen them before. He thought for a moment, trying to remember, and suddenly it came to him. Jack had made it to the surface, so Pax shoved the photo into his shirt pocket and started climbing.

Jack's aching lungs gasped for breath as he watched Pax deftly climb to the surface, making the ascent look easy. Once on top Pax pulled the photo from his pocket and showed it to Flores as he spoke rapidly in

Spanish. Travis moved over for a closer look. Jack did not understand what was being said but moved closer anyway to see if he could figure out what the fuss was about. He recognized the photo and reached in his empty pocket, wondering how it had come into Pax's possession.

"How did you get that?" snapped Jack as he snatched the photograph from Pax's fingers.

"He said it fell from your pocket as you were climbing," said Flores.

"*Gracias,*" replied an embarrassed Jack as he slipped the photo back into his pocket.

"Jack, is the woman in the photograph your wife?" asked Flores.

"Yes," replied Jack.

"Pax says he saw her and Gus at the place where he worked before he came to Cobá," stated Flores.

It took Jack a moment to comprehend the meaning of Flores' words. "Where? . . . where did he see them?" stammered Jack.

"The estate of Ricardo Reyes," answered Flores.

CHAPTER 29

Josephine Phillips lay on her back, empty of emotion, her senses numb. Her eyes were open but not focused on anything in particular, not the thatched roof, not the slowly revolving ceiling fan, and not the mosquito netting draped above the bed. Over the last few days she had experienced a full range of dark emotions: fear, anger, grief, and depression. Her time had been spent waiting for the final moment that would end her misery. The moment had not come, though, and it appeared she was going to have to deal with living for a while longer.

Since that morning in Mérida her life had been a blur, one long nightmarish blur. Jack had only been gone a few minutes when there was a knock at the door and she opened it to be greeted by three men claiming to be Mexican Federal Police. The one who appeared to be in charge, a dark handsome man with a scar on his neck, asked if they could speak with her a moment. Somewhat intimidated and unable to think of an excuse to decline, she invited the officers into the room. Wasting no time, they showed her the morning paper with a photograph of Steve Potter on the front page. According to the paper, Steve was a drug smuggler named Sam Peters who was responsible for the shootings on the Punta Sam ferry. She was stunned when the dark one calmly told her that she and Jack could be considered accomplices to Peters' crimes. She tried to explain how they had only met the man a few days earlier and had no way of knowing about his criminal past. The officers shook their heads in pity as they listened to Jo.

Jo was ready to do just about anything to prove her innocence when the one with the scar told her that if she would help them apprehend Peters it would put both her and Jack in a better light. Scared and confused, Jo asked them to wait for Jack to return before making a decision, but they pressured her, claiming they had to move immediately. If she helped, they would have a chance of taking Peters without bloodshed. Seeming to have no other choice, she agreed to help; after all, Potter or Peters or whatever his name was a murderer.

She had surprised herself with how calm she remained while waiting for her opportunity, making small talk with Peters, acting her part. What happened when she let the so-called lawmen into Peters' room was not what she expected. No attempt was made to take Peters alive. Shocked by the brutality of what she had witnessed, Jo did not question the one with the scar when he ordered her to come with them. It was not until they were leaving the hotel through the rear entrance that it occurred to Josephine that these men might not be police. She told them that she should not leave the hotel until her husband returned, but they insisted that she come with them. Gripped with fear, she tried to go back into the hotel. Her way was blocked, though, by the barrel-chested man wearing the ill-fitting suit. She started to scream, but was silenced by a blow to the back of her head. The world went black.

Her memory of how she arrived at the estate of Ricardo Reyes was fuzzy; she had an almost dreamlike recollection of traveling in the back seat of a car. Her first solid memory found her lying on the concrete slab floor of a small enclosed *palapa*. Except for a couple of blankets, the *palapa* was empty. Jo had not been there long when the man with the scar began his interrogations. The sessions would last for what seemed like hours, an endless stream of questions concerning her, Gus, Jack, and Steve Potter. The man would then leave her alone only to return a couple of hours later and ask the same questions over again. She was unsure how long this went on; it seemed like days, the never-ending questions broken up with short periods of fitful sleep. She began to answer the questions with whatever she thought the man wanted to hear, hoping that the proper answers would end this torture.

Her torment reached a crescendo when Scarface took her from the *palapa* for the first time. The midmorning sun had blinded her unadjusted eyes as he led her down a sparkling beach. Near the water's edge they came upon a crumpled human form that lay unmoving on the hot sand. She recoiled at what she immediately realized was a dead body. Flies buzzed about the bloody intestines that spilled out of the gutted man. A heavy odor filled her nostrils. Her empty stomach was attempting to climb up her throat when she recognized the glazed lifeless eyes and the scraggly beard of Gus Wise.

The dark one took her back to the *palapa* and began the questioning again. Her mental state was now completely shattered, her dignity stripped, and her soul laid bare. This was the final interrogation, and she remembered it as a distorted jumble of questions about Gus. There was nothing left; she had no answers. She lay sobbing on the bare concrete floor wishing for the end.

The sound of a strange voice had brought Jo out of her hysterical state. She had looked up through swollen eyes to see a short, slightly built man staring back at her. There was a concerned expression on the dignified face. After introducing himself as Ricardo Reyes, he began to apologize for the treatment she had received, explaining that he had been away for a few days and what had occurred had not been ordered by him. With Reyes was an attractive woman who looked young enough to be the man's granddaughter. The woman's copper-colored skin and black hair suggested an Indian ancestry, but her high cheek-bones and blue eyes indicated European blood. The mixture had combined to form a beautiful woman. Reyes and the woman helped Jo to her feet and moved her to new quarters. It was another *palapa*, but this one had superior appointments: a double bed with a mosquito net canopy, ceiling fan, a small sink (with hot and cold running water), and even a short chest of drawers. She wondered what she would put in the drawers as her wardrobe was somewhere in Mérida. On top of the dresser were a clean folded towel and an unlit mosquito coil. Compared to her previous lodgings this looked like plush living.

"I must go now as I have some important business to attend to, but I will leave you in the capable hands of Juanita. You're free to enjoy the facilities. If there is anything you desire, ask and I will do my best. Right now, I'm sure you would like a hot shower, a good meal, and some rest," concluded Reyes.

Jo was almost as shocked by the sudden hospitality as she had been by the mistreatment. Unsure of what this change in attitude meant, she had remained silent, hoping that it was not another attempt to screw with her mind.

Juanita led Jo to a communal bathhouse complete with showers and flush toilets. The building appeared to serve a half-dozen nearby *palapas*, including her own. Not having bathed since Mérida, the hot water was a godsend. When Jo had finished toweling off, Juanita handed Jo a pair of shorts, a loose-fitting cotton blouse, and a pair of sandals. The woman walked Jo back to her *palapa* and then excused herself. Jo was unsure of what to think of Juanita. The woman was not exactly cold, but she had not been very friendly either.

Inside her room Jo had found a bowl of soup and some bread and fruit set out on the dresser. She devoured the meal then slept for the next twelve hours.

It was now late afternoon, and she lay on the bed as she had most of the day, staring at the ceiling. The only interruption had been Juanita bringing a midmorning meal. Unable to understand her own situation, Jo contemplated what had happened to her husband and prayed that he had not met the same fate as Gus.

Her despair was interrupted by a knock at the door. She opened the door and was surprised to find a strange woman; she had expected Juanita.

"Hi, I'm Sandy. I thought I'd come introduce myself," said a stunning strawberry blonde with a magnolia accent.

Flustered by the appearance of this beautiful woman, Jo stood holding the door open, unsure of what to say.

"I was hoping we could talk. Hell, it has been a long time since I've seen another gringo," said the woman as she awkwardly tried to fill the silence.

"Excuse me, I'm sorry. I'm very confused. I just don't understand what is happening to me," stammered Jo, her voice quavering, a tear trickling down her cheek.

"You poor thing. I know how it is. I remember when I was first brought here," exclaimed Sandy, her voice full of sympathy.

"Please, come in," said Josephine as she wiped the tear from her cheek with the back of her hand. They sat next to each other on the edge of the bed.

"I guess you don't realize why you're here yet?" quizzed Sandy.

Jo slowly shook her head in reply.

"They left me confused for a couple of weeks," continued Sandy. "I thought I had been kidnaped for ransom or something. It didn't make sense, though. Neither my family nor my husband's have the kind of money to make kidnaping me worthwhile. I thought they had me confused with someone else, sure they would kill me once they found out I was no good to them. I was wrong, though; they had wanted me, or I should say Ricardo wanted me, and now Ricardo also wants you."

"What do you mean Ricardo wants me?" asked a confused Jo.

"He wants you to be one of his women," replied Sandy as she stared down at the floor.

"Are you telling me that I've been selected to be one of this man's concubines?" sputtered Jo in disbelief.

"I'm sorry. I know how hard this is. I went through it myself, but believe me, you're better off knowing what you're in for from the start. I spent my first two weeks here lost, not understanding what they wanted from me. For a while I tried to deny what was happening, then I tried to fight it. I wasn't going to give in. If I couldn't escape, I decided I would let them kill me. It was all just a fantasy; escape is impossible. This place is surrounded by miles of jungle, and the only road into here is heavily guarded. After a while, I realized that I didn't have the guts to do anything that would get me killed. I accepted my fate."

"So you became one of his women." stated Jo, the distaste evident in her voice.

"I know this sounds terrible, but it's not like he rapes you. He takes his time. I was here for two months before I shared his bed for the first time. He won't force himself on you physically; it's more like brainwashing. He treated me nice. He was the only one here who seemed to care about me. I soon found myself wanting to be with him. It's not like love, but I do like feeling needed."

Jo listened in shocked silence, remembering how grateful she had felt the day before when Reyes had rescued her from her prison. She now felt sickened by her gratefulness. His plan was already being implemented; the brainwashing had started. Some things were starting to come into focus.

"So, did Ricardo send you here to get an idea of how best to go about breaking me in?" asked Jo directly.

"Oh, no!" exclaimed Sandy. "I wouldn't do that. This conversation is just between us. I need someone to confide in as much as you probably do. I've been here for almost a year now, and in all that time there hasn't been anyone I could talk with about how I feel."

Tears were welling up in Sandy's eyes as she spoke. "The Mexican girls are nice enough, but they only know a few words of English, and my Spanish still isn't very good. Besides, most of them seem honored to be here. I was just hoping we could talk, maybe be friends."

The tears were now streaming down the woman's velvety cheeks. Jo felt a pang of guilt over her last comment. This girl was not here by choice. Jo wanted to console Sandy, but her own emptiness prevented her from speaking. She did manage to grip the girl's hand. She studied Sandy as the girl wiped back her tears. Originally, Jo thought the young woman was in her late twenties but was beginning to suspect she was much younger.

"If you don't mind my asking, how old are you?" asked Jo.

"I'll be twenty-two next month."

"Practically a kid," thought Josephine, a very beautiful kid.

"I really would like to be able to go home. I'd leave in a flash if I thought I could get out of here with my life. I admit that in a way I'm very fond of Ricardo; it would be hard for me to hurt him, but I also have not forgotten what he has done to me," explained Sandy.

Jo sensed the girl needed to unload something, so she held this stranger's hand and listened to her story.

"My husband and I came down here on our honeymoon last year. We had already been married for six months, but we had waited until Jeff was discharged from the navy to take this trip. It was going to be a month spent lounging around the tropics: eating, sleeping, and making love. The first two weeks were fabulous. We had a grass shack right on the beach. It was like we were the last two people on earth and we were living in paradise. Our third week, we decided to rent a car and travel inland; Jeff wanted to visit some of the ruin sites. On our way to Cobá the car broke down in the middle of nowhere. We hadn't been there long when a passing car stopped. It was a big fancy car, and when the rear window lowered it was Ricardo on the other side. He told us he would go to Fellipe Carillo Puerto and send a tow truck for us. We were relieved to have found help so quickly.

"About twenty minutes passed when two police cars pulled up. There were two officers in each car, and they all got out. One of the officers asked to see our travel papers, which we presented to him. We tried to explain our situation, but he did not seem to understand English. He kept saying 'cocaine, marijuana' and pointing at us like we were some kind of criminals. Jeff figured they were looking for a payoff and offered the officer some cash, but the man laughed. They started to search our car, going through our things. One of them held up a bag of white powder he claimed to have found in one of our bags. It wasn't ours, though. Neither Jeff nor I have ever been into drugs. When they put us in handcuffs I started to lose it. I've never been so scared in my life. Jeff stayed calm, though. He told me not to worry; we hadn't done anything wrong. But when they took me to one car and Jeff to another, he started to get angry. He asked them to put us in the same car, but they only laughed at him. He tried to come to me, but one of the men hit him on the back of the head. Jeff fell to his knees. He had this funny confused look on his face that I will never forget. They picked him up and shoved him into the rear seat of the police car. It was the last time I ever saw him."

Sandy was silent a moment, as if the words had become too painful to speak. She took a deep breath and then concluded, "They put me in the other car and brought me here, and I've been here ever since." She paused. "Listen to me ramble. You don't need to hear all of my problems; you have enough of your own," said Sandy as she wiped back the tears dribbling down her cheeks.

"Oh, I wouldn't say that," replied Jo. "Misery loves company."

Jo was deeply moved by this young woman's tragedy. She found it cathartic to listen to someone else's problems, especially when they were similar to her own. Jo was also starting to understand what was happening.

"Did you ever learn what became of your husband?" asked Jo.

"I had been here a month when Ramon gave me a newspaper clipping. I'm sure you've met Ramon, dark and handsome with a scar under his chin?"

"I didn't know his name, but I'm acquainted with the bastard," interjected Jo.

"'Bastard' is too nice of a word for him," added Sandy. "Anyway, the clipping reported a shootout between two car thieves and the *Federales*. Both men were killed, but a car was recovered. The car was the one Jeff and I had rented. The article stated that the *Federales* suspected the thieves had murdered Jeff and me in order to steal the car. It also stated that they had little hope of ever recovering our bodies. Until I read that article, I had hoped that Jeff would somehow escape and then come rescue me, but now I knew that Jeff was dead, and as far as the rest of the world was concerned, so was I."

Jo felt a sense of loss as she wondered if Jack had met a fate similar to Sandy's Jeff. For the moment she did not want to contemplate Jack's fate. Afraid of being overwhelmed by her emotions, she moved the conversation in another direction.

"Exactly how many women are in Ricardo's personal harem?"

"Four Mexican girls, plus me," answered Sandy.

"And I make six. Almost a different woman for every night of the week," added Jo.

"Actually, he does have a woman for every night. There's Juanita his personal maid. She has a room in the main house, and I'm sure he sleeps with her."

They continued talking for the next hour, mostly light stuff. Jo learned that Sandy grew up in a small town near Savannah, Georgia. She was a southern belle who had married her high school sweetheart, and if her life had worked out the way she had planned she'd be home in Georgia making babies. Jo sensed Sandy was interested in hearing how she came to be here, but Jo was not ready to share her experience, and Sandy did not push.

It was early evening when Sandy finally left the *palapa*, leaving Jo alone with her thoughts. The conversation with the young woman had been painful, but it did help to explain much of what had happened. Jo lowered the mosquito netting and laid down on the bed. The evening darkness slowly descended on the room. She had much to think about.

CHAPTER 30

It was late afternoon when Carlton first arrived at his office. He had slept until noon and would probably still be in bed except for the paperwork he had to destroy. Upon the termination of Carlton's investigation, the State Department ordered Carlton to destroy all files and written material pertaining to his investigation of Operation Raven. Carlton, however, had secreted away copies of some of the material. If it became known that he had ignored orders, he could expect more than a slap on the wrist, more likely an extended stay in a federal penitentiary. And it would not be one with tennis courts and swimming pools.

He entered the office kicking his way past an empty doughnut box and sat down at his desk. Unmoving, he stared at the wall trying to organize his thoughts through a screaming hangover. After his meeting with the Senator he had gone home and polished off a third of a bottle of Kentucky bourbon. Last night the whiskey had tasted good. It had been his first drink of hard stuff in a week. He drank while watching the second half of a Monday night football game. The Redskins were up by ten points going into the fourth quarter, when Steve Young threw two touchdown passes to steal the game away from the 'Skins. Carlton was feeling old; he wondered if Young was ever going to get old? After the game he started watching an old Jimmy Stewart movie, the one about the invisible rabbit. Sometime during the movie he fell asleep, and his next conscious moment was waking up in bed fully clothed with a queasy stomach and a pounding headache.

Sitting at his desk his head still pounded and his whole body hurt. It was as if every cell in his body was screaming, "no more whiskey!" or maybe they were screaming, "more Whiskey!" It was hard to tell. Carlton wondered if it was time he got out of this business. Hell, technically he was already out of it. His job was a fabrication with no meaning; no one even cared if he showed up at the office. The only reason he had held on this long was that in two years he would be able to collect full retirement benefits. If he stayed on, though, would he live long enough to collect any of those benefits?

He lit a cigarette then unlocked his bottom desk drawer. The smoke tasted like shit in his sour mouth, but he kept on puffing as he pulled files from the drawer. He went through the papers, occasionally reading bits and pieces of the documents. Coming across the file on Ricardo Reyes, he skimmed over a page of basic biographical data—birthplace, age, accomplishments, et cetera—when something under the heading of education caught his eye. It stated that Reyes, a business major, had graduated from the University of Southern California in 1962. USC 1962, Carlton thought. He had seen that school and date somewhere else, but where? He could not get past the fuzz in his brain, his mind still thick from last night's whiskey. Carlton had read Reyes' file more than once with a clear head, and "USC 1962," had not meant a thing to him, so why now? The school and date looped through his mind searching for a connection to an earlier memory, stuck in a revolving door with no exit: USC 1962, USC 1962, USC 1962 . . . In frustration he slammed the file shut and stacked it on top of the others piled on his desk. Why was he torturing himself? It was over; he had to let go.

He quickly finished cleaning out his bottom drawer files, then searched the other drawers to make sure they contained nothing of importance. Collecting all the paperwork into his arms, he headed to the shredding room. The paper was turned into confetti and fell into a plastic container. At the end of each day the container was taken to the basement and its contents dumped into an incinerator.

Carlton checked his watch and saw that it was a quarter after four. He decided he had been at the office long enough for one day. He also decided he could use a drink to take the edge off his hangover.

*   *   *

The painful effects of his hangover faded as one drink turned into four. Carlton sat in a booth at one of his favorite drinking establishments. The place was a hole in the wall. A wooden bar stretched along the length of one wall, worn metal bar stools in front and a mirrored wall behind. Along the opposite wall were two small booths. Two nautical prints that hung on the wall above the booths were the only decorations. The interior of the place had not changed since the Thirties. This was a bar for the serious drinker who did not want frills, just stiff drinks and cheap prices. It was one of the two reasons Carlton was a regular patron, the second reason being that he did not have to worry about running into anyone he knew professionally here. This was an old man's bar; most of the customers were retired and living on fixed incomes. The place was sort of a social club for them. He knew most of the regulars as the bar represented 90 percent of his social life over the past two years. Usually he sat at the bar where they bullshitted about football, baseball, or whatever other sport was in season. Today, however, he sat alone smoking Camels and drinking highballs.

Since Elizabeth's death Carlton had lived with almost constant depression, but some days were worse than others. Tonight was one of those times when the automatic in his shoulder holster weighed heavily on him. Prior to the Raven investigation he had gotten in the habit of keeping his gun locked up at the office, fearing what he might do with it during one of his binges. When he stopped drinking the hard stuff, he started wearing the gun again. It seemed prudent since the case did involve one violent death and the attempted assassination of a United States Senator. Now he wished the gun were back in his office.

Elizabeth haunted his thoughts tonight, the memory of her death tormenting him. He was punishing himself by replaying the events, as if reliving the hell of that night might remove the guilt. He carried the guilt around like a cross. In his mind's eye he could still see her as she looked that night before they left for the party. It was an early summer evening, and she wore a peach-colored dress that accentuated her figure, which was good for a woman of forty-eight. Hell, she had a figure that a woman of any age would covet. Her brown hair fell down to her shoulders, accented by a few streaks of gray (which she refused to color). Her face had also held up well; the laugh lines and crow's feet were starting to form but they only seemed to complement the sparkle in her eyes. Elizabeth's eyes had always been magical to Carlton. No matter how down he might be, gazing into her eyes would always raise his spirits.

The last few weeks before her death he had talked about leaving the fieldwork behind. With the end of the cold war the Agency was increasingly shifting its emphasis from classic espionage aimed at the Russians to a new role in the war against drugs. Carlton did not feel comfortable with the agency's new direction, and this led to a dampening of his appetite for fieldwork. He was offered a promotion to a new position that would have been based in Washington with normal hours and little travel. Elizabeth was looking forward to having him around more, and he was starting to like the idea himself. He had even managed to remain monogamous over the past year. They were as close as they had ever been, but their happiness was about to be shattered.

They were traveling down the expressway on their way to the dinner party when a burgundy-colored Cadillac pulled up alongside them. Out of the corner of his eye, Carlton noticed the rear passenger window being lowered and then saw the muzzle of the pistol. Reacting immediately he slammed on the brakes, sending the Buick into a sideways skid. He saw a flash from the pistol's muzzle as his driver's side window exploded in a spray of glass. The Cadillac sped away as he tried to correct the skid and keep the Buick from rolling. Somehow, he managed to get the car under control without running into anyone else.

Feeling lucky to have escaped a sniper's bullet, he looked across at Elizabeth to see that her throat had been ripped from her neck. Blood poured from the wound down onto her peach-colored dress. She clutched at her throat as her mouth formed a scream, but no sound came. In this whole macabre scene, what had burned deepest into his memory was the shocked look in her eyes. The sparkle had been replaced by a look of horror.

He ripped off his shirt and wrapped the cloth around the wound in an attempt to stem the bleeding. With her head in his lap he sped off for the hospital. He drove wildly through the streets, her hand gripping his thigh. Elizabeth's grip was strong at first, and he encouraged her to hang on. His encouragements turned to pleading, but as he got closer to the hospital her grip weakened until there was just the dead weight of her hand on his thigh. Tears flooded down his face as he pulled up to the emergency entrance. He looked down at her head in his lap. Her eyes were blank, like two dark marbles. The sparkle was gone. Sometimes he would awaken at night, his body shaking, and he could feel her grip on his thigh and her warm blood in his lap.

Carlton came out of his reverie, his heart pounding, his shaking hands holding an empty tumbler that had contained his fifth drink of the evening. His guilt consumed him. He felt as responsible for her death as if he had pulled the trigger himself. The bullet that had killed her had been meant for him. Weeks earlier he had uncovered evidence that the KGB was involved in the Mexican drug trade on a massive scale. It appeared that the Russian intelligence organization was making a nice profit running drugs into the United States. Carlton's discovery had come at the same time U.S.-Russian relations were at a historic juncture: The Cold War was ending, but with the breakup of the Soviet Union the Russian government was on unstable ground. The State Department did not want the Russians embarrassed at such a critical time; too much was on the line politically to threaten it all with rumors of a KGB-controlled drug trade. Carlton disagreed; he wanted to dig deeper. Pressure was brought to bear on him; the administration at that time wanted him silenced. Somehow the KGB found out what Carlton had discovered and solved the problem in their own way. They had missed Carlton, but in taking out his wife they destroyed his will to fight. The U.S. government ignored the KGB hit for fear of harming relations with the Russian government. Carlton was moved out of the CIA and into a phony State Department job, a place to hide him while letting him finish out his career.

Carlton was about to get up and order another drink when a young man entering the bar caught his attention. He looked to be more a boy than a man, probably not more than twenty-one years old. The boy appeared to be of Latin descent with clean cut good looks, his dark hair cut short. He had the kind of face that only needed to see a razor once a week. Dressed like most young people of the day, he wore expensive high-top sneakers, jeans, and a baggy Washington Redskins football jacket.

Carlton's intuition immediately went on alert. Something about the kid was odd. This was an old man's bar, so what could interest the kid in this place? Maybe his grandfather hung out here and the kid was looking for him to bring the old drunk home for dinner. Possible, but not likely, thought Carlton.

Standing halfway between the bar and the door, the kid scanned the half-dozen patrons lined up at the bar as if he were looking for someone in particular. The old men gazed back over their shoulders through red-rimmed eyes as if they were waiting for the kid to announce himself. Glancing back to the booths, the kid's eyes locked on Carlton. Carlton saw the recognition in the boy's eyes; he had seen that look before. If the kid had been any good, Carlton would not have had a chance, but even half-drunk he could read the kid's intentions. The boy had come to kill him. Immediately, the kid averted his gaze, looking nervously back toward the bar.

The patrons at the bar were beginning to sense a problem. Carlton slipped the automatic out of its holster and held the gun under the table. Reaching into his jacket pocket with his right hand, the kid pulled out a pistol and shouted, "This is a holdup! Nobody moves, nobody gets hurt!"

"Bullshit," thought Carlton to himself. "You're here for my ass."

Even as the kid shouted his command, Carlton could see him craning his head around, ready to sight his pistol on Carlton. There was no time to think; instincts took over. His gun came up from under the table and was leveled at the kid's chest. He automatically snapped off three rounds, the report of the gun ripping through the silence. The kid attempted to come around with his weapon but was too slow. Carlton's first shot was high, entering the kid's open mouth instead of his chest. His head jerked back and the young man staggered and fell. Carlton's second and third shots drifted up even higher, lodging in the opposite wall. It did not matter; the kid was dead before he hit the floor.

Gun smoke hung in the air; the old familiar smell burned Carlton's nostrils. The old men looked on in shocked silence until one old lush uttered, "Holy Jesus."

Carlton now had to think fast. He wished he were sober. At least the adrenaline surge was helping to clear his fogged mind. He had to get to someplace safe, somewhere he could think. First, he had to get out of this place; he was not going to wait around for the cops. Getting up from the booth, still holding his gun, he looked down at the young man's head lying in a pool of blood. The dull eyes stared at the ceiling.

"Just a damned kid," he thought to himself.

He did not dare leave by the front entrance, for there could be others waiting outside. The back door appeared to be his best option. Carlton moved off down a small hallway at the rear of the bar. The strong odor of disinfectant and urine assaulted his sense of smell as he passed the bathroom and came to the rear door. He cracked open the door and was greeted by a dark alley that appeared deserted. Shoving the automatic into his coat pocket but still gripping the butt of the gun, he headed out into the night.

CHAPTER 31

Jack sat on the ground his back resting against the wing-like root buttress of a giant Ceiba tree. His muscles ached for rest while his stomach growled for nourishment. Exhausted, he craved a bed and a pillow upon which to lay his head. A part of him wanted to say to hell with it, fall asleep and not wake up; but he now knew that Josephine might be alive. At least she had been alive a few days ago, and he needed to know the truth.

Alongside Jack were Pax and Hector Flores. They were hidden in the thick vegetation that surrounded the parking lot at the tourist entry to the Cobá ruin site. After an arduous trek through the jungle, they had found their way here only minutes earlier, at which time Travis told them to take five while he reconnoitered the area. It was almost dark and the only sign of life was a solitary uniformed man pacing back and forth across the graveled lot. It seemed like years but had only been a few days since Jack had first arrived at Cobá and walked over this same parking lot into the restaurant/souvenir shop located across from where he now sat.

Jack's legs and arms were scraped and bleeding from the tramp through the jungle. The thick foliage had not been kind to his uncovered appendages. The hike had been made in silence so as to avoid Ortiz's agents who were surely searching the jungle for them. It had been difficult for Jack to keep silent. He was dying to quiz Pax about Jo and the situation at Reyes' estate. For now he had to remain silent and wait for Travis to return.

The wait was not long as Travis had suddenly appeared on the opposite side of the parking lot. Displaying the badge he had stolen from Inspector Ortiz, Travis approached the lone man. A moment later the man lay unconscious. Travis called for Jack and the others to come out of hiding. They handcuffed and gagged the *Federale* and dragged him into the underbrush.

There were two cars parked on the lot, a brown Ford sedan and a patrol car with the seal of the Mexican Federal Judiciary Police on the door. Travis opened the trunk on the Ford and pulled out a red duffel bag, which Jack immediately recognized.

"We'll need some traveling money," remarked Travis as he opened the rear door of the patrol car and dropped the bag of money on the seat. "We'll leave my car here," Travis nodded to the Ford. "As Jack already knows, I prefer traveling in official vehicles."

"Won't we be somewhat obvious driving out of here in a police car?" asked an incredulous Flores.

"However we leave, I imagine we will be somewhat obvious," returned Travis as he walked around the patrol car and got behind the wheel.

"There is sure to be a roadblock before we reach Highway 307. How do you expect to pass through in a stolen police car?" questioned an anxious Flores.

The keys were in the ignition. Travis started the car, then backed up to where the others stood. He leaned his head out the window and said, "This is exactly how we will get through any roadblocks. Hopefully they won't be searching fellow officers of the law."

"They will be once they discover one of their agents has been mugged and a patrol car is missing. It is over thirty miles between here and the highway," replied a clearly uncomfortable Flores.

"You're right there," agreed Travis. "And that is why we better get moving."

Flores looked to Jack hoping for some backup, but Jack only shrugged and deadpanned, "He's got the badge; he might as well have the car."

"I recommend you get in the rear seat, Jack, and if we get stopped, keep your head down. Remember, everyone in Mexico knows what you look like now," explained Travis.

Jack and Pax sat in the rear while a still-grumbling Flores took the front passenger seat. Travis put the car in gear and maneuvered the vehicle out of the parking lot. They soon passed through the small settlement just outside the archeological zone. Two patrol cars were parked on the side of the road. The cars appeared empty and they saw no one on the street.

They relaxed a bit after they had gone a few miles without any flashing lights rushing up behind them. Jack figured he might as well use this time to question Pax about Josephine and the situation at Reyes' estate. He was fearful of what he might learn but knew he would be better off if he understood the truth.

Flores acted as interpreter between Jack and Pax. Initially, Jack could see that the young man was uncomfortable. Flores started out by explaining something to Pax; he then related what he had said to Jack. "I told Pax that the man in the photograph is a good friend of ours and that the woman is your wife. I explained that we would very much like to find these people, and that any information he has could be useful.

He seems a little nervous, like maybe he knows something he wishes he did not."

"I don't want to sound like I'm running the show," interrupted Travis. "But if you want to keep the confusion to a minimum have the boy start from the beginning. Chronological order can be very important, plus it will give him a chance to warm up to the telling."

Flores began the questioning. Every so often he would stop to inform Jack of what had been said. Jack's Spanish had improved to the point where he was able to understand snatches and pieces of the conversation, though most of the time he was lost until Flores translated.

Pax started by telling how he hired on as laborer at Reyes' estate two months ago. For a few pesos a day plus room and board he worked six days a week with Sundays off. The work consisted of odd jobs, from digging ditches to gardening. From the first day he did not like the place. He wanted to leave, but jobs are scarce in Quintana Roo.

He saw Jo first. She was brought to the estate by the man with the scar. Pax explained that this man was very evil and that all of the workers feared him. She looked drunk when they got her out of the car. They took her to an isolated *palapa,* and Pax did not see her again until the day he left. That night he had heard the screams of a woman coming from the *palapa.*

The next day the *Federales* arrived with Gus and he, too, was locked up. Pax desperately wanted to terminate his employment; there were too many men with guns, but he was afraid of what might happen if they caught him trying to leave.

Early the next morning, Pax and some other workers were replacing a damaged walkway near the main house when there was a commotion down on the beach. Pax looked up to see some of Reyes' guards pulling Gus Wise from the surf. He was too far away to hear what was said, but he saw the dark one with the scar use a knife to cut open the other man's belly. Pax was upset, but the other workers pretended not to see what had happened. One of the older men told him to forget what he had seen as it could only bring him trouble. He could not forget, though, and decided he would leave that night; no job was worth this. The day was not yet over, though; the body of Gus Wise was left to rot on the beach, and a couple of hours later Scarface brought the woman down to view the body. The lady had screamed hysterically and then collapsed. Scarface had to carry her away. That was the last time Pax saw Jo, for that night he escaped into the jungle. He arrived at Cobá the next day looking for work.

Jack's head was swimming as he listened to the archeologist interpret Pax's story. His best friend had been gutted like a fish. In spite of his suspicions about Gus and Josephine, Jack still felt the loss. He would never see that crazy bastard smile again. The same gangsters that killed Gus also had his wife. He did not want to imagine what they might have done to her.

The next few miles passed by in silence; after listening to Pax's story no one felt like talking.

"Maybe there won't be a roadblock. It is not more than a mile to the highway," said a hopeful Flores.

He had no sooner spoken when two cars parked across the road came into view. The silhouettes of a half-dozen men were captured in the headlights. Some of the men had what appeared to be rifles or possibly shotguns cradled in their arms. Jack hoped Travis had a plan.

"I want you to lie down, Jack. Put your head in Pax's lap and start moaning like you've been shot in the gut," ordered Travis.

"What!?" shouted a confused Jack.

"Just do as I say and make it sound convincing, or I really will shoot you in the gut."

Jack did as he was told. He lay across Pax's lap holding his belly and groaning loudly.

"I hope you know what you are doing," said Flores grimly.

"Not really," replied Travis. "Just play along, and don't say too much."

Jack felt the car slow down as they approached the roadblock. Since he was rolling around the back seat playing the dying man, he was unable to see what was going on outside the car, but he did hear Travis shouting in Spanish. Jack waited for the gunfire to start as he continued to writhe in imaginary pain. The car was stopped for less than a minute when Jack felt the vehicle accelerating again. No shots were fired. He was still squirming and moaning when Travis informed him he could quit acting.

"Academy Award-winning performance, Jack. For a moment there you had me believing," exclaimed Travis.

"Thank you, I guess. What the hell happened back there?" asked Jack as he sat up.

"I told them that the suspects were pinned down about five miles back and that they were exchanging gunfire with the *Federales*. I also told them that you had been shot and were in need of immediate medical attention. I ordered half of them to take one car and go assist in the capture of the suspects, the others were to remain at the roadblock and shoot anyone who tried to get through. I came at them so fast they didn't have time to question what I was saying," explained Travis.

"How long do you think it will be before they question why three apparently healthy men are running away from this supposed shoot-out?" asked Flores.

"Not long," replied Travis. "We need to find a place to spend the night. How familiar are you with the surrounding area, Señor Flores?"

"Outside of the archeological zone, I am as lost as you are," replied Flores.

They had come to the intersection of Highway 307, and Travis brought the car to a stop. The deserted jungle highway stretched north and south into the darkness.

"We need to make a decision, ladies!" stated Travis.

"Pax might know a place. He grew up along this section of coast," said Flores.

Flores spoke rapidly in Spanish. Pax listened, then thought a moment. His eyes brightened and he answered back excitedly. Jack was able to pick out two words "*norte*" and "*playa.*"

"How does a little R and R on the beach sound, Jack?" asked Travis as he turned the car left onto 307.

CHAPTER 32

Carlton had slept fitfully for the last six hours; a boy with a gun kept entering his dreams. Dehydrated from the booze, he awoke fuzzy-headed and thirsty. His tongue, swollen and dry, felt like sandpaper. His first waking act was to pop three aspirin tabs and wash them down with two glasses of water. On the bedstand was his pack of smokes. Breaking his normal morning routine, he did not light up, as his head was still smoked up from last night.

This was an economy motel of the kind found along interstates outside most American cities. A sparse but clean cell with cable T.V. and a bathroom. The room smelled of stale cigarette smoke and motel disinfectant. On the bathroom counter was a two-cup kettle for heating water and next to the kettle were two Styrofoam cups. One of the cups contained packets of instant coffee, creamer, and sugar. Carlton filled the small kettle and plugged it in. He then removed his underwear and stepped into the shower.

For a full fifteen minutes, he stood motionless under the hot spray. The flow of warm water melted away some of the cobwebs, allowing him to think more clearly. He had been pretty drunk, but the events of last night were not forgotten. A kid with the back of his head spread out on a barroom floor, a kid who had come to end Carlton's life. He wondered if this kid had ever tended bar?

His shower completed, he toweled off and made himself a cup of coffee. He turned on the television and switched the channel to CNN, then sat down on the bed his back against the headboard. Not really paying attention to what was on the tube, he sipped coffee while trying to gather his thoughts. The coffee tasted terrible but warmed his mouth enough for a morning smoke. He reached for a Camel and lit up, sucking the smoke deep into his lungs.

After he fled the bar last night he had taken a ride on a city bus and then a taxi, making sure he was not followed. The trip around the city had given him time to think. The shooting had changed things; if he was going to survive, he would have to figure out who wanted him dead and why. To do this he would need a clear head. He realized he could not go back to his apartment, but he needed a place to get some sleep and sober up. One of the most important things he had learned as a CIA field agent was to keep well rested; fatigue is a merciless opponent. He had found his way to the motel around midnight, arriving half-drunk and exhausted.

Now sober and rested, Carlton was still confused. It did not take a genius to conclude that his assassin was probably sent by the same people who had ordered Buck and Allen taken out, but why had they suddenly decided that Nelson Carlton had to be eliminated? What had changed?

He snuffed out his cigarette, only half smoked; it tasted like shit and was not helping his headache.

Last night Carlton had been apprehensive about going to the authorities, and the light of day and a sober mind had done nothing to diminish his anxiety. Two VIPs had already been murdered and Carlton did not want to become the next statistic. He needed help, but he would have to find someone he could trust, someone who would believe his story. Hell, he was not sure he believed it himself. He had no hard evidence, only supposition and intuition. It would even be difficult to explain last night's shooting as anything more than the interruption of a holdup.

Carlton wondered if he had read the situation properly. After all, he was pretty drunk. Maybe it was only a scared kid trying to get some easy money. The eyes, though, the eyes never lie. Deep down he was certain the kid had come to kill him, but would anyone believe him?

His worries were abruptly interrupted when he noticed that his face was plastered across the television screen. With his heart hammering in his chest he stumbled over to the T.V. and with a trembling hand turned up the volume. He sat on the edge of the bed and listened to the male voice:

"...after the shooting, Carlton fled the scene and his whereabouts are currently unknown. The State Department has acknowledged that Carlton is under investigation for what officials term as 'erratic behavior.' The possibility of alcohol abuse was mentioned.

"According to sources inside both the State Department and the CIA, Carlton had become increasingly unstable since the death of his wife. Elizabeth Carlton was shot to death two years ago on a Washington expressway. No suspect was ever apprehended, but it was suspected that the real target had been her husband, who had a twenty-five year career with the CIA.

"Officials are worried about the threat Carlton may pose to the public. Federal authorities are asking citizens to be on the lookout for Nelson Carlton. He should be considered armed and dangerous. If you suspect you have seen this man, contact authorities immediately."

Carlton was stunned; not only were the bad guys after him, but now the good guys were too. Everyone wanted him out of the picture. His first inclination was to run. He had a little money stashed away in a Cayman bank account, but how would he get out of the country? They would be watching for him at all the international airports. His thoughts of escape were interrupted when he saw that a reporter was now interviewing Senator Jason James Hightower on the steps of the Capitol building.

> *"I did meet the man a few times in connection with an investigation into the death of Ron Allen. He appeared competent; I do not remember anything unusual about him. Once the investigation was closed, though, he continued to contact me. I even met with him once. He had concocted some wild conspiracy theories. It was at this point that I suspected the man had problems. He became more insistent with his views, to the point of becoming unreasonable."*
>
> *"It is really sad to see what this man has become after spending over twenty years in service to his country. I think some of the blame has to go to the CIA and the State Department for not recognizing the stress this man was under. The intelligence community has been operating under their own rules for far too long. Too much freedom without enough checks against abuses. It may be time to reform the agency under new guidelines to meet today's needs. The Cold War is over . . . "*

The Senator carried on about the CIA for another ten seconds while Carlton watched in disbelief. This was a blitz. They wanted him destroyed; there would be no surrender. Why was Hightower spouting this bullshit? The bastard was hanging him out to dry.

When the Senator had finished his monologue, he held his hand up toward the camera indicating the interview was over and then started up the Capitol steps with reporters shouting questions after him. In the split second the Senator had his hand in front of the camera, Carlton could see the class ring on the Senator's middle finger. In that moment it all became clear. The simplicity of it hit him like a cold slap in the face. With the shock came a chill that numbed; he now knew who his enemies were, and they were on both sides of the law. The tickling in the back of his mind was validated.

Carlton was aware of another urgency; he had to check out of the motel. When he checked in, he had paid for the room with a credit card. Last night he was only worried about Reyes, but now the feds were after him. Credit cards could be traced, and in the computer age, it did not take long. The hounds probably had his scent and were on their way. He called the front desk and asked for a taxi to the airport. Dressing quickly, he left the room headed for the motel office.

CHAPTER 33

Jack awoke slowly from a deep sleep, the sound of surf on an unknown beach gently rolling through his dreams, the smell of salt air mixed with the ocean sounds creating a comfortable state of somnolence. As conscious thoughts took hold, he realized that the rhythmic sound was not part of a dream, but reality. He sat straight up in his sandy bed wondering where he was and how he came to be here. The early morning light revealed an unfamiliar stretch of deserted beach. The last few weeks he had awakened in too many strange places, and it was becoming increasingly difficult to remember where he had fallen asleep. Sprawled out beside him in the sand he recognized the prone figures of Flores, Pax Chi, and Travis Horn. The sight of these men jogged his memory and he began to recall their late night arrival at this place.

It was Pax who had directed them here. They needed a place to hide out for the night and it just so happened that Pax's Uncle Jorge owned a half-mile section of deserted coastline. They had arrived sometime around midnight after traveling two miles on a rough four-wheel drive track overgrown with vegetation. It was a nerve-racking experience; the cop car was not designed for such terrain. They were greeted at the end of the tract by a short, yet sturdily built older man holding a large rifle. Luckily, Pax was able to convince his uncle not to shoot them. The uncle lived in a tumbled-down shack set back in the jungle. He scraped out a living harvesting coconuts, though the 1988 hurricane had wiped out a good portion of the coco palms on his small plantation. He was now trying to hold onto his land long enough to sell it to a resort developer. It appeared that Uncle Jorge would be waiting many years. He was too far south from Cancún and Cozumel, and his access road needed some work, but his beach did make a great outlaw hideout.

Jorge had appeared apprehensive about strangers but allowed them to sleep on the beach. Travis hid the police car by driving it deep into the underbrush, then they had all passed out in the sand.

Reoriented with his place on the planet, Jack stared out over the Caribbean. The sun was still below the horizon, but the eastern sky was tinted with the first hint of blue. Above and to the west the darkness was still filled with stars. Jack yawned at the morning sky as he combed his fingers through his greasy hair. The thick texture between his fingers reminded him he had not bathed in the last thirty- six hours. He got to his feet and made his way down to the water's edge. He walked along the shoreline for a couple hundred yards, then stripped off his shorts and shirt and waded naked into the surf. The briny water would not be very effective in cleaning his grimy body—soap would be required for that—but at least the water would be refreshing.

Wading out past the small breakers, he lay down in three feet of water and floated on his back. On one side, the waters of the Caribbean reached to the now yellow-orange horizon, on the other, waves rolled onto a brilliantly white beach fringed with coco palms that eventually gave way to a green wall of vegetation. The warm water felt good on his aching muscles and soaked the scabs and scratches his exposed arms and legs had received the day before. Rocked by the small swells, he watched the night sky turn a misty blue as the stars winked out one by one. Even with his current troubles, it was difficult to not enjoy the beauty of this place and this moment.

It had been almost two weeks since he last wetted himself in the waters of the Caribbean. It had been Jo and his last day on Isle Mujeres. So much had happened since. Late in the afternoon they had gone to town for a last browse through the market. It was hot, and they soon found themselves in the blue waters off Playa Norte, just north of town. They swam and played, and shared passionate kisses. Later, back on the beach after the sun had set, they had made love in the sand. These were powerful memories, but there was also the letter; Jack could not forget those words that burned. Could his wife have been faking her passion? Was his love so strong he was unable to detect her deceit? Gus was dead, but why? Had Jo met the same fate? Would he ever know the truth? If only he could find her, hold her in his arms, and look into those dark-green eyes while she explained. In spite of everything that he suspected or feared, he realized that he still loved her. But this mattered little, for he would never get near her. If still alive, she was in an armed fortress surrounded by miles of jungle.

The swells had pushed Jack back to shore, and his heart was not into pushing himself back out. He stood and walked to where his clothes lay in a pile. He slipped on his shorts and then sat down in the sand. The sun had crested the horizon, and in its yellow light was the outline of a cruise ship steaming south. Jack thought about the people on the promenade deck, drinking their morning coffee while watching the world glide by. They were close to him in terms of space and time, but their reality was worlds away from his. He longed for Jo to be by his side and share this beautiful morning. He stared trance-like at the rising ball of fire and the ship headed south. His gaze was unwavering; the sun climbed higher and the ship moved on, but his sight remained fixed on the same point of the horizon.

Jack was unsure how much time had passed when he heard the voice of Travis Horn. "Sorry to barge in on you, Jack, but we don't have much time, and decisions have to be made."

Travis came up from behind him and offered him a mug of hot coffee as he sat beside him. "Uncle Jorge's coffee," explained Travis. "Hope you like it thick and black."

Jack stared at Travis as if he had not understood the man. He then took the mug of coffee and muttered a thank you.

"I've been discussing our situation with Pax and Flores, and I now think I have a good idea as to what has happened," said Travis getting straight to business.

"That's good to hear," replied Jack halfheartedly. "I've been out here trying to figure things out myself, but I am as confused as I ever have been."

"Still feeling betrayed?" asked Travis.

"I guess I am. It's hard to accept that my best friend and my wife could be involved in something like this. I tried like hell to hate them, but now Gus is dead and Jo probably is . . . " Jack halted mid-sentence, unable to finish.

"I don't know what happened between your wife and Gus Wise, and at this point I don't care. The reason you're here has more to do with being in the wrong place at the wrong time than with any conspiracy between your wife and Wise. Your personal involvement is clouding your ability to think objectively. You need to listen to me now so you can understand how things really are," implored Travis.

Jack stared out over the ocean, the pain evident on his face, as he nodded his head in acquiescence.

"To start with, you have to accept that Ricardo Reyes is the mystery man the DEA was after. Sam's last contact raised the suspicion, and Pax's description of life on Reyes' estate adds more evidence. Honest businessmen generally don't need small armies for protection. The murder of Wise confirmed for me that Reyes is the mystery man. Another assumption that has to be made is that Sam did not sell out or become compromised. I have no problem with this assumption, for the man was a personal friend; it wasn't his style. For now, just accept my assumptions; I think when I am finished you will be in agreement.

"The shooting on the Punta Sam Ferry was what started this chain of events. Sam was to buy some cocaine from a man thought to be linked to the mystery man, whom we now assume to be Reyes. Instead of doing business, though, a gun battle ensued and only Peters survived. What actually took place we will probably never know, but given our assumptions it would appear that Reyes had found out about Sam and wanted him eliminated. The big question is how did Reyes find out about Peters? I'm sure after Sam escaped from the ferry he asked himself the same question. If he suspected that the operation had been compromised, he would have been fearful of making contact; going underground would have been his only option.

"This is where Mr. Wise comes in. From what Señor Flores has told us, Gus admitted to being a DEA operative. I think that Wise and Sam were already acquainted and that Wise may have been the one person that Sam trusted."

Travis stopped his narrative for a moment in order to catch his breath and to let his words sink in. Jack was listening intently as he sipped his coffee.

"As I inferred yesterday, your meeting Sam at the Cancún bus station was probably not an accident. Even if it was, you would have met him before leaving Chichén Itzá, Gus would have made sure of it. What better cover for Sam than traveling with a couple of unsuspecting tourists? Gus knew your itinerary; he only had to tell Sam where to go. I don't know what their final plan was. It died with Sam in that Mérida hotel room.

"I do know that the day after Gus showed up at Chichén Itzá, Washington received its final contact from Sam, and I suspect that message was relayed by Wise. The surprise visit to Chichén Itzá had nothing to do with you and your wife. Wise was there to meet with Sam, but your being there was a great cover.

"What happened next Sam did not count on. Someone leaked information to the Mexican government linking Sam to the shooting on the Punta Sam Ferry. The information included descriptions and photos along with a record of Sam's criminal activities. It was soon on the front page of every newspaper in Mexico."

"Who'd have released this information?" interrupted a confused Jack.

"It had to be someone back in Washington. It wouldn't have been hard to do; Sam had been posing as a drug smuggler for the past two years."

"But why?" asked a still-confused Jack.

"The men in Washington were probably afraid that Sam had been compromised or sold out or maybe had flipped his lid. He was a wild card that was better off eliminated. My guess is that one of Sam's superiors is Reyes' informant, and that this man pushed for the termination orders. Remember, the only reason I was brought into this in the first place was because one of Sam's superiors had become wary of the termination talk.

"However it happened, Sam was now a known entity. It didn't take long for someone to identify him and then for Reyes' men to show up and finish the job they had started on the ferry. The only problem is they discover he was traveling with two unknown people. They couldn't afford any loose ends, so they took your wife with them; they had to find out who she was and what she knew. The only reason you survived that morning was that you left the hotel moments before they made their move. After you were arrested they attempted to take you out at the police station. They could not wait, or the U.S. Consulate would have gotten involved and you might have started talking."

"But I didn't know anything! Why waste their time on me?" interjected Jack.

"They had no idea who you were, and they could not afford to take any chances. We both know what happened at the police station, so there is no need to rehash that. The next morning Gus was arrested and dropped off at Reyes' estate. I have an idea that Reyes already suspected Wise was involved with Peters, but what was learned during your interrogation by Ortiz would have led to Wise anyway. We know that Reyes owns candidate Cervantes, and that Cervantes' position as director of the Mexican Federal Judiciary Police would make him privy to information gathered during the interrogation, but the information got to Reyes too fast for it to have come through Cervantes. I suspect that the information came from Ortiz or someone close to him.

"Are you still with me, Jack?" asked Travis, as he noted Jack shaking his head.

"I can't disagree with what you've said. This stuff is so foreign to me anyway, but it seems like you are using a lot of words like probably and assume," answered Jack as he set his empty coffee mug down on the sand.

"I won't argue with you about that, but at least it all fits together with what we know. Let's look at the key question here: How did Reyes find out about Sam Peters? Yesterday you sounded convinced that your wife and Mr. Wise were somehow responsible. I guess you figured that Wise had sold out to Reyes, and that he was going to use the money to run away with your wife. This doesn't make sense any way you look at it. For one, if your wife really wanted to leave you, would she go through all of this Machiavellian shit? Why wouldn't she just pack her bags and go?"

Jack had to admit that would be more Jo's style.

"Another problem I have with your line of thinking is that if Gus had sold out, I don't think Sam would ever have made it to Mérida. Everything Gus did helped Sam. It just doesn't fit."

"You make some good points," replied Jack. "But you are relying on a lot of assumptions, and I still have that letter to deal with."

"I am not going to lie to you, Jack. Your wife and Wise may have had something going on the side, but I doubt it has anything to do with what has occurred over the last two weeks," explained Travis.

Jack's eyes were fixed on the distant cruise ship as he chewed on his thumbnail. "I just don't know what to think anymore," he claimed in exasperation. "Before we found the tomb yesterday, I had decided to go back home. I figured Jo had left me or was dead. Shit! I guess the hows, whats, and whys don't matter anymore; however you look at it, she's dead."

"I'm not so sure she is," stated Travis matter-of-factly.

"What in the hell are you saying? We know they killed Gus. Why would they spare Jo?" replied a confused Jack.

"While talking with Pax this morning, I learned that Reyes likes the ladies. Apparently, he keeps his own personal harem on his estate, and rumor is that Jo is the latest addition."

"Bullshit! Jo wouldn't go for something like that," interjected Jack.

"I don't think she would have a choice. According to Pax, not all of Reyes' women are there by choice. Reyes probably figured there was no problem keeping her once they found out that she knew nothing. She appears to be a good-looking lady."

Jack was stunned, unsure of how to react. Jo was possibly alive, but only to be this bastard's concubine?

"Remember, there is no guarantee that she is alive, only a possibility," added Travis.

"What do we do now?" asked a dazed Jack as he tried to process this new information.

"Flores is headed for Mérida. His family is well-connected, and he thinks they can put some pressure on the government to take action against Reyes. He also wants to protect his find at Cobá. It's eating him up that Ortiz and his men could be pawing through the tomb, and he doesn't even want to imagine Reyes getting his hands on the find. I guess he has the reputation of being a grave robber. Me, I'm going to pay a visit to Señor Reyes and hopefully find out who his friend in Washington is," informed Travis.

"I'm going with you," stated Jack, though he was sure Travis would not allow it.

"I figured you would want to go, and I've been trying to decide what to do. Flores wants you to go with him, which makes a lot of sense. The only problem is I don't think you would make it through the first roadblock. You are too well-known. Dropping in on Ricardo will be dangerous business, but I reckon your chances are not much better just trying to make it to Mérida. You've survived this long; you might as well join me," said Travis as he watched the small waves roll onto the sand.

Jack had not expected this reply from Travis; it caught him by surprise. At first he was strangely excited, but this turned to a more somber mood when he thought about the task before them.

"How are we going to get onto the estate? Pax made it sound like an impenetrable fortress surrounded by miles of jungle," asked Jack.

"Actually, that will be the easy part," explained Travis, as a smart ass crooked grin spread across his face. "We will arrive by sea."

CHAPTER 34

Carlton strode through the crowded airport terminal, his suit wrinkled and a half-smoked Camel between his lips, just another tired business traveler fresh off the red-eye. He walked with his head down, keeping as far away from the security cameras as possible. In spite of the crowds, he knew that airport terminals were not good places to hide with too much security already in place and the flow of people in and out easily surveyed. He continued on, appearing relaxed, even though his heart was in his throat.

Passing a newsstand, he was chilled by the sight of his own mug staring back at him from the front page of the *Washington Post*. This was not good; they were farther ahead then he thought. His face had already been plastered all over the television and now it was on the cover of all the newspapers. He could be fingered by anyone. He would have to rely on his chameleon-like ability to blend into a crowd; it had served him well in the past.

With his credit card, he had just purchased three tickets on three different airlines to three separate destinations: Chicago, Atlanta, and Los Angeles. Carlton would have liked to have bought an international ticket, but he was sure that the international ticket counters and terminals would be the first places staked out. None of the tickets would be used; they were only purchased to keep his pursuers busy for the next few hours. Those hunting him would be suspicious of him actually using any of the tickets, but they would still have to check out each flight. Even more problematic for them was the possibility that he purchased a fourth ticket with cash or a bogus credit card.

Carlton wanted out of the terminal. He had to fight the urge to break into a trot and head for an exit. He was not safe here. If the airport was not already under full surveillance, it soon would be. It was only a matter of time. There was one more task he wanted to accomplish before leaving. Walking up to an automatic teller machine, he stuck his card into the slot. The machine greedily sucked in the card. He punched in his personal identification number and made his selection, a withdrawal of three hundred dollars. There was less than fifty dollars in his pocket, and he would need some walking-around money. Instead of producing cash, a message flashed on the screen: "Invalid Card". The machine spit his card back out. It could be coincidence; this would not be the first time he had an ATM card malfunction. The other possibility was that his accounts had been frozen. If so, he had just set off the alarm bells. He decided to try the credit card he had used to purchase the tickets, which had been valid a few minutes ago. Slipping the card into the designated slot, he punched in his PIN number and selected a transaction. Carlton waited anxiously, anticipating the sound of the machine dispensing the cash. He knew that law enforcement agencies sometimes left credit cards active in hopes of the suspect leaving a paper trail. He relaxed somewhat when he heard the gears of the machine whirring and twenty-dollar bills began sliding out of the dispensing slot.

Eventually, he would need more cash, but this would get him through the next few hours. Back in his days with the CIA, he had set up a couple of secret bank accounts under assumed names. The accounts were for emergencies such as now. Carlton hoped the accounts had remained secret, for without money he would not last long.

Stuffing the wad of bills into his wallet, he started for the nearest exit. He passed through the glass doors and out onto the sidewalk. The cool morning air was refreshing after the crowded confines of the terminal. As he hailed a taxi he noted a familiar face. It was an average looking man in his late twenties dressed in blue jeans, a bulky gray sweater, and tennis shoes. The man stood nonchalantly on the sidewalk smoking a cigarette as if he were waiting for Aunt Nellie to arrive. But was the man waiting? Or was he watching? Carlton could not place the face with a name or an event. Was he CIA or was he State Department, or maybe he was just a guy who lived on the third floor of his apartment building? Another coincidence? Carlton was not sure, but he knew if he wanted to stay alive, he could not trust coincidence. The fellow did not take note of Carlton; his attention seemed to be focused on people coming, not going. He felt the old familiar rush as the cab pulled out into traffic leaving the airport terminal behind; Carlton had passed undetected right under their noses.

He had the cab driver take him to a sprawling suburban mall outside of Chevy Chase. This did not figure to be a place they would look for him, but he still needed to be careful while his image was plugged into the national psyche. He could be recognized by anyone. For Carlton, this was not an impossible situation. His average features were one of the reasons he had lasted so long as a CIA field agent. Only subtle changes were required to transform his appearance. Small things like wearing a hat or taking on an accent could change a person's perception of him. Some of these things could also draw attention, but as long as he kept changing into something else, it made it very difficult for others to track him. Other things could also be done with body language: taking on the stride of an old man or carrying himself like a shy introvert. In the past he had also used more standard disguise techniques like changing hair color or wearing colored contact lenses, which worked well with his gray eyes. In a matter of seconds his eyes could go from blue to brown. He generally stayed away from using elaborate disguises such as fake mustaches or stage makeup. Like in an old Peter Sellers movie, bringing attention to a drooping mustache at an inopportune time was a very real possibility. Keeping things simple was usually best, though Carlton did manage to leave Buenos Aires once disguised as a matronly woman.

He strolled through the mall making a number of clothing purchases. He would not be able to go back to his apartment, and he could not wear the same suit day after day. The purchases were made with an eye toward future disguises: jogging sweats for the athletic look, work shirt and blue jeans for the construction worker look. He also picked out a couple of casual shirts and a pair of khaki slacks.

Carlton was starting to feel more comfortable with his current situation after he had been in half-dozen shops and no one seemed to take more than the usual notice of him. In spite of the media blitz, most people were not going to spend their day looking for a wanted criminal, especially one wearing a suit and tie.

The shopping had given him some time to think, to organize his thoughts. He decided to make a phone call. Finding an empty phone booth in a quiet corner of the mall, he fed the pay phone a number of quarters, then punched in a number. The call was answered after the first ring. "Special Agent Schovich speaking."

Bingo! He was hoping he would get directly through to Don Schovich. "Hello, Don, this is an old friend," returned Carlton.

"Oh, shit!" replied Schovich as he immediately recognized Carlton's voice. "I figured you would be calling, but I was kind of hoping you would leave me out of this. You've stepped into a massive pile of shit, my friend."

"I've been framed," replied Carlton.

"I'm sure you have, but you're still in a pile of shit."

"I need a favor."

"I'm not sure I should get involved. This is too big; you have some VIPs very pissed off," said Schovich, his voice strained.

"I have nowhere else to go."

"If you have somewhere to hide permanently, I'd go there," suggested Schovich. "Otherwise, I'd throw myself at their mercy."

"All I want is for you to meet with me and listen to what I have to say. If you don't want to get involved, that's fine, but you may have some ideas about who else I might go to."

There was silence on the line; he did not want to have to start pleading. The silence only lasted about five seconds, but it seemed like an eternity to Carlton.

"Fuck!" exclaimed the FBI agent, breaking the silence. "I shouldn't do this, but I'll listen to you this one time. Where and when?"

"Remember where and when we met last time?" asked Carlton, referring to The Senate.

"Yes," answered Schovich.

"Meet me there today at approximately the same time. I have one other small favor to ask you. I would like you to get a list of 1961 through 1963 class seniors at USC who belonged to the Sigma Alpha Gama fraternity. I'll explain why when we meet tonight."

"I'll see what I can do," replied Schovich with a sigh. He then added, "Nelson, be careful."

CHAPTER 35

Josephine walked out on the beach that fronted Ricardo Reyes' estate. A black one-piece swimsuit hugged her body like a second skin, and her dark chestnut curls fell loose onto her shoulders. She picked a spot in the sand and opened the beach chair she was carrying then settled down under the Caribbean sun. From behind a pair of dark sunglasses, she watched the waves roll smoothly onto the sparkling white sand. She was feeling stronger; the day of rest and good food had done wonders for both her physical and mental state. The conversation with Sandy had also helped her sort things out. Her situation was still grim, but at least she now had some understanding of what was happening.

From what she could piece together, it appeared that Steve Potter and this gangster Reyes had some kind of problem. She wasn't certain, but she had an idea that it involved illegal drugs. Whatever it was, it was important enough for Reyes to send his goons to dispose of Potter. The goons also found her when they came to kill Potter and decided they better take her with them so they could find out what she knew. Their plan was probably to interrogate her then kill her. They did interrogate her, but as luck would have it they did not kill her. Instead, Señor Reyes decided to add her to his collection of women. What had happened was not fair, but life was not fair, which she had learned long ago when she lost her parents. That had been a difficult experience, but it had made her stronger. She would try and do the same with her current situation. Jo had survived thus far; she had no choice but to play the cards dealt to her.

She had not been soaking in the sun long when she was startled by the sound of a peach and magnolia-laced voice, "You mind if I join you?"

Jo looked up through her dark sunglasses to see Sandy standing above her. "Sure," replied Jo.

Jo admired the girl's body as she spread out her beach towel. Sandy wore a pink bikini that did not leave much to the imagination. Her large, perfectly formed breasts seemed to defy the laws of gravity, causing Jo to wonder—a bit jealously—if they were all her own. The girl could have just stepped out of a centerfold. She should be in Hollywood, not here as the plaything of some horny old goat, thought Jo.

"I try and catch the morning sun; I read someplace that it's the least damaging to your skin. You never want to lie out during the middle of the day, especially if you have fair skin," informed Sandy as she lay down on her stomach.

Jo started to laugh at Sandy's comment but cut herself short; with all of her current problems the last thing Jo was going to worry about was skin cancer. Sandy caught the bemused expression on Jo's face.

"Did I say something funny?" she asked in her sweet Georgia drawl.

"No, I just had a funny thought," lied Jo.

Jo was not sure how much she could trust the girl. Her instincts told her that Sandy had probably been straight so far, but she also knew that Reyes must have a strong influence on the girl. It was in her best interest to keep her feelings to herself.

"Ricardo has invited you to brunch with him on the patio," said Sandy.

"I thought you said he wasn't going to rush me," responded Jo.

Sandy replied softly, almost as if she were hurt. "You don't have to go. It was an invitation, not an order."

"What happens if I decline?"

"Nothing for now, but eventually you'll have to spend some time with him," answered Sandy.

Jo sighed in resignation then remarked, "I might as well get to know who I am dealing with. When do we brunch?"

"Be on the patio in twenty minutes," instructed Sandy.

The degrading circumstances aside, Jo had to admit there was something flattering about this man selecting her to become one of his women. The ladies she had met so far were all gorgeous, the type men fantasize about and women dream of becoming. Did Reyes really think she compared with his other women? She had never considered herself to be any great beauty; she had her share of dates through high school and college but had never suffered from any undue attention. She had known certain women who could draw men to them with their beauty, but she had never put herself in this class. Deep inside she knew there was a part of her that enjoyed Reyes' attention, and this made her uncomfortable.

"Thanks for talking with me last night. I babbled on about my problems for so long that I never listened to yours. It's just been such a long time since I could sit and gab with another woman," commented Sandy in an attempt to keep the conversation going.

"I appreciated your company. It helps to know that I'm not the only one suffering," replied Jo as she gazed out over the ocean. At the moment, she did not feel like talking.

Jo was surprised by the sight of a cruise ship headed south. She leaned forward in her chair and sputtered, "There's a ship out there!"

Her first thought was that the ship was not that far out, if she could get to it, she could be saved. She quickly realized her foolishness; the ship was much farther out than it appeared, at least too far to swim.

"It's a cruise ship. They pass by every so often," said Sandy, who sat up to get a better look at the ship.

Jo's gaze wandered down the beach to a small fiberglass boat moored to the shore. Sandy noted Jo's interest in the craft. "They don't leave gas in the boats," remarked Sandy. "I've thought about it many times. Besides, even if I had the fuel, I wouldn't know how to start the dang thing."

Jo was no expert, but she had operated the outboard motor on her dad's boat many times as a kid. That was a long time ago, but she could not imagine it being too difficult to remember. How would she get fuel, though? She would have to keep her eyes open and learn where the gasoline was stored.

"I know the feeling; if it has more than two buttons I'm lost. Besides I get seasick," lied Jo, she would keep her options to herself.

"I used to hate watching the boats go by," remarked Sandy as she gazed out over the water. "I'd wonder if there were people on board from back home. It was difficult to have the outside world so close and all I could do was watch it slide by. Now I like to see the ships once in awhile; they remind me that there is an outside world."

Sandy looked away from the water to see Jo studying her with a sympathetic eye. A blush crossed over her smooth complexion and she looked down at the sand. "You must think I'm crazy," said Sandy.

"No," replied Jo. "I am amazed you've been able to keep your sanity."

Sandy looked up, her expression changed, "You better get along to the patio. Ricardo doesn't like to be kept waiting."

The girl's sudden concern in meeting Reyes' timetable irritated Jo. How could such a beautiful and seemingly sensitive young woman let herself become a slave to the wants and desires of this old letch? She seemed too accepting of the situation; Jo wanted to see a little more fight.

"Any last-minute advice?" asked Jo as she rose to her feet.

"Ricardo is pretty understanding, especially when he's first getting to know you. If you treat him nice, he'll treat you like a queen. I know this sounds crazy, but I think you'll like him," replied Sandy.

Jo nodded her head and without a word started up the beach toward the main house. She could not imagine having any feelings other than disgust for Ricardo Reyes, but she kept this thought to herself.

The main house stretched out in front of her. The long low building had a commanding presence over the beach and yet seemed to be part of the beach. The building's flat roof was supported by stone pillars, the space between the pillars filled with glass. A large stone terrace extended in front of the windows and was almost as long as the building. A wide stairway descended from the patio onto the sand and was bordered by a pair of giant stone serpents. The fierce-looking heads rested on the sand as if guarding the lower steps from unwanted visitors. To Jo, the building looked like an updated version of a Mayan palace.

Stopping for a moment at the bottom of the stairs, she placed her right hand on the feathered head of one of the snarling stone reptiles. She looked up the stairway toward the terrace. At the top of the stairs a chacmool statue looked forebodingly out to sea, holding the sacrificial offering plate on its belly. Suddenly, she did not feel so sure of herself. Her legs a bit rubbery, a queasy feeling in her stomach, she slowly made her way up the stone steps, like a convicted man climbing the gallows.

Stepping out onto the terrace she saw that it was decorated with patio furniture woven from palm and bamboo. On one corner of the terrace was a small table with a round glass top, the base of which was constructed of the same jungle materials as the rest of the furniture. The table was arranged with two place settings, a small bowl of fruit, and a ceramic pot from which a wisp of steam curled out of its spout. The rich aroma of coffee filled the morning air.

Standing alone and feeling out of place, she wondered why she was here. She certainly was not hungry. Turning to take in the ocean view, she waited for something to happen.

The sound of a door opening interrupted the quiet of the patio and sent a burst of adrenaline coursing through Jo's veins. She managed to retain a look of indifference as she turned toward the sound.

"Good morning, Josephine! I am pleased that you have chosen to join me," said the rich voice of Ricardo Reyes. His voice reminded Jo of the old Latin actor who used to pitch the cars with the Corinthian leather; she could not remember the actor's name though.

The smiling countenance of Ricardo Reyes warmly greeted her. He was dressed comfortably in white, light-weight cotton slacks and a white shirt with the first two buttons undone, exposing a moderately hairy chest. Refined and delicate, the round open face was decorated with a pencil-thin mustache and a receding hairline of jet black hair pasted straight back over his head. The almost cherubic face was incongruous with the sonorous voice. He was much shorter than she remembered him being two days ago. There was something about his eyes that belied his mild-mannered exterior. She sensed a Napoleonic complex.

"Thank you for the invitation," replied Jo, trying to sound pleasant. Part of her was still trying to remember the name of the actor with the Corinthian leather.

"Please, let us sit," said Reyes in Spanish as he motioned toward the table.

Jo pretended she did not understand. She figured it would be to her advantage for Reyes to assume she was ignorant of the language.

"I will speak English if that is what you prefer, but I would think a Spanish teacher at an American university would understand the language," said Reyes in English.

Her face flushed at being caught in an attempt to mislead. She did not try to explain; he already had put her off balance and assumed control, no use digging a deeper hole.

When she approached the table Reyes smoothly pulled a chair out for her. It was refreshing to be treated like a lady. She could not remember the last time a man, including her husband, had held a chair out for her. Reyes scooted the chair into place then sat on the other side of the table from Jo.

"Coffee?" offered Reyes as he picked up the steaming pot.

"Please," answered Jo. She did not really want any but figured it would give her something to do with her hands.

"Sugar or cream?" asked Reyes as he filled Jo's cup.

"I drink it black, thank you," replied Jo.

Reyes nodded his head in approval as he filled his own cup. They sipped their coffee, which was strong and robust the way she liked it. Reyes stared at her over his cup, a reflective expression on his face. She felt uncomfortable under his gaze and found herself wishing he would speak. Talk would break the tension. Jo was not going to give anything away unnecessarily by speaking too quickly; she would leave it up to Reyes to direct the conversation.

"I hope you have found your new accommodations comfortable?" said Reyes breaking the silence.

"I've no complaints. It's an improvement over where I spent my first few nights here," responded Jo, trying not to sound like a smart-ass.

"I apologize for how you were treated. I was away for a few days, and I am afraid Ramon got a little carried away," explained Reyes.

The last statement almost caused Jo to choke on her coffee. If Ramon had only been "a little carried a way," what was he like when he got really serious about something? Reyes definitely had a way with understatement.

Before any more was said, an older woman arrived at the table pushing a trolley cart loaded with food. There were pastries, toast, bacon, eggs, salsa, pitchers of juice and milk, enough food, it seemed, to feed a dozen people.

"I did not know what you would like, so I had a selection prepared," explained Reyes.

Jo was not hungry but took a pastry and some fruit so she would not appear unappreciative. Reyes took two hard-boiled eggs and a slice of toast. Once the selections were made, the old woman left the patio with the cart.

"We have some important matters to discuss, but first let us enjoy our meal," instructed Reyes

Reyes dissected and ingested his eggs and toast, while Jo picked at her fruit and pastry. She forced herself to appear to be enjoying the meal. They ate in silence, Jo passing the time trying to remember the name of the Latin actor. She kept wanting to say Ricky Ricardo, but that was Lucy's husband. The guy she was thinking of had a television series that took place on a tropical island with a funny-looking dwarf for a sidekick. The name was on the tip of her tongue, and not remembering it was starting to drive her crazy. It was meaningless information, and at the moment she had much more important things to worry about.

The meal finished, Reyes offered Jo more coffee, which she accepted. He topped off his own cup, then leaned back in his chair holding the cup in both hands, appearing quite at ease. "You are a very attractive woman," complemented Reyes as he stared at Jo over his steaming cup.

She tried not to blush at this comment, which was surely the response he was trying to incite. In spite of her efforts, she could feel the rosy glow spreading across her cheeks. It made her feel like some silly schoolgirl. Unsure of how to respond, Jo stammered, "Thank you," as she turned her gaze toward the sea and tried to regain her composure. She suddenly wished she were dressed in something other than a swimsuit.

Reyes followed her gaze out to the ocean. He sighed and then said, "This is a beautiful place. Every time I look out on this view, I think about how lucky I am. I hope that you will eventually have similar feelings."

Jo clearly understood the underlying meaning of this last statement: this is to be your new home, so you might as well enjoy it.

"You have your own piece of paradise here," complemented Jo with forced enthusiasm.

"I suppose you would like to know why you are here. From what I've been told, you are a very intelligent and strong-willed person, so I will be as honest as I can. You and your husband unwittingly became involved with the wrong people, people involved in a very dangerous business. Some of these people are very powerful, and they now want to see you dead. I regret to inform you that your husband has already met this fate."

Reyes' last sentence hit Jo like a fist in the gut. She had feared the worst for Jack, but now the awful truth had been spoken out loud.

"I had feared as much," said Jo, hiding her pain under a cloak of indifference. Inside she was a boiling pot of emotions, but she was not going to show herself to this bastard. Somehow, Reyes' bringing up Jack's name gave her strength.

"I must admit, I thought the news of your husband's demise might cause a more emotional response," said Reyes truthfully.

"As I said, I was already fairly sure he had been killed. It may sound a bit cold, but one must deal with life the way it is. You can't change the past, you can only live in the present and plan for the future. Both my parents died when I was in high school, and I learned to carry on at a young age," explained Jo.

"You have a very practical view of life," replied Reyes, apparently pleased by her explanation.

Jo realized there was only one thing she had left: her body. She understood that if Reyes had not found her attractive she would be dead. Through most of her life she had never been highly attuned to men's desires. She had known women who blatantly used their wiles to get what they wanted from men, and now she wished she had paid more attention to their ways. It was something she would have to get better at; her survival would depend on it.

"Now that we have decided that I am a practical woman, why don't you finish explaining the situation here," asked Jo as she looked directly at Reyes. She was going to use her attributes to her full advantage.

"There is not much more to say, except that if you left here your life would be very cheap. I propose that you stay here with me permanently. I think you would find life here very enjoyable. Little would be asked of you, and you would be free to pursue your own interests, within reason. Above all you would be safe here."

"Is that what you told Gus?" asked Jo, unable to resist a jab.

Reyes stared down at his lap. For the first time the man looked uncomfortable. "I apologize for your being subjected to that scene. Ramon is good at what he does, but he can be heavy-handed at times. Mr. Wise was more deeply involved in all this then you may realize. In fact, if it were not for him, you and your husband would probably be lying on the beach right now planning your trip back home. I cannot tell you more, but believe me, Mr. Wise was responsible for his own death."

"What kind of business are you in?" asked Jo, changing the subject, to avoid thinking of Gus.

"I'm involved in many ventures, but they are no concern of yours. Understanding my enterprises will not improve your situation, and in the long run could place you in jeopardy. What I do makes me a wealthy man and pays for everything around you," said Reyes as he spread his arms in an expansive gesture. "That is all you need to know."

This was a bullshit answer, but Jo could see that it was all she was going to get. Whatever Reyes was involved in, Jo was pretty sure it was not legal.

"You said little would be expected of me; exactly what would be expected of me?" asked Jo.

"For now, I would like you to relax and enjoy the facilities here. I want some time for us to get to know one another better," replied Reyes, not really answering her question.

"It appears that I don't have much choice but to go along with what you want. I guess a person could get used to living in a place like this," said Jo, with a trace of a smile. "I have one request though," she continued, the smile now gone. "Ramon is to stay away from me. I don't want him speaking to me, I don't even want to see him."

"He will stay away from you, I give you my word," assured Reyes. "I must leave you now, as I have some things to attend to, but before I go I have a request of you: will you join me for the evening meal?"

"Yes," answered Jo. After all, he had granted her favor.

"Excellent," said a pleased Reyes. "Talk with Sandy. She will help you find a suitable dress for tonight."

Inside Jo did a slow burn; she did not like the way her life was being directed. For now, though, she had no choice but to go along. One thing she was certain of, she wanted to survive.

Ricardo excused himself, and Jo started down the steps to the beach. All things considered, she felt she had handled the situation fairly well. At least she had managed to get Reyes to promise to keep Ramon away from her, which was worth something.

As she stepped out onto the beach it suddenly came to her, "Ricardo—fucking—Montalban!"

CHAPTER 36

Jack lay in the sand, his back propped up on a fallen palm tree. Beside him, stretched out in a similar position, was Travis Horn. The shade of a still-standing palm combined with a slight breeze from off the Caribbean gave them some relief from the afternoon heat. A dozen feet away, in the shade of another palm tree, slept Pax Chi, unaware of the two flies strolling across his exposed cheek. Jack marveled at how the young man was able to sleep with zero hour so close at hand. Travis had recommended they all try and get some sleep, but Jack was too wired. Soon it would be nightfall, and they would set out to sea in Uncle Jorge's small boat headed for the estate of Ricardo Reyes. Jack was filled with a mixture of apprehension and excitement. Hopefully, he would find Josephine and bring about some kind of closure to his present situation. He ached to hold her in his arms, look into her eyes, and know the truth. There was also danger; he might be shot at and he might have to shoot back. How would he react? Would he be up to the task?

Travis had spent the morning educating Jack and Pax on how to handle and shoot a handgun. Travis had collected two guns during the previous day's travails, one from Jesus, the other from the *Federale* he had ambushed in the Cobá parking lot. Both were .38 revolvers. Jack had never held a gun, let alone shot one, but with instructions from Travis he found that he was soon comfortable with the weapon and that he had a good eye. Back home Jack had always been for gun control, believing that the average citizen should not be allowed to own a handgun. For the last two weeks, though, he had one person or another sticking a gun into his face; this, along with the instruction he had received from Travis, had changed his perspective on the gun control issue. He now understood the true power of a firearm. The unarmed man lived under the tyranny of the armed. He would now be able to shoot back.

Jack glanced at Travis, who lay beside him dressed only in a pair of brown-striped boxer shorts with a blue ball cap perched atop his head. The big man had the body of an aging athlete; the muscle definition was still there, but a slight paunch was developing around the waistline. His skin had a light bronze cast to it, a perpetual tan that went well with his dark brown hair. The stubble- covered face had a chiseled look with a strong jaw line and green eyes that could twinkle with humor one moment and be stone cold killer the next. Jack was not sure of the man's age but guessed early forties by the lines etched into the skin at the corner of Travis's eyes and the flecks of gray around his temples and into his sideburns. Travis had saved his life twice, and tonight they were going into the lion's den together, yet this man was still a stranger.

"You keep staring at me like that, and you're going to make me nervous," cracked Travis as one eye stared back at Jack from beneath the blue ball cap.

"I was just wondering who you are," replied Jack.

"I've already told you too much," said Travis as he pulled his cap down over his eyes.

"I wasn't referring to your work. It doesn't take a genius to figure out that you're with the CIA or the DEA or some other government organization identified by three initials."

"I'm on my own on this," interrupted Travis.

"Whatever," continued Jack. "I was thinking more like: where did you grow up? Are you married? Do you have any kids? Do you follow baseball? You know, the things that make you, you. It would be interesting to know a little something about the person with whom I might die."

"My life really isn't that interesting. Besides you should get some sleep," replied Travis in an effort to end the conversation.

"I guarantee that I won't be able to sleep until this thing is over with," returned Jack.

"You have a point there. I've always had a hard time sleeping before a difficult operation. It's a bad habit. In Special Forces training they hammer it into you, 'rest as a weapon.' Try and keep the enemy from getting any sleep while you stay well rested. Fortunately, I don't need a lot of shut-eye," explained Travis.

"So you were in Special Forces," said Jack, surprised Travis had revealed this information.

"I was," corrected Travis. "There are quite a few Special Forces graduates in my line of work."

"Which is?" volleyed Jack.

Travis did not answer. He looked at Jack with a crooked smile and shook his head. He then closed his eyes and folded his hands across his chest indicating he was through talking.

"Where did you grow up?" persisted Jack.

Travis did not respond; his eyes remained closed as if he were asleep. Undaunted Jack pushed on. "When did you lose your virginity?" he asked, trying to get a reaction.

Travis cocked one eye open and peered up at Jack as if he were looking at a crazy man, but he still did not verbally respond.

"You're not still a virgin, are you?" quipped Jack, an expression of mock surprise on his face.

This question cracked through the veneer. Travis chuckled as a smile spread across his face. "I'd probably be better off if I was," stated Travis.

"What was her name?" inquired Jack, taking advantage of the opening.

"Kathleen O'Kerrigan," replied Travis. "The prettiest girl at my high school. A tall, blue-eyed blonde who got straight As. I couldn't believe that she was interested in me. We went steady for most of our senior year, but semi on the sly. Her father was an Irishman who owned the hardware store. He would not have been happy to learn his daughter was dating a half-breed. It was spring time, we were both seventeen . . . "

Travis paused, a distant look in his eye, "Two weeks later I was in Marine Corps Boot Camp. I haven't seen her since the day I graduated from high school."

"Where did all this take place?" asked Jack.

"Manhattan," answered Travis.

"Manhattan?" repeated Jack. "It sounded more like somewhere in Kansas."

"Manhattan, Montana," added Travis

"Whatever became of Miss O'Kerrigan?" asked Jack.

"Last I heard she was living in Bozeman, married with two kids. I sometimes wonder what might have happened if I had stayed around. Maybe I'd be living in Bozeman with two kids."

A half smile curled Travis's lips as he stared out over the ocean, remembering.

"So, you're half Native American?" said Jack, changing the direction of the conversation.

"I'm only one-eighth injun; my grandmother's mother was full-blooded Cheyenne. That's on my dad's side of the family. The rest is a mixture of European blood. My grandfather is German and Irish. My mother's side I'm not too sure of. She left my father soon after I was born, and I've never met her, but her last name was Simon, which I think is French."

"You never met your mother?" asked an incredulous Jack.

"No, she and my old man were a one-night stand. I was conceived in the back of a pickup truck after a rodeo dance. She didn't have any long run interest in me or my father. As soon as I was born she hit the road. I never really got to know my father either; he died when I was five. Hit some black ice on his way back home from the bar one night and wrapped his pickup truck around a telephone pole. I never really thought much about my mother, but I would have liked to known my father better. From what I've heard he was a pretty good guy, just a little too young and too wild to be raising a kid on his own. He was a good saddle bronc rider, but the difference between good and great in the rodeo business is the difference between making a living and starving."

"It sounds like you had a rough childhood," said Jack, unable to think of anything else to say.

"Actually, I had a great childhood, thanks to my grandparents. As far as I'm concerned they're my real parents. My grandfather has a cattle ranch, nothing big, but enough to take care of a family, 400 to 500 head of mother cows. There's not a better place for a boy to grow up than on a ranch. The old man still runs the ranch, though it is getting to be more than he can handle. Sometimes I think about moving back and taking over."

"Why don't you?" asked Jack.

"If I make it through this I just might, and if we both make it, you'll have to come up and go fishing sometime. We'll fish the Madison River and catch brown trout as long as your arm," said Travis.

Jack was touched by the invitation. He was starting to genuinely like Travis. "I hope that's not an idle invitation. I've done quite a bit of fly fishing in the Sierras. I've always wanted to fish Montana."

"You're a fly fisherman!" said Travis, his eyes lighting up. "Oh man, is there anything better than a day on the river with a fly rod in hand?"

They had found common ground. For the next thirty minutes they talked nothing but fishing, and for a while both men were able to forget the danger that awaited them. Jack could see that Travis loved his home state and its trout-filled rivers. It was a subject the man enjoyed talking about. It soon became obvious to Jack, however, that Travis had not spent much time back home since he was a kid.

The conversation dwindled as the sun dropped lower in the sky behind them. Jack's thoughts turned back to what faced them tonight. He found himself wishing that time would slow down. It was moving too fast; soon they would be heading out onto the open ocean. A nervous excitement was building inside him. He wondered if Hector had made it to Cancún. Would he be able to get the Mexican government to take action?

"You think Flores will be able to get help to us tonight?" asked Jack.

"I wouldn't count on it," replied Travis truthfully.

* * *

The bus rumbled around the sleepy *zocalo* of Playa Del Carmen, belching out a cloud of black diesel smoke. It screeched to a halt in front of the small bus station and disgorged a load of human cargo. Inside, Hector 'Flores gladly took a seat in the rear of the bus. It had been standing-room-only since he boarded the bus over an hour ago. This was a second-class bus, which meant that passengers were allowed on board as long as nobody was sticking out of a window or a door too far. He would have preferred to travel first-class where everyone gets a seat, but after four first-class buses had blown by his attempts to wave them down, he figured he could not afford to be picky. When the second-class bus pulled off the deserted jungle highway and stopped in front of him, Flores decided he better get on board.

He felt guilty about leaving Jack and Travis; part of him wanted to go with them tonight. It was a suicidal course of action, though. The proper thing to do was go to the authorities and let them handle it. Of course, he probably should have gone to the authorities when Gus first vanished. Maybe then things would not have gotten so out of hand. He had let his work take precedence; the precious artifacts of a lost civilization were more important to him than a missing friend. In a way, he felt responsible for Gus's death. Hopefully, he could get to the right people in time so that Jack and Travis would not meet the same fate. He also wanted to protect his find. It made him ill to think of Ortiz's men pawing through the tomb, even worse if any of the artifacts were to come into the hands of Ricardo Reyes.

It would be another hour to Cancún, where, hopefully, he could begin to straighten out this mess. If he had to, he would fly to Mérida. He thought about renting a car. Playa Del Carmen was a small town that survived mostly on tourist trade; surely there was a way to rent a car here. The problem was that he had very little money and no credit cards or identification, plus he was now wanted by the police. It figured that the *Federales* would keep an eye on the rental car places when they were searching for fugitives. He decided it was best to remain on the bus, which would get him to Cancún soon enough and where it was easy to blend in with the locals.

Hector stared out the open window across the plaza to the beach and ocean beyond. Down at the dock he could see the jet boat ferry loading up with tourists for its next run to Cozumel. Playa had originally been nothing more than a place to catch the ferry to Cozumel, but the stretches of long, white secluded beaches eventually started attracting an international beach-bum crowd. The beaches had become so popular that the town fathers were now having to decide on the next stage of development. Would it keep the beach-bum flavor of simple *palapas* strung out along the beach, or would it go the way of Cancún and Cozumel? Flores hoped the beach bums won out.

Hector smiled at the sight of half-dozen soldiers standing on the sidewalk. The soldiers were from Playa's own army base. No one in the ragtag group appeared to be older than eighteen. Once a day the commandant would send a group of his men out to patrol the town and the beach. The sight of the soldiers, with their rifles on their shoulders (or dragging behind them if they were tired), would usually put a little scare into the tourists. What the tourists did not know was that the commandant did not let his men have bullets for their guns. There would have to be a very serious situation before he would turn his boys loose with loaded weapons.

Hector's smile turned to a frown when he noticed two *Federales* standing with the soldiers. They were checking passengers as they got off the bus. Once they had checked all the disembarking passengers, one of the *Federales* climbed on board the bus and began to slowly walk the aisle. Flores' stomach dropped into his lower intestine as the man approached; Flores imagined that he looked guilty as hell.

The man was dressed in the tan uniform of the Judicial Police; the area of the shirt under the arms was stained with sweat. His face, which sported a moustache and three-day-old stubble, had a weary look.

Flores stared out the window, attempting to look bored. He feared that if he made eye contact with the man, his identity would be known. As the cop walked up to him, he felt certain he had been identified. Goose bumps rose on his skin, and he started to tremble. He clasped his hands tightly in his lap in an effort to control the shaking. Frozen, afraid to move, he continued to stare out the window. The cop passed by him then turned around and headed back to the front of the bus. Flores felt a wave of relief wash over him as the *Federale* exited the bus.

His heart was hammering in his chest, but even so he felt almost giddy. He had escaped their notice. Of what had he been so fearful? They were searching for two gringos. He leaned his head back and closed his eyes. He was not used to this fugitive business; he had to learn to keep his cool or the stress would kill him.

"Señor Flores?"

Hector's eyes popped open, shocked to hear his name spoken. Above him stood the *Federale* with the moustache and stubble, but now his partner was with him. Hector had been so wrapped up in his relief that he did not hear them reenter the bus. The archeologist sat there with his mouth open, unable to speak. He was not going to make it to Cancún.

CHAPTER 37

Carlton had been sitting alone in a dark corner booth of The Senate for over thirty minutes, slowly nursing a beer. Five minutes ago, Don Schovich had arrived and taken a seat at the bar. When the FBI man entered, he had searched the crowded room with his eyes; at one point his gaze had been directly on Carlton, but there had been no recognition. Carlton was disguised simply: his hair was greased back and he wore a pair of horned-rim glasses with thick lenses. He was dressed in a pair of pleated cotton slacks and a slightly wrinkled, vertical-striped button-down shirt with a solid brown tie. Carlton considered this to be his professorial look, or at least he looked like someone who owned a lot of books. He had not expected to fool Schovich, but he was pleased that he had.

He had arrived early so that he could watch the crowd and attempt to spot anyone who might be tailing him or waiting for him. The place was more crowded than it had been during his previous visit, which made things more difficult, but so far he had not spotted any suspicious or familiar characters. He was now letting the room soak, watching for anyone who might be following Schovich. Carlton trusted Don, but one could not be too careful.

Deciding the place was as safe as it was going to get, Carlton stood and approached the bar, leaving his half-empty glass of beer on the table. Schovich was working on a neat bourbon and eyeing the entrance to The Senate when Carlton sat beside him.

"Are you going to buy me a beer, or do I have to do it myself?" asked Carlton good-naturedly.

Schovich turned quickly toward the sound of the familiar voice, almost falling off his stool. The FBI man held himself steady by gripping the edge of the bar with both hands.

"Holy shit! You scared me. I didn't recognize you," exclaimed Schovich, somehow managing to keep his voice low.

"Sorry, but I can't afford not to be careful," explained Carlton.

He ordered a beer and fired up a smoke. Schovich pushed forward a pile of bills that were sitting on the bar, indicating that he was buying. The barkeep set up Carlton, then took the required amount out of Schovich's pile of money.

"Did you get the list of fraternity members?" asked Carlton as soon as the barkeep had moved on to the next customer.

"Yes, but how about a little explanation as to what's going on here," answered Schovich.

"I'll tell you more than you want to know, but let me see the list first. If it shows what I think it does, it will make explaining a lot easier."

Schovich pulled some folded faxcimile paper from his pocket and handed it to his friend. Carlton unfolded the paper, a list of graduating seniors belonging to the SAG fraternity at USC from the years 1961 through 1963. The list was broken down by year graduated, with the graduates of each year listed in alphabetical order. He searched through the year 1961 first and did not find either of the names he was looking for. He moved on to 1962 and about halfway down the list came across the name Jason James Hightower. Circling the Senator's name with a pen, he then dropped down to the Rs where he found the other name he was looking for: Ricardo Reyes.

Finding the names together sent an adrenaline spike through Carlton's system. He finally had something stronger than murky supposition to go on. Reyes and Hightower belonging to the same fraternity and graduating from the same school in the same year had to be considered more than a mere coincidence. This was the connection he had been searching for.

His feelings of triumph did not last long; as they were soon overshadowed by thoughts of how foolish he had been in going to Hightower with his speculations. It was no accident that things had started to heat up after his meeting with the Senator; the son-of-a-bitch was in league with Reyes. It all made sense now. Hightower was the only one left alive; he had to be the leak in Operation Raven. What had thrown him off from the beginning was the attempt on the Senator's life. It had compelled Carlton to consider the man a victim and not a suspect. Evidently the car bombing had been staged, the only victim being the substitute chauffeur who was vaporized. This would explain why Hightower had been keeping such a high profile; he knew that he was not in any real danger.

The information Carlton now had was not enough to bring the Senator down, but it could get the process started. A full investigation would certainly turn up enough dirt to bury Hightower. All he had to do was get this information into the hands of the right people.

"Did you find what you what you are looking for?" asked Schovich.

"I think so. Now I have some explaining to do."

Keeping his voice low so only Don could hear him, Carlton started from the beginning, not leaving anything out: Operation Raven, Sam

Peters, Hightower, and Reyes. He revealed how he contrived their first meeting at The Senate. He told of his last meeting with Hightower and of the kid who tried to end his life last night, and he concluded with the college connection between Hightower and Reyes.

"Holy shit! Hightower is on the short list for Vice President," stated Schovich in a hushed voice.

"What are you talking about?" asked a confused Carlton.

"I guess you haven't heard yet. The news was just breaking as I was driving over here. The Vice President has announced he is declining to run for a second term. I'm sure you've heard the rumors floating around that the President was pressuring the VP to step down; he wants to bring in some new blood. The President has slipped so far in the polls he is willing to try anything. Supposedly the short list is very short, and the Senator's name is at the top," explained Schovich.

The stakes had been raised. Carlton was now trying to bring down not just a United States Senator, but a possible Vice Presidential candidate.

"This information has to get into the hands of the right people, or my life is not worth shit," claimed Carlton.

"And now that you have enlightened me, I'm in the same boat," added Schovich.

"I'm sorry for bringing you into this, but I had nowhere else to go. It won't last long now. I think I have enough information to convince Secretary of State Goreman, if I can get a meeting with him. Once the big boys get involved, we can breathe easier," explained Carlton, attempting to put their situation in the best light.

Schovich slugged down the rest of his drink, as if to steady himself, and then said, "I have something to tell you now. The big boys are already involved, and we're taking you in."

At first Carlton did not comprehend what Schovich had said. It took a moment for the meaning to sink in.

"Take me in?" said Carlton, "I don't think I am quite ready for that. Let's wait until there is a little better separation between the good guys and the bad guys. You show up with me at Buzzard's Point, and I'll be shot by some rookie agent fresh out of the academy."

"I'm not kidding, Nelson. You're coming in with me," stated Schovich.

"And what if I choose not to come?" challenged Carlton.

"You don't have a choice," answered the FBI man as he tilted his head toward the door.

Standing at the entrance to the bar, Carlton saw a clean-cut young man dressed in a blue suit. The man returned Carlton's stare. Carlton slowly turned his head to look behind him. Standing at the rear door he saw a duplicate of the man watching the front entrance.

"You're a fucking asshole!" hissed Carlton.

"I'm sorry. I didn't want to do it this way, but these bastards put the pressure on me. They said if I didn't cooperate, I'd be busted out of the Bureau, no pension, no nothing. I had no choice. Besides they are after the same thing you are. With what you have, they will put Hightower and Reyes out of business and protect you in the meantime."

Carlton was stunned; he had not expected this from Schovich. His options were limited. Hemmed in and outnumbered, he had no choice but to go along and hope these men were who Don said they were.

"It's time for us to go. You follow me out. There will be a car out front; we'll get in the rear seat. Don't make a scene or try anything cute; these guys don't need much of an excuse to drop you."

Carlton did not doubt the FBI man's words. He followed Schovich to the door. The agent who had been standing sentinel at the front door exited immediately in front of Schovich, and the other agent followed closely behind Carlton. Outside the bar a dark-blue Cadillac was parked at the curb. The front agent held the caddy's rear door open, and Schovich ducked into the back seat, immediately followed by Carlton. Carlton thought the car was a bit ostentatious for the Bureau, but this appeared to be a high-powered unit. The rear agent slid into the rear seat, sandwiching Carlton between Schovich and the agent. After shutting the rear door, the front agent opened the front passenger side door and climbed into the shotgun seat. A driver was seated behind the wheel of the vehicle, but Carlton was unable to see the man's face.

"You're going to have to hand over your weapon. Lift your coat back, and I'll remove your piece," instructed Schovich.

Carlton did as he was told and allowed Schovich to pull the pistol from his shoulder holster. Schovich handed the weapon to the agent in the front seat. The driver then turned around to face the passengers in the rear seat, a pistol in his hand. Carlton's blood turned to ice when he recognized the smiling face of Armando Galvan, Hightower's private chauffeur. Why had his friend set him up this way? He glanced at Schovich and saw a shocked expression on the man's face.

"You will now hand me your weapon, agent Schovich," ordered Galvan in an accented voice.

"What's going on?" sputtered a flustered Schovich.

"I will ask you for your weapon one last time. If you do not produce it, I will kill you," explained Galvan calmly.

Schovich did as he was told this time, handing his weapon over to the pseudo-agent in the front seat.

"Now we are going for a little drive," said Galvan as he started the car.

CHAPTER 38

A Montechristo number four between his lips and a tumbler of Comemorativo in his hand, Ricardo Reyes sat in his living room enjoying the ocean view out the giant picture window. It was late afternoon and in a couple of hours he would be dining with a beautiful woman, someone new. Life was good.

For the first time, polls showed that candidate Cervantes was leading in the presidential race. Soon Cervantes would be the most powerful man in Mexico, and he would owe his standing to Ricardo Reyes. In the United States, the U.S. President was going to ask Senator Jason James Hightower to replace the current Vice President, who was declining to run for a second term. The Senator was also in debt to Reyes and in four years, maybe sooner, Hightower could be the most powerful man in the world.

For Reyes the future was full of possibilities. Soon the war on drugs would be turned up another notch, his competitors hounded, harassed, and hopefully put out of business. He alone would be able to operate under complete anonymity of both the U.S. and Mexican governments. The doors to more legitimate businesses would now open to him. Reyes was becoming a very powerful man. Life should continue to be good.

Reyes puffed on his cigar as he contemplated the future. The problem of Jack Phillips appeared to be nearing an end. Inspector Ortiz had called earlier and informed him that Hector Flores had been apprehended in the small coastal town of Playa Del Carmen. He had been alone; there was no sign of Jack Phillips or the big man, but it was only a matter of time until they were also apprehended or eliminated. Reyes was confident he could manipulate the archeologist into helping track down Phillips. If not, there was always Ramon with his special talent of persuading people to confide in him.

Reyes glanced at his watch; Ortiz should be arriving soon. He had sensed that the Inspector did not want to bring Flores to him, but Ortiz would not question Reyes' wishes, especially after getting caught in his lie about what happened at the Merida Police Station. The Inspector had been pulled deep into Reyes' web, entangled to the point where extrication was impossible. This is where Reyes liked to have people.

Juanita's voice interrupted his reverie. "Inspector Ortiz is here."

"Send him in!" said a beaming Reyes as he rose from his chair.

Reyes remained standing as he anxiously waited for Juanita to return with the Inspector and Hector Flores. When they finally entered the room, Reyes was stunned by the sight of a ragged-looking Flores, his hands cuffed behind his back. Reyes had imagined exchanging theories on ancient Mayan culture with the archeologist as they leisurely inspected his collection of antiquities. He had almost forgotten that Flores was not a willing visitor to his home.

"Are the handcuffs necessary?" asked Reyes.

"He is a prisoner of the Mexican Government," explained Ortiz.

"He is a guest in my house," returned Reyes.

Ortiz got the message and removed the cuffs.

A confused Flores rubbed his sore wrists as he glanced warily at Reyes. Hector had expected to be taken to some medieval torture chamber, not the seaside estate of Ricardo Reyes. In spite of the plush accommodations currently surrounding him, he had a feeling the torture chamber was not far away.

"Juanita, would you have Ramon report to me," Reyes instructed the young woman before she left the room.

"Please take a seat," said Reyes, pointing toward a long off-white sofa.

The sofa was situated so that it afforded those sitting on it a view through the wall of glass. Flores sat on the couch, but Ortiz ambled over to the window where he gazed out to the ocean.

With the cuffs removed and Ortiz's attention averted, Flores considered making a run for it. Could he make it out the front door before being caught by Ortiz? He quickly realized how foolish this idea was, for even if he managed to outrun the Inspector, he had nowhere to go. The estate was surrounded by miles of dense jungle, and the only road in or out was heavily guarded.

"I apologize if you have been treated poorly. You need not fear now, for you are with an admirer," said Reyes, a smile stretched across his face.

Flores was in a mild state of shock, uncertain of how he should react. His gut feeling was to tell Reyes to "shove it!" Luckily, he still had enough of his wits in place to keep a hold of his tongue and smile back at the bastard.

"Would you like something to drink?" asked Reyes.

Flores was about to refuse, then thought better; a beer would taste good after the day he was having. "*Leon Negra, por favor.*"

"My pleasure," said Reyes as he walked across the room to a small wet bar tucked into the wall. "I assume the usual for you, Inspector?" asked Reyes as he opened the small refrigerator behind the bar.

"Actually, I think I'll have a beer tonight," answered Ortiz, who was still staring out the window.

While the host poured the beer, Flores studied his surroundings. The room was sparsely decorated; muted tones predominated. The floor was a gray slate tile, the walls a cream-colored textured plaster. Scattered about the room were pieces of Mayan art. He had not yet been close enough to any of the works to identify if they were genuine, but he would have been surprised if they were not. The focal point of the room was the wall of glass that allowed views of a broad stretch of fine white sand and the blue Caribbean beyond. On the other side of the glass was a large patio area, on the far edge of which was centered what appeared to be an original chacmool statue. The reclining figure was facing the ocean holding the sacrificial platter on its belly.

Reyes, playing the gracious host, returned with the glasses of beer. He passed out the drinks, then joined Flores on the couch.

"As I already stated, you have nothing to fear from me," started Reyes. "But I cannot speak for the Judicial Police. According to Inspector Ortiz, you are suspected of harboring a fugitive, a gringo named Jack Phillips. Is this not right, Inspector?"

"No charges have been filed, but we are very interested in what Señor Flores has to say on the subject of Jack Phillips," answered Ortiz between swallows of beer.

"I must tell you that the Inspector did not want to bring you here," continued Reyes. "He does not like me interfering in his business. The government tends to be heavy-handed with cases like this. You could be facing difficult interrogations and interminable jail time. I may have a way to keep you from these hardships and keep the Inspector happy. Before we get to business though, I would like to show you something."

Reyes rose from the couch and said, "Please, follow me."

As Flores stood, he noticed Reyes silently nodding to Ortiz, indicating that the Inspector was to follow. Flores guessed that Reyes did not want to be alone with him. He also detected tension between the two men; he sensed that they did not like each other.

Reyes led them down a long hallway, the end of which held a closed metal door with a ten-digit key pad above the knob. Flores wondered what could be behind the door that required this kind of security. Reyes entered a set of numbers into the key pad, and the mechanism emitted a short electronic beep. He then opened the door and flicked on a light switch. The light revealed a large room, approximately 30 feet by 60 feet, which was set up like a museum. It was filled with glass display cases, the walls covered with objects of Mayan art, and suspended from the ceiling were other articles of curiosity.

"My hobby room," said a smiling Reyes as he motioned them inside.

Flores quickly forgot about his present predicament as he inspected the room's treasures. It was a warehouse of pre-Colombian art and artifacts. There appeared to be samples from all of the great ancient civilizations of Mexico. Ceremonial greenstone axes carved into the "Were Jaguar" figure, with flaming eyebrows and cleft forehead, were Olmec from the Gulf Coast. Another greenstone figure portrayed an Olmec holding an infant deity, the rain deity, if he remembered correctly. He had seen similar figures recovered from Las Limas. There was a ceramic incense burner shaped in the form of a temple, and inside the temple was the face of a god. Immediately, he recognized that it was from Teotihuacan. He gazed upon a jade bat mask that at one time must have graced the waist of some Mayan king. Against one wall was the carved relief of a Mayan nobleman, the delicate, perfectly proportioned style suggested that it came from Palenque. He noted a gold figurine that was Aztec in style. Flores was awed by the size and diversity of the collection. Important pieces from each era were represented, many of them priceless.

It was driving him crazy not knowing if they had uncovered the tomb of the Bearded Man, but he did not dare broach the subject for fear of leading them to his find. So far, he was relieved not to find anything from the tomb within Reyes' collection. This gave him some hope that the tomb and its contents remained undisturbed.

Flores inspected a large gold disk depicting three warriors wearing gaudy quetzal-feathered headdresses, spears in hand, with a large serpent at their feet.

"That was found by scuba divers in the sacred well at Chichén Itzá," informed Reyes.

Flores was not sure he wanted to know how the gold disk came into Reyes possession.

"I helped finance the *cenote* dive project, and this was a gift from the head archeologist," explained Reyes.

Hector doubted that any archeologist would give such a significant piece away, even to an important contributor, but he decided it was best to keep these doubts to himself. In fact, Flores had his doubts about much of what he was seeing. He questioned how Reyes could have legally amassed such an extensive collection of antiquities. Only at the Museum of Anthropology in Mexico City had Hector seen a superior assemblage of pre-Colombian artifacts.

When Hector stared down into the next display case he froze in stunned disbelief; under the glass was Lord Pacal's Jade Death Mask! This mask had been stolen from the Museum of Anthropology on

Christmas Eve 1985. After his initial shock, anger surged through the archeologist. This was too much. This man had no right to such a thing; it belonged in a museum. Managing to keep his anger hidden, he moved on to the next display case as if he had not noticed what the mask was. He could not afford to show his anger.

"Your collection is quite impressive, but what does it have to do with me and my situation with the police?" asked Flores as he continued down the line of display cases.

"I wanted to impress upon you my commitment to preserving Mexico's ancient past as it relates to a proposal I want you to consider."

"Commitment to stealing it all for yourself," thought Hector.

"Your partner Gus Wise and his friend Jack Phillips were part of a drug smuggling scheme. This was the reason for the raids at Cobá. Originally, the *Federales* did not think you were involved, but they are now beginning to question this assumption. I happen to think that they are jumping to conclusions."

Reyes paused a couple of beats for effect, letting the meaning of his words sink in.

"I'd like to think that an important scientist like yourself would not become entangled in such matters. I think it would be a terrible loss to the country if you were to spend the rest of your life in prison; your services are too valuable to the archeological world. The problem is, unless you help the government apprehend Mr. Phillips, it won't matter what I think.

"I am sure you feel some loyalty to your supposed friends, but I assure you it is misplaced loyalty. Now, if you were to help the Inspector, I'm sure I could convince him to drop any pending charges against you. I also could become very interested in helping to fund future archeological projects."

"So you can add to your personal collection," shot back Flores unable to contain his emotions any longer. "This room is a record of over twenty years of grave robbing."

The look in Reyes' eyes suddenly became very hard, while a perplexed expression passed over the Inspector's face. Flores realized too late that he had said too much. The Inspector was looking down into the display case containing Pacal's Mask; for a brief moment his expression changed from puzzlement to shocked recognition. Had the Inspector recognized what he was looking at?

"You wanted to see me, Señor Reyes?" came a voice from across the room, breaking the tension.

Hector turned around to see a handsome, dark-haired man standing in the doorway.

"Yes, Ramon, I wanted you to meet Hector Flores. He will be staying with us tonight," said Reyes.

Ramon strode confidently up to Hector and stuck out his hand. Reluctantly, Hector gripped the cold hand while trying not to stare at the line of pink scar tissue under the man's chin. The man exuded a darkness that sent a shiver through Hector.

"I am pleased to meet you," greeted Ramon. Hector could imagine Ramon being just as pleased to cut his throat.

Hector did not answer verbally. A slight nod was his only reply, but inside he was seething.

There was an awkward silence as they stood amongst the relics of the past.

"Inspector, you may leave if you like. Come back in the morning, and I am sure we will be able to conclude this unpleasantness," suggested Reyes, but it was a suggestion not meant to be questioned.

Ortiz bit his lower lip as he glanced at Flores then back at Reyes. He appeared uncomfortable. He nodded his head and then ambled out of the room.

Hector had swallowed back his anger. He knew his only hope was to hold on until Travis and Jack arrived. To do this he would have to play along.

"Let's not play games, Señor Flores," started Reyes, once the Inspector had left the room. "Mr. Phillips is a wanted man, and the *Federales* have evidence that he has been living at your Cobá base camp for the past week. This is serious; you could end up wasting your life in prison. You can avoid this if you will tell me where Jack Phillips is."

"I don't know!" replied Flores as sincerely as he could muster.

"We know you were with him yesterday afternoon. Tell me the last place you saw him." demanded Reyes.

Hector was not sure how he should answer this question. How much did Reyes already know? He did not want to say anything that would lead them to his friends or to the tomb of the Bearded Man. Unable to make a decision, he remained silent.

"Come now, Señor Flores. You could not have forgotten yesterday? Such important finds only come along once in a very lucky lifetime," baited Reyes.

Hector immediately got a sick feeling in his stomach. This was not fair. "That is an extremely important site! I hope the *Federales* did not disturb it," he said, his voice quavering as he hoped against hope.

"Your find is protected. I have had most of it boxed up and moved to a safe place," replied Reyes.

Flores could not believe what he was hearing. "You bastard! That was an undisturbed, intact site, untouched for over a thousand years, and you have your men go in and remove the artifacts! Do you understand what has been lost?" screamed Flores, his face inches from Reyes' face.

Flores was shaking, his body boiling with anger. Suddenly there was a sharp pain in his lower back and his lungs felt as if they had collapsed. He dropped to his knees, gasping for breath; his lungs would not function. Ramon had delivered a blow to his kidney.

Hector looked up into the unsympathetic eyes of Ricardo Reyes. "Take our guest to his quarters," ordered Reyes. "Perhaps you could teach him some manners."

CHAPTER 39

The small boat cut through the surf, taking them out past the breakwater; they were finally off. Jack watched as the wide strip of white sand and the green line of jungle disappeared into the glare of the setting sun. He glanced down at the gun in his hand; it felt heavy and awkward. For the first time, the enormity of what they were attempting grabbed hold of him, and he began to question himself. Maybe this was not the best way. Maybe Flores was right. Let the authorities handle the situation. What did he know about armed assaults or nighttime operations? A few shooting lessons did not make him a commando. Jack tried to push these thoughts of self-speculation from his mind; after all, it was too late to turn back.

Pax's Uncle Jorge steered the twelve-foot fiberglass boat south through the small swells. Against Travis's wishes, the old man had been a last-minute addition to the crew. Jorge had spent the afternoon prowling up and down the beach with his large homemade rifle. Even to Jack's untrained eye the weapon did not appear safe. The long barrel looked to be a length of common pipe attached to a rough-hewn wooden stock, and the hammer action was nothing more than a rubber band. He had seen such rifles strapped to the backs of men bicycling along the jungle highways. According to Pax, the rifles were used to hunt wild pigs and deer. The scene of this old man protecting them from all evil with his near Stone Age weapon, had provided Travis and Jack a source of comic relief throughout the afternoon; that was until it came time to leave and they found Jorge seated in the boat with his rifle beside him. At first Jack thought the old man had decided not to let them use the boat. This turned out not to be the case. Jorge wanted to go along, and if he could not go, then the boat stayed.

Travis had appeared quite irritated as he spoke rapidly in Spanish to Jorge, but the old man had remained stoically seated, refusing to discuss the situation. Jack could not understand the conversation, though it was obvious that Travis was not getting his way.

"What the hell am I doing!? A college professor, a kid, and now a crazy old man with a homemade cannon. We will be lucky if he doesn't blow us all up with that thing," complained Travis to Jack as they boarded the boat with Jorge still at the throttle.

Jorge was actually Pax's great-uncle. Jack figured the old man was at least sixty years old, as Pax had explained that Jorge was his grandfather's older brother. Even so, Jack did not doubt the man's toughness. He was thick-chested with a sturdy, compact body that had been toned by years of physical labor. His skin was remarkably smooth for a man who had spent so many years on, in, or near the ocean; only the thin lines at the corners of his eyes began to tell of the countless days out in the elements. The old man wore his age well. He had a timeless quality about him; it was as if he were an immutable part of the coastline.

The sun had dropped below the western horizon, and the black silhouette of the mainland had become distinguishable. To Jack the dark coastline all looked the same. "You think Jorge and Pax will be able to find Reyes' estate? The coastline all looks the same," commented Jack to Travis.

"Actually, it should be pretty hard to miss, probably the only lights we'll see," replied Travis, an edge to his voice.

Jack felt like an idiot for asking such a stupid question. Now that he thought about it, he realized he could probably find the estate all by himself. This only made him feel more uncomfortable. Throughout the day he had felt like this was the right thing to do; now, though, he was beginning to waver. It was not a problem of courage, Jack had plenty of reasons to face the task before him, but did he have the ability to complete the task? If it came to shooting, would he react properly? Would he react at all? Earlier in the day it had seemed like an adventure; there was excitement ahead. Travis had been serious in explaining the use of the pistol and in how Jack should handle himself, but there had also been some good humor. The mood was different now; Travis seemed more focused, and there was no time for amusement.

"What is our plan tonight?" asked Jack

Travis stared back at Jack, not answering immediately, making Jack feel like he had just asked another stupid question.

"We find your wife and then we find Reyes so I can have a little talk with the man. As to how we accomplish this, I am not sure. Like I said last night, I'm making this up as I go along." For a moment, Travis's crooked smile was back on his face, which somehow made Jack feel a little better.

They rode on in silence, the only sounds being the constant drone of the outboard motor and the slapping of the sea against the boat's fiberglass hull. With the salty smell, the empty ocean, and the deserted coastline, they could have been the last people on earth. The light in the western sky had dimmed enough to allow a clearer view of the coastline; rocky points, small inlets, and hidden beaches were now visible. It was the day's last light, that rosy brilliance that can make the world sparkle in an ethereal glow. Jack relaxed somewhat as he watched the east coast of the Yucatán slide by.

Without warning, Jorge suddenly turned the boat sharply to starboard and cut the motor. Jack sat up straight, his insides churning. It was now quiet except for the water lapping at the hull.

"What are we doing?" asked a confused Jack.

Travis pointed south toward the coast. A couple of miles away Jack saw the lights of Reyes' estate interrupting the dark coastline.

"What are we waiting for?" asked Jack, still confused.

"It's still too light, they might see us coming," replied Travis, "We'll wait for it to get darker."

CHAPTER 40

Nelson Carlton sat in the rear seat of the Cadillac, sandwiched between the bogus FBI agent and a sweating Donald Schovich, hoping that this was not to be his final ride. He recalled the times he had spent with the barrel of a gun in his mouth, contemplating pulling the trigger, and now realized how full of shit he had been on those tormented nights. It had all been an act, a self-indulgence. Genuinely faced with his demise, his mind had gone into high gear trying to figure a way to save himself. Schovich would be no help; he had the deer-in-the-headlights look. For now, Carlton would have to wait and hope for an opportunity.

Armando Galvan maneuvered the Cadillac through the late afternoon traffic, making good time but staying within the speed limit. Carlton thought of attempting something while they were still in traffic. If he could draw some attention, cause a wreck, he could at least go down fighting. Every scenario he devised, though, ended with bullets being deposited into his brain. His prospects with Galvan did not appear much better; these men planned to kill him.

They had moved into an industrial section of the city made up of gray concrete and rusted metal buildings, many of which appeared deserted. The term "urban renewal" did not immediately come to mind. Galvan steered the vehicle into an alley and parked in a small parking lot behind a metal warehouse building. The lot was empty.

Carlton and Schovich were ordered out of the car and marched through a door into the large warehouse. Schovich went in first, then Carlton, followed by Galvan and one of the men who had posed as an FBI agent. The other impostor stayed with the Caddy, Carlton assumed to keep watch.

The building was wood frame with a metal shell. An array of small wood frame windowpanes filled the upper quarter of the western wall. The last rays of the setting sun filtered through the dusty, fly speckled glass, casting the empty interior of the ancient warehouse in a dusky orange-red glow. Their footfalls on the concrete floor echoed off the metal walls.

They had walked approximately thirty feet toward the center of the warehouse when Schovich stopped and said, "I'm not taking another step until you assholes tell me what this is all about."

His question was answered by an ear-shattering blast. Don Schovich dropped face first onto the concrete, with a neat, round, red hole in the back of his head.

Carlton jerked to a stop, his eyes locked on the quivering body. He lost control of his bladder as he waited for the shot that would end his life. Warm urine soaked his legs. Armando Galvan's laughter filled his ears.

"My friend, I am not going to shoot you," said Galvan as he slowly walked toward Carlton. "This man was stupid; he could not be trusted. I'm sure you are much smarter." The Mexican was now facing him approximately ten feet away. "Look at you—you have wet yourself! Are you so old now that you can no longer control yourself?" chided an amused Galvan.

Carlton did not react to the taunt; it was all he could do to keep from trembling. He pulled his gaze from Don Schovich. He had to get himself together, and staring at the lifeless flesh of his friend would not help. The brutal murder he just witnessed had to be pushed from his thoughts.

Galvan fished a cigarette out of his coat pocket with his left hand, then pulled out a lighter and lit up, all while keeping the gun in his right hand pointed at Carlton.

"May I get a smoke?" asked Carlton as he pointed at his pants' pocket.

"Have one of mine. You've pissed all over yours," replied Galvan.

"I'd rather have a Camel. I never did care for filtered cigarettes," explained Carlton, sounding much calmer then he felt.

Galvan nodded, indicating it was all right for Carlton to take the cigarettes from his pocket.

"Thanks," said Carlton as he pulled out a smoke and lit up. He sucked the smoke deep into his lungs, hoping the nicotine would help to settle his rattled nerves. His mind was racing trying to figure his options and forget about the hole in Schovich's head.

"You do not have to end up like your friend," said Galvan as he motioned to the lump on the floor. "If you cooperate, we are willing to let you live. We can give you a new identity; you could retire somewhere in South America and live out your golden years in relative comfort. For this to happen, you are going to have to help us. We know that you are a smart man and that you have surely protected yourself. If you want to continue living, you are going to have to hand over all documents you have pertaining to Senator Hightower and Senior Reyes. We also want the names of anyone with whom you may have shared this information. If you help us, we will take care of you; after all, you could be a valuable source for information in the future."

It was all out on the table now. Carlton's suspicions were validated: Hightower and Reyes were partners. Until tonight he had no hard evidence against the Senator, only some hard-to-ignore coincidences and a theory that fit a strange set of circumstances. The only other person he had shared this information with was now dead. Galvan could dust him right now, and their troubles would be over. Evidently they thought he knew more than he did; this was Carlton's only bargaining chip, and it was all bluff.

"Let's cut the crap! No matter what I do or say you're going to drop me," replied Carlton, his Camel bobbing in the corner of his mouth. A plan of action was forming in his mind. It was a thousand-to-one shot, but Carlton was not going to get any better odds tonight.

A slow, easy laugh escaped through Galvan's lips. He laughed as if he had just been caught in the middle of a practical joke. "I told them you were too smart to swallow some line of shit. You are right; you are a dead man, but there are easy ways to die and there are hard ways to die. If you come clean, I will make it easy."

Now it was Carlton's turn to laugh. "Why don't you go fuck yourself," he said calmly. Dropping his cigarette on the concrete, he then crushed the butt out with the sole of his shoe, and in this same motion he took a step toward his captor.

Galvan was put off balance by Carlton's sudden attitude change. He also did not like Carlton moving in so close, but it would not have been macho to back away, especially since he had the gun.

"My death will be as slow as possible, because you won't be able to believe anything I tell you. As long as I am breathing, you will continue to torture me, trying to extract another morsel of information that will either prove or disprove what I've already said. I'm not sure how I'm going to hold up under this; maybe you will learn something, maybe you won't. But here is something to think about—if I die, Hightower will be exposed," warned Carlton, as he eased another foot closer to Galvan.

For the first time this evening, Galvan did not seem so sure of himself. He had not expected such a reaction from Carlton. Galvan had ended a few lives; the victim's initial reactions were almost always shock and terror. If he gave them time to think about it, they usually went to pleading. Men were the worst; it embarrassed him to watch strong men on their knees crying like babies. He had found that women usually accepted their fate in a more dignified manner. Danielle, the hooker who killed Ron Allen, was a good example; she had accepted her death without a big fuss. It really did not matter to Galvan how Carlton reacted; he would have the man on his knees begging before the night was over. Carlton was not going to die easily.

"It is too bad that you cannot be more reasonable. I am not going to enjoy this," lied Galvan. He was going to enjoy it very much.

Carlton moved even closer, but this time Galvan shot him a hard look, as if to say the fun was now over. Galvan's eyes left Carlton for a split second as he motioned for his accomplice to move in. In that split second, Carlton made his move. He was betting his life on the assumption that he was not to be killed until thoroughly pumped for information and that his comment about exposing Hightower would be in the back of Galvan's mind. It also helped that at six foot two inches and 210 pounds Galvan probably assumed he could easily handle the smaller thinner man. Carlton would have preferred to have been closer before making his attack, but this appeared to be his only chance.

Coming at Galvan with an open palm upper cut, Carlton drove the base of his right palm toward the man's chin. He was not as quick as he had been in his youth, and Galvan was fast. A smile formed on the big man's lips as he easily blocked the attack with his left arm. He seemed to find it humorous that this smaller, older man would try and take him on physically. Galvan swung his right hand, which held the gun, at Carlton's head.

The frontal attack had been a diversion. Carlton anticipated the right and managed to get a grip on the weapon as it crashed into the side of his face. In one motion, Carlton twisted around, swinging his right arm over Galvan's right arm, pinning it to his body. With his back now to Galvan and his left hand still gripping the gun, Carlton clamped his jaws around Galvan's right wrist. A guttural scream echoed through the warehouse as Carlton's back was pounded by hammering blows from Galvan's left fist. Carlton hung on like a pit bull terrier, refusing to let go. The steely taste of blood filled his mouth as his teeth cut through the salty skin and ground against bone. His hands pulled furiously at the gun in a desperate attempt to free the weapon from Galvan's grip. He knew at any moment the bogus FBI agent would be on top of him.

They were locked in a stalemate, neither man able to overpower the other. Galvan's assistant had rushed up in front of the two combatants. Carlton could sense that this third man was about to deliver the deciding blow when his finger found the trigger. The world suddenly exploded. A blinding flash and crushing blow to his face occurred simultaneously. Carlton's first thought was that the weapon had exploded, taking a good portion of his face with it. What had actually happened was the gun's slide had discharged into his left cheekbone when the weapon fired.

The Mexican lost his grip on the gun, which then slipped through Carlton's hands and clattered to the floor. A foggy black numbness was floating over Carlton's consciousness, threatening to engulf him. His vision blurred, his hearing shattered by the blast, he fought back the darkness as his hands scrambled for the weapon now lying on the concrete.

His right hand found the butt of the pistol and his fingers gripped the weapon as if it were the last handhold on a ladder to nowhere.

He came up holding the gun out in front of himself. Through his haze he was able to make out the crumpled form of the bogus FBI agent. The man lay on his back, his hands clutching a bloody red blotch on his belly. Carlton's numb ears could not hear the man's screams.

"Where is Galvan?" thought Carlton as he frantically tried to spin around, the gun still out in front of him. His brain was not fully communicating with his legs, and he stumbled down onto one knee. A large blurred shape was above him, coming down on him. Reacting, he pulled the trigger, the gun fired, and the shape dropped back away from him. The world was spinning faster, his guts churning. Fighting against waves of nauseating darkness that threatened to pull him under, Carlton tried to get to his feet. If he could only rise up through the gray fuzz that surrounded him. He stumbled, and the world went black.

CHAPTER 41

Pax Chi leapt from the bow of the boat as the fiberglass hull ground into the sand. He secured the bowline to the nearest palm tree; Jorge had already dropped the anchor off the stern. Once the craft was secured, Jack followed Travis through knee-deep water and onto the deserted beach. A half moon hung in the sky, giving off enough light so that they could distinguish shape from shadow. They were approximately one mile north of Reyes's estate.

Travis ordered Jorge to stay behind and guard the boat. The old man did not appear to like this, but he did not argue the point.

"The old bastard can get into too much trouble out here by himself," remarked Travis to Jack as they started following Pax down the beach.

Jack's feelings of angst had calmed since landing on the beach. Maybe it was because they were now taking action with a job to do, or maybe it was because Josephine was so close. The gun still felt awkward in his hand, but he was no longer questioning himself.

They made good time by walking on the packed wet sand along the surf line. The lights of the estate grew brighter with each step. They were within a quarter mile of the estate when Travis had them move up into the tree line. It was harder work trudging through the loose sand, but the trees offered cover if they came upon anyone.

They had traveled on another couple of hundred yards when they came upon a group of weary looking *palapas*. The small palm- thatched buildings appeared to be deserted, except for one that had a man standing in front of it smoking a cigarette, a rifle cradled in his arms. Their position in the trees was well-hidden, and there was little chance of the man seeing them.

Travis and Pax whispered back and forth in Spanish, then Travis explained to Jack, "Pax says this is the place they were holding your wife. I'm going to take the guard out. I think he is by himself, and he doesn't appear too worried about intruders. You and Pax wait here until you hear me whistle for you."

"What do we do if the guard takes you out?" asked Jack.

"He won't, but if you hear a gunshot it would mean that my plan hasn't worked. In that case, shoot the guard. Don't ask questions just shoot him, preferably in the head. Hopefully, you'll find your wife inside. Take her back to the boat and shove off as quickly as possible. If there is gunplay you won't have much time," explained Travis.

As he spoke, Travis lifted up his right pant leg to check the sheathed knife strapped to his calf. He then made sure his pistol was secure in his shoulder holster. "See you in a bit," whispered Travis, before he moved off through the trees, silently vanishing into the night.

Jack was filled with hopeful anxiety; the impossible had suddenly become possible. Was Jo alive and in that grass shack just a few yards away? He was beginning to believe she was. As the minutes passed, Jack's anticipation was tempered by a feeling of awkwardness. Another man was putting his life on the line to rescue Jo while he remained hidden in the trees. It did not feel right, but, ego aside, Jack understood that Travis had a much better chance of disarming the guard than he did.

From their hiding place, Jack and Pax watched the shack and waited. He was beginning to worry about Travis when he saw something moving in the jungle to the rear of the shack. The guard remained unaware as the dark shape of a man moved stealthily out of the trees and into position behind the *palapa*. Jack nervously bit on the tip of his thumb, hardly able to contain himself as he watched the scene play out before him.

Slipping around the far side of the shack, the shadowy figure disappeared from view. The next few minutes passed excruciatingly slow as Jack waited for Travis to act. Still appearing relaxed, the guard leaned against the *palapa* smoking his cigarette. All at once, the guard went rigid, his body rose up from the wall as an unintelligible grunt carried across the night air. It was too dark and had happened too fast for Jack to see exactly what had occurred, but the guard had vanished either behind or into the *palapa*. The night was quiet, and he saw no other movement around the shack. Time stretched as he waited for the whistle, prayed for the whistle. Then he heard what could have been a bird whistle—two short and high-pitched trills.

Jack felt a mixture of exuberance and fear as he and Pax left the hiding place and moved swiftly to the *palapa*. The closer he got to the shack, the greater his expectations became. By the time he rushed through the door, he was positive he would find Josephine.

Once inside the dark interior he came to a stop. All he could see was indistinct shapes. It took a moment for his eyes to adjust. A foul odor was heavy in the room, a human fecal smell that was somehow familiar. It reminded him of a hotel room in Mérida. His exuberance quickly drained out of him as his stomach turned.

"Travis?" whispered Jack. In front of him he was able to make out the shape of a man kneeling down next to a person seated on the floor. He prayed that the seated person was Jo.

"She's not here, Jack," Travis whispered back. "But Flores is, and he's in bad shape."

"Flores?" sputtered Jack as he tried to process this unexpected information.

The room began to spin around Jack, nausea forming in the pit of his stomach. Was it the sudden change in circumstance or the putrid smell? He looked down to his left. Just inside the doorway the body of the guard was sprawled out on the floor. The moonlight spilling through the open doorway illuminated the bulging eyes and slashed throat. The head was practically decapitated from the body. Sticky blood poured down from the wound, soaking the dead man's shirt. The warm smell rising off the lifeless flesh was overpowering. Jack turned and left the *palapa,* then promptly tossed the contents of his stomach onto the sand.

Jack wiped his chin as he stood up, feeling somewhat better. Travis stepped up behind him and asked, "You alright?"

"Yeah, just something I ate. It's gone now," replied Jack as he swallowed back the bile in his throat. "How did Flores get here?" he croaked.

"He says the *Federales* caught him on the bus at Playa Del Carmen. Ortiz brought him here to Reyes. He's been worked over pretty good. Nothing that won't heal, but I think he has a couple of broken ribs. He won't be moving anywhere fast. I want you to take him back to the boat. Pax and I will find your wife."

Jack ground his teeth as his cheeks flushed warm. The anger helped to burn off some of the lingering nausea. "Send Pax back with him. I'm not leaving here without my wife," replied Jack curtly.

"Look, Jack, we don't have time to fuck around. They could change guards or be coming back for another round of interrogation at any time. It makes more sense for Pax to come with me. He knows the layout of the estate. Besides I can't have you puking your guts out every time things get bloody. You're going back with Flores," commanded Travis.

"I'm not turning around. You can shoot me if you like, but I won't go back to the boat," explained a resolute Jack.

Travis looked hard into Jack's eyes, as if he were searching for something. He did not like being forced into making poor decisions.

The discussion was interrupted by Flores, who had made it to his feet and limped out the door of the *palapa.* "You know, I feel pretty good," grunted the archeologist.

Flores stood stiffly, his upper body tilted to the right. Even in the dark, Jack could see that Hector's face was swollen. There was a nasty-looking gash above his left eye and dried blood crusted on the side of his face. The archeologist's smile only made his face appear more macabre.

"Am I glad to see you, *amigos*," rasped Flores. "The only reason I was able to keep my mouth shut was that I knew you were coming. My biggest fear was that you would come and go without realizing I was here."

Travis and Pax had a brief conversation in Spanish, then Travis said to Jack, "Pax will take Flores to the boat." He paused a beat and stared down at Jack. "And you'll come with me."

Jack was relieved that Travis had not decided to shoot him. "What's our next move?" he asked trying to sound confident.

"Right to the top," replied Travis.

"What about Jo? How are we going to find her?" pressed Jack.

"We don't have a lot of time to go searching around. Pax says there is a group of *palapas* closer to the main house that are occupied by Reyes's women. We'll check it out on our way to the main house, but we can't afford to waste a lot of time there. If we don't find her, we go straight to Reyes; if anyone will know where she is, it'll be Reyes."

"Jack," Travis paused. "There is one thing you need to keep clear, and that is you might not like what we find, but no matter what happens, you have got to keep it together. Understood?"

"Understood," replied Jack.

"Alright. We don't have much time, let's move out," ordered Travis.

"Hold up," croaked Flores. "Ortiz and his men found the tomb at Cobá. Reyes claims to have removed the contents of the tomb and stashed them at a location known only to him. You must find out where!"

"I just might bring the bastard back with me and let you ask him yourself," responded Travis, a crooked grin spreading across his face.

"There is something else," continued an excited Flores. "Reyes showed me his private collection of Mexican antiquities. Most of the items were probably stolen. It's been rumored that Reyes revived the family fortune by dealing in the black market sale of pre-Colombian art. There is one piece in particular that could put him in jail for a long time; it's Pacal's Jade Death Mask, stolen from the National Museum of Anthropology in 1985. If you could bring back that piece, the government would be forced to listen to us."

"I'll do my best, but you need to get moving. The boat is a good mile from here; you're going to need every second," answered Travis.

Jack lightly placed his hand on his injured friend's shoulder and looked into his eyes, "You take care. We'll see you in a bit."

Flores nodded his head and smiled, "You, too, Jack."

Jack turned and followed Travis into the night.

CHAPTER 42

His consciousness had slowly risen from a formless black void into a fuzzy gray realm of awareness. A voice within pushed him to shake off the fog that clouded his mind. Why this was important, he could not recall, but he sensed danger. Lying on his back, he felt cold concrete beneath him; he could not remember where he was, but somehow he knew it was concrete beneath him. He attempted to open his eyes but was not sure if he had been successful; all he could see was blurred grayness. He tried to recall his last conscious moments: a struggle, but with whom? His recollection was as indistinct as his vision; he knew something was there, but it had no form. For a brief moment the distinct shapes of wood framing and corrugated metal coalesced above him. This vision drifted in and out of the fuzz a few times before finally stabilizing. He suddenly realized he was staring at the warehouse ceiling and, at the same moment, Nelson Carlton recalled his struggle with Galvan.

Prodded awake by his memories, Carlton rose to a sitting position. The sudden movement almost caused him to pass out again, but he managed to hold onto consciousness. His head felt swollen and his mouth thick. His vision was again blurred, but slowly the interior of the warehouse came into focus. Off to his right, the bogus FBI man lay motionless in a crimson pool, his belly soaked in blood. Carlton did not have to look any closer; he was sure the man was dead. To his left, and lying on his side, was Galvan. The man's right shoulder was bloody. Galvan's labored breathing indicated that he was still part of the living. Past Galvan, the body of Don Schovich lay face down on the concrete floor; there would be no Winnebago, no cross-country travels. Carlton looked away from his dead friend and immediately in front of him saw Galvan's gun resting on the concrete. He picked up the weapon with his right hand, feeling more in control now that he possessed the gun.

Carlton sat motionless for a few minutes, feeling wobbly, trying to regain full use of his senses. His head felt like an anvil that was in use, his ears ringing with each strike of the hammer. Slowly, he became aware that his left cheek felt heavy. Reaching up with his left hand, he cautiously touched the side of his face; the flesh was swollen and numb. When he pulled his hand back his fingers were sticky with blood. He remembered the gun exploding, but it could not have exploded; he was holding the weapon in his hand. Then he realized that the gun's slide had smashed into his face when the weapon fired. There was now an inch-long gash across his left cheek. Luckily, his cheekbone did not feel broken, and the wound was only slowly weeping blood.

Carlton was not sure how long he had been unconscious. The orange-red glow that had earlier filled the interior of the warehouse had been replaced by a dull gray light, but through the window panes along the top of the wall he could see a burnt-red sky. He concluded that he could not have been out for more than twenty minutes.

Miraculously, he had escaped torture and death at the hands of Galvan, but he was not so sure his situation had improved much. He was a wanted man holding a gun that had just been used to shoot three people, and two of them were dead. There were also at least a dozen people who had witnessed Schovich and him leaving The Senate together. He might have a difficult time explaining what had taken place, and he was pretty sure that Galvan was not going to back up his story. Carlton would not get many chances to tell his story. There were powerful people on both sides of the law who would go to great lengths to silence him.

The urge to run, to get out of the country, was strong. He had some money stashed away, enough to live on comfortably, but where could he go? Where would he be safe? Did he want to live the rest of his life looking over his shoulder? The prospects of a fugitive's life did not intrigue him.

He needed to decide on a course of action. Up to this point, he had only been reacting to the situations confronting him. Attacking Galvan had not been the result of any great plan or bravery, it had been his only option. It was pure luck he had survived. Now it was time to capitalize on his luck. He had to devise a way to get his story out before he could be silenced or discredited. Acting quickly would be critical, but he was anxious about calling in the authorities. Who would believe him? Whom could he trust?

Slowly a possibility began to form in his mind. A way out began taking shape. It would be a gamble, but any decision he made at this point would be a gamble. First, he would have a little talk with Galvan's other bogus FBI agent, who he hoped was still out with the car. He was going to need to borrow the man's phone.

CHAPTER 43

Hidden by the darkness, Jack and Travis stood with their backs against the wall of a large *palapa*. The sound of someone showering and a toilet being flushed informed them that this building was some kind of community bathroom. A heavy odor suggested a sewage problem. On the other side of the bathroom was a group of smaller *palapas* arranged in a semicircle around a central courtyard area. As he peered around the corner of the building, Travis saw a woman leave the bathroom and walk across the courtyard.

"I can't tell if it's your wife, but that doesn't mean much. I've only seen that one photograph of her," whispered Travis.

"What does she look like?" Jack whispered back, as he was not in position to be able to see around the corner of the building.

"Gorgeous blond with long legs, definitely a gringo," replied Travis, as he watched the woman enter one of the nearby *palapas*.

"Jo is a brunette," declared Jack.

"Like you don't have dark roots," pointed out Travis.

"Only my hairdresser knows for sure," quipped Jack, as he moved past Travis so he could see around the corner of the building. The courtyard was now empty. "Damn, I wish I could have seen her," said Jack.

"Well, let's go introduce ourselves. If she's not your wife, I might marry her," stated Travis.

"If she is not my wife, she'll probably scream bloody murder when she sees us. Won't that expose us?" questioned Jack.

"Only if she has the chance to scream, which she won't," assured Travis. "The tricky part will be crossing the courtyard; we'll be out in the open. Let's hope we don't bump into anyone. Put your gun in your shorts so we don't look so obvious."

Jack did as he was instructed, pulling his shirttail out so it covered the butt of the gun. Travis took off his shoulder holster and then his shirt. He then put both items back on, this time with the shoulder holster hidden under the shirt.

Travis looked around the corner of the bathhouse; the courtyard was still empty. Pipes rattled as whoever had been taking a shower turned off the water. "Let's go," whispered Travis as he started around the corner of the building.

Jack followed Travis across the small courtyard to the *palapa* the blonde woman had entered. The place had a resort atmosphere. Patio furniture and flowering tropical plants were arranged around the courtyard while colorful hammocks hung from the small front porches of the *palapas*. Jack had the bizarre feeling that they were sneaking around a Club Med resort.

Travis knocked on the door. A few seconds passed and the door was opened by the blonde woman. She was only allowed a momentary look of confusion as Travis rushed forward and placed a hand across her mouth while using his other arm to restrain her. Jack stood outside the door, a dumbfounded expression on his face. The woman was not Josephine.

"Get in here and shut the door," ordered Travis.

Jack moved into the *palapa* closing the door behind him. The woman, who was initially too stunned to resist, was now trying to free herself from Travis's grip. "Hold still! I'm not going to hurt you," said Travis as he struggled to keep hold of the woman. She was stronger than she looked.

She bit his finger and kicked him in the shin. "Son-of-a-bitch!" cursed Travis under his breath. He manhandled her over to the bed and pinned her down. "If you will hold still and listen to me, I might let you go," explained Travis.

The woman quit struggling and stared up at Travis with a wild look of fear in her eyes. "If you'll promise to keep quiet, I'll let you up," he assured her. Her look of fear slowly turned to one of confusion. "You promise?" asked Travis again.

She nodded her head affirmatively.

"You break your promise and I'll break your pretty neck," warned Travis as he cautiously lifted his hand from her mouth. He then released his hold on the young woman and stood up next to the bed.

The young woman rubbed her throat as she rose to a sitting position. She kept a wary eye on Travis. Jack saw that the lady was a true beauty. She also appeared to be quite young, twenty one or twenty two, Jack guessed. Her smooth skin was tan, and her blonde mane was the color of the sun. She wore a peach-colored, v-neck T-shirt that revealed the tops of two healthy breasts and tan shorts from which a pair of shapely legs extended. The young woman had that wholesome girl-next-door look that gave most men between the ages of thirteen and ninety three unwholesome thoughts.

"Who are you?" asked the woman, her upper lip trembling. She had a silky Southern drawl.

"We're here to find someone," answered Travis. "An Anglo woman, a pretty brunette. She would have arrived here recently."

An expression of recognition passed over the young woman's face. "You're here for Jo," she said excitedly.

Hearing his wife's name, Jack was unable to keep quiet. "Where is she?" he demanded as he step forward.

The woman tensed at Jack's sudden advance. "Are you her husband?" she asked warily, as she looked Jack square in the eye.

"I am. Now, where is she?" asked Jack again.

"Shut up, Jack!" ordered Travis. "Let me do the questioning. The idea is to get information, not give it away."

"No, it's OK," interrupted the young woman. "I'll help you find her, but I want you to take me with you. I want out of this place."

"Where is Mrs. Phillips?" asked Travis as he stared appraisingly at the woman.

"She's having dinner with Ricardo at the main house. I'll take you there."

Jack did not like what he was hearing. How could Jo be dinning with this man? He remained silent, his emotions a mixture of disgust and embarrassment.

"What's your name?" inquired Travis. The look in his eyes indicated he was mulling the situation over.

"Sandy Lake," answered the magnolia scented voice.

*   *   *

Josephine sat alone on the patio terrace, gazing at a half-moon hanging over the Caribbean. Minutes earlier Reyes had excused himself from the evening meal claiming that he would be right back. She wore a simple cream-colored cotton dress that Sandy had helped her pick out. The dress was casual, but still revealed more leg and cleavage than Jo was comfortable with. Sandy had been insistent, though. She said it was important to make a good impression on Ricardo. Sandy had also helped Jo with her hair and makeup, and when Jo looked into the mirror before leaving for dinner she saw a stunningly beautiful woman. Jo was pleased by her reflection but was not sure this was the image she wanted to convey to Reyes.

A candle-lit table was covered with the remnants of the evening meal. She hated to admit it, but dinner had been delicious, with lobster dripping in butter served with a dry white wine. To make matters worse she had found Reyes to be a charming dinner companion. She kept having to remind herself of what this man had done and was beginning to understand how Sandy could have feelings for Ricardo Reyes.

A pleasurable evening was not what she had expected. The setting on the patio overlooking the beach, the sound of the surf, the star-filled sky, the smell of the ocean, and the wine had combined to form a sensual ambience that she found all too enjoyable. Her aroused emotions frightened her. She was terrified of the Patty Hearst syndrome: kidnap victims who start to identify, and even sympathize, with their captors.

Rising from the table, she strolled to the edge of the patio, a half-empty wine glass in her hand. Jo stared out toward the ocean trying to clear her head. Memories of her husband swirling about her. The wine combined with her emotions, and her eyes filled until a tear trickled down her cheek. Brushing off the line of moisture with her forefinger, she tilted her head back in an attempt to keep the tears within their orbs, hoping they would be reabsorbed.

"It pains my heart to see such a beautiful woman cry."

Jo was startled by Reyes' voice; she had not heard him return. She turned to see him standing beside her.

"I'm sure I don't look so beautiful with these streaks down my face," replied Jo as she rubbed back her tears with the palm of her hand, hoping that she was not smearing her mascara and then wondering why she cared.

"A truly beautiful woman is beautiful even with her tears," stated Reyes as he offered a handkerchief.

Reyes' statement was sophistry, but it somehow made her feel a little better. She accepted the hanky and dabbed at the corner of her eyes. Her tears were soon under control, but a lonesome empty feeling remained. Reyes must have sensed her condition, for he attempted to comfort her by placing his arm around her shoulder. Almost against her will, she found herself leaning into his chest. She craved a pair of understanding arms.

"It is all right to cry, my darling. Ricardo will take care of you," soothed Reyes as he pulled her close.

*   *   *

Jack, Travis, and Sandy lay on their bellies in the low shrubbery along the side of the patio. Travis had decided to take Sandy with them. He really had only two choices: take her along or kill her. He did not want to wring her gorgeous neck, but he also could not afford to leave her behind for fear she might sound the alarm. So far she had proved herself useful, bringing them straight to the two people for whom they were looking.

From their hiding place they had been spying on Reyes and Josephine for the last few minutes. Jack could not hear what was being said, but what he was seeing was ripping his guts out. His first shock had been to witness Jo and Reyes finishing what appeared to have been a very romantic dinner. Jo was wearing a skimpy dress that showed off some of her best attributes and sipping on a glass of wine, a contented smile on her face. He had seen this expression before, only he had been the man on the other side of the candlelight. Jack felt ill as he watched but still held out hope for an explanation.

Reyes then went into the house, leaving Jo alone on the patio. She got up from the table, her wineglass in hand, and walked to the edge of the terrace and looked out to sea. Jack could tell by the way she moved that she'd had more than two glasses of wine. He wished she would run down the patio steps and onto the beach, at least make an effort to get away. This did not happen. Reyes returned and put his arm around Jo. She leaned against him and they embraced.

Jack was flushed hot with embarrassment, the warmth rushing up his neck and onto his face, seeming to burn the tips of his ears. He had come here to rescue his wife, only to find her happily ensconced in the arms of her captor. Was his wife a tramp? First his best friend and now this bastard. How many others had there been? Had their relationship been one big lie? His embarrassment turned to burning anger. He was starting to like the feel of the gun in his hand.

"It's time, Jack," whispered Travis. "Do exactly as I say, and we just might pull this off. I'll do the talking and cover Reyes, you watch our backsides. Keep an eye out for anyone coming up from the beach or anyone inside the house.

"Sandy, you stay between Jack and me and keep quiet; and please don't do anything that would cause me to do something I'd regret."

Travis was quickly on his feet in a crouching position, his pistol in hand. Jack followed Sandy who followed Travis as they made their way through the shrubbery toward the patio.

"Excuse me," hailed Travis, as he stepped out onto the patio, his gun pointed at Reyes.

Reyes jerked around at the sound of Travis's voice, an irritated expression on his face. The expression turned to one of puzzlement when he did not recognize the intruders but noticed the gun pointed at him.

"Our yacht has run aground on your beach, and we were wondering if we could borrow your phone to call for help," explained Travis in a mock British accent.

Reyes stared back incredulously, completely confused. Unable to discern the truth, he remained silent.

"Jack?" stammered a stunned Josephine. Who was this blonde man who looked like her husband?

Jack did not answer. He stared back at his wife, his heart hammering in his chest.

"Oh my!" gasped Jo as she realized that her husband was not dead.

An expression of understanding passed over Reyes face as he processed Jo's reaction.

"It is a beautiful night, but I think we will be more comfortable indoors," said Travis as he motioned toward the door with his gun hand.

"It *is* you!" gushed Jo as she started to move toward Jack.

"You stay with Señor Reyes, ma'am," instructed Travis as he stuck his arm out and directed Jo toward the door. "A moment ago you looked pretty content to be wrapped up with him."

Jack remained stoically silent as he swallowed back his anger. It hurt to ignore Jo this way; part of him still wanted to take her into his arms, but he had seen what he had seen.

Once they were all in the living room, Reyes turned to Travis and spoke for the first time. "I would like to get this over with as quickly as possible. What can I do for you?" Reyes spoke calmly; he appeared to have regained his composure.

"I like your attitude. If you cooperate, this won't take long," replied Travis. "Have a seat, and we will get down to business."

Reyes sat on the couch while Travis remained standing, his gun pointed at the man's head. A shocked Josephine sat beside Reyes. Jack remained silent, but beneath his quiet exterior anger boiled. He could not bear to look at Jo; he kept his gaze trained out the large picture window.

"Is there anyone else in the house?" asked Travis.

"No, I sent the cook to her quarters after dinner was served. There is no one else here," replied Reyes.

"And you're not expecting any visitors tonight?"

"No, but you never know when someone might drop by," answered Reyes, a trace of a smirk forming on his lips.

"You better hope no one does, because if there is any trouble, I'm going to shoot you first," informed Travis.

"He normally sends all the help away and asks not be disturbed when he is entertaining one of us girls," Sandy explained in a tentative voice.

Reyes glared up at Sandy, his eyes hard. The girl shrunk back from his gaze, a timorous expression on her face.

"A couple of rules we are going to live by as long as I have the gun," started Travis, seemingly oblivious to the tension between Reyes and the girl. "First, you will keep your mouth shut unless I ask you to talk. If I ask you a question, you will answer quickly and truthfully. If you follow these simple rules you might survive the night."

Reyes followed rule number one and did not reply, but he looked like someone who had just been forced to eat his own shit.

"I know that you have been getting information from someone within the United States intelligence community. I want you to tell me who this person is?" ordered Travis.

"I do not know what you are talking about," replied Reyes calmly.

"Wrong answer!" cried Travis as he delivered a brutal backhand across Reyes' face.

Reyes was surprised by the blow. Bringing his fingers up to his now split lip, he stared with pure hatred at Travis.

"Now, before you again try and answer my question, I want you to understand something. I'm here on personal business. Sam Peters was a good friend of mine, and you had him killed," stated Travis, who then paused to let the meaning of his words sink in. "It would be very satisfying to put a bullet in your brain, but then I might never find who was truly responsible for Sam's death. I want the name of the traitorous bastard who set Sam up. Don't tell me you don't know or give me the wrong guy's name, because I have a pretty good idea who I am looking for. The name you give me better fit with what I already know. I want you to think real hard, because if you give me another wrong answer I'm not going to yell and scream or knock you around, I'm going to kill you."

"Once I give you the information you seek what is to keep you from killing me anyway?" asked Reyes, an edge of fear creeping into his voice.

"That's a chance you'll have to take. The one thing that is certain is if you do not give me the right name in the next thirty seconds, you will be dead."

Reyes licked a spot of blood from his split lip as beads of sweat popped out of his forehead. Strands of hair now stuck straight out of his originally slicked back coiffure. Jack could not tell if it was anger or fear, possibly both, but the man looked as if he were about to explode. The seconds ticked by, and for a moment Jack thought Reyes was going to remain silent. If he did, Jack had no doubts that Travis would kill him, which was fine with Jack.

"Jason Hightower," blurted Reyes, breaking his silence.

"Senator Hightower?" asked a stunned Travis.

Jack did not connect with the name Jason Hightower, it was vaguely familiar, but Senator Hightower was immediately recognizable. Hell, he had voted for the man a couple of times.

"I want some supporting information. Explain the connection between Hightower and Sam Peters," demanded a critical Travis.

Reyes was grinding his teeth while staring stubbornly past Travis, as if he were trying to ignore him. He did not reply.

"A name without corroborating evidence is worth horseshit. If it makes it any easier, I already know that you're a middleman between the Columbia cartels and U.S. wholesalers, and I'm not the only one who knows. No matter what I do, your little party is about to be broken up.

Soon you won't have anything left to protect. It's time to cut your losses and head for parts unknown. You won't be heading anywhere, though, unless you play it straight with me."

Travis had taken the little he knew to be true and woven it into a probable set of circumstances. By the look of fear and surprise in Reyes' eyes, Travis realized he must be close to reality. He knew what had really set Reyes back on his heels was the possibility that others had knowledge of his activities.

"Hightower was a member of a secret committee set up by your President. Their supposed purpose was to eliminate me, though they had no idea who I was. Peters was one of their agents; he was getting close, so he was eliminated," explained Reyes grudgingly.

"Who else was involved in this operation?" asked Travis.

"I don't have a lot of names, but Ron Allen and Andrew Buck were involved," replied Reyes, barely able to control his anger.

"And you had them eliminated?" asked Travis.

Reyes did not reply. His ears turned red as he again stared past Travis.

Travis took this to be an affirmative answer and went on to his next question. "How did Gus Wise fit in to all of this?"

"I am not really sure, but he appeared to be working with Peters. We only found out about him very recently," explained Reyes.

Travis was silent a moment, lost in deep thought. "Son-of-a-bitch!" he finally muttered to himself.

He faced Reyes again and continued. "Let's say you're telling me the truth—and for your sake you'd better be—why is the Senator sharing this information? What's in it for him?"

"I share information back. I am also a generous contributor to the Senator's campaign fund," replied Reyes evenly.

"You're bullshitting me, Ricardo. That's not enough reason for him to risk his career. Come clean or die," ordered Travis.

Reyes gazed dejectedly at the floor, sighed, and shook his head. His empire was crumbling. "We belonged to the same fraternity at USC. His senior year he got a coed pregnant. He did not wish to marry the girl and she did not want to have an abortion. Jason was the golden boy football star, and this threatened his image. Remember, it was a different world back in the early sixties. I found out about his dilemma and decided to make an investment in Jason. In spite of belonging to the same fraternity, we hardly knew each other. Jason was busy being a football star, and I was the fraternity's token foreign student.

"I came up with enough money to convince the girl that an abortion would be best for all concerned. Jason and I drove her down to Tijuana where she had the operation. Jason was in my debt, but our relationship was cemented a week later when the young lady died from an infection. I now owned Jason's soul."

"And you helped him get into politics?" asked Travis.

"I suggested it, and when he made the decision, I contributed to his campaigns. The Senator has not been a totally unwilling subject; he has gained much through our relationship," explained Reyes.

"So, you are telling me that Hightower never tried to cut his ties to you? I find that hard to believe," questioned a skeptical Travis.

"Once, after Jason was first elected to the Senate, he made overtures, hinting that it would be best if our relationship were to end. I sent him a copy of a film that starred him enjoying the company of two teenage girls. There was no more talk of ending our relationship," explained Reyes. The man actually seemed to enjoy relating his conquest of the Senator. A classic case of megalomania.

"I want to chew on your story for a while," said Travis as he regarded Reyes with a critical eye. "In the meantime, why don't you give me a tour of your private museum. I'm looking for a jade death mask to hang on my living room wall."

Reyes was caught off guard by Travis's request. How did this stranger know about his private collection?

"I believe it is located at the end of that hallway," continued Travis, as he motioned toward the hallway at the far end of the living room.

Reyes's cheeks were flushed and his body trembling as he got to his feet. For him this was the final insult.

"Sandy, why don't you come with Ricardo and me. You might enjoy the collection, and it will give the Phillips a few minutes alone to get reacquainted," suggested Travis. He then looked at Jack and said, "If anyone shows up while were gone, shoot them." Travis and Sandy then followed the petulant Reyes out of the room.

For the first time since that ill-fated morning in Mérida, Jack was alone with his wife, and he did not know what to say. Those last few hours they had spent together in that Mérida hotel room now seemed to be part of another life, another time. Could things ever be the same between them? The woman he loved had become a stranger, and his heart felt like a chunk of ice. Unable to deal with her presence, he stared sullenly out the wall of glass, his gaze fixed on the stone chacmool figure reclining on the terrace.

"I still can't believe it's you! I thought I would never see you again," sputtered Jo in an attempt to start a conversation.

Jack looked down on her for a moment, an expression of contempt on his face, then shifted his gaze back out the window.

"I thought you were dead," continued Jo as she groped for the right words.

"Yeah, I saw you mourning your loss," cracked Jack, finally breaking his silence.

Jo's tears had started again. She still had Reyes' hanky and used it to dab the corner of her eyes and wipe her nose. "Jack, that wasn't what it looked liked. I'm being held prisoner here," claimed Jo between sniffles.

"Listen! There is no need to play games anymore! I know about you and Gus. I was at Cobá, and I went through Gus's things. I found a letter you sent him. The letter made it sound like you two were pretty cozy. I don't know what exactly is going on here, but evidently you've now decided to get cozy with Señor Reyes. I guess what really bothers me is how ignorant I was. How many others have there been, Jo?" demanded Jack. He was now trembling, on the verge of losing all control. "Tell me! How many have there been?"

The pain and confusion in Jo's eyes were quickly being replaced by fierceness; she was only going to be pushed so far. "I don't deserve this! I haven't done anything to be ashamed of. I've been through hell this last week, and I'm not going to put up with this crap," she struck back.

"Shut up, bitch!" spat Jack, the ugliness of his words echoing in the silence.

He thought the word "bitch" would feel good rolling off his tongue, but it left a bilious taste in his mouth and an uneasy feeling in his stomach. Instead of giving him the intended vindication, Jack was left with a low-down mean feeling. A part of him wished he could take back what he just said, but there was no going back; the conversation was over. Jack went back to staring out the window while Jo gazed at the floor, her confusion and sorrow now mixed with anger and resentment.

The silence was abruptly interrupted. "Do not move!" instructed a heavily accented voice that came from behind Jack.

Jack froze in place at the sound of the voice. His anger quickly drained out of him as he realized someone probably had a gun pointed at his head. He did not look back, but out of the corner of his eye he could see Jo seated on the couch. She was positioned so that she could see the intruder; her expression was one of fear.

"Slowly place your gun on the floor," ordered the voice.

Jack did as he was told. He was then instructed to place his hands on his head. He wondered where the hell Travis was.

"Turn around, but keep your hands on your head."

Jack turned around and saw that there were actually three men behind him, all of them armed. The man closest to him was in a shooter's stance, his weapon aimed at Jack. A pair of cold black eyes stared back at Jack from behind the gun sight. A line of ugly scar tissue, along the top of his neck, marred the man's otherwise handsome features. He realized that this must be the one Pax had told them about, the one who had murdered Gus Wise. The other two men stood behind the one with the scar. One was a heavyset man dressed in a blue polo shirt and a pair of baggy white shorts, the other was an average-looking fellow wearing a nondescript gray uniform and clutching a 20-gauge pump.

"Are these friends of yours, darling?" wisecracked Jack.

"Why, yes. These are the nice men who brought me to this tropical paradise," replied Jo in a sweet voice dripping with sarcasm. "I don't know Fatso's name; we were never properly introduced. But the one with his gun stuck in your face is Ramon Martinez."

Jack was not sure why, but Jo's sarcasm made him feel better.

"Ramon, I would like you to meet my husband, Jack Phillips." Jo then looked at her husband and said, "Welcome to hell, Jack."

"Shut up!" ordered Ramon. The edge to his voice and the cold expression on his face chilled the black humor. "Where is Señor Reyes?" he demanded.

Jack did not want to answer this question. His one hope was that Travis could surprise these men and reverse the situation. In fact, he was confident that this would be the case once the big man showed up. Jack had already witnessed more than one example of Travis's talents in matters of this kind. Hell, he was not even sure if it was fair; after all, there were only three of them. For the moment he would have to stall Ramon without giving Travis's presence away. He decided to try humor, as he had seen Travis use it effectively in similar situations.

"We ran out of beer! Ricardo ran down to the Quick Stop for another six-pack."

Jack found out that Ramon had a poor sense of humor when the man slammed the butt of his pistol into Jack's mouth. The blow left his teeth in place but split his upper lip. Blood filled his mouth and dribbled down his chin as his lip began to swell.

"You son-of-a-bitch!" cried Jo as she leapt up from the couch and began wiping the blood from Jack's mouth with Reyes' hanky.

Jack was surprised by Jo's reaction, especially after what he had said to her only minutes ago. Despite his bitter feelings he found he liked having her standing close, tenderly wiping the blood from his chin; the warm scent of her body evoked memories of what had been. He wanted to take her in his arms and hold her.

The moment was broken when Ramon stepped forward and with one hand pushed Jo roughly back onto the couch. He then stuck the barrel of his gun into Jack's bloody mouth. "I will ask you one more time. Where is Señor Reyes?"

Jack was paralyzed with fear, but he had made up his mind; he was not going to give this asshole anything. He closed his eyes and waited for the end.

"They're in the back of the house, looking at Reyes' collection."

He recognized Jo's voice. Jack opened his eyes and yelled a muffled, "No!" around the barrel of the pistol. Ramon rammed the barrel deeper into Jack's mouth in an effort to silence him. Jack gagged on the cold steel.

"Who is with him?" demanded Ramon, as he looked down at Jo.

"A big man. I don't know his name. And Sandy," replied Jo in a strained voice.

"Is the man armed?" inquired Ramon.

Jo did not answer immediately. She looked up at Jack through moist eyes, then stared down at the floor and nodded her head affirmatively.

Ramon reached down and snatched the hanky out of Jo's hand. He then removed the barrel of his gun from Jack's mouth and replaced it with the wadded-up hanky. Ramon signaled the uniformed man forward. He said a few words of Spanish to the man, then relieved him of the shotgun. The uniformed man produced a pair of handcuffs and cuffed Jack's hands behind his back. Without warning Ramon drove the butt of the shotgun into Jack's belly. Jack fell to his knees gasping for air, choking on the wadded-up cloth in his mouth.

Ramon pumped a shell into the chamber of the shotgun and then motioned for Fatso to follow him. They moved to the far side of the room, and took up positions against the wall at the corner where the hallway and the living room intersected. They were hidden by the living room wall from anyone in the hallway. Ramon was closest to the hallway, and he carefully peered around the corner, then immediately jerked his head back.

Jack could hear the footsteps approaching from down the hall. He wanted to scream, to warn Travis, but his burning lungs were not functioning. A muffled grunt was all he could manage. The uniformed man grabbed him by the hair and pulled his head back, shoving the barrel of his pistol against the side of Jack's face. His mind was in a frenzy, but his body was paralyzed from lack of oxygen. If only he could have occupied Ramon for a few more minutes.

"Ricardo's collection is quite extensive, I picked out a magnificent jade mask," he heard Travis say in a mocking voice.

Jack watched in horror as Reyes entered the room first. Jack attempted to rise to his feet, but was held down by the uniformed man.

Reyes instantly processed the situation before him and dropped to the floor, exposing a wide-eyed Travis. Ramon, standing immediately to the right of Travis, aimed his weapon at Travis's gun hand and pulled the trigger. The blast of the shotgun, sent Travis's pistol flying into the opposite wall along with a good portion of his right hand. A woman's scream filled the room as Ramon then stepped forward and brutally clubbed Travis in the face with the butt of the shotgun. Jack saw his last hope crushed as Travis dropped to the floor.

CHAPTER 44

The uniformed man allowed Jack to rise to his feet. He managed to spit out the handkerchief that was stuffed in his mouth and now stood stooped over sucking air into his oxygen-starved lungs. Across the room he could see the broken body of Travis Horn writhing on the floor. Farther down the hall, a wide-eyed Sandy leaned against the wall, her hands covering her face. Ramon and Fatso stood above Travis, their weapons at the ready. Jack was shocked by how easily they had taken Travis down. It occurred to Jack that he might soon be dead. A strange calm had come over him, an acceptance of his fate. They had made their run and played their cards, but it was now over.

Reyes was now on his feet and taking charge of the situation. He began to shout orders in Spanish as two more uniformed men entered the room with their guns drawn. He spoke rapidly in Spanish to Ramon, pointing down at the prone Travis. Ramon reached down and picked up the leather case Travis had been carrying in his left hand, and handed the case to Reyes. Jack guessed that the leather case held Pacal's Jade Death Mask. They had come so close; Travis had the golden ring in his hand.

His hands still cuffed behind his back, Jack was moved outside onto the terrace where he was allowed to sit in a chair. The original uniformed man stood guard over him. In spite of the warm night air a cold chill settled over his body. Through the picture window he could see Jo still seated on the couch with her head down and her hands in her lap. He imagined that she would continue to be one of Reyes' women, and this thought made him ill. His will to continue drained; he hoped the end would come quickly.

The figure of Travis stumbling across the living room brought Jack out of his semi-catatonic state. He was astonished to see the man on his feet. Travis's hands were cuffed together in front of him, his right hand a mangled mess of flesh and bone, his nose broken and bleeding. Jack felt a pang of guilt as he watched Travis struggle forward.

One of the uniformed men pushed Travis out onto the patio where he was made to sit in a chair next to Jack. "You were supposed to watch my back," choked Travis.

Jack knew he was to blame for his friend's present condition. He was supposed to have been watching for intruders, but he had let personal matters interfere with his concentration. "You were right, I should have gone back to the boat. I'm getting us both killed, and there was nothing waiting for me here anyway," replied Jack as a flood of guilt washed over him.

"Hey! I'm ribbing you," gasped Travis. "There were three of them. There wasn't much you could do, short of getting yourself killed."

Travis's words did not make Jack feel any better; in a way they made him feel worse. The man's face was pale, his nose smashed and bloody, and a good portion of his right hand shot off; it did not look good for Travis. Yet here he was trying to buck up Jack, even when Jack was at least partially responsible for his present condition.

"Before they brought me out here I heard them talking," continued Travis. "They caught the others on the beach and found our boat. They knew we were here; we weren't going anywhere."

"How did they find them? The beach was deserted," asked a perplexed Jack.

"Evidently they found the dead guard and Flores missing and went to have a look around," explained Travis.

Through the window Jack could see Reyes and Ramon in deep conversation. Jo sat motionlessly on the couch.

"I guess it doesn't matter how it happened. We're all dead men now," stated Jack as he continued to stare into the living room.

"I wouldn't say that," croaked Travis.

In spite of the grim situation Jack found Travis's last statement almost humorous. Here was a man suffering traumatic shock and on the verge of bleeding to death, telling him there might be a way out.

"What are we going to do, make a run for it?" inquired Jack, with a dark grin. "I hate to burst your bubble, but you're not going anywhere. You have more blood on you than in you."

Travis glared back at Jack. "You may be right, Jack, we may be dead men; but like the man said, I refuse to go quietly into that good night."

At first Jack did not know what to make of this last statement; it was over, why continue to fight? But then the true meaning of Travis's words became clear to him. The struggle to survive never ends, even when the end is near. And it is in fact how one faces the darkness: when all hope is lost, that is the truest measure of one's self.

He looked back into the living room where he saw that Reyes was now speaking to Jo. Her head was down; she appeared to be staring at the floor. When she looked up there was an expression on her face with which Jack was well acquainted. It was a smart-ass, "what dumbfucks men are" expression that she was so good at. It pleased him to see it directed at Reyes. Words were traded between Reyes and Jo, but Jack could not hear them through the glass. With a swift movement Reyes reached out and viciously slapped Jo across the face. The blow twisted her head around, but when she turned back to face Reyes she was smiling. The violence toward his wife sparked an anger in Jack. He rose from his seat, but was pushed back down by the guard.

"Relax, Jack," whispered Travis. He then added, "She's got some spunk."

One of the uniformed men went to Jo, cuffed her hands behind her back, and escorted her out onto the terrace. A patio chair was procured for her and she was seated beside Jack.

"What happened?" asked a confused Jack.

"I told Reyes he was an asshole," stated Jo flatly, her eyes glassy.

"Why?" sputtered Jack.

"It looked like you guys were having more fun out here."

The meaning of her words swept Jack up in a swirling mixture of emotions. He felt guilty that he had lost faith in his wife and was ashamed of the harsh words he had spoken. She was giving up her chance to live in order to die with him. He wanted to laugh at the way Jo had told off that pompous ass Ricardo Reyes, but at the same time there was anger. He wished he could spend some time alone with Reyes, see how brave the bastard was when he was not smacking a woman around. Great sadness also filled him, for soon they would be killed. These feelings coalesced to form a kaleidoscope of emotions that pulled at his id and tugged at his ego, but none was more potent than that which came from his heart. It was all so clear now; he wondered how he ever doubted her in the first place.

"I've been a fool!" confessed Jack as looked into her eyes for the first time that evening. "I love you, Jo."

"I love you, Jack," returned Jo, as she gazed into his eyes. Nothing else needed to be said.

The moment was broken by the sound of foot falls on the stone steps leading up from the beach. Jack looked back to see Hector Flores and Pax Chi stepping onto the patio, their hands cuffed behind their backs. Two more uniformed men came up behind them. Jack wondered just how large was Reyes' personal army.

"Hector Flores," Jack whispered to Jo. "The other man is Pax Chi. Until about a week ago, he worked here as a laborer. He told us that you and Gus were here."

Still under his own power, a swollen-faced Flores limped across the terrace. Pax and Flores were made to sit on the patio next to the others; no chairs were offered. Flores exchanged nods and knowing glances with both Jack and Travis. No words were spoken; they all understood the situation.

Reyes, Ramon, and Fatso strolled out onto the terrace, Reyes looking like the cat who ate the canary. "I want to thank you all for coming. It is a relief to see all of my recent worries wrapped up in one place," explained Reyes with a smug smile, his arms open wide.

Reyes swaggered over to where Hector and Pax sat. He peered down at the archeologist's swollen face and said, "Señor Flores, have you taken a bad fall?"

Flores did not answer.

"You must be more careful," continued Reyes. "I have been told that you were leaving my humble estate without saying goodbye. Do you not appreciate my gracious hospitality? Have I offended you?"

"I wasn't going anywhere, I just felt like a moonlight stroll on the beach. I needed some fresh air," replied Flores.

Reyes leaned his head back and laughed loudly. He then said, "You are a funny man, Señor Flores. It is too bad you did not accept my offer; we would have been a great team."

"Who's this young man?" asked Reyes as he pointed down at Pax.

Ramon stepped forward and whispered into Reyes' ear. Reyes nodded his head in understanding and then said something in Spanish to Pax that Jack could not understand. Pax remained silent as he stared past Reyes.

"I give the man a job and see the thanks I get," said Reyes in English.

Reyes moved to his left so that he was now standing above Travis. "Without a gun in your hand your attitude has changed," noted Reyes, with an expression of mock bewilderment. "You seem more subdued."

"Now that you have the guns, I play by your rules," explained a smiling Travis.

"You are a very pragmatic man," observed Reyes as he signaled to one of the guards. The guard handed over his revolver. Reyes shoved the barrel of the weapon up against Travis's forehead and cocked the hammer. "Now you will answer some of my questions. Same rules as before; one wrong answer and you're dead."

"Stuff it, Ricardo. I already told you that this is personal business for me. I'm not answering any of your bullshit questions so you might as well shoot me. I'm about to bleed to death anyway," declared Travis calmly, as if there were no gun pointed at his head.

"Oh, Mr. Horn, you are a brave man," laughed Reyes.

Jack was somewhat surprised that Reyes knew Travis's last name, he could only assume that Flores had mentioned it during his beating.

"I probably know more about you and why you are here than you know yourself. I believe the recently demised Andrew Buck has something to do with your presence on the Yucatán," said Reyes as he let the pistol's hammer down, then handed it back to the guard.

"The Senator keeps you well updated," rasped Travis.

"Yes, the Senator, or should I say the Vice President keeps me informed," agreed Reyes smugly.

"Vice President?" interjected a confused Jack.

"Yes, your current V.P. announced he is stepping down after this term. It is rumored that Senator Hightower will be named his successor," explained Reyes. "It is funny how such a little investment early on in life can pay such big dividends years later."

For the first time Jack was beginning to truly see that things were much bigger than what happened to Jo or him. They were only flotsam caught up in the currents of much larger events, along for the ride, but having little causal effect on the final outcome. It was difficult for him to imagine that this gangster would have a direct line to the Vice President of the United States, one heartbeat away from the President. Jack was pulled into the intrigue; at the very least he wanted to understand why he would be killed. At the moment Reyes was full of himself; he liked to hear himself talk. The man enjoyed relating his grand scheme, something he could only afford to do for the condemned.

"So if Cervantes wins, you'll have your man as President of Mexico and Hightower as Vice President of the United States. You will be very well connected," stated Jack, hoping to elicit a response from Reyes.

"Yes, I will be well connected," said a smiling Reyes, a faraway look in his eyes. "Cervantes is doing well in the polls, especially after his Judicial Police uncovered the corruption at the Cobá ruin site. Imagine, archaeologists Wise and Flores find a subterranean tomb, the final resting place of some long forgotten Mayan nobleman. What amazing artifacts did it hold? We will never know, for these two well-respected archaeologists pirated the tomb and vanished with unknown wealth. Not to worry, though, for director Cervantes and his loyal agents of the Judicial Police are working hard to apprehend these despicable men who steal Mexico's ancient past. I think that will play well with the people," concluded Reyes with a satisfied smile.

"You bastard!" exclaimed Flores who had struggled to his feet. "You've raped my find! What have you done with it?"

Fatso moved quickly between Flores and Reyes, punching the archeologist in the area of his broken ribs. Flores dropped to his knees, his face twisted in agony, then fell over on his side groaning and gasping for breath.

"Do not worry about your precious find. It is safely hidden away in a location known only by me," informed Reyes, a bitterness in his voice.

Jack wondered how Reyes could be the only one to know the exact location of the hiding place. Someone had to move the items. Jack could not picture Reyes moving the artifacts himself. It then occurred to Jack that Reyes could have had the movers killed.

Flores' outburst seemed to have dimmed Reyes' buoyant mood. Jack hoped he could keep the man talking a little longer; there were still things he wanted to learn.

"I don't quite understand why you would want both Cervantes and Hightower in power. I mean they are both strong advocates of the so-called 'War on Drugs.' It seems that in your business you would want people in power with the opposite idea," commented Jack.

"In my business?" remarked Reyes, "Are you insinuating that I am somehow involved in the illegal drug trade? You should not speak so forwardly of such things." Reyes paused as he eyed Jack suspiciously.

"Oh, I want the 'War on Drugs' to continue, even increased, as long as the purveyors of this aggression do not target me. If the government eliminates my competition, I will be able to corner the market; I may eventually become the market. I have a degree in economics from USC, you can see that it has served me well," said Reyes with a pompous grin.

It was now all clear to Jack, though little good it would do him, for there was no chance that Reyes would let them leave the estate alive.

"You ask a lot of questions, Jack Phillips," stated a more serious Reyes. "Now it is time for you to answer some of mine. You are still somewhat of a mystery to me. You may be, as your wife claims, an innocent traveler who got caught up in events beyond your own control. But maybe you are part of something else? One can never be too careful in such matters."

Jack immediately understood to what Reyes was alluding. It was what had dogged him from the very beginning but also what had probably kept him alive: the notion that he had information or was some kind of player in what was going down. Whether it was Ortiz, Travis, or now Reyes, they all asked the same questions: What did he know, who had he talked with, and where was he from? Jack was a mystery. No one knew anything about him because he was who he said he was, "Joe Tourist." He realized that if he could convince Reyes he had critical information he might buy a few more hours.

"What I know stays with me. But I'll tell you this, you can't stop what's coming," declared Jack as he tried to look impenetrable.

"You are not a very convincing liar, Mr. Phillips. I do not think you know anything, but now I will have to be sure. If you are doing this in an attempt to buy a few more hours of life you are going to be very sorry, for they will be very painful hours," warned Reyes.

Jack suddenly did not feel very good. Reyes turned to Ramon and spoke in a hushed whisper. Ramon nodded his head in understanding. "I must go now, but I leave you in Ramon's most capable hands," said Reyes, who then turned and walked back into the house.

Ramon and his men hustled their prisoners to their feet. Flores required assistance, and Travis did not look like he would be standing for long. They were marched down the terrace steps, past the fierce-looking serpent heads, and out onto the beach where a jeep was parked in the sand. Pax Chi was forced into the front passenger seat of the jeep while Flores was helped into a rear seat. Jack could see that Travis was slipping; he had stumbled up to the jeep looking as if his next step might be his last. Travis's shirt was soaked in blood and even in the dim light Jack could see his pallid complexion.

Fatso motioned for Travis to get into the jeep, but Travis did not step forward. He stood in place weaving slowly back and forth, his eyes glazed over. Fatso stepped toward the dazed man as he shouted obscenities in Spanish. Travis's knees buckled, and he fell forward into Fatso. The fat man pushed Travis away, but not before his shirt was smeared with blood. Unable to keep his balance, Travis stumbled away and fell face first onto the sand. Cursing the fact that his tennis shirt was ruined, Fatso stomped his foot down on Travis's injured right hand, eliciting an anguished howl from the fallen man.

Two of the uniformed men picked up Travis and tossed him in the back of the jeep. One of the men then got behind the wheel, while the other climbed up on the back of the jeep, his feet straddling the comatose Travis. Fatso took the remaining rear seat. Jack, Josephine, and Ramon were left standing on the beach.

"What about us?" asked Jack.

"You stay with me," replied Ramon.

Ramon gave a signal to the driver, who then started the jeep and put it into gear.

"Where are they being taken?" asked Jack, though he already knew the answer.

Ramon did not reply, he stared back at Jack with a sneering smile on his lips.

As the jeep pulled away into the night, Jack thought he saw Travis's eyes open, and there appeared to be a crooked grin on his face. He could not be sure; it was pretty dark, but he thought Travis gave him a knowing wink. Jack blinked and looked again, but now he saw that Travis's eyes were shut, his face slack. Jack's mind was playing tricks on him. He watched as the jeep disappeared into the darkness. Travis Horn would never make it back to those Montana trout streams.

CHAPTER 45

Darkness had fallen on the city, but the interior of the warehouse was illuminated by the yellow glow of the antique light fixtures suspended from the ceiling. Only about half of the saucer-shaped lamps were functioning. Carlton stood off by himself, a fresh Camel between his lips, surrounded by a cone of light. The vision in his left eye was blurred, his head throbbed with a dull ache, and his left cheek had swollen to the size and consistency of a ripe plum. All in all, it felt pretty good to still be able to suck on a smoke.

Fifty feet away Special Agent Patricia Lance of the FBI and Bill Pritchard of the State Department were in deep conversation over what to do with Carlton. Both had cellular phones pressed to their ears. Carlton found this scene somewhat comical. He was certain that the Bureau Director was on the line with Lance, and that Lester Goreman was screaming into the right ear of Bill Pritchard— it had to be one hell of a confusing conference call. He might have laughed, except for the sobering thought that these people were deciding his future; would he be declared an enemy of the state or decorated as a hero for exposing a traitor? He would settle for unknown State Department hack who retires early on a full pension.

Immediately in front of Carlton the blanket-covered bodies of Don Schovich and Galvan's unnamed accomplice lay where they had fallen. There was a tight feeling in his chest like he had swallowed a stone, when he thought of Schovich. At the moment it was not hard for Carlton to imagine his own body lying on the concrete, covered by a cheap blanket.

On the other side of the dead bodies, Armando Galvan lay on the floor, his back propped up against the wall. A pair of EMTs tended to his wounded shoulder. The man was semiconscious and in obvious pain. The only other people in the building were Randy Stickle from Channel Six News and his cameraman. Galvan's other assistant, the one who had been left behind with the Caddy, was tied up in a small office just off the main entrance to the building. Outside the warehouse there was a small circus of cops, FBI agents, and competing news services.

Carlton's fate was now in the hands of the FBI and the State Department, which was not a comforting thought. Before he had called in the law he had considered vacating the premises and letting the cops sort out what happened. But he quickly realized he could not leave unexplained dead bodies lying around. The people who wanted him silenced would make sure that the killings were blamed on him; then there would be no turning back. He would be a fugitive of the state, living the remainder of his life constantly looking over his shoulder. Unable to run from what had happened, he decided to meet the government head on and lay the cards out on the table. He hoped they would believe enough of his story to start an investigation on Hightower.

Of course, Carlton did not invite the State Department and the FBI in without taking some precautions. The first call he had made on the Cadillac's car phone, after subduing Galvan's goon and securing him in the warehouse office, was to Randy Stickle. Stickle had been a left-leaning, gonzo-style journalist during the 70s, whose political philosophy had been smoothed with age and moved to the right by the Reagan years. (He considered himself a Libertarian.) The journalist had started out the 1980s with an almost unequaled hatred of Ronald Reagan. But always one to buck the mainstream media, he ended up being an unabashed Reagan defender by midway through the decade of greed. (He could never be a Reagan supporter, for he disagreed with much of the former president's ideology.) For the past ten years Stickle had made his living as an investigative television reporter who was not afraid to take risks. He loved using the video camera to go after society's invisible crooks. From congressmen to welfare cheats, no one was safe once in Stickle's spotlight. In the greater Washington metro area, a call from Randy Stickle could create as much fear as a call from "Sixty Minutes". Years ago Carlton had helped Stickle with some information on the Soviet Embassy. It was information the CIA wanted leaked anyway, but Carlton had chosen to give Stickle the first shot at it, and now it was time for Carlton to collect on the favor. He wanted his story to be in the public domain before he could be silenced, and Stickle was a man who could accomplish this.

With Stickle's video cam rolling, Carlton had persuaded Galvan to talk about the connection between Hightower and Ricardo Reyes. The man confessed to setting up the murders of Ron Allen and Andrew Buck, and even admitted to shooting the whore he had hired to kill Ron Allen. He also explained how the bombing of Hightower's limo had been staged. The taped confessions of a severely wounded man would not be given much credence in a court of law, but Carlton believed what he had heard and was certain Galvan would continue to sing if faced with a plea bargain situation.

The still-living bogus FBI agent, currently tied up in the warehouse office, had also been willing to talk, but he claimed to have no knowledge of the Senator or Reyes. The man was only a hired gun with no knowledge of who was signing his paycheck. But he did confirm on videotape that Carlton had been taken from The Senate under false pretenses and admitted that he had impersonated a federal agent.

Carlton felt that under normal circumstances he had enough circumstantial evidence against Hightower to activate a serious police investigation, if not get an indictment, but these were not normal circumstances. Galvan was the key; the man would have to be pressured. Whether or not this was to happen would depend on the decision the State Department and FBI were about to make, and this decision could depend on how deeply the President was involved. Carlton's story, which was going to be broadcast on Channel Six's eleven o'clock news, did not put the President in a good light. It would be revealed that the President had handpicked the people in charge of Operation Raven, a government operation that smuggled cocaine onto United States soil. Except for Senator Hightower, all of the major players in Operation Raven had come to mysterious ends. Hightower was possibly linked to a Mexican drug lord, and now the President was about to select the Senator to be his running mate in the next election. For all Carlton knew, the President was as deeply involved in this as the Senator. It seemed farfetched, but he would have thought the same thing about Hightower a week ago. Even if the President was totally innocent of any wrongdoing, the pressure would be to cover-up, which would mean silencing and discrediting Carlton.

Carlton was counting on three things to prevent a cover-up: one was the strength of his evidence, which would be presented to the public tonight. Once the proverbial cat was out of the bag, it would be extremely difficult to put back, thus making a cover-up difficult. Secondly, he had no interest in bringing down the President; he wanted Hightower. The President had not yet officially announced his selection for a running mate, so it would not cause irreparable damage to cut the Senator loose. Plus, presidents had survived similar scandals; Reagan and Iran-Contra was a good example. It would have been a more difficult situation if the President had already declared Hightower his choice. The third thing Carlton was counting on to avoid a cover-up was also his long-term insurance policy. He had led Pritchard and Lance to believe he had more evidence that could be very damaging to certain people and that this evidence might become public if he were to suddenly vanish. In reality he had no such evidence, but those who might want to eliminate Carlton would have to consider his threat.

In exchange for his future cooperation on this matter, Carlton had made only two requests: one was full retirement from the State Department, effective immediately. His second request had come to him as he stared at the blanket-covered body of Don Schovich. He wanted a new motor home.

Bill Pritchard had removed the phone from his ear and shoved it into his coat pocket. He started walking toward Carlton, leaving an impatient Special Agent Lance behind. Pritchard had short curly hair, sad eyes, and a weak chin. The weary expression on his face was nothing new for Pritchard, the man always looked as if he suffered from terminal sleep deprivation. He was Lester Gorman's right-hand man, and in spite of his appearance he was not a man to be taken lightly.

"The FBI wants to debrief you, they also want to bring in Hightower," said Pritchard. He talked as if the State Department and the FBI had not yet come to a decision as to what to do. Carlton knew this was bullshit. "I think they believe you," added Pritchard.

"What about my retirement?" asked Carlton as he dropped his cigarette butt onto the concrete and snuffed it out with the toe of his shoe.

"The early retirement shouldn't be a problem. To be truthful we have wanted you out for a long time; we never thought to pay you off. Gorman said no to the Winnebago, but he is willing to offer you a fifty-thousand dollar retirement bonus. That ought to be a nice down payment on the recreational vehicle of your choice. Of course, the bonus will only be paid if Hightower is indicted," explained Pritchard, as if the matter were settled.

"I have one more request," said Carlton.

Pritchard rolled his sad eyes toward the ceiling.

CHAPTER 46

The interior of the small *palapa* was illuminated by two bare light bulbs that hung from the center of the roof. Against one wall stood Jack Phillips. His hands were cuffed above his head around an open roof beam, and his legs were strapped to a wooden wall post. Directly across the sandy floor from him, Josephine was secured to the opposing wall in the same manner. Jack's eyes stung with the sweat that rolled off his forehead, while the weight of his weary arms pulled the sore and abraded flesh around his wrists against the unyielding metal of the handcuffs.

To Jack's right, Ramon sat on a wooden chair just inside the open doorway. The man who had gutted Gus Wise like a fish and then left the body to rot on the beach wore a detached, dispassionate expression. Ramon had not spoken since they left the beach. The thick line of pink scar tissue across the man's neck gave Jack the impression that Ramon had been decapitated and his head sewn back on. This Frankenstein monster, though, was not a hideous clumsy beast but dark and handsome with catlike reflexes and cold-black soulless eyes.

Jack could hardly bear to look across at the pathetic figure of his wife. Her tear-stained cheeks were in contrast to the fiery glint in her eyes. It ripped at his heart to see that she was still willing to fight when only torture and death awaited. He somehow felt responsible for their present situation; how could he have let this happen? He had failed her.

"I'm sorry, Jo," he apologized.

"For what?" shot back Jo. "You have nothing to be sorry for. You're not responsible for what these bastards have done to us. Jack, you have given me seven wonderful years of your love. If this is it, then so be it. Fuck these assholes!"

Jo's words were punctuated by the distant sound of gunfire. The echoing blasts had a finality about them. Three lives had been extinguished. Jack had hoped for a miracle to save his friends, but now he realized there would be no miracles.

For the first time this night Ramon showed emotion as a smile crossed his lips. Jack was disgusted by the sight of this smirking jackal who took pleasure in the destruction of human life. He had never felt such pure hatred for another individual.

The next few minutes passed in a bitter haze as Jack wished for the end to come quickly. The haze partially lifted when Ricardo Reyes entered the *palapa*, a lit cigar between the fat fingers of his left hand.

"Sorry to keep you waiting," greeted Reyes cheerfully as he closed the door to the *palapa*.

"That's OK. We've enjoyed hanging around your plush accommodations," remarked Jo.

A surprised Jack could not help but smile at his wife's sarcasm. He should not have been surprised, as he had felt her sharp tongue more than once over the years. It lifted his spirits to see her not back down. He was reminded of Travis's quote from the Dylan Thomas poem, "I refuse to go quietly into that good night!" It would have been easier to have gone down with the others, but if she was willing to put up a fight, so was he.

Reyes ignored Jo's comment and turned to Ramon, who was now standing. He handed Ramon a large cigar. "I know how much you like these. Enjoy one with me in celebration," said Reyes.

Reyes pulled a gold lighter from his pocket, flicked it on, and held the yellow flame against the end of Ramon's cigar. Ramon puffed until a cloud of gray smoke rose around his head. "*Gracias*," said Ramon as he sat back down with the cigar clenched between his teeth.

Reyes walked forward until he was standing directly between Josephine and Jack. He glanced at Jo and then at Jack as he took a drag on his cigar. He slowly blew a stream of smoke toward the ceiling and then spoke. "I usually leave this sort of thing to Ramon; he is very good at it, but tonight is very special. It is the culmination of much hard work, and I wanted to be a part of it. Plus, it is a pleasure to see the lovely Josephine one last time."

"Lucky me," cracked Jo.

Reyes shot a sharp-eyed glance at Jo, an uncertain expression on his face. Such was the man's opinion of himself, he was not sure if Jo was being funny or if she truly felt lucky. Jack could not help but laugh at the man's reaction to Jo's comment. Reyes shifted his gaze to Jack, his expression one of confused irritation. A sneer formed on Reyes' lips, which slowly turned to a chuckle.

"I am happy to see you are in such a good mood; it should make things go much easier. In fact, let's make this easy on all of us, Jack, and tell me who you really are?" asked Reyes.

"Oh hell, we might as well get this over with," exclaimed Jack in mock surrender. "I'm a DEA agent sent down here to scout you out. Tomorrow one hundred DEA agents and a contingent of United States

Marines will be landing on your beach, and if they don't find me alive they are going to be very pissed off."

"I guess they will be very pissed off," replied Reyes calmly, a bemused expression on his face.

Reyes' remark took much of the humor out of the situation for Jack. It was difficult to be sarcastic when faced with the end of one's existence.

"I really don't think you are anything but a tourist in the Yucatán, a tourist who has lost his way. One can never be too careful, though. We will soon know all about you," said Reyes ominously.

"Boy, are you going to be bored," remarked Jo as she glared at Reyes, an insolent expression on her face.

Jack did not laugh this time. He sensed that the time to be funny had passed. The dynamics of the situation had shifted. There was a sinking feeling in his stomach.

Reyes chuckled at Jo's remark as he turned toward her. The cloud of tobacco smoke swirled around his head as he moved.

"You are a funny lady. I appreciate a good sense of humor. I am sad you chose not to stay with me. You would have found life here quite pleasurable," said Reyes, who then blew a stream of smoke into Jo's face.

Jo glared back through the heavy cigar smoke, looking as if she were staring at dog crap on the bottom of her shoe. "You have a nice place here, Ricardo. I thought about staying, but all the men I have met here are a bunch of limp dicks. I began to wonder, who would I fuck? A girl has to have a love life, and if I stayed here I'd have been faced with a lot of self-gratification."

Reyes had been pretending to ignore Jo's taunts up to this point, but the last comment had hit him between the legs, an area about which he was very sensitive. The smile vanished from his lips as the muscles around his jaw tightened. Reyes gripped Jo's dress at the neck line, above her breasts, and ripped the dress from her body. A grunt- like gasp rushed from her lungs, as a look of shocked fear replaced her mocking expression. Except for bra and panties, she stood revealed, the remains of her dress draped across her feet.

This was too much for Jack; it was destroying him to watch his wife receive such brutal treatment, but he had no option. He struggled wildly against his shackles. "Leave her alone, you son-of-a-bitch!" He screamed. "I'm the one you have a problem with. Fuck with me, but leave her out of it."

Reyes stared back at Jack with a satisfied, superior grin. He appeared pleased by Jack's reaction. "Please do not feel left out, my friend. I will get to you, but first let me have a moment to admire your beautiful wife," informed Reyes in a condescending tone.

"You piece of shit!" cried Jack, his fury overwhelming him. "You're a brave man picking on a lady. How about trying me?" He was willing to do anything to focus Reyes' attention on him rather than Jo.

Reyes giggled, his amusement growing with Jack's agitation. Reaching out to the squirming Josephine, he unhooked the clasp on the front of her bra. Her breasts fell free from the constraints of the garment.

"Jack, Jack, let me put you at ease," purred Reyes as he gently stroked Jo's left breast. "Josephine will be well taken care of; in fact, I have already found her employment. The oilmen of Villahermosa will pay much to spend a few carnal minutes with your lovely wife."

Jo's eyes grew wide and her lips curled in disgust as she comprehended the meaning of what Reyes had said. "I'll kill myself," stated Josephine as she choked back a sob.

"Do not cry, pretty lady. You will learn to love your new profession. Once you've been introduced to the pleasures of heroin, you will suck cock all day long for your fix," cooed Reyes as his hand slipped inside her panties.

Tears flowed from Jo's tightly shut eyes, her red cheeks twisted in misery, and a pitiful moan sputtered out from between her lips. Feeling emasculated and impotent, Jack watched in agony as his wife's spirit was crushed.

The room began to spin slowly around Jack as the sinking feeling in his stomach turned to nausea. With each revolution, the faces of the others in the room passed before him: the leering Reyes with his hand between Jo's legs, Josephine withering in horror, and Ramon seated by the door smiling behind his big cigar like one of Satan's laughing minions. His heart hammered wildly in his chest, the pounding pulse filling his head making his ears ring. The world spun faster, a nightmarish carnival ride gone out of control. Jo's words from earlier in the evening circulated through his mind, taunting him, "Welcome to hell, Jack!"

Jack was about to tumble completely off the edge of sanity when the door to the *palapa* suddenly flew open. At first he thought he had fallen into dementia, for in the doorway stood Travis Horn, resurrected from the dead, his broken nose swollen and bloody and a sneer on his lips. Travis's right hand was wrapped in a bloody bandage and in his left hand was a gun, the muzzle of which was stuck in Ramon's left ear.

Ramon had been caught completely by surprise, he had been too busy enjoying the torture session. He raised his hands up in surrender, his eyes wide in shocked terror.

"You're dead!" stammered a dumbfounded Reyes.

"That's what I thought, but they wouldn't let me into heaven, and I was too much competition for the devil. I'm a reject until they figure out what to do with me," rasped a wild-eyed Travis. "I was informed that they do have a place for you, Ramon, and it isn't sitting beside Saint Peter."

Ramon appeared confused by Travis's statement. His eyes moved nervously from side to side, like a wild animal looking for an escape route. Behind Travis, Jack could now see Pax Chi, who was also armed with a pistol. He was beginning to believe that this was not a dream.

"This is for Sam," stated Travis as he raised the pistol above his head.

For a brief moment Ramon fully comprehended his fate, causing his look of confusion to turn to panic. The moment ended abruptly as Travis brutally smashed the butt of the pistol against the top of Ramon's head. The impact of the pistol butt with the man's skull produced a sound similar to that of an axe splitting dry oak. Ramon's eyes crossed as he tumbled off the chair and fell face first onto the sand. The body convulsed as the individual cells fought over the remaining elements of life. Jack was filled with a rush of dark pleasure; he only wished he could have delivered the mortal blow himself. This was a feeling he could not have imagined a week ago. Ramon's cigar lay in the sand near his still-twitching fingers.

"Is that a Cohiba?" remarked Travis. He stuck his gun under his wounded arm, then reached down and picked up the still-smoldering cigar. Biting off the end that had been in contact with Ramon's mouth, he spat the butt onto the dying man's back. He puffed vigorously, creating billows of smoke and turning the end of the cigar into a red ingot.

"God damn, there is nothing like a hand-rolled Cuban," remarked Travis, a satisfied look on his sweat-soaked and blood-stained face.

Jack was amazed by Travis's hardy condition; less than an hour ago he appeared to be on death's doorstep. Evidently he was a bit of a Thespian.

"Now, if you would take a few steps back, Señor shithead, so Pax can release my *compadres*," ordered Travis, the cigar now clenched between his teeth and his gun pointed at Reyes.

Without argument Reyes backed up against the far wall of the *palapa*.

"I thought you were dead. Once I heard the gunshots, I figured it was over. What happened?" asked Jack, bewildered by the turn of events.

"Did you forget about the old man?" Jack had forgotten about Jorge. "He pulled a little surprise attack on the beach. Turns out he doesn't miss with that homemade cannon of his. I'm sure glad I had the good sense to bring the old bastard along," replied Travis with a crooked grin.

Pax stepped forward but came to a stop between Jack and Josephine. Jack could see the young man was troubled and immediately realized what it was. The lady should be helped first, but she was naked, and Pax was too embarrassed to even look in her direction.

"Pax," said Jack as he glanced up at his cuffed hands indicating it was all right to undo him first.

"How about Flores?" asked Jack as Pax unlocked the handcuffs.

"He'll survive, but he is not moving anywhere fast. We left him on the beach. Jorge is watching over him and the boat," answered Travis.

Once released, Jack took the handcuff key from Pax and rushed to his wife. He removed the cuffs and untied her feet. She sagged against him, burying her tear-stained face in his chest. He took off his shirt and wrapped it around her shoulders. A tear rolled down his own cheek as he held her quivering body in his arms. He had almost lost her, lost everything. But even worse, he had lost faith in her. He promised himself to never do that again.

"Now, Señor shithead, I want you to take off your pants," commanded Travis.

Reyes looked at Travis as if he had been asked to commit an unholy act. "You're crazy," he replied.

"You're not telling me anything I don't already know. Now take your pants off," came back Travis.

"You won't make it out of here alive without my help. Perhaps we can make a deal?" pushed Reyes, trying a different tack.

"This isn't a round table discussion. Take your pants off!" ordered Travis.

Reluctantly, Reyes did as he was told, revealing stubby white legs and a pair of neon orange and yellow tiger-striped jockey shorts.

"Nice jockeys, *el Jefe*," commented Travis as the Mexican's face turned red.

Travis handed the pants to Josephine. The length was about right, but she had to use the cord that had been strapped to her feet as a makeshift belt in order to keep the pants around her waist. She buttoned up Jack's shirt and tucked it into the pants. Jo had stopped crying and a look of determination was back in her eyes. Jack was grateful that his wife had quickly regained her composure; it was still a long way home.

Having taken care of Jo, Jack walked over to where Reyes stood. Under normal circumstances he would have found the sight of a paunchy middle-aged man in tiger-striped shorts quite humorous, but at the moment he was filled with rage.

"Let's see how tough you are with someone who can fight back," snarled Jack as he hurled himself at Reyes, immediately knocking the older man to the ground. Down on his knees, his legs straddling Reyes' waist, he pounded the man's face with his fists. Jack had never been much of a fighter, but right now it did not matter, his boiling anger drove his wild punches. He wanted to crush this man.

The attack only lasted a few seconds as Pax and Travis pulled Jack off of the prone Reyes. "I want you to enjoy yourself, but I need the bastard alive," said Travis as he backed Jack up against the far wall.

Jack leaned against the wall, his hands on his hips, his chest heaving. If it had not been for Travis, he would not have stopped the beating until Reyes lay dead beneath him. The desire to kill was a new emotional experience for Jack; it had overwhelmed him. Something primitive within him enjoyed the violence, but at the same time he was terrified by the loss of control.

"What's the plan now?" asked Jack between deep breaths.

"We head back to the boat and get the hell out of here. The jeep is parked close by so it won't take us long," replied Travis.

"What about Señor shithead?" asked Jack as he motioned toward Reyes.

"*El Jefe* comes with us. Flores needs him alive so he can re-find his find," explained Travis.

"If that is all you want, I'll tell you right now. Then you would not have to take me with you. Tie me up and gag me; you will be long gone before anyone finds me," pleaded Reyes as he sat in the sand, attempting to wipe the blood from his face with the sleeve of his shirt.

"And I'm sure you would tell us the truth," returned Travis. "I'd shoot your sorry ass right now, but Flores wants you alive."

The discussion was over. Pax helped Reyes to his feet as Travis gave one last piece of advice to his prisoner. "If we run into any of your men, and there is any shooting, I'm going to make sure you're the first one dead."

They left the *palapa* and headed out into the night. Travis and Reyes were followed by Jack and Jo, while Pax brought up the rear. The outside world was a shadowy gray, partially illuminated by a half moon. Jack was glad to have been rescued, but he would not feel comfortable until they were off of Reyes' estate.

They had not gone far when a voice called out from the darkness. The voice was accompanied by a metallic click-clack sound of weapons being readied to fire. Jack did not understand the Spanish, but he froze along with the rest of the group. The voice called out again, this time in English, "This is the Mexican Federal Judiciary Police. Drop your weapons!" The voice sounded familiar.

Jack's eyes were not yet totally adjusted to the darkness, but he was slowly able to make out a number of vague human forms surrounding them. He felt Jo's hands gripping his left arm. Suddenly, a flood of light was directed at them. The blinding light was coming from three sides, making it impossible to see anything outside the semicircle of light. The effect made Jack dizzy.

Travis had the muzzle of his pistol buried in Reyes' right ear. The Mexican stood with his teeth clenched, looking uncomfortable. Jack could not hear what was said, but he saw Travis whisper something to his prisoner.

"Now you listen to me! I'm not dropping anything," shouted Travis as he squinted into the bright lights. "If you want Reyes to continue breathing, you and your men are going to back off and let us pass through. You will do this very quietly and very carefully, for if I hear so much as a sneeze or a fart, Reyes gets a lobotomy."

"Drop your weapons and raise your hands above your heads, or we will be forced to fire," replied the accented voice. "I am here to place Ricardo Reyes under arrest. I would rather have him alive, but if you insist on shooting him I will take him dead. However, if you fire your weapon, my men will be forced to return fire. The choice is yours; drop your weapon or die."

Travis stood unmoving, seemingly unable to make up his mind. All eyes were on his trigger finger. Jack could sense the surrounding firepower; his skin twitched in dreadful anticipation. He had no say in this matter—not that he wanted to surrender—but this was Travis's call.

"We want Reyes, not you. If you've broken no laws, you've nothing to fear. You will be given a fair hearing," assured the voice.

Travis looked over at Pax and nodded his head. He then tossed his pistol onto the sand in front of him and raised his good hand above his head. Pax did the same, and Jack and Jo also placed their hands above their heads. Jack did not like this; his freedom had been short-lived. His only hope was that the voice spoke the truth. The ends of Reyes' pencil-thin moustache pointed up toward his eyes as a Cheshire cat grin spread across his face.

The silhouette of a large figure ambled toward them from outside the light. Jack saw something familiar in the ambling gate; he recognized that it went with the voice. Given a few more seconds of contemplation, he would have connected the voice and the ambling gate; to a name, but the face of Inspector Ortiz came into focus before he had a chance to do this.

CHAPTER 47

With the appearance of Ortiz, Jack's giddy feelings of freedom were castrated and replaced by hopeless despair. Ricardo Reyes was at the opposite end of the emotional spectrum.

"Inspector, you are a brilliant man," cried an ebullient Reyes. "Although I must admit you had me worried."

Jack noticed that Reyes was shaken by his experience. His hands trembled, and his voice was an octave higher. Reyes placed his hands on his hips, his arms akimbo, in what Jack saw as an attempt to hide his quivering hands.

Ortiz stood motionless and silent, his eyes staring down at Reyes from an expressionless face. His stare seemed to make Reyes more uncomfortable.

"Inspector, I think you are about to become a very prosperous man," continued a smiling Reyes as he stepped toward Ortiz.

"Stay where you are!" commanded Ortiz.

"What is the matter?" asked a confused Reyes, a forced smile on his lips, his hands in front of him, palms to the sky.

"Place your hands on your head, Señor Reyes. You are under arrest," ordered Ortiz.

This was not something Jack had expected. It did not make sense. Ortiz was one of Reyes' goons, only with a badge.

"Surely, you joke," asked Reyes as beads of sweat popped out along his brow.

"This is no joke," returned the Inspector. "You are under arrest."

"But what laws have I broken?" asked Reyes, an edge creeping into his voice.

"Which laws haven't you broken?" came back Ortiz. "What is bringing you down, though, is your private collection of Mayan artifacts. I guess you figured a stupid cop would never have heard of Lord Pacal's Death Mask, or maybe you thought you owned me. Either way, you are now under arrest for possession of stolen cultural artifacts."

"You are making a large career error, Inspector Ortiz. I have many connections in high places; my arrest could cost you dearly. Do you forget that Director Cervantes is a friend of mine?" threatened Reyes, his voice cracking.

"Your powerful friends will want nothing to do with you. You have been the subject of a secret investigation for over two years. With the discovery of your private museum, we now have enough evidence to bury you and Cervantes."

Reyes' face had turned a bright red, his lip quivered. "You fool! I can have you eliminated!" he shouted. He was beginning to lose control.

"Do not threaten me," replied Ortiz, starting to show some emotion. "Your days of ordering people killed are over. You have caused too much pain. If it was not you, then it was a man like you who ordered the assassination of Javier Vasquez. He was a good man who wanted to protect Mexico's heritage, but those who saw only personal gain in the ancient past had him killed. I would enjoy taking your life, but I think I will take more pleasure watching you spend the rest of your life in prison. Your fellow inmates will love your fancy ass."

Reyes' face was now twisted in pure terror. A man who lived for total control now had none. In desperation, he lunged for the gun Travis had dropped in the sand.

"Stop!" screamed Ortiz.

There was no more stopping for Ricardo Reyes. The gun was in his hand, a crazed expression on his face. A staccato burst of gunfire erupted outside the semicircle of light. The first bullet tore into Reyes' chest, thrusting him backwards. A second bullet impacted his right shoulder, creating an opposing force that spun him around like some frenzied ballerina. As Reyes twisted into the sand, a final slug smashed into his right temple, causing the top of his head to pop off like an exploding watermelon.

A hushed silence descended on the scene as the gunfire echoed off into the night. The body of Ricardo Reyes lay face up in the sand, the glazed eyes reflecting the harsh lights, the mouth open in a silent scream.

CHAPTER 48

Nelson Carlton and Special Agent Patricia Lance stood at the entrance to the large ballroom. The place was filled with people dressed in formal wear and dining on rubber chicken. Carlton recognized the faces of a few congressmen and senators amongst the crowd. "What a collection of crooks," whispered Carlton to Lance. She smiled at the comment.

This was a "thousand dollar a plate" party fund raiser. The featured speaker, Senator Jason James Hightower, had just completed an upbeat speech on the outlook for his political party in the upcoming election year and was rewarded with a standing ovation. The charismatic Senator's oratory had been sprinkled with witty innuendo concerning who might be the country's next Vice President. His speech completed, he returned to his table next to the rostrum.

"You ready?" asked Lance.

Carlton looked over at her and nodded his head. Lance was a good-looking woman in a buttoned-down sort of way. So far she seemed to be the "by-the-book" type, but Carlton found himself wondering what she was like when she unloaded her gun at the end of the day. He had noted the wedding ring on her finger and figured that romance was out of the question, but he did find this to be an unusual situation to rediscover his long-lost libido.

"Let's go get him," announced Lance.

Carlton led the way around the perimeter of the giant hall, followed by Lance and another agent. Agents had also been deployed at all of the ballroom exits.

Carlton's swollen and bandaged face elicited double-takes and repulsed expressions as he made his way through the crowd. His cheek had ballooned to the point where he was practically blind in his left eye. One of the EMTs who had been attending to Galvan had cleaned and bandaged the wound before Carlton left the warehouse. Not that the bandage did much good, but at least it kept the torn flesh hidden from public view. The wound needed stitching, but Carlton had wanted to be here; it was his final request.

They passed a C-Span camera crew that had been recording the night's speeches for the masses. "You might want to keep that thing rolling," tipped Carlton as he passed by the cameraman. The man, who was in the process of taking down his equipment, glanced up to see Carlton stride past, followed by the two FBI agents. He then looked at his sound man, who shrugged his shoulders. The cameraman nodded his head, and they began to hook back up.

Hightower was seated at a round table with four other well-dressed people, two men and two women. Carlton recognized both of the men; one was the President's chief of staff and the other was CEO of one of the world's largest corporations. He approached the table from behind the Senator, who was in the middle of an animated conversation with a handsome middle-aged woman seated to his left.

"Senator Hightower," stated Carlton as he came to stop.

The Senator turned around, his left arm over the back of the chair. His initial expression was one of perturbation at having been interrupted, which quickly turned to disgust by the sight of Carlton's badly swollen face. At first he did not recognize the misshapen face, but slowly it became more familiar.

"What the hell?" gasped Hightower as he realized who he was looking at.

Carlton stared down at the Senator, the image of Don Schovich spread out on the concrete floor of the warehouse heavy on his mind. "You're busted, asshole!"

EPILOGUE

Nelson Carlton looked out over the Pacific Ocean as the sun set on the western horizon. There was a stiff breeze blowing in off the sea, the air cold and salty. Two hundred feet below where he stood, surf crashed wildly against a rocky shore. Behind him, parked on a California Highway One turnout, was a brand new Winnebago. He was somewhere between San Luis Obispo and Monterey; he was not sure of his exact location, and he did not care. The last six months had been spent driving cross-country. If it had not been for Don Schovich, he probably would have never thought of traveling this way. When he first started out, he wondered if buying a motor home was such a wise decision; how could he expect to live out another man's dream? But he found that he was enjoying life on the road.

The latest news from Washington was that Senator J.J. Hightower had been found dead in his cell this morning, his wrists slashed. Carlton figured this end was for the best; it would save the taxpayers the cost of a drawn-out trial. The President, unable to weather the storm of public outrage created over Operation Raven, announced last week that he would not seek a second term in office. Carlton decided that once in a great while the good guys do win.

He took in the view one last time, then climbed back into the Winnebago. He had met a lady who lived in Carmel while he was visiting the Grand Canyon. They had ridden mules down to the bottom of the canyon together and had struck up a friendship. She was a nice woman about his age, and he would not mind if they became more than friends. He was in no hurry, though. He had plenty of time.

He steered the massive vehicle onto the highway and started north toward Monterey.

*   *   *

The Phillipses were lucky in that their house was on the edge of town and their lot backed up to open farmland. On spring evenings, when the sky has been scrubbed clean by the north winds, the snow-capped peaks of the Sierra Nevada could be viewed from their rear patio. Tonight the view was spectacular as the last of the sunlight painted the distant peaks with a red glow. There were only a few evenings like this a year in the Sacramento Valley, mostly in the late winter or early spring. During the summer and fall, temperature inversions trapped the valley smog, while in the winter, tule fog covered the ground; both climatic situations blocked the mountain view. Jack sat alone on his rear patio sipping a Sierra Nevada Pale Ale, enjoying the spring evening.

He had just finished reading a letter from Travis Horn. It was the first contact from Travis since Mexico. The letter was short, and little mention was made of their experiences together in Mexico. Travis had evidently retired from the nonexistent government agency that he did not work for and moved back to Montana. His grandfather had passed away during the winter, and Travis was now running the ranch. The prospect of working the ranch on his own was daunting, but he sounded as if he were looking forward to the task. His right hand, which had been mangled by the shotgun blast, had been amputated at the wrist. Travis had his stump fitted with a special metal hook that allowed him to hold a fly pole. He called it his built-in hay hook. He wanted to know when Jack was going to come up and beat the waters with him; big trout were being pulled out of the Madison River.

Six months had passed since that terrible night on Reyes' estate. Inspector Ortiz had kept his word; Jack and Jo were given a fair hearing, and after three days of intensive interrogation, they were allowed to return to California. The Inspector had been part of a special task force within MFJP that was investigating both MFJP Director Cervantes and his connection with organized crime. Ortiz had been appointed Acting Director of the MFJP, while Cervantes would be spending the remainder of his life in prison.

Upon arriving at LAX, the Phillipses were subjected to a few more days of extensive grilling by the U.S. State Department and the DEA. Their own government actually gave them a harder time than the Mexican Judicial Police. Jack quickly became disgusted with the endless questions and refused to cooperate unless he was allowed to have an attorney present. The next day they were allowed to return home.

Home proved to be no refuge as they were immediately forced to deal with their fifteen minutes of fame. The Phillipses were welcomed home by a frenzy of unwelcome media attention. Newspeople camped out in their front yard and crowded outside their offices at the university. It became so bad at one point that they rented a cabin in Tahoe and moved to the mountains for a few weeks. Luckily, the media's attention span was short, and over the last couple of months, the Phillipses had been allowed to fade back into semi-obscurity, though once or twice a week they still had to turn down a movie offer or an appearance on Oprah.

This period of time had taken a toll on their marriage; not only did they have to deal with the media, but they also had to come to terms with their relationship. Over the winter they spent a lot of time with a marriage counselor. Josephine admitted that when she and Jack were having their problems she contemplated taking off to Mexico to see Gus, but that Gus had talked her into staying home and trying to work things out with Jack. She also admitted that her interest in Gus had been more than purely platonic, and that it was Gus who had not let things go too far. In time she had rediscovered her love for her husband and was thankful Gus had kept her from doing something she would have regretted. By the time of their Mexico vacation her interlude with Gus Wise was something she hoped was a forgotten part of her past.

It had been difficult for Jack to deal with some of this information. There were still times when he felt his wife had betrayed him. When his anger burned too hot, though, he would remember that night when she chose what seemed like certain death to be by his side. Jack was learning that Mexico had not been an end or a beginning, only part of a continuum, and that happily-ever-after required some effort.

The Phillipses had not heard personally from Sandy Lake, but the young lady did not appear to have a problem with the media attention. She had not been back in the States long when she signed a deal to star as herself in a television docu-drama. There were also rumors of a spread in Playboy. Sandy was definitely taking advantage of the opportunities her situation presented.

Hector Flores had proved to be a good correspondent, writing twice and even phoning once. He recovered quickly from the beating he had received from Reyes' men and began scouring the Yucatán, searching for the lost contents of the Tomb of the Bearded Man. Pax Chi was working as his assistant.

The tomb had been cleaned out. Only the sarcophagus lid remained; even the remains inside the sarcophagus were gone. In his last letter, the archeologist seemed to be resigned to the fact that Reyes probably was the only one who knew where the tomb's artifacts had been hidden, and that its treasures may lie hidden for another thousand years. Without the contents of the tomb, the importance of the find was greatly reduced. For now, there would be no speculation of a Viking ship that may have sailed the Caribbean. In his mind, Jack could still see the tomb as they found it. He would always wonder what fantastic story the inscriptions on the tablets might have told. He hoped someday they would be found and the mystery of the tablets revealed.

The sound of the sliding glass door opening behind him, interrupted Jack's thoughts. He turned his head to see Jo stepping out onto the patio. She was dressed in a pair of his old gym shorts and a large gray sweatshirt. Even dressed like this she looked good. She walked over to where he sat and put a hand on his shoulder as she looked toward the mountains. "I wish the view was always like this," she remarked.

Jack reached up and took her hand in his. "It is a pretty view but not as pretty as you," he said as he looked up at his wife.

She smiled back at him, then leaned down and kissed him on the lips. He pulled her down onto his lap. They embraced and exchanged wet kisses. He loved her smell. She saw the letter still in his hand and asked, "Who is that from?"

He looked into her eyes, a crooked grin on his face and replied, "You want to go fishing?"

The End

Author's note

The 1985 Christmas Eve heist of artifacts from the National Museum of Anthropology in Mexico City actually occurred. Thankfully, most of the priceless pre-Colombian works of art, including Pacal's death mask, have since been recovered. Every once in awhile the good guys do win!

About the author

James is a sixth-generation Californian. When not exploring the Mexican Outback, he can be found in the wilderness of California's Sierra Nevada mountain range, leading a string of mules through the high lonesome. He spends his winters on the central coast of California.